GREATER
THAN A WALL

Akkadia Press Ltd
www.akkadiapress.uk.com
ISBN 978-0-9935845-6-5
Designed by Larry Issa
Illustrated by Sasan Saidi
Typeset in Palatino
Printed in the UK by Clays Ltd.

I would like to express my gratitude to the many people
who read earlier drafts of this novel and provided unstinting
encouragement, especially my agents, Heather Adams and
Mike Bryan; and to my editor, Michelle Wallin. Special thanks also
to Larry Issa for designing and shaping this book so ingeniously.

GREATER
THAN A WALL

CARL GIBEILY

AKKADIA
PRESS

Greater than a Wall

Carl Gibeily was born in Lebanon in 1966. After school in Beirut, he read engineering at Cambridge University, and worked as a confectionery salesman in Dubai, a journalist and UN editor in Beirut and Bahrain, and a Bloomsbury editor in Doha. Carl is now about as Scottish as anyone in Edinburgh, where he lives with his wife and two children. His first novel, *Blueprint for a Prophet*, was published by Doubleday to critical acclaim.

Author's Note

As a matter of form, novels usually run disclaimers to emphasize the fictitious nature of the characters and events, stressing that any similarity to actual events or persons is purely coincidental. In this case this is not completely true. While the story of the Israeli family is entirely a work of fiction, that of the Palestinian family is partly factual if fully dramatized: the rapid sequence of events that stemmed from the construction of the separation wall between Israel and the West Bank is all too true. I came across the story of that family in the course of editing and fact-checking a particular UN document, and my only legal tweak has been to change all the names of the members of that family. Theirs is only one story among so many countless others, and if history teaches us anything — including the most recent history of Brexit and Trump's US — it is that events that seem to happen at breakneck speed are in fact the climax of years of simmering complacency and xenophobia.

Carl Gibeily
Edinburgh, June 2017

For Anne, Elissa, Terry, Albert, Caius and Kyrâh:
a cluster of cedars among pines

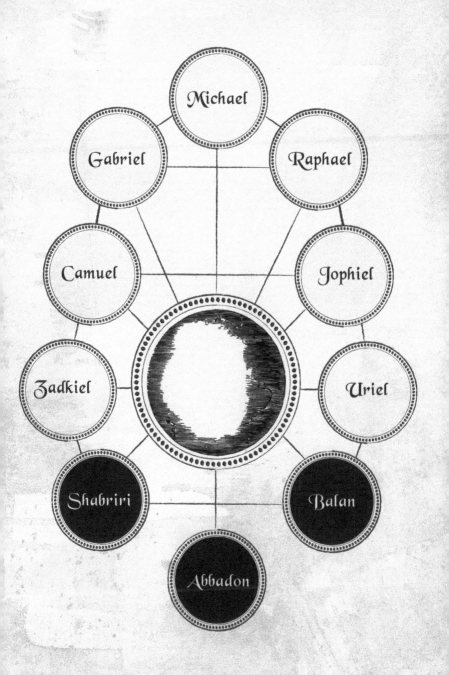

Budapest, 1956

THE HOSPITAL'S TANNOY relayed the radio broadcast, filling the wards and corridors with patriotic songs non-stop for two days, with only brief interruptions for newsflashes. On this, the third day, the tone changed abruptly and the rolling drums faded into a gentle melody of hope and prayer. In the maternity wing, a man paced the corridor nervously, waiting for news of his wife's delivery. He heard the change and stopped in his tracks to stare at the closest speaker. He reached into a pocket of his grey suit for a cigarette, which he put mechanically in his mouth. His eyes still on the speaker, he lit his cigarette and inhaled deeply.

It was an old Christmas carol that was being played two months before Christmas. The man hummed the tune and exhaled through his nose, the smoke dancing with the words from the tannoy: '*Csoda fia szarvas, ezer ága boga* —' *Boy stag of wonder, with horns of a thousand branches* —

He turned to look at the only other person in the corridor, whose wife had been rushed into the delivery room at the same time as his. The man was seated on one of three wooden chairs, his legs crossed and cheek resting on a hand. His beard was so thick and bushy that the fingers of his hand seemed consumed by it. But it was the man's calm disposition that attracted the smoker's attention: oblivious to the song and to the sound of the angry crowds on the street below, the man's eyes were riveted to a sheet of paper on the middle seat.

Outside, flags and banners had invaded the streets of the city for a third consecutive day. Some of the protesters had hunting rifles and old muskets. But the vast majority were armed only with rocks, which they threw in defiance at the advancing tanks. The crowd roared when the leading tank rumbled to a halt, and then fell abruptly silent as the turret was lowered to aim point blank at them.

'*A thousand branches and of a thousand bright candles* —'

The bearded man blinked at his sheet and let out a deep sigh.

The demonstrators hurled stones, which, in an instant, were lost in a sea of sound, pyrotechnics, flesh and collapsed masonry. And, for that instant, the banners and flags blew more fiercely in the apparent wind.

'*Among its horns it carries the light of the blessed sun. On its forehead is a star, on its chest the moon* —'

Driven by curiosity, the man in the grey suit drew closer

to peer at the sheet. It was a list of names, arranged in a neat oval around a larger name, like a snapshot of a planet with its family of moons. He read the central name, written in bold: Áron Lunzer. 'A fine time to bring a baby into the world, eh?' he said, blowing smoke down.

A cloud of dust rose high above the banners, grew arches that were more pointed than the Gothic towers of Parliament House, and slowly turned eastwards, away from the green Danube.

'And it starts along the banks of the shining heavenly Danube — '

Józsi Lunzer looked up and, moving his hand away from his beard, declined the cigarette that was being offered.

'We haven't chosen a name yet either,' said the man. He paused to hum a snatch of the song before adding, 'A strange time to be choosing a name, no?'

Barely a mile away, due east from Parliament Square, the windows of the Central Hospital on the corner of Varosligeti and Fasor Avenues shook dangerously.

'That it may be the messenger of heaven and bringer of news — '

Both men jumped at the sound of the first explosion, and the man in the grey suit sat suddenly on the third chair as his knees gave way.

'Áron,' said Józsi simply.

'Hmm?' There was a shocked lull after that first explosion; even the radio had been momentarily silenced. The man gazed at the tannoy with dismay.

'I am expecting a son,' explained Józsi, 'and he will be called Áron.'

The station repeated the Christmas carol and the man lit another cigarette with the stub of the first. He gave a non-committal shrug and, picking up the sheet of paper between them to József's suprise, pointed at one of the names in orbit. 'Why not this one?' he asked. 'That's a good name. It was my grandfather's name. We might choose it if we get a son.'

József looked over at the name in the first quadrant of mid-heaven. 'Raphael is an exceedingly good name,' he agreed. 'He is the angel of healing.'

Now the explosions were coming in rapid succession, causing the windows to resonate dangerously.

József continued undeterred, 'And we will need a lot of healing after today.' He tugged at his beard as he added darkly, 'My brother is out there.'

The man nodded and they sat in silence for a while.

The choice of song, now repeated in an endless loop, was worth a thousand commentaries.

It was an old Christmas carol that had come to haunt them from a deeper, purer past when bards still roamed the streets of the great Empire. It sang of an era when there were no communists, of an age that was untainted by the anti-co-mintern pact with Germany, and of a time well before the annexations and dismemberments of Hungarian territories by Czechoslovakia, Romania, Russia and Yugoslavia.

'Szarva közöt hozza áldot napnak fényét —'

Moreover, it was an old Christmas carol that was being played two months to the day before Christmas of 1956 as though the radio station, in addition to every ordinary Hungarian, instinctively knew that the song would be banned this and many other Nativities to come.

The man in the grey suit handed the sheet back and broke the silence. 'Just get your family home safely today. That's more important than names.'

József shook his head fervently. 'Nothing except God is more important. Without names we are unthinking and unloving beasts.'

The man shrugged again. 'You think the Soviets outside will only kill Konráds and Konstantins?'

'It's not enough to have a given name.' József pointed at the central name in bold and then indicated the scattering of names. 'Every living human soul has an ascending name whether they are conscious of it or not. Parents choose the given name and society selects the family name, but it is God who disposes the point of purpose. That is the ascending name. That is the true first name.'

'What do you mean?' The man was only half listening; he was more interested in the voices outside that were growing more urgent.

Like a hounded beast, an acrid black plume was slowly engulfing Budapest.

Still indicating the names around Áron Lunzer, József said, 'These are the principal angels and fallen angels, each with a characteristic. And each child that is born to the world comes with the gift or curse of that characteristic for all eternity.'

'So — like astrology?'

The black smoke turned to the maternity wing of the Central Hospital.

'This has nothing to do with stars,' replied Józsi tersely and fell abruptly quiet.

'So?' prompted the man after some time.

It was Józsi's turn to shrug. 'It's complicated,' he said simply. It was also secret. He had almost shared, in a moment of weakness, what had taken the finest Talmudic minds many generations to work out. In the constant state of war between the sons of light and the sons of darkness, if you were born blessed with Raphael or Gabriel as your ascending master, then you would forever fight those who carried the mark of the fallen angels, such as Shabriri, the demon of blindness, and Abaddon the destroyer.

As if on cue, a shell exploded on Fasor Avenue causing all the windows to buckle and shatter and the building to shake. This was followed, two seconds later, by a swarm of flying shrapnel pocking the outer walls of the hospital.

'I just can't see,' breathed Józsi with genuine fear. The God-given name for any human soul could only be glimpsed through prayer and meditation — the letters on a page eventually glowing brighter than the other angelic names. He had used this venerable knowledge to infer the names of his closest kin, such as his kind brother, Áron, after whom he was naming his son, who was guided by Camuel, the angel of tolerance and love; and Dorika, his wife, born with the angel of ministration — Uriel — in her spirits. 'For the first time since I know the way, I can't see. And it's my own son's name that is hidden,' he moaned. He realized suddenly that he had said this out loud and he turned to glance at his neighbour.

But the man had stopped listening with the blast. Curled up in his seat, both hands were buried in his ears.

Inside the delivery room, Dorika screamed as the obstetrician almost casually extracted a blue baby boy.

The acrid smoke that had blown in from Parliament Square paused for barely a second at the broken window and the venetian blind that had been kept shut. A black finger tentatively moved between the slats and entered the room in time to fill the newborn's lungs with its first breath of air.

The baby opened his mouth and coughed.

Dorika sat up. 'What's wrong?' she cried, 'Why is he coughing, doctor?'

'Poor thing. What a shame,' murmured the attending nurse and she whisked the baby away, repeating, '*De kar.*'

1

Jerusalem, 1997

ARON LUNZER AND HIS SON, Avi, waited to be admitted to the
Western Wall plaza. Access to the site, the holiest in Judaism,
was usually effortless. The large concrete security gates at the
entrance to the plaza had been specifically designed to provide protection from would-be suicide bombers while catering for a steady stream of Jewish pilgrims, devout habitués,
bar mitzvah parties and foreign tourists.

But on the morning of 1 January 1997, the sheer number
of visitors had put a spoke in the system, causing a tight bottleneck at the gate. It seemed to Aron that at least half the
city's residents and all its foreign tourists had spontaneously resolved to mark the new Gregorian year by visiting the
Wailing Wall. They waited in a line that was as chaotic and
tortuous as the adjoining alleyways of the Jewish quarter,
shuffling forward a painful shuffle every five minutes.

Aron hated crowds almost as much as he hated wearing a yarmulke. It wasn't so much the hubbub of a thousand conversations taking place simultaneously, or the way that crowds moved in discrete pockets, like particles collecting in a pipe before being impelled onward by the next cluster. Aron certainly found those irritating enough, but what he absolutely could not tolerate with a visceral vengeance was the smell that crowds always seemed to exude. Crowd odours moved through space just like background noise, through crests and troughs along much the same air channels. It was as if people in groups lost their distinctive odours to a collective super-stench that gathered in whorls around Aron's head.

The resulting mixture affected him to such a degree that he couldn't make out individual smells even in his immediate vicinity. He was therefore about as likely to trace the cheap cologne to the American tourist behind him or the unwashed smell to the group of ultra-orthodox Jews in front of him as he was of picking out any single conversation from the mass. He began to breathe through his mouth in order to ward off an all-too-familiar itch.

It wasn't his olfactory system that was under assault; it was his throat. If anything, breathing through the mouth provided a more direct route to the back of his throat — where the hard Semitic ĥ is formed — and therefore only hastened the inevitable.

He gave a little cough, hoping to clear his throat. The ultra-orthodox *haredim* in front, dressed in black, shuffled forward.

Ever since childhood, Aron's body reacted to invisible particles in the air — strong smells and especially dust. It would start in the throat and emerge in the range of a mild cough to a gut-splitting retch. On very rare occasions, the cough had even developed into a stream of vomit.

Aron coughed a couple more times, causing one of the *haredim* to glance at him unkindly and to indicate the security gate several metres away as if to say there was no cause to be impatient.

Smells alone usually didn't cause the balance to tip to the retch scale. But Aron's constitution had chosen that particular day and moment to prove the rule. His hand shot into a pocket for an inhaler as he felt the onset of a fit. Unlike asthmatics, it was his throat that suffered from regular bouts of inflammation. His lungs and bronchial tubes were as healthy as any non-smoker's living in the ambient pollution of Jerusalem. While stress could induce these spasms, more than anything else it was plain dust or strong fumes that caused Aron to heave. So the inhaler was more for the psychological comfort it accorded him than for any actual physiological benefit. It could not tame the cough, but it did sometimes prevent it from developing into an all-consuming retch.

Now the coughs were coming seconds apart and with increasing intensity.

'Soon pass,' Aron spluttered mechanically to no one in particular.

But he started to cough so violently that everyone within earshot turned sharply in his direction. In this age of suicide maniacs, every loud noise was immediately suspicious and put people on edge. Those who were close enough focused on the child with the man and noted that he seemed completely unperturbed by the fit.

Aron was now doubled over, coughing and retching helplessly.

The sea of people took a synchronized step away, parting on either side of the man, who, if not possessed, was visibly suffering from some mysterious biological ailment.

The American with the cheap cologne cupped a hand to his mouth to urge the people ahead to move faster through security, and then used the same hand as a makeshift mask. His call was picked up by several others, including the ultra-orthodox *haredim*.

Between coughs, Aron could hear his young son, Avi, explaining his dust and smell allergy to complete strangers.

'It's true,' Avi repeated to two soldiers who appeared at the scene to investigate the commotion. 'He's just allergic to dust.' He nodded fervently as if to confirm a clearly outlandish lie and added one of Aron's pet phrases: 'A patented dustometre — that's what he is.'

There were a few advantages to being a patented dustometre. For instance, Aron had been allowed to work mostly from home, where he had a diligent cleaner who understood his particular affliction and who went about the flat searching and destroying all the dust particles in their hideouts. His allergy also provided a perfect excuse to turn down invitations to boring office parties or school gatherings. He would shake his head sadly and provide some weary response that would elicit an immediate apology from the inviter, as though they should have known better than to put him in this awkward position by inviting him.

Being a leper in the middle of a crowd also meant that no one batted an eyelid — actually there was a collective sigh of relief — when the two soldiers led Aron and Avi to the front of the queue and straight through security.

'Cool,' said Avi delighted, with a backward glance.

Aron's throat became marginally less inflamed as they stepped onto the large plaza and away from the mass of bodies at the gate, but his voice was still hoarse and his agreement sounded more like a grunt.

The Western Wall plaza, the largest open space in all of Jerusalem, was massive enough to accommodate thousands without the jostle of elbows and smells. Aron was just relieved to be away from the crowd and he sniffed cautiously at the air.

The disadvantages to Aron's mystifying ailment fully outweighed any minor benefits, in the way that an elephant stomping in the jungle can be said to live far more than a mouse under a kitchen sink. For Aron, hell in Jerusalem was a long season that began in mid-March and lasted till end-October. This was when the high temperatures stimulated the city's resident crickets to rub their wings madly and caused the ambient dust and exhaust fumes from all the traffic to grow spirals that rested as a faintly ochre halo above the capital.

He always looked forward to December and January, when the heavy rains ended the reign of dust, shooting down the legions of filth and grime. It had rained the night before and Aron dared to open his lungs to the crisp, almost wintry air.

He put his inhaler away and brought out his yarmulke. He gave a final cough and watched as his son, his head already covered, led the way to the eastern side of the Wailing Wall where the biggest bush grew out from between cracks.

Aron hated wearing a yarmulke even more than he hated crowds. It always seemed to accentuate his allergy, like a circumflex above a letter, as though he were adding a thin layer of dust to his skull. While his father, Józsi, was fiercely Jewish and could quote entire passages of the Tanach with the ease of a trained rabbi, Aron was more *hiloni* than *haredi*, that is an Israeli with little time for the rituals of orthodox Judaism. He succumbed only on rare occasions. That morning, he was wearing a skullcap and had braved the stinking crowds at the gate for his Avi, who had begged to visit the Wailing Wall as a treat for his twelfth birthday.

Aron caught up with his son and placed a hand on his shoulder.

Avi looked up at him and grinned. 'Aren't you pleased we came, Dad?'

He shrugged and mimicked Józsi's pronounced Hungarian accent: 'What's the point of living in Jerusalem if you won't visit the Temple, eh?'

The Wailing Wall is all that remains of the ancient fortification that once surrounded the Temple, which was destroyed by the Romans in 70 AD. This was often called the second Temple to set it apart from Solomon's Temple, the first Holy House, which was built on the same site and destroyed by the Babylonians in 586 BC.

To superstitious Jews like Józsi and the *haredim*, these two events, separated by more than half a millennium, occurred on exactly the same date in the Jewish calendar: the ninth day of the fifth month — 9 Av, or *Tisha B'Av*.

This was why the first of that month, *Rosh Chodesh Av*, marked the beginning of the lowest point in the Jewish calendar. As a child, Aron remembered how, gathered in the obscurity of his parent's dining room, Józsi would quote the Talmud to proclaim to his wife and son: 'As Av enters, we diminish joy.' And while they would still say *Hallel*, Psalms 113 through 118 — as they did for every new Jewish month — the tone was always more demure, more of a wail than a chant. They would move on to the Book of Lamentations, sitting on the floor and weeping with the Prophet Jeremiah over the lost Temple.

During that period, his parent's gloomy flat in North London became all but a mortuary. The mourning would grow in intensity to culminate in *Tisha B'Av*, 9 Av, when the bans were so stringent that even certain portions of the Torah and Talmud were prohibited on that day.

Back then, Aron had been the dutiful son. *Tisha B'Av* had not yet become the most horrible day of the most horrible month in his calendar.

There was an uninterrupted line of bobbing and covered

heads by the Wall; some of the men also wore prayer shawls and read from scrolls and open books. Behind them were rows of white plastic chairs for those waiting their turn at the Wall or taking a breather from the praying.

Only men and boys were allowed in this main section of the Western Wall. The entire site came under the control of the Ministry of Religious Affairs, which had grudgingly allocated a far smaller area to the right for women, split from the main section by a dividing screen.

Standing by the Wailing Wall brought back far too many painful memories, and Aron put his hand in the pocket with the inhaler just for reassurance.

He'd visited the site only once before since making aliyah from London in 1982 — ascending to Israel, which is how the act of return is dubbed in Hebrew.

He had been wearing his yarmulke for two full weeks anyway and, leaving one-year-old Avi with his mother-in-law, he had braved the crowds in order to come to the Wailing Wall as a special tribute to his S'faradi wife. This had been during her *siete*, as he sat a second shiva for her death. It had also been the fortnight during which he was so quick to tears anyway that there was no pretence as his own head moved up and down.

Avi had his mother's thick, curly black hair that seemed to resist the skullcap every time he swayed his head. He also had Sela's healthy olive complexion so that, were it not for the doleful green eyes from Aron's Ashkenazi side, no one would have doubted the boy's S'faradi roots.

This was Avi's birthday — poor, beautiful Avi — celebrating his twelfth birthday without a mother but with a grumpy father who couldn't even breathe like a normal human being.

Avi had found a vacant patch of the Wall a few metres from the screen between a group of black-clad believers, swaying their entire torsos rhythmically, and the male relatives of a boy celebrating his bar mitzvah — who was therefore exactly a year older than Avi. They were all dressed in their finest clothes and even the adults took their cue from the oldest of the party, most probably the grandfather.

Avi closed his eyes and his hand reached out to touch the ancient stones as if to caress and comfort some crestfallen creature. He even started to nod gently back and forth in exactly the way Aron had never taught him.

Aron was standing several paces behind and he turned his attention to the bar mitzvah boy. He could hear him talking and giggling to his female relatives on the other side of the screen. This caused a sharp rebuke from the grandfather. 'Look.' The old man gestured towards Avi. 'Is it his bar mitzvah? Is this the day he becomes a man — ten times better, ten times wiser?'

Thus scolded, the boy turned to a scroll and started bobbing his head with little conviction. Every so often, he threw Avi a look of absolute loathing.

Avi was completely unaware that he was the subject of comparison and while he continued to stroke the slabs of limestone, the other boy tapped forcefully the mother lode for spiritual inspiration.

All along the wall, every conceivable crack in the limestone was filled with folded pieces of paper so that, close up, it looked as if the site had been subjected to an invasion of inconsiderate litterers and a year-long strike by dustmen.

These were actually written prayers to God that were collected twice a year for the Ministry of Religious Affairs by volunteers who carried out full-body ablutions beforehand so that they could reach into every crevice without offending God, their fingers stretching that much closer to the holy of holies. And since all these notes were addressed to God, they were ceremoniously buried nearby in the Mount of Olives.

As he stroked the wall, Avi was careful not to let his fingers slip into the cracks so as not to interfere with other people's wishes and hopes.

The grandfather scolded the bar mitzvah boy again when he saw his fingers in a crack. 'Are your hands clean?' he stated crossly.

Avi took out his own sheet of paper from a pocket, which he unfolded, read a couple of times, nodded, folded again and carefully wedged into a crack.

The other boy had either forgotten his prayer or had not prepared one, and he turned to his grandfather with a look of contrition.

How the grandfather reacted to the boy's lapse was lost on Aron, for just then there was a loud commotion and he instinctively turned his gaze upwards to the top of the Wall where he could see some Arabs looking down at the Jews. He immediately assumed that the shouts were coming from irate Muslims.

What Jews venerate and know as the Temple Mount is equally venerated and known by Muslims as *al-Haram ash-Sharif*, the Noble Sanctuary. Given that the Western Wall forms part of the wall that surrounds al-Aqsa Mosque, there have been many cases of enraged Muslim worshippers hurling rocks down at worshipping Jews, and Jews responding in kind despite their geographical disadvantage. Indeed, Arabs had lost every war against Israel, but they always had the upperhand in the stone-throwing battles of the Temple Mount.

However, the shouts, which were getting progressively louder, were not coming from above.

Aron turned to his right in time to see a rip appear suddenly in the screen.

Two women stepped into the men's section dressed in prayer shawls and carrying scrolls. One of them in particular caught Aron's eye: she seemed to be in her early twenties and her face was so freckled it looked like it had been left to sun-dry for years.

But the newcomers weren't the source of the racket. It was the women they had left behind who were shouting their disapproval, calling them sinful and un-Jewish, urging the two to return to their side of the screen.

The two women ignored the calls and, facing the wall, began to recite to themselves from the scriptures.

In unison, the men stopped bobbing and praying and for a while, most of them seemed capable of doing little more than gawp at this flagrant breach in religious protocol.

Aron was the first to move and instinctively covered the distance to his son in three long strides. The bar mitzvah party, being closest to the intruders, did the opposite, stepping briskly away and thereby offering more wall space to the women.

However, not all the men were slow in their response. On Aron's left, a group in civilian clothes came running out of nowhere to form a tight semicircle around the women, while on his right the large group of *haredim* began to stir. 'What do you think you're doing?' one of them demanded incredulously.

Speaking from behind her male supporters, the woman with the freckled face looked up from the scroll and retorted, 'We have every right to be here. We are as Jewish as you.'

Aron tried to lead his son away, but another group of ultra-orthodox Jews appeared and blocked his path.

'Get out! Get out!' they shouted.

The first *haredi* spat at the woman, 'And just who do you think you are?'

She replied immediately, 'We are Evshel. We stand for justice for Jews. Join us, brother.' She added with a defiant shout, 'The whole of Israel for all Israelis!'

This was clearly a well-rehearsed slogan for it was immediately picked up by the young woman's companions around her, and by various other groups dotted all around the plaza.

There are as many woolly parties in Israel as there are holy days in the Jewish calendar. Aron had heard of Evshel, which he thought consisted of little more than a close-knit band of loons and goons sequestered in remote settler outposts. He was surprised the party had been able to muster so many activists. The very name, Evshel, was derived from *Esrim v'Shevah Elef*, or 27,000, which represented the total surface area of Biblical Israel and Judea in square kilometres and which the esrimists — as Aron preferred to call them — believed was their God-given inheritance down to the last square millimetre.

'The whole of Israel for all Israelis!' The smaller groups started to band together like ponds adding to a lake, and more women began to cross into the main section. They also chanted: 'The Western Wall must be liberated!'

The ultra-orthodox Jews were so incensed that they came up with their own improvised battle cry: 'Nazis, Christians, whores!'

Aron also hated how crowds could so spontaneously turn into mobs. Holding Avi firmly by the hand, they tried to dash across the plaza to the exit, but found themselves suddenly in the eye of the storm.

Aron stopped and looked around at the sea of faces, all twisted with fury, all yelling menacingly.

There weren't enough soldiers in the plaza to control the situation, and the ones at the gate had been pushed back by a sudden influx of local *haredim* from the Jewish quarter.

Aron and Avi witnessed the first blow: a black-clad believer picked up a chair and swung it squarely into two *evshelim*. One of the them collapsed, blood pouring out of his nose and mouth.

Aron shielded his son as, all around them, the battle erupted, with flying chairs, fists and boots, screams of rage and pain, and the smell of blood and sweat everywhere forming an invisible mist.

He had to think quickly. Of the two armies in this conflict, only one wore a uniform, and the homogenous *haredim* were now lashing out at anyone who was not dressed in black. So Aron turned back towards the Western Wall and to the right in order to cross the Evshel line. His progress was hampered by the fact that he still held Avi firmly to his chest with one arm, using the other arm to block any punches and flying chairs.

He could see his goal: the rip in the screen to the women's section where, he hoped, the battle had not yet spread to and from where they could use the side exit.

But as soon as they were in the midst of the *evshelim*, someone pushed Aron forcefully from the back, causing him to trip along with Avi, and collide into two others. All four fell to the ground in a messy heap, and Avi was briefly on top of the woman with freckles who had provoked this battle.

Her prayer shawl was knocked back to reveal long blond hair in a ponytail and piercing blue eyes. Her fists were clenched and she seemed about to punch Avi.

'Don't you dare touch him,' roared Aron, jumping to his feet and deftly lifting Avi off her.

Still staring at her, Avi mumbled something.

'What did you say?' she said, nonplussed.

Aron was already leading his son away, the path to the screen now clear.

'What did he say to me?' insisted the woman, addressing Aron.

Aron felt like replying, 'You stupid fucking cow', but instead he just shook his head and pulled Avi along.

Avi looked straight into her eyes and repeated his one word. He had to say it loudly to be heard above the din.

'What?' She frowned. It was a strange word to come up with in the middle of all this fighting; the fact that it was in English made it all that much more curious. 'That's right, kid,' she shouted after them, once father and son had reached the rip in the screen. 'This is all a great big carnival.'

Her eyes were brimming with excitement.

Later that morning, the *evshelim* were finally forced out of the plaza by riot police. As they withdrew down the adjoining streets in the Jewish quarter, the *haredim* spat on them from their balconies and pelted them with rubbish and excrement.

It was early afternoon by the time Aron and his son finally returned to their flat at the other end of town. Meanwhile, in the Old City, the *haredim* were still too rattled and needed a release from all that pent-up fury. So they turned their rage on the Muslim quarter, smashing Palestinian cars and attacking passers-by. Bands of Jewish youths sprayed tear gas and threw stones at the police and at Palestinians well into the early evening.

Avi took a deep breath, closed his eyes to make a wish and blew out all twelve candles on a smartly decorated chocolate cake.

'You are S'faradi, dear,' Avi's grandmother said warmly. 'You are 200 per cent your mother's son.' She handed him his birthday presents.

Büyük-anne Lilah demanded only two things of her grandson: that he call her büyük-anne, Turkish for grandmother, and that he consider himself S'faradi like his mother, Sela, rather than Ashkenazi like his father.

'And so your dad is at work,' she said testily, 'when he should be at home for his son's birthday.'

Avi cut two slices of cake. 'They asked him to go in because of what happened this morning.'

Aron was a political commentator and journalist for the conservative daily *Adlai*, and the next edition had had to be changed at the eleventh hour in order to cover the ongoing events at the Wailing Wall.

Büyük-anne Lilah was always perfectly coiffed and manicured and had an all-year-round tan so that, with age, her flabby arms — that a younger Avi had imagined were filled with yoghurt — became blotchy and deeply wrinkled. While she couldn't stop her forearms from spreading, she believed she could limit the droop of her chin by constantly chewing gum. 'Thank you, dear,' she said as he handed her some cake, taking the gum out of her mouth and placing it delicately on the side of the plate. 'Well we shall have your birthday without him.' She nodded at the gift-wrapped presents and added, 'Go on, open them.'

When she moved those arms, the gold bangles at both wrists jingled, which they did now as her fingers moved through the boy's curly black hair.

'He didn't cough,' Avi said suddenly.

'Hmm?'

'Back at the Wailing Wall, when things got really bad and we were on the ground, Dad was OK.' He added, 'Maybe he's not a patented dustometre.'

Her hand moved away from his head with a dingle. 'What do you mean "on the ground"?' she asked with sudden concern. 'Who pushed you on the ground?'

'Dad,' replied Avi, adding quickly, 'But he was pushed. Everyone was being pushed.'

'Hmm.' She wasn't convinced. 'And anyway, that doesn't excuse his absence.' She shook her head. 'If you'd been a girl, this would have been your bat mitzvah.' She indicated the empty living room with a jingling sweep of the hand, a finger pausing to point at the cake on the coffee table that she'd brought and that was far too big for just the two of them. 'And where are the guests? Where are your friends from school? Why didn't you invite that girl from the building, what's-her-name?'

'Matea,' said Avi sullenly. 'She wouldn't want to come.'

'Oh, don't worry.' She nodded. 'Did I ever tell you that one of my best birthdays was only with my father?'

Büyük-anne Lilah loved to talk about history, her family's history, and usually Avi loved to listen. Like Aron, she was a first-generation Israeli, who had made aliyah from Istanbul in the 1950s to escape from the endless military coups. But unlike Aron, she was proud of her roots. She claimed to be able to trace her family tree all the way back to 1492, when King Ferdinand expelled her ancestors from Spain.

'Come on, Avi,' she said impatiently. 'Open your presents.'

Avi tore through the wrapping paper of the first of three presents on the table. It was a Megatron transformer, an angular grey robot, which, according to the blurb on the box, was capable of untold destruction thanks to the energy blasts that could be fired from its cannon.

'I'm told that's what all boys your age like these days,' she said happily.

'Thanks, Büyük-anne,' he said unenthusiastically and reached over to kiss her.

He was about to open her second present to him when she indicated the third, which was considerably smaller than the others. 'Open that one,' she said. 'Let's see what your father found for you.'

'That's not from Dad,' said Avi, opening the packet. 'That's from Samiha.' Avi smiled when he saw the latest set of Pogs; Samiha knew how much he loved to collect Pog discs.

Lilah was suddenly very cross. Even their Palestinian housecleaner had been kind enough to buy Avi a gift, but nothing from Aron. 'I'll have a word with your father,' she said under her breath.

'But Dad did take me to the Wailing Wall,' Avi said quickly in his father's defence.

'Yes, where he pushed you to the ground. And if you'd been seriously hurt, what then?'

She was still brooding over her inconsiderate son-in-law when she heard Avi whoop with delight. 'Oh thank you, Büyük-anne.'

Avi had just opened the last present to reveal a framed portrait of an ancient warrior and the boy's mood changed instantly. He gazed at the grainy black-and-white photograph. 'Thank you,' he repeated with a broad grin.

Avi had certainly inherited his mother's fascination with history. Where Aron was a dry journalist who had neither time nor humour for things dead and buried — nor, apparently, for buying a birthday present for his only son — her Sela had been an archaeologist who had specialized in Roman history. In fact, she had been invited to a conference in Rome on her last trip to present a paper on the subtly different Roman architecture of the Levant.

'Tell me about him, Büyük-anne,' pleaded Avi.

'Again?' She feigned impatience.

The boy nodded.

Büyük-anne Lilah was deeply pleased that Avi seemed to be following in her daughter's footsteps and was more than happy to oblige when he had asked her for a print of her grandfather's portrait. The original photograph had remained in Istanbul, so Avi's copy, now cradled in his arms like a baby, was actually a reprint of her copy that graced her living room.

Avi loved to hear about Büyük-anne's grandfather, a decorated Janissary in the Ottoman army, whose grave had been robbed shortly after his burial on account of the full military dress and gilded sword that had accompanied him.

'Show me where you'll put it,' she said to him, picking the chewing gum off her plate and returning it to her mouth.

With the picture firmly against his chest, Avi led the way to his bedroom. He pointed at the high wall opposite the bed, which was plain white and interrupted only by a framed picture and an old newspaper article.

'I want to put them together,' said Avi simply.

'Oh?' She was surprised to see another picture.

'My great-great-grandfathers,' explained Avi. 'Hungarian and Turk — don't you think that's cool, Büyük-anne?'

The other black-and-white portrait was just as grainy, and both men were in military uniforms and stared with haughty expressions. While the Janissary sported a well-groomed beard, his Western counterpart showed off a perfectly symmetrical and curled moustache like the horns of a water buffalo.

'Who gave you that picture?' she asked.

'My grandparents sent it to me for my birthday,' replied Avi happily. 'I received it yesterday. Isn't it great? Now, I've got both of them.'

Büyük-anne Lilah had never seen the *other* grandparents, Józsi and Dorika, and she didn't think much of them. It was bad enough that they had never met Sela or even their grandson, but it was downright sinful that they hadn't come to Israel to sit shiva with them when Sela died.

'He has the European look of your father,' she said, staring at the Hungarian officer.

Avi wasn't listening. He had already marked a spot on the wall with a pencil for the Janissary and had left the bedroom to get a hammer and a nail.

She turned her attention to the newspaper article and gasped. It was the lead picture in the full-page feature that almost caused her to swallow her gum: a snapshot of four soldiers grinning and drinking beer with six corpses lying haphazardly at their feet. She read the headline: *The Human Face of Evil*.

She waited for her grandson to return to the room.

'Does your father know you've put this horrible thing on your wall?' she demanded crossly.

'It is my father's.' He grinned cheekily. 'He wrote it.'

She returned to frown at the article, chewing so furiously that her second chin flapped. She looked for Aron Lunzer's name and found instead the byline of Arnold Lounger. She recognized the name. Her Sela had fallen in love with Arnold Lounger, who had changed his name to Aron Lunzer by the time they were married.

'This is not appropriate for a boy,' she said finally. 'I will speak to your father.' She would have to make a list of all the things she needed to raise with him. She added, almost as an afterthought, 'Your mother would not want you to go to sleep every night looking at this.'

The article remained tacked to the wall. But that night, curled up in bed, Avi focused only on the portraits of his great-great-grandfathers, flickering in the city lights, side by side and united for the first time.

Avi loved to hear about Büyük-anne's grandfather because he imagined links with his father's own colourful family history. This had been transmitted to him indirectly and in snippets from his paternal grandparents, Nagypapa Józsi and Nagymama Dorika, who insisted on their Hungarian appellations whenever they phoned. He was able to piece these together with the little that Aron had told him to form a hazy picture.

From his grandfather, he discovered that Aron was born in Budapest on 25 October 1956, in the dying days of the Hungarian October Revolution; and that Józsi and Dorika Lunzer moved to London when he was barely more than a week old, forced to seek political asylum in the West. The Lunzers became the Loungers, and Aron became Arnold. However, Józsi hadn't chosen to anglicize their own first names — the promise and hope of a new beginning had applied only to his newborn.

From his father, he learnt that Aron was raised from a dreary life in North London, making aliyah on 3 June 1982 on the eve of the Israeli invasion of Lebanon. He followed the IDF into Lebanon, becoming a stringer for *The Daily Telegraph* on the back of his British citizenship as Arnold Lounger, and supplementing his income with freelance commissions to local Israeli publications, including *Adlai*, under the byline of Aron Lunzer. His father had changed his identity and reverted to his original name with which he had first entered Britain as a ten-day-old infant on Dorika's Hungarian passport.

Avi had hung Büyük-anne's Janissary to the right of Nagypapa Józsi's grandfather, the decorated officer in the Austro-Hungarian army who had fought against the Ottomans.

He imagined a meeting between these arch rivals, now related and connected in the blood that coursed through his veins more than a century later. This was how old enemies finally became true brothers. He couldn't help but wonder if, a hundred years from now, a boy would be born with both his blood and that of a Palestinian ancestor.

Avi closed his eyes and imagined he could even meet that future Arab brother and they would talk about how petty the conflict had been and how distant it had all become.

Almost asleep, one word came drifting into his mind. It was the same word that had driven him to beg Aron to take him to the Wailing Wall, and that had been carefully written on a sheet of paper and left in a crack.

'Carnival,' he mumbled drowsily. He hoped God would get that message.

Aron returned home late that night, once the storm had passed and the Old City was enveloped in an uneasy calm. The marauding *haredim* had caused the deaths of two Arabs, including a four-year-old girl. Al-Aqsa Martyrs' Brigade promptly issued a statement to declare that they would avenge the murder of little Salwa.

He stepped in with a cough to clear his throat of any lingering dust from outside. He removed his shoes in the hall, placed them tidily on a rack, used a clothes brush that hung on a nail by the entrance to brush his sleeves and trouser legs, and washed his hands in the guest bathroom before moving on to the rest of the house.

This was the ritual for entering the Lunzer flat, the unwritten rules for residents and visitors alike. This therefore applied particularly to three people: Aron, Avi and the only regular visitor to the flat, Samiha, who let herself in at 8:00 am sharp and out at 5:00 pm, six days a week. Blessed Samiha, who spent all day and every day keeping the flat pure of dust, making this sanctum sanctorum the only place in the world where he didn't have to take short breaths like a wretched animal.

Among the less frequent visitors were the very occasional babysitter, whom he now paid and sent home, and his mother-in-law, Lilah, who visited every Sunday afternoon, after a morning spent playing cards with her group of friends, and on Hanukkah and Avi's birthday. She once let slip that she might have visited more often had Aron been less anal about all that dust nonsense. She was in fact the only visitor to the Lunzer residence who was allowed to dispense with the routine at the door, turning her nose up at the tidy rack of shoes and clothes brush every time she came.

Aron even suspected that Lilah had reshuffled her card-playing session to coincide with the only day in the week when he worked all day away from home at his regular editorial meetings.

But in terms of extended family, she was his son's only living relative in Israel, so he overlooked her shortcomings for Avi's sake.

He forgave her banal conversations, the steady stream of snide comments, and her irritatingly idealized attachment to the halcyon days of her family in Turkey. If it was so bleeding grand in Istanbul, he always wanted to ask her, why did you make aliyah?

But he was always polite for Avi's benefit, and at all times considerate in memory of Sela. Whenever she phoned, which was how most of their exchanges took place, he would grit his teeth and remind himself that he would have had even more interactions with her had his wife still been alive.

That evening, she had phoned him at work just as he was putting the finishing touches to his column. The production department was waiting to close the commentary page and the subeditor was pinging his monitor every five minutes for his piece like a maddening countdown. With an eye on the clock in the newsroom, Aron answered her call and got an earful of complaints. He carried on working on his piece, mashing the keys until she reached the end of her litany. Then, in rapid succession, he told her that the nature of journalism was such that you sometimes had to work even on your day off, and that obviously he wished the events at the Wailing Wall had occurred a day after Avi's birthday; that the boy had never been in any serious danger; that Avi was now old enough to have whatever he wanted on his bedroom wall; and that — just for the record — he had already bought his son a birthday present, which, given the hectic day, had been forgotten in a closet.

He said it all very sweetly and proceeded to thank her for spending the afternoon with Avi and wished her an excellent night.

And then he hung up, returned to his monitor and thought of a title for the commentary: *When Extremists Meet Esrimists, Who You Gonna Call?*

He went over his piece one last time and pressed the send button, thereby dispatching it to the sub's desktop and causing several monitors in production to ping simultaneously.

The political spectrum in other Western democracies was visible in clear, discrete bands, and to foreign observers, the events at the Wailing Wall would seem little more than an altercation between two equally batty fringes of the far right, a battle of the ultras. But in Israel, the colours were more blurred and the rainbow of politics was more like a set with progressively dimmer secondary, tertiary and even quaternary arcs that were so faint that most people didn't even see them in normal daylight.

Aron's piece argued that the events of that day were momentous for several reasons. For a start, it was an undeniably spectacular show of strength by ultranationalist Evshel, the party that until recently had been so minor in Israeli politics that it would have had trouble filling a shed with activists let alone the largest plaza in Jerusalem. The battle had in fact been more about flexing these newfound muscles than about pushing for gender equality at the holy site. They had turned up in their hundreds — which with hindsight explained the unexpected crowd at the entrance — and had wilfully provoked the far more established ultra-religious party on its home turf. The *haredim* had then turned on Palestinians both out of deep frustration and as a subtle if violent reminder to the Israeli public that they would forever stand for true Zion.

The piece also touched on the spectre of more running battles between the scary fringes, especially if mainstream politics slipped from the current centre or centre-right — *Adlai*'s main readership. At that point, even the defenders of the modern state — the heroic ghostbusters of Israel — would have their hands too full of psychoreactive slime to answer the phone.

Aron had strapped on this last bit to his column after Lilah's call.

He went straight to the closet where he'd hidden Avi's birthday present. The large gift-wrapped box contained an ornate Mahogany chess set, which he'd bought several months earlier on his last trip to the UK. He'd kept it hidden all this time precisely so as to spring this fabulous chess set on Avi for his big day and, according to the original plan, straight after an uneventful trip to the Wailing Wall by way of a Häagen-Dazs treat. But he'd got the call from *Adlai* when they were still in the Jewish quarter, having only just emerged from the side exit of the plaza, and he kicked himself now for having forgotten both the gift and the ice cream.

Avi loved chess as much as he loved history. Aron had bought this particular set not only because it was the most attractive in the shop, but especially because the chess pieces were faithful replicas of the Isle of Lewis chessmen: the squat Viking pieces that were discovered in Scotland, each with a distinctive face, complete with the wild-eyed berserkers biting their shields with battle fury. He really wished he hadn't forgotten, as the gift would have had that much more of an impact if he'd given it straight after their run-in with the crazies at the Wailing Wall.

He carried the chess set, entered Avi's bedroom and placed it gently on the floor by the bed so that it would be the first thing the boy woke up to.

For a while, he just stared at his sleeping Avi.

In the dark and with his green eyes shut, he looked just like Sela.

He blinked as he remembered how he had held him in the plaza and how, out of nowhere, he had been scared witless for his son. He had lied to Lilah; the danger had been very real. When the *evsheli* cow had clenched her fists and seemed about to strike Avi, Aron had been ready to pounce. He could have killed her. He would have buried his boot in her face. He could have scratched her, bitten her with bestial instinct.

It was such an extreme gut reaction that it troubled him to think about it even now. In this one conflicting moment of fear and rage, nothing else had mattered, not even his allergy.

He focused again on his sleeping boy and, not for the first time, he asked his dead wife how he could be doing a better job as a parent.

Then, ever so softly, he whispered the Hungarian lullaby that his mother used to sing to him and slipped out of the room:

'*Csoda fia szarvas, ezer ága boga* —' *Boy stag of wonder, with horns of a thousand branches* —

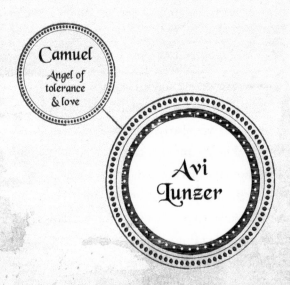

Camuel
Angel of tolerance & love

Avi Lunzer

2

SOMETIMES, AVI WISHED he'd been born in another family and raised in a different house — in Matea's family and home, to be exact. Matea, who was also twelve years old and had celebrated her bat mitzvah a few months earlier, lived in the same apartment block, both flats facing east, hers on the first floor and his on the loftier third of a four-storey building. Their kitchen balconies were connected by a hotline — as Avi had called it when he'd finished rigging it up — which was meant to allow them to communicate through polystyrene cups and a hanging wire. Unfortunately, much as they strained to hear, pressing cups to ears, not even the thinnest garbled voice came through.

'Are you sure you can't hear me now?' Avi yelled down the wire.

'No,' Matea shouted back, leaning dangerously over the railing.

So that while it was always easier to holler their communication between balconies, to the annoyance of Mrs Spiegel on the second floor who lived in her kitchen, they kept the line upon Avi's insistence. It provided him with a sense of physical attachment to Matea's home, even if it was hanging by a thread.

But it wasn't Matea herself that he was drawn to, or any particular member of her family. Rather, it was the complete bundle that she represented: her three siblings, two parents and, over the holidays, four grandparents and a wholesale number of uncles, aunts and cousins all packed into a real house.

Structurally, their flats were identical, with an equal number of walls enclosing four bedrooms, a large living room, dining room and kitchen. But they were identical in the way of twins who are separated at birth and raised in, respectively, happy and melancholic settings. Matea's house was vibrant with endless mess in every corner, walls stained by years of grimy kiddy handprints, and excited voices filling up every room so that, at any one time, you could listen to four conversations simultaneously.

Avi's fondest memory ever was of a Hanukkah holiday when Aron was compelled to travel to the UK for work and when Matea's family insisted that he should stay with them, adopting him for two days and a night. For all too brief a time, Avi was one of theirs, receiving gifts even from the grandparents, uncles and aunts and, at night in the bedroom allocated to the boys, participating in a farting contest with Matea's brothers and cousins.

By stark contrast, Avi and Aron lived in a mausoleum. They were the only occupants of the flat, and since the third bedroom was Aron's study and the fourth was the TV room, they rarely used the large living room and adjoining dining room, which had long ago been converted into a bar. Despite a spectacular view of Jerusalem from the third floor, the heavy green drapes were usually drawn in those two rooms so that that they appeared to drift in and out of them, submerged in the constant half-light of a Gothic set.

Indeed, where it was always Hanukkah at Matea's, it was forever *Rosh Chodesh Av* or *Yom Kippur* at the Lunzers — the pumped up gloom of heavyweight festivals.

As a younger child, Avi had dreaded all the ghoulish things that could appear from those rooms. In the near-constant obscurity, the bar was a wooden beast that spanned a full four metres from scaly head to flaking tail, complete with its brood of seven matching stools. Even now, he only dared to enter when Samiha was in there and with the curtains drawn back. In a brighter light, the ghosts appeared less malevolent; they sat at their stools, sipped cocktails and filled the area with spirited chatter.

Sela had ordered the bar to provide a focal point to soirees with friends. But the truth was that their friends were actually her friends. When she died, so too did the dinner parties. Having long outgrown its use, the bar now looked set to await the Messiah with Semitic stoicism.

Also barely visible in the constant twilight was a large mirror covered in the flag of Israel, the Star of David, which hung on the wall behind the bar. Over the years, the flag itself had become a shroud dissolved into its shadowy environment to the extent that the bright blue had turned greenish grey and the yellowing white had splotches of darker patches of grime to delineate continents of an alien atlas.

For a younger Avi, the mirror and bar worked their black magic hand in hand. The bar had been a very real sleeping beast that could feed off the enchanted mirror and that would awaken to consume everything in its path if anyone was foolish enough to remove the protective shroud. Or that the mirror was so potently wicked that, uncovered, it could suck in and forever trap your brain, leaving a husk of a body.

Only once, with Samiha busy at the other end of the room, did Avi summon up the courage to touch the cloth and feel tentatively the wrought iron frame that it concealed.

According to the unwritten rules of the Lunzer residence, it was the only object in the flat that could never be cleaned. In that, it was at odds with the rest of the house with its pervasive smell of disinfectant, and its polished surfaces and bleached sheets. While those house rules and the endless war against dirt and dust were aimed at creating a more hospitable environment for Aron, they also created an increasingly stifling one for Avi.

Avi removed his shoes and brushed himself down. 'You don't have to use this,' he said to Matea, indicating the brush. 'Just take your shoes off.'

They went to his bedroom and Matea immediately made for the shelf with his comprehensive collection of Tom and Jerry comic books.

'I wish I had this many,' she marvelled. She chose one and jumped on his bed.

Ordinarily, they would be in her house, jostling for space with her two brothers and sister, and talking loudly in order to be heard above the interference from other voices. Here, even a whisper sounded like an awkward shout.

But Avi wanted to write his word on the wall, just below the great-great grandfathers, and he wanted Matea to write it because she had lovely handwriting.

Avi also had an ulterior motive in inviting her to his house. For a full week now, he'd fantasized about her and about this very moment. The fantasy was short and not at all as developed as some of his favourite daydreams like, for instance, the one where he was a young Briton who was abducted by a band of marauding Vikings and ended up befriending the son of the chief or, as a variation, a Crusader squire who was taken by the young and charismatic son of Saladin.

He joined her on the bed. Their legs were now touching and with the comic book across their laps, Avi waited for her to reach the end of the page before saying, 'Do you want to help me write on the wall?'

She shook her head, causing her ponytail to wag. 'Not yet.'

Just then, Samiha entered with two glasses of juice and two slices of his birthday cake. She placed the tray on Avi's desk and, in her broken Hebrew, told them not to enter the kitchen as she was washing the floor.

Glaring at the chocolate cake, Matea waited for the housecleaner to leave before she uttered, 'Who does she think she is? Your mother?'

'She's OK,' he said dismissively. Samiha had been a full-time housecleaner at the Lunzers for thirteen years; to Avi, she had always been a lot more than a cleaner, as integral to his universe as the house itself and everything within it.

'She's Arab.'

He shrugged.

'Aren't you scared,' continued Matea, 'that she's going to steal something or do something?'

'Of course not. Why should she?'

'Because she's Arab,' groaned Matea as though it was the most obviously dim question anyone could ever ask. 'They're all like that. Everyone knows that.'

He didn't feel like sticking up for Samiha and he looked over guiltily at his new Pogs on the floor next to his cool new chess set. He tried to change the subject. 'Do you want to play chess?' he asked, picking up a chessman. 'You'll love their faces — they all look horrible.'

She looked away from the chess piece and indicated the juice and cake. 'I'm not having any of it,' she said sullenly. 'So anyway, what do you want to write on the wall?'

He told her.

'What?'

He repeated: 'Carnival.'

She said with derision, 'But that's so boring.'

'I've got lots of different colours,' he said quickly, 'and we can make the letters as big as you want.'

'But why?'

He hesitated. 'It's a secret code,' he said finally. 'It's funny.' He'd known Matea all his life, but only in the last week had he thought about kissing her.

'It's not funny. It's just weird.' She pouted as her stare returned to the chocolate cake. 'But I'll do it,' she said, perking up suddenly, and adding sweetly, 'if you get your dad to fire her.'

He looked at Matea and frowned.

She returned his look and added earnestly, '*You* know more than anyone how bad *they* are.'

He knew what she was referring to, but asked anyway, 'Why me?'

Matea groaned, 'Because *they* killed your mum.'

Everyone in the neighbourhood knew about Sela Lunzer, the innocent victim of a terrorist attack who was shot by Palestinian gunmen in Rome. Avi had been one month away from his first birthday when Sela travelled to Italy on business, and four days shy of it when she returned to Israel, her coffin draped in the Star of David. She and the fifteen other civilians had been offered full military honours as fallen heroes of Israel. Just about everyone in the neighbourhood had turned up for the funeral, many even choosing to sit shiva with Aron.

'Can I see it?' Matea asked suddenly.

'Wh-what?' Avi was confused. He was still trying to understand why she'd think Samiha was related to his mother's murderers.

'You know,' said Matea, smiling sweetly. 'The flag.'

'Oh.'

'Can I?'

'I guess.'

He led the way to the bar and pointed at the wall.

Matea gasped. Even in the poor light she could see that the years had not been kind to the flag. 'But it's a martyr's flag,' she exclaimed, adding disappointedly, 'My mum told me it was special.' She drew closer to it. 'You should keep it in a drawer or something. That's what your mum would want.'

Matea touched the fabric reverently and felt the iron frame underneath. 'What's that?' she asked.

'A mirror,' Avi replied simply. He was feeling uneasy and wanted them to return to his bedroom.

'Why is it covered?'

'For my mum. Don't touch it.'

Matea groaned again. 'Don't you know anything?' She chuckled. 'You're supposed to cover mirrors only for seven days — for shiva — not for a million years.'

The flag was tacked to the back of the mirror at the four corners so Matea pulled the mirror back on its hook in order to reach one of the staples.

Avi was shocked. 'What are you doing?'

'Have you ever seen it?'

Avi shook his head. The mirror had always remained covered.

'Aren't you curious?' Matea was now driven by two purposes — to liberate the flag and to see the mirror. She had succeeded in prizing a staple back with her nails and was now attempting to pull it off.

Avi could have physically stopped her. But part of him was curious, a small part of him did want to see the mirror for the first time. 'But what if something bad happens,' he said weakly, his words betraying his thoughts.

The staple proved too resilient so she was forced to pull the mirror back further to straighten the wire and free the corner.

The sudden image of his father discovering the exposed mirror and yelling filled Avi with panic. 'Stop,' he said, this time urgently and tugging at her arm.

'Don't be such a baby.' She brushed his hand away and peeled the corner back.

It was just as a sliver of the mirror appeared at the bottom corner that Avi blurted out: 'If you stop now I'll kiss you on the mouth.'

That got Matea's attention.

With Avi's hand back on her arm, she recoiled from him so suddenly that the mirror followed her, shifting off its hook. For an instant, it appeared frozen in midair, the freed corner of the flag preparing to flap.

In that instant, it seemed that the young girl would be able to hold up the wrought iron frame. When it fell, it did so almost gracefully, as if it had always been destined to end in a loud explosion and a thousand shards.

Matea screamed. Samiha came running and the girl screamed even louder.

Even though a small piece of the mirror, no larger than a coin, had bounced up and had done little more than graze her leg, she shrieked as if a piece of shrapnel had gone right through her.

Samiha was the epitome of calm. She ordered the children to step away from the glass and she would have cleaned the girl's superficial wound, but Matea would have none of that. Sobbing uncontrollably, she limped to the door and down the two flights of stairs to her house, leaving her shoes behind.

Avi was completely unhurt. The fact that most of the flag had still been fastened to the mirror had limited the spread of the broken glass.

'Poor Abi,' tutted Samiha.

Avi was now on the other side of the bar, standing by the stools and transfixed by the section of the wall where the mirror had been. 'You mean, poor Dad. He's the one who liked it.' Avi added anxiously, 'He's going to kill me.'

'He like it,' agreed Samiha in Hebrew as she checked him for pieces of glass. 'But poor Abi.' She sent the boy to his room and went about cleaning the mess and praying that the jinn that had been trapped in the mirror would not plague the two children with bad luck.

In the event, Aron did not kill his son and didn't even punish him — not at first. He told him off about being careless, especially since the neighbour's child had been injured, but was otherwise philosophical about the incident. 'Man thrives on accidents,' he told his son. 'Just try to make it the right kind of accident next time.'

It was as if Aron had waited all those years for someone else to remove the mirror and the last stronghold of dust in the flat. He instructed Samiha to wash the flag and thought no more about the event until the following day.

Avi was at the bedroom wall with a pencil, dragging his hand along an arc under the great-great grandfathers so that the word would appear like a banner. He was trying to write in as ornate and large a script as possible. He stopped every so often to rub out a stroke or to correct a wavy line or add a flamboyant loop.

Aron watched his son in silence for a while, indulgently allowing the mess on the bedroom wall to grow. Then he turned his attention to the last piece he wrote for *The Daily Telegraph* as Arnold Lounger and for which he had received the most acclaim as a freelancer.

'Your grandmother phoned me about this,' he said. 'She feels it might be giving you nightmares.' The full-page feature was a scoop on a Christian Lebanese militiaman who had participated in the massacre of Palestinians in the Sabra refugee camp. 'She thinks you should take it down.'

'But I like it, Dad. I think it's the best thing you've ever written.'

He chuckled. He wasn't sure it was his best ever, but it had certainly been instrumental in convincing the publishers of *Adlai* of his investigative skills and, more importantly, of his affiliations. By the time the IDF prepared to lift its siege of West Beirut in March 1983, Aron had accepted their offer of full-time correspondent, and Sela had agreed to marry him. 'Not too scary for bedtime?'

'Dad,' Avi groaned. 'I'm not a baby.'

Aron spotted a more recent article: an op-ed he'd written for *Adlai* under his Israeli name. It had been tacked to the wall furthest from the Janissary ancestor since Lilah's last visit. He read an excerpt: 'Just imagine that you are born with a penchant for cheddar cheese. Would you go to a French supermarket and choose the one, comparatively inferior cheddar among the 200 different cheeses on offer? Or would you go to an American supermarket where the choice is largely limited to the 200 varieties of cheddar? Your tastes are an active function of your makeup. If you are aware of and true to your tastes, the choice becomes academic. Similarly, there is little more than intellectual curiosity in comparing the different mutational paths of dinosaurs and humans, or of the widely varying narratives of Palestinians and Israelis...'

He stopped reading; it was one of his earliest commentaries and far from his best.

Aron believed that excellence could only be achieved through confrontation and a predisposed kind of choice. But he had explored that notion of choice in other, less cheesy op-eds. 'I do think you should take this down,' he said. 'I'll print out a different piece for you. How about a recent one about what happened the other day at the Wailing Wall?'

Avi shook his head. 'I like the cheese.' He took a step back from the wall and then, like an artist examining his oeuvre, he indicated the central portraits as he explained, 'You see, they're having a conversation.'

It was only upon closer inspection that Aron could make out the pencil marks around both articles. Each was set within bubbles pointing towards the respective great-great grandparent such that it seemed as if the Janissary was expounding on the human face of evil, while his Hungarian counterpart retaliated with a discourse on cheddar.

Now that Avi had stepped back from the wall, Aron could read the bold letters that he'd written in an arc:

CARNIVAL

Avi saw him reading the banner under the portraits, which had become a caption to a wall-sized cartoon. 'Matea thought it was weird,' he said glumly.

'I see,' said Aron. It was certainly an unusual word to deface a wall with. He wondered whether Avi would be drawing clowns next or a couple of floats. 'Why a carnival?'

Avi shook his head vigorously. 'It's not *a* carnival — it's just *carnival*.' He went back to the wall to put some finishing touches with the pencil before turning to his colouring pens.

Aron frowned as he remembered that his son had used that word on the *evsheli* cow at the Western Wall.

He suddenly felt guilty that he hadn't considered how traumatic the whole experience must have been for a twelve-year-old. 'Avi, you know that people do bad things,' he began lamely. He glanced at the picture of the Butcher of Sabra. 'Very bad things.' He began to suspect that maybe Lilah had been right about its negative effect on Avi. 'You do know that what happened the other day at the Temple Mount was bad, really wrong.'

Avi turned to look at him and with a twinkle in his eye, he said 'really' in Hebrew, '*Mamash*.'

'I'm being serious, Avi.'

'So am I, Dad.'

'It wasn't a carnival.'

'Just carnival,' he corrected again.

'For God's sake,' Aron said impatiently, 'it wasn't fun. It wasn't exciting. It was just a bunch of crackpots going at each other. You do know that, don't you?'

Avi nodded. '*Mamash*,' he repeated. Aron was about to get cross with him, so he added quickly, 'I learnt that word at in the Chabad.' He fell silent and went back to colouring his letters.

At the beginning of term, Avi's class had spent a couple of nights in a Chabad, a spiritual retreat for adults and children, by Lake Merom in Galilee. The boy had returned so exhilarated and had spoken so enthusiastically about his experience that Aron had almost been tempted to see it for himself. But the whole Chabad setup reminded him too much of the rituals of orthodox Judaism and of his parent's flat in North London, especially Józsi's three cardinal rules that were 'as easy as A-B-D': the Hebrew *'ahavat Torah*, love for the Torah; the Yiddish *bentch*, give blessing after a meal; and *daven*, pray with emotion. It was especially the *davening* that Aron hated.

Avi hadn't explained anything and Aron grew tired of waiting. 'So?' he prompted.

'We learnt about Rabbi Schneur Zalman,' said Avi, reaching for a different colouring pencil. 'He added one word in the book of Job and changed the whole meaning.' He paused and glanced at Aron. 'Isn't that amazing, Dad?' he said with a contagious smile. 'He changed the world with one word. Before that, people didn't get that they were part of God — I mean really part of Him. But after he added that word, people started to understand that their souls weren't just *like* God — they *really* were divine.'

'And what was the word?'

For the first time in his life, Avi looked at his dad as though he were being slow-witted. '*Really.*'

'Really?'

'Yes, really.'

Aron couldn't help it; he started to laugh. 'God, sometimes you sound just like my dad. Really.'

But Avi wasn't laughing. He was pointing at his two great-great grandfathers. 'They were stupid because they fought when they could have been friends. And they fought because they believed such hateful things about each other. We're just like them.'

Avi was going to change the world with his word. And he thought he sounded very grownup when he added, 'This is my wailing wall — look, there's even a crack in it.'

The following day Büyük-anne Lilah almost wailed when she saw the broken mirror. 'How could you do that?' she moaned to Avi, her deeply freckled hands moving to her cheeks in shock.

'I didn't, Büyük-anne. It was Matea.'

She remained silent for a while, taking in the metal frame with its ornate lattice pattern, now fully uncovered and empty of magic, leaning disenchanted against a chair in the hall. The flag itself had to be washed twice, hand-scrubbed by Samiha to remove eleven years of grime, and was ironed and stored away in the cupboard in the TV room where all the useless junk ended up.

'How could you,' she repeated sadly. 'It was my wedding gift to your parents.'

The gold bangles at both wrists jingled as she caressed the iron frame. 'My father bought it for my mother,' she said sadly. 'And look how it is because she gave it to me and I gave it to your mother.'

'It just needs a new mirror. That's all,' said Avi.

She shook her head. 'And how do you replace a mirror that was made in the nineteenth century in Limoges?'

'Well it was always covered up anyway,' he pouted.

The hand on the frame moved back to close into a tight fist. 'Yes.' She felt that the boy's father should have returned the gift after her Sela died, rather than leave it to fester. 'Yes, yes.' She moved away abruptly with a tinkle. 'Tell Samiha I'll have coffee in the living room,' adding, 'and do open the curtains, will you dear? What's the point of living on a third floor if you won't let the view in?'

She told him that she hoped he would take more care of the Janissary and asked whether he had taken down that 'horrible article' in his room. Then she launched into her family's history, recounting anecdotes of the pioneers who had fled Spain in the fifteenth century.

Büyük-anne Lilah ended her account abruptly as soon as she heard Aron's cough, which preceded the sound of the key in the door. He spluttered as he entered the flat, closing the door on the dust and the traffic outside.

'Hi, Dad,' called Avi from the living room.

'Hmm,' came the response.

Büyük-anne Lilah waited patiently for her son-in-law to finish his ablutions. She got up to leave when he came into the room, raising her eyebrows ever so slightly at his socks. 'Hello, Aron.'

'Lilah.' Aron forced a smile and said a bit too affably, 'Did you win today?'

Büyük-anne and her friends played for money, with a pot that never exceeded a few shekels just to make it interesting. Her bangles clinked as she gave a noncommittal wave. 'And how was your meeting?' she asked politely.

'As usual.'

'Well then.' She kissed Avi and aimed for the hall. 'I'll

see you next week, dear,' adding pointedly, 'and you'd better close the curtain now. You wouldn't want to be in trouble now.'

'He's already in trouble,' said Aron.

'What, for that old thing?' Büyük-anne indicated the deßjected frame. 'Give it to me and I'll find the perfect mirror for it.'

'Then take it,' said Aron. 'It's yours, Lilah.'

She smiled, delighted, and told him her handyman would pick it up tomorrow. 'Sela will be pleased.'

Aron waited for her to leave before turning to his son. 'It's not about the mirror,' he said, his green eyes turning grey. 'I saw Matea's mum in the stairwell. Is there anything you want to tell me?'

Avi shook his head.

Aron shouted when he was very cross. But when he was furious, his tone turned icy cold. 'So you're depraved now? Is that it?'

'No, Dad.' Avi was confused. Try as he might, he couldn't stop his tears from welling up in his eyes.

'And why did you lie to me about how it broke?' he demanded.

'I didn't, Dad, I swear.'

'You will go to your room,' ordered Aron, 'and you will write 200 words on what happened and about how sorry you are. And then, you will go downstairs and hand that essay to Matea's mum. Do I make myself clear?'

Avi was forced to nod as he wept.

In Matea's retelling of the events, Avi had whipped out his penis and had wanted her to show him her privates. When she refused, Avi pushed her against the mirror, which somehow caused it to fall off its hook.

Avi cried because his father hadn't even wanted to hear his side of the story. Matea was a filthy liar. He'd never shown her his penis and didn't want to see her naked — he'd just wanted to kiss her. When he wrote that, Aron duly corrected it in red ink, and sent him back to write progressively different accounts, which, with every version, was more toned with her tale and more replete with contrition.

When, finally, a suitable apology had been handwritten on a clean sheet of paper, Avi went downstairs, rang the doorbell, handed his essay to Matea's mum and mumbled: 'This is to say I'm sorry.'

She nodded. 'And I'm really sad,' she said at the door as she took the sheets of paper. 'You were like a brother to Matea.' She stared first at the sheet and then at him as though waiting for him to apologize once more for good measure. 'You know, Avi, you were lucky you didn't hurt her. That broken glass could have cut her very seriously. And we — ' Her voice trailed off.

Behind her, Avi could hear the voluble noises of the house and he yearned to enter.

'Thank you for this,' she said at length, waving the sheets. 'And send my best regards to your father.' Ever so slowly, she closed the door in his face.

Avi turned bright red and ran back to his house and his bedroom where he counted the ways he hated Matea and prayed she'd live to regret her lies. He was so furious with her that he even came close to cutting the hotline linking their two kitchen balconies.

But he missed her house.

And with every passing day after that, he would linger progressively longer at their door on his way out or back, hoping someone would open it and that all would be forgiven to return to how it was before the accident. On one occasion, he arrived from school at the same time as Matea's older brother and they climbed the stairs together in complete silence.

When Avi hesitated at their door, the older boy asked him, 'What do you want?'

'Can I see Matea?'

'Which part of her?' The boy found his joke so funny that Avi could still hear his laughter as he entered and shut the door.

It was a full three weeks later before Avi saw Matea again. She was waiting in the lobby.

'Hi,' said Avi.

'Hi,' she replied, looking away at the main entrance.

'What're you doing?'

'Waiting for my dad.'

'You want to play a game?'

She just shook her head without looking at him, causing her ponytail to swing.

There was an awkward silence.

At first, he'd meant to confront her with her lie, to ask her why she'd said those horrible things and to seek an apology from her. But that wouldn't have made things right between them. Avi could think of only one way to make her like him again: by lying himself. 'I told my dad to fire our cleaner.'

Matea spun around to face him. 'Really?'

'Yeah.'

She smiled. 'What did he say?'

'He said he'd consider it.'

She wanted more and urged him with her eyebrows. Avi had already fabricated a tall tale, so he had to wrap it up and sell it.

'He said that in any case he was thinking of getting a new cleaner because she's too big to do housework.'

'You mean she's too fat.' She had a broad grin.

Avi nodded, adding under his breath, 'And too Arab.'

Just then, Matea's father pulled up at the main entrance and honked his horn.

'My dad's here,' she said, turning to the door. 'He's dropping me off at the mall.'

'Can I come?'

'No, I'm meeting my girlfriends.' She hesitated at the door and, turning to Avi, added sweetly, 'But after that, maybe I'll come to your house.'

But he just wanted to go to hers. 'Or we could go to your house.'

She shook her head. 'Yours,' she insisted coyly. 'That way I can write that word on the wall for you. Or maybe you'll want to show me whatever you want.'

Avi watched her skip to her father's car, her ponytail bobbing up and down.

Samiha was mopping the guest bathroom when Avi rushed in. 'Wait, Abi,' she said, indicating his feet on the wet floor.

He looked down at his socks then frowned at her. 'You're always telling me what to do,' he said, almost shouting. 'You're not my mother. And my dad always wants us to wash our hands when we come in.' He moved resolutely to the sink, leaving his footprints on the floor.

She looked at him with surprise. '*Allah*,' she breathed.

Avi waited for Matea anxiously all afternoon.

He was actually pleased when she didn't come before 5:00 pm, which was when Samiha left the flat. He brushed his teeth, forced a comb through his unruly hair and applied some of Aron's deodorant. He even kept checking himself in the mirror of the main bathroom.

At 5:15, he started to suspect that she had stood him up.

Matea was just a liar and he began to dislike her again.

With every passing minute, he also felt increasingly guilty that he had lied about Samiha just so that Matea would like him again. How could he even have talked about firing her, he thought ashamedly, when she kept their house together.

'Carnival,' he muttered to himself.

The shame was in every person and in every situation.

The word in English, which Avi believed could transform the world, had its roots in Hungarian and Hebrew.

Those distant grandparents spoke with a Hungarian-Hebrew stress that had always delighted the boy. It was like a secret code invented by them and shared with a grandson they had never met. Thus, *jó* and *tov*, which meant 'good' in Hungarian and Hebrew, respectively, became *jó-tov* for 'excellent' and *nem-lo*, or 'no-no', was 'never ever'.

But *de kar haval*, 'pity-pity', denoted the ultimate in shame and pain and was used sparingly and only to represent a sense of outrage. It applied to Aron's grandfather and other relatives who were murdered in the Holocaust; to Józsi's younger brother and after whom Aron had initially been named, who perished in Budapest during the October Revolution; and it applied to Aron's mysterious ailment because he had popped out coughing instead of crying, like a newborn being thrust into the wrong atmosphere. But then, according to Dorika, it was precisely that sinfully alien environment at Aron's time and date of birth that literally seized his throat and caused that first of a lifetime of coughing fits.

Avi had rendered Nagymama Dorika's *de kar haval* into the more manageable 'carnival', and he had broadened the meaning to cover all injustices, such as the Arab-Israeli conflict and the death of his mother.

But it was far more than that, and Avi sat at his desk

and reached for a pen and paper to write down his defini-
tion of carnival.

*Carnival is about knowing — really knowing — the shame-
ful things you do and understanding that you can only stop
doing them if you recognize they're wrong in the first place.*

He read what he'd just written. That didn't sound right
at all. He knew what carnival meant, and he knew that
God would understand what he meant by it when the note
from the Wailing Wall would be delivered. But he had
trouble describing it in words. It was a bit like *mamash*.
The Chabad leader had explained how it meant so much
more than 'really', more than 'literally' or 'tangibly' — *mamash* was all of those and still meant something more. His
carnival was a bit like that.

He tried again:

*Carnival is about being aware — really aware — of the shame
that makes people what they are, so that they can become more
understanding of others.*

That was marginally better.

Matea was still a filthy liar, but then so was everyone
else. He just had to tell her 'carnival', actually say it to her
face for the Jewish magic to work. Then she would realize,
with blinding clarity, how wrong she was about Arabs and
become a happier person for it.

He scrubbed out the previous definitions and wrote:

Carnival: To recognize shame really.

He nodded and then looked up when he heard wails of anguish in the stairwell.

At 5:45, Aron entered his bedroom with a pale expression.

Even without Matea, Avi was invited back to her house the following morning and for the last time. After that, even the hotline had to be cut.

Neatly folded in his suit pocket was the spell to change the world and Matea's life. It was considerably shorter than 200 words and he didn't intend to give to anyone. This time, Aron came down the stairs with him.

Samiha immediately dropped her broom when they left and headed for Avi's bedroom. Finding her spot next to the desk, she prostrated herself a short distance from the wall. It wasn't the right time for prayer but Samiha made the most of the fact that she was alone in the flat. She was in the boy's bedroom because, of all the rooms, this was marginally the closest to the Kaaba in Mecca. She raised her hands to her shoulders, fingers stretching to the earlobes. Then, with the first *Allahu Akbar* completed, she folded her hands over her stomach with the right hand covering the left hand to restrict every movement. Her eyes fixed the exact spot on the floor where her forehead rested during prostration. At a length of three forearms, in the direction of the Kaaba, the wall with the Hungarian and Turk acted as her sutra, the compulsory barrier between a worshipper and the rest of the world.

Aron wore a yarmulke only when he had to and usually in order to add gravitas to momentous events, such as 13 March 1983, the day he married Sela; 1 January 1985, the day Avi was born; and 27 December 1985, the day his Sela died along with fifteen others during simultaneous twin terrorist attacks at Rome and Vienna airports by the Abu Nidal organization.

That morning, he was in a yarmulke for Matea.

Samiha prayed: 'God set me apart from my sins as east and west are apart from each other.' She paused and noted with concern that her eyes had strayed. She forced them back to the exact spot on the floor and emptied her mind of common thoughts, including and especially thoughts about that poor little girl and the evil jinn who had killed her.

The door to the flat was already open as father and son stepped inside. Even though every room was packed with people, there was a creepy silence as if the house itself had ascended to the third floor and lost the will to reflect the voices.

A tight band had formed around Matea's mum, propping her up, whose face had frozen into a crescent-shaped groan.

Matea never returned from the shopping mall. She died there along with twenty-three others in a suicide attack by al-Aqsa Martyrs' Brigade to avenge the death of little Salwa.

The three mirrors in Matea's living room and dining room were covered in black shrouds because everyone was created in God's image, and since each death diminished that image, covering mirrors could adequately reflect the loss.

God is the greatest.

With this final *Allahu Akbar* completed, Samiha prepared to leave Avi's bedroom.

She paused only briefly to take in the latest additions to the wall.

The image, closest to the Hungarian ancestor, was of a devastated shopping mall with a focus on a paramedic, squatting helplessly and his head buried in his hands. Below that image was a short poem Avi had written for Matea along with her passport picture.

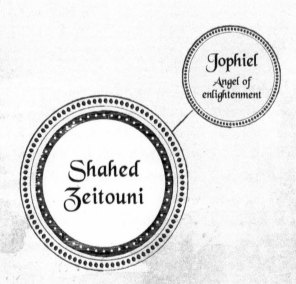

Jophiel
Angel of
enlightenment

Shahed
Zeitouni

3

West Bank

SHAHED ZEITOUNI WAS twelve when he explained the Solar System to his mother and Earth's place within it. Leading her outside by the hand, he pointed at the night sky. 'And there! Look over there,' he said with a contagious sense of wonder. 'That's Mars. You can tell because it's a bit redder than the other planets.'

'Oh, yes,' she said, squinting. 'That's true. I'd never noticed before.'

'Of course no one lives there and there's not enough air,' he said. 'But just imagine if we could have a whole planet to ourselves.' He paused to consider that and then added, 'We'd look back at this planet and have a good laugh at all the people living on a blue dot.'

'Blue?'

'The Earth looks blue from space.'

'Oh.'

'We'd be so far away, Mama, we wouldn't be able to see even the whole Middle East.'

While Ibtihage Zeitouni, known as Imm Nidal, was proud of her son's largely self-taught knowledge, she would have liked a few more religious texts in his assortment of books — works that revealed the magnificence of creation from an Islamic perspective, rather than from purely a scientific one.

And over the years, it seemed that the more the boy read and the more books appeared in his bedroom, the more Shahed changed from a confident boy and youth to a shy young man.

There was one book in particular that Shahed read and reread religiously, a novel that could not be further removed from the reality of Palestine. Entitled *Flatland* and written in English in the nineteenth century, the book tells the story of a sphere that pushes a square out of his plane to show him the beauty of three-dimensional space.

'You read it as though it were the Holy Koran,' Imm Nidal complained to her son one day, shortly after his seventeenth birthday. She was in his bedroom and took in the mess in one sweep: clothes everywhere on the floor and endless sheets of paper scattered on his desk and at the foot of his bed. 'I spend my life cleaning,' she grumbled. 'Why don't you go outside, Shahed? Why will you never help your father on the farm for a change?'

Shahed, lying on his bed, looked up briefly from his book and said, 'I'm working.'

'*Allah*,' she moaned softly. 'Then why don't you come and help me in the kitchen. I'm preparing a special lunch for your brother-in-law.'

'I'm working, Mama,' he repeated.

'That's not work,' she said with a dismissive wave. 'That work you do will never feed a family.' She turned to leave and on the way out, she spotted the map tacked to Shahed's wall and breathed, '*Bismillah*.'

This was the stronger of the two invocations that Imm Nidal used to guard against the demons. Thus, she moaned '*Allah*' whenever she entered the toilet next to the kitchen or undressed at night to prevent the evil spirits from seeing her naked body. '*Bismillah*' was usually reserved for things that entered her body, including food, drink and — back when they had intercourse — her husband's penis. Those nights, she'd also ensured that her body was at right angles to the eastern wall of the bedroom so that the sex would be blessed. Uttering the phrase created a barrier that stopped Satan and his minions from partaking in her meals and sexual activity.

Shahed looked up again and shook his head at his superstitious mother with sad regret. Then he glanced at the map before returning to his book.

There were as many maps of historic Palestine as there were Palestinian households in the occupied territories and in the many refugee camps littered across the Levant. Reproduced from an original published in the early 1940s, before the Catastrophe, this map featured the Arabic names of all the towns, villages and hamlets from the west bank of the River Jordan to the Mediterranean Sea and, lengthwise, from Lebanon in the north to Egypt in the south. It was usually stuck to the wall in the entrance or living room to provide a constant reminder of the land that once was and to reflect the loss of a collective inheritance. Where the maps were always the same, their arrangement varied widely. In some Palestinian houses, it was framed or garlanded with plastic flowers and set next to portraits of dead kin, appearing as a member of the household who was equally mourned. In other houses, an entire wall was consecrated to it, allowing it to develop into a shrine. This was the case of the first of two maps in the Zeitouni farm, which looked down on the dining room.

This second map in Shahed's bedroom was like none in any Palestinian household. Shahed had asked for and received that map for his fifteenth birthday to the delight of his father, who at first mistook his son's zeal.

This particular map of historic Palestine had progressively changed over two years. Using a red marker pen, Shahed had drawn idealized borders, confining the entire land to an elongated polygon with many smaller square cantons and, with the help of a map of Israel downloaded from the Internet, he had painstakingly deleted all the Arab towns and villages that no longer existed, added all the new Israeli settlements, and corrected or updated all the English transliterations, including, for example, Tel Abib to Tel Aviv.

This second map was not a passive reminder to lament the Catastrophe, and the young man who had stuck it on the wall did not feel as duty bound as others his age to dream of the stolen land. And unlike the one in the dining room, which had pride of place, this map had to compete for wall space with various sheets and charts of geometric figures and algebraic formulae.

Shahed was not lying; he was in fact really working.

He had spent most of his free time over the past two years struggling with equations, measuring various objects, including his own surface area, timing all sorts of events, and jotting down all his notes. He was working on his theorem, which he called Flatland after the book that continued to inspire him. This theorem would prove mathematically and beyond a shadow of a doubt how Palestinians and Israelis could live in peace side by side.

According to his model, people and countries could be represented by idealized squares or circles and, therefore, that conflicts between them could be reduced to bare geometric problems with real solutions.

In his case, he lived in the West Bank, a relative square to the relative circle that was Israel, and in a family where he stuck out like a circle among squares.

Resolving conflicts therefore required ways of reconciling the two shapes: finding corners on a circle or adding curvature to a square. In that light, even the most intractable of conflicts — Arabs versus Israelis — was merely a mathematical conundrum, albeit one that had eluded the best scientific minds for the better part of 4,000 years: squaring the circle.

At first, he attempted to square the circle using nothing more than imagination and pure geometry as the ancient Greeks and Arabs had tried eons ago. But there was no static solution; squares and circles were intrinsically too dissimilar to be matched by a formula. Shahed's eureka occurred when he considered a dynamic solution, adding a time factor. It came to him one day as he was shirking his chores around the farm. Hiding from his father, he had sneaked into the building that housed the family's olive press and had squatted on the ground, entranced by the large millstones that thundered at twenty revolutions per minute to turn olives into paste. When they were at rest, the grooves on the millstones, half submerged in a giant red receptacle, seemed like so many sides to interrupt the circular forms.

Inspired, he built a model that, once completed, took up most of the space on his desk: a square wooden block through which, at its centre of gravity, an elastic band passed to end at two hooks. When the block was turned, tightening the elastic, it could then be released such that the square spun perfectly on its axis. Looking directly across at the whizzing block, the four corners of the square all but vanished and the straight sides grew curved in the spin.

He'd written the final mathematical solution in bold black letters and symbols on the map itself, over the blue of the Mediterranean Sea. To turn Palestine into Israel, 'spin'

Palestine by a factor of the surface area of historic Palestine, the surface area of a smaller future Palestine, the size of the population and the time in years since the creation of Israel. Conversely, to turn Israel into Palestine, 'slow' it down by the same amount.

It was particularly ironic that his inspiration should have come — even if indirectly — from his father, the king of squares, whose interests were limited to turning olives into olive oil and to acts of favouritism towards Shahed's older sister, Nidal. As a farmer's son without the slightest inclination for the business, Shahed had grown up with the constant comparison crammed down his throat.

Accordingly, Nidal's hands were not 'as soft' as his, she knew 'an olive from a date' and she was a 'true Arab'. Even physically, Nidal and their kid brother, Saddam, inherited their father's olive complexion and straight black hair, while Shahed had added a thin layer of white to his mother's light skin tone to enhance the chestnut curls on his head. The three shared only the brown eyes that, on Shahed, had a perpetual doughy sheen. His fairness had that quality of being generically Mediterranean. He could easily pass for Spanish, Italian or even Israeli.

Nidal was always given the important tasks around the farm, cleaning the millstones thoroughly after every batch to prevent souring of the olive paste in subsequent batches, and timing the grinding process just enough for the olive drops to join to form the largest droplets of oil and to allow the fruit enzymes to produce some of the oil aromas and taste.

Even the olives that Shahed picked during harvest were never sufficiently ripe or fleshy enough for his father's taste. Shahed accepted every criticism with bowed head, which further exacerbated Abu Nidal. 'Stand tall!' he would roar. 'Real Palestinian men don't tremble like leaves.'

But with time, he stopped caring about Shahed's perceived weaknesses and limited his involvement in the business, which suited Shahed grandly as it allowed him time to work on Flatland.

It therefore came as no surprise to anyone, least of all to Shahed, when Abu Nidal offered his daughter and her new husband, Fouad Ash-shuja', an Israeli Arab from Haifa, all the land and the farmhouse to be validated upon his death so that, he'd argued, the Zeitouni farm would remain intact and because Nidal was simply better all-round than Shahed. This notarized wedding present and dowry flew in the face of tradition given that, according to Muslim custom, the farm should have been shared unequally among Nidal and her two brothers, with the boys inheriting twice her share. Abu Nidal had discussed his decision with the family back in June 2001, a fortnight before the wedding. It would also precede the Nationality and Entry into Israel Law, No. 5763-2003, which would forbid Israelis — Jews and Muslims alike — from marrying residents of the occupied territories.

This wedding gift was liberating for Shahed. It formalized the fact that his father had come round to his way of thinking, namely, that Shahed could never evolve into a farmer. His father had finally given up the secret hope that his son would become more interested in olive oil. In a Flatland sense, a small part of the four-sided figure had become more flexible with time, curving slightly at one corner to allow Shahed to pursue a different career.

In fact, if anything, it was Saddam, eleven days shy of his eleventh birthday, who had felt betrayed by his father's gift and deprived of his rightful inheritance. He'd run away on the day of the wedding and was discovered in the early evening two kilometres away, caked in mud and fighting with a younger boy, eight-year-old Mohsen Brahimi, outside the other boy's farm. Shahed had found him and dragged him by the ear the entire distance between the Brahimi and Zeitouni farms.

Shahed wanted to be a teacher, not a farmer. But in the interim, he had found the perfect job to get him away from the farm in an Internet café in Qalqiliya, which was the closest town five kilometres away due west.

'*Indranet*?' repeated his mother, frowning with clear disapproval when he informed the family.

They were in the dining room having lunch. Fouad was slumped in his seat opposite Shahed, with a hand on his wife of nine months. At either end of the table, Abu Nidal and Saddam were devouring generous portions of lamb, like father and son, as though fearful their plates might be snatched away from them.

Shahed was explaining the Internet to his mother, who shook her head with consternation, when his father looked up and asked, 'When do you start?'

'Tomorrow, Baba.'

He nodded briefly, which constituted an oblique blessing, and resumed his meal.

Saddam also looked up from his plate and said, 'But that's where losers hang out.'

Nidal ignored him, cleared her throat and declared, 'I've got some news as well.'

'That's where all the kids who are too scared of Israelis go to hide,' added Saddam, but no one was listening to him so he returned to his meal with renewed vigour.

All eyes were on Nidal, but Nidal had eyes only for her father. 'I'm pregnant, Baba,' she said beaming.

A smile crept over his face as Imm Nidal clapped and ululated briefly.

'Pregnant?' His tone could not mask his sudden joy. 'Pregnant, eh?' He mulled the prospect of becoming a grandfather and started to laugh. 'So you want to make me a *Jiddo*?' he asked his daughter. He nodded happily and smiled. 'About time. Come give me a kiss.'

Shahed offered his warmest *mabrouk*, congratulations, to his sister and said, 'It will grow into the best Zeitouni farmer ever.'

'Yes,' agreed Abu Nidal. 'My grandson's hands will be as tough as my Nidal's.' He brought one of her hands to his lips. Reluctantly, he had to let go of her hand to shake Fouad's hand.

'It could be a girl,' Shahed pointed out.

'No, it will be a boy.' Abu Nidal was too happy with his daughter to be bothered with Shahed. 'A boy as true as Palestine,' he spoke lovingly to Nidal.

'Just so long as he cares about olives.' Shahed spoke so softly that no one heard him. He glanced at the wall behind his father, at the traditional map of Palestine. Unlike the map in Shahed's room, this map had only one mark, added in black: a minuscule polygon to delineate the extent of the Zeitouni farm.

The view from the porch of the farmhouse embraced the fields of olive trees. In bright sunlight, the trees lost their individualities, spreading uniformly across the horizon in a mass of boughs and trunks. But at dawn every weekday, each tree reacted to the end of night in its own discrete way: some immediately yawned and stretched their branches, unfurling to celebrate the day; others creaked inwards like nocturnal creatures moaning at the light.

According to Abu Nidal, the oldest tree from the vantage of the porch, which even Shahed affectionately called Jiddo, had been an olive pip in the eighteenth century, and had grown so knobbed and twisted that in the early light it seemed to prostrate itself, using the farmhouse as a sutra to Mecca.

The farm consisted of almost three acres of olive trees that had remained comparatively unscathed by the turbulent century. Thus, Abu Nidal's father reaped the olive harvest in the 1940s, a particularly bountiful decade, as tens of thousands of families shifted their meagre possessions by the cartload to temporary addresses that would, with each passing generation, turn into permanent refugee camps all across the region.

The family business prospered in the subsequent two decades that followed the Catastrophe. The West Bank, including their farm, fell under Jordanian control, paving the way for exports of their olive oil to Jordan and the Gulf beyond. And while 1967 itself was a disastrous year, both on account of the fleshless pips that the trees yielded that season and for the Arab defeat in the Six-Day War, the 1970s was relatively favourable as exports picked up again, shifting instead to Israel and Europe beyond. Even the neighbouring Jewish settlement of Alfe Menashe, developed in the 1980s, provided an additional boost to the local demand for olive oil.

But Abu Nidal believed he was more nationalist than most of his generation — he repeated it often enough to his children. While he could sell his produce to Israelis, even sitting with their merchants over coffee to discuss prices and deliveries, he shook their hands as any gentleman must to conclude a deal, waited for them to leave, and then spat on his offending hand.

'May the oil turn to acid in their throats.' That particular curse was used so often it lost all its potency. 'May I live to see the day we won't need the Zionist shekel.'

But in terms of actual deeds, Abu Nidal's acts of defiance were largely irrelevant and vainglorious. His show of solidarity to the Arab cause was mostly limited to the names he had chosen for their three children:

Nidal, born on 4 June 1982, means struggle and defensive battle in Arabic and was his way of offering moral support to the Palestinian brethren in Lebanon on the eve of the Israeli invasion.

Shahed, born on 1 January 1985, signifies witness and justice in the afterlife and was chosen for its sense of divine retribution and despair. When the midwife presented Abu Nidal with this second child, the Arab world was still reeling from yet another military defeat. The PLO had been driven out of Lebanon and the massacres of Palestinians in the Sabra and Shatila refugee camps were still vivid in the collective psyche.

And *Saddam*, born on 10 August 1990, was named after a person rather than for any Arabic connotation. Their third child was born on the day Saddam Hussein of Iraq declared a jihad against America and Israel. He was very nearly the male carbon copy of Nidal — both physically and temperamentally — as though nature had tossed a thousand and one dice and all except the last had returned the same result.

According to Arab custom, Abu and Imm Nidal — Father and Mother of Struggle — should have changed their appellations to Abu and Imm Shahed when their first son was born. But upon his insistence, they kept the first, more belligerent name. 'I am in the resistance,' he said defiantly. 'I will change my name to Abu Shahed the day we win our freedom.'

He chose to remain Abu Nidal also as a conscious way of giving his approval to the Palestinian organization by the same name that had won so many victories against Israeli targets.

So it was by that name that the contractors addressed him when they arrived on 15 June 2002, armed with theodolites and posters. The posters, which they stapled to olive trees, fences and wherever else they could find space, were written in Hebrew and Arabic, and featured a map of the land being expropriated for the Wall.

Imm Nidal rushed to the contractors, her black abbaya swishing in the apparent wind. She immediately tore down the poster stapled to Jiddo and confronted the two Israelis and their Palestinian guide. 'What is this?' she demanded, tapping the map.

'Read it if you can,' said one of the Israelis, duly translated by his guide.

'I can read it. I just don't understand.'

Abu Nidal arrived on his tractor from one of the fields, saw her look of consternation, took one look at the poster and started to laugh. 'This is a joke,' he said at length, repeating it to the contractors.

'No joke, Abu Nidal,' they replied coldly.

'But there's obviously a mistake,' he insisted. 'Look again at your maps.'

'No mistake,' said the contractors through their guide.

He walked with them. 'Of course there's a mistake,' he said.

'Then take it up with the Ministry of Defence.'

He pointed at the section of the plan around his farm. 'This is facing east.'

'No mistake,' they repeated.

'But Israel is west of here.'

'So?'

His grin returned momentarily. 'So if I'm a suicide bomber, your wall will just stop me from blowing myself up in Ramallah.'

The Israelis stopped in their tracks and one of them actually grinned back. 'Don't worry,' he said, nodding towards the west. 'This barrier will join the one we're building in Qalqiliya. That should stop you.'

It did. Abu Nidal never laughed again.

As soon as the Israeli contractors sped off in their military jeep, he instructed Shahed and Saddam to walk all the way to Qalqiliya and tear down every poster that they found along the way, promising to thrash them soundly if they missed a single one.

It was one stroke of a red pen on a map that drove Abu Nidal insane. Had the line been drawn just a couple of degrees on either side, the farm would have survived.

The contractors did not follow their own maps; they took much more land than on the plan. More than thirty-three per cent of the land around Qalqiliya was expropriated to allow the Wall to coil around, dipping deep into the West Bank.

They chopped down the century-old olive trees, including Jiddo, that had been unfortunate enough to find themselves in the path of the red pen. Then they abandoned the shorn trunks and branches, stacking them high like firewood.

Abu Nidal instructed his boys to join him as he took his case straight to the mayor of Qalqiliya, the helpless representative of the Palestinian Authority who couldn't stop shaking his head sadly. 'Consider yourself lucky you still have a home. All Palestinian property within thirty-five metres of the wall has been destroyed.'

'Consider yourself lucky?' roared Abu Nidal. 'Consider yourself lucky I don't cut your throat with a kitchen knife.'

'I'm sorry, but what do you want me to do?'

Abu Nidal snapped: 'I want you to go home, undress your mother and then fuck her.'

But he reserved the best of his profanities for the Palestinian workers hired to build the Wall, some of whom he even recognized as residents of Qalqiliya.

At first, he tried to reason with them, arguing that Jews were too proud to do menial labour and that if Arabs were to quit en masse the Wall would never be built. And, when they replied that they needed the money to feed their families, he tried to bribe them. 'How much are the Zionists paying you? One shekel a day? Two? Whatever it is I'll double it if you just stand and do nothing.'

On several occasions, the Israeli soldiers assigned to protect the builders had to push him back using their guns as staffs.

'Your wardens have sold your balls to their dogs,' he shouted. 'You're nothing but castrated prisoners building your own prisons.'

An inverse proportionality was at play throughout the summer of 2002 whereby the more the Wall neared its completion, the less Abu Nidal found the energy to swear.

When the cement base was still wet, he and Nidal were busy cursing the builders as Shahed came to stand beside them.

'May your nightmares last until Hell,' shouted Nidal.

'Look,' said Abu Nidal. 'Look at all that slime poisoning our land.'

'Yes,' said Shahed sadly. His gaze swept across the horizon as he added, 'It's going to be twice as high as the Berlin Wall and five times as long.'

Abu Nidal thought he misheard. He frowned at his son. 'Than where?'

'The Berlin Wall,' mimicked Nidal viciously. Hugging her belly that was only just starting to show signs of her pregnancy, she added to her father, 'You'll soon be a grandfather to a real Palestinian.'

But Abu Nidal was busy slapping Shahed around the head, which caused several builders to laugh.

'Berlin,' he growled at Imm Nidal as she rushed to intervene. 'They're stealing our land and your son talks of bloody Germany — *Allemanya*.'

'He's only sixteen,' she said placatingly, 'What does he know?'

'He's seventeen,' corrected Nidal.

'He's an ass,' snapped Abu Nidal. 'What does the moron know? *Allemany-ayr*!' For emphasis, he grabbed his crotch and roared, 'My *ayr* is in Berlin!'

Nidal glared at her mother. 'He knows enough to say it's going to be ten times bigger than Berlin.'

Shahed, still red-faced, corrected, 'Five times.'

Abu Nidal raised his hand to slap his son again when he heard more builders laughing. He stopped, reached down for some stones and started to pelt them. Saddam came running and joined his father, his aim almost as true as the man's.

'That's right, boy. That's good. That's how you treat fucking collaborators.'

'Fucking collaborators,' shouted Saddam; his serious tone could not mask the boy's look of utter excitement.

Words had not stopped the workers, nor could sticks and stones; they were desperate for money to feed their families. The unemployment rate in the West Bank, which was already in the high double digits, had soared following Israel's decision to stop all migrant blue-collar workers from the occupied territories. Shahed was one of the fortunate few who still had a full-time job and had willingly accepted a cut in his modest income just to keep it. Even Aunt Samiha, Imm Nidal's sister who lived in Ramallah with her family and who had worked for the same Israeli family for seventeen years, had recently been denied leave to enter Israel.

Aunt Samiha would spend a day with them every six months or so, ostensibly to see them, although her visits always included a trip to the broom factory down the road, the Brahimi farm, where she always bought her brooms. While Imm Nidal and her sister could disagree on just about everything, constantly bickering on such subjects as the most effective detergents or the nature of jinn, they did at least see eye to eye on brooms: the Brahimis weaved the best in the world.

Once construction around Qalqiliya was finished, its 42,000 residents woke up to discover they now inhabited a round concrete bottle with a long neck whose cork was guarded by an Israeli checkpoint. The soldiers were also clearly visible in the round watchtowers, their binoculars reflecting sunlight like strobes. These had been erected every 200 metres with fat triangular tops, giving the illusion that the town had, in a matter of months, been transformed into a medieval fortress and could now boast the largest inhabited barbican in the world.

An extra section to the Wall was also added so that, were suicide bombers to head off from the Zeitouni farm, they now had to cross the Wall at two separate points to complete their missions in Israel.

These seizures had been cunningly designed to take the land without the people. Throughout the West Bank, the route of the Wall embraced and came as close as logistically feasible to Palestinian towns, villages and farms, thereby leaving Arab land in areas now de facto annexed into Israel. This was the case with the Zeitouni farm.

Abu Nidal lost considerably more than thirty-three per cent of his property. While the Wall itself had consumed less than ten per cent of his land, its route was such that the farmhouse was on its western flank and the fields of olive trees and the building that housed the olive press were now in Israel.

The ramifications of this was that he was compelled to circumvent the Alfe Menashe settlement, avoiding the Israeli bypass road, to reach the agricultural gate next to Arab Ramadin seven kilometres away, only to follow the Wall all the way back to his land on the eastern flank.

In all, then, a trip from the farmhouse to the first olive trees that used to take three minutes by foot would have become a commute of fifty-five minutes by tractor.

Abu Nidal would have suffered the humility, the hours to get to and from his land had he only been given half a chance. But after barely a week of sporadic opening, the agricultural gate was closed permanently. No justifications were given, and farmers with land on the Israeli side were advised to move on several kilometres down the road to the vehicular gate at Hable.

The Hable gate was open three times a day — 7:00–8:00 am, 12:00–1:00 pm and 4:00–5:00 pm — and only for Israeli-plated cars and commercial Palestinian vehicles with valid permits. Given that his tractor was neither registered in Israel nor a commercial Palestinian vehicle, his application for a permit was summarily rejected.

In a very real sense, Abu Nidal now lived in one country while his land was relocated to another — to a country that turned down all applications for entry visas. For all intents and purposes, the construction of the Wall had resulted in the seizure of more than ninety per cent of the Zeitouni estate.

By 10 November 2002, with the grey pre-fabricated slabs firmly hoisted into place, Abu Nidal hardly flinched when his son casually informed the family that the Wall was costing the Israeli government one million dollars per kilometre. He didn't even hear Shahed explaining how the Wall was a blessing in disguise. His groan was directed at the sheet of paper where he was calculating the family's diminishing resources. 'We'll have to sell the tractor,' he said softly and mostly to himself.

Saddam was busy trying to pop Nidal's navel back in. 'Look,' he said, tweaking the loose flesh, 'it's like Shahed's pricklet.'

Nidal slapped him good-naturedly and then guided his hand to her protruding belly. 'Can you feel him kicking?'

Shahed stood in the middle of the room like a teacher before an unruly class. 'The world is starting to understand the deep injustice,' he was saying. 'To the international community, Israel has become like South Africa during the Apartheid years.'

'How do you know it's a boy?' asked Saddam.

'Because I want a boy,' she replied.

Only his mother seemed to be listening to him, so he turned to her as he added, 'And this was actually disclosed in a secret report by Israel's Foreign Ministry.'

'Great,' said Saddam, happily. 'I'll be able to teach him lots of things.'

'With the exception of America, the world now considers Israeli policies as racist as those of the white supremacists. The report was especially alarmed by changed perceptions in the European Union.'

Imm Nidal looked straight at Shahed and asked, 'How do you know all that?'

'The report was leaked and is widely available on the Internet.'

'*Indranet,*' repeated Imm Nidal incredulously.

'And what could this little pipsqueak teach my boy?' teased Nidal.

'I can teach him to spit and to throw stones,' replied Saddam, causing both of them to laugh.

'Is it Dastmastur who told you?'

It was the first time she'd ever mentioned the name and Shahed's look of complete surprise was not lost on her other children.

'Who?' asked Nidal and Saddam simultaneously.

Behind them, Abu Nidal muttered, 'In 1995, it was worth $20,000.'

Shahed was stunned into silence.

'We'd be lucky to get $10,000.'

'Who's Dasturmast?' asked Nidal, intrigued by Shahed's discomfort.

'Yeah,' said Saddam.

'I'd probably settle for $5,000.'

Shahed turned to his father. 'Baba, if you want,' he said, hesitating, 'I could find a buyer for the tractor on the Internet.'

Abu Nidal looked up. 'So now my son is interested in farm matters,' he said sourly, 'now that there is no farm and no money.' He returned to his accounts sullenly.

'So who's Basturma, Mama?' asked Saddam.

She began, 'Dastmastur is — '

'None of your business,' Shahed completed her sentence and snapped, 'And the next time you want to go through my things, Mama, ask me first.' He withdrew to his bedroom.

'*Bismillah*,' muttered Imm Nidal.

With time, Imm Nidal had come to believe that a malevolent jinni lived in Shahed's bedroom and was responsible for her son's transformation from a confident boy to a shy young man. She even had proof of his existence: the evil demon went by the name of Dastmastur and communicated directly with her Shahed — she had found several sheets of paper with that name, hidden under Shahed's underwear. This was why she said '*Bismillah*' every time she entered and left his room, or even thought about that bedroom.

It was written that every child of Adam would be assigned a *qareen*, a faithful companion from among the jinn. Humans and jinn were supposed to complement one another. It was God's way of maintaining checks and balances in the universe. But it was a delicate equilibrium and sometimes a single event could turn the most God-fearing Muslim into the most abject kafir. What she didn't know, therefore, was whether the sprite had been a faithful companion to her son before being turned into a kafir by all the violence; or whether he'd lived in an olive tree — maybe even in Jiddo — that had been chopped down to make way for the Wall. Either way, the arrival of Dastmastur coincided with the construction of the Wall, and would bring the deepest harm and suffering into the farmhouse.

Nidal and Saddam pressed her for more information, but she shook her head and got up resolutely to prepare lunch.

Given that it was a Sunday, she lined up the ingredients to prepare a *hummus balila* — a plain dish of whole chick peas in olive oil, served warm. She began by sprinkling some salt on four cloves of garlic in the mortar and pounding them into a fine puree. Imm Nidal added the crushed garlic to the bowl of cooked chick peas, a dash of lemon juice, and pinches of cumin and cinnamon. The trick to a good *hummus balila* was the topping of fried pine kernels and the quantity and quality of the olive oil added at the end of the preparation. There had to be enough oil so that the mixture appeared as an atoll in an olive-green sea. With so much dressing involved, high-grade oil was essential.

Imm Nidal's *balila* suffered when their reserves of oil ran out and when, for the first time in generations of Zeitounis, they were forced to buy olive oil, cheaply and by the bottle. And given the steep price of pine kernels, these were among the first items to be excluded from shopping lists. But she didn't mind that her wide culinary repertoire from before the Wall had been clipped to a dozen basic dishes. It only served to emphasize her faith every day. Only the covetous and indolent needed more than a basic diet. True believers could live on a handful of ingredients.

But Abu Nidal believed differently. He jumped to his feet when he heard his son-in-law's car in the driveway and stepped outside. He was going to ask him the mother of all favours that would save the farm.

Raphael

Angel of
healing

Bernadette
Shakour

4

BERNADETTE SHAKER WAS a product of the modern world and sometimes hated herself for it.

She was single, with a love life that was packed with casual flings and embroidered imagination, and she had a minuscule and dysfunctional family that had almost become the archetype of families in any major city in the West. Even her surname was a lie: Shakour had been mistakenly Anglicized to Shaker by the registrar during her freshman year of university, which she had chosen not to rectify.

Like most middle-class Beirutis, she prided herself on being trilingual; but, like most, her Arabic was limited to the colloquial version of spoken Lebanese and to a basic grasp of journalese Arabic, the language used by the media across the region. The third and purest form — Classical Arabic — remained largely indecipherable to her. She'd therefore stretched the truth somewhat when she applied to the United Nations Relief and Works Agency for Palestine Refugees in the Near East and declared perfect oral as well as written fluency in three of the six official UN languages — a modest fabrication that eventually secured her the job of Projects Officer in the West Bank.

Bernadette had accepted the offer by UNRWA and had relocated to the West Bank partly to rediscover the Arab roots of her ancestors. But in one way, at least, she was in synch with the world of Arab traditions and rituals. From the age of fifteen, Bernadette had replaced lunch with the Lord's Prayer — a habit that she found impossible to break. She wasn't particularly religious nor did she believe that prayers could atone for sins, but come every lunchtime, she fasted and said the Lord's Prayer with the passion of an Antonine nun to remind herself of past entanglements.

She said it in its original Aramaic as Jesus had intended, and not as it had been rendered by countless translations first into Greek, then into Latin and later into the modern languages. She liked the sound of Aramaic, but she especially enjoyed the sense and spirit of the original prayer that had been lost over the centuries:

Aboon dabashmaya nethkadash shamak. Tetha malkoothak newe tzevyanak aykan dabashmaya af bara — Cosmic creator of all radiance and vibration, soften the ground of our being and carve out a space within us where your presence can abide —

Bernadette completed her lunchtime prayer and waited patiently in line at a checkpoint midway between Ramallah and Qalqiliya behind an old Mercedes that was serving as a communal taxi. In addition to the driver, she could count seven heads in the car. A little girl in the back leaned over the seat and was peering at her.

Bernadette smiled and the little girl returned a coy grin. Still grinning, she held out her doll for Bernadette to admire. The doll in the Mercedes started to dance and then paused.

Bernadette was doomed to remember every detail of her own doll, even though she had played with it for less than fifteen days.

The young girl in the backseat checked to see the reaction. Bernadette took her hands off the steering wheel to clap. Thus encouraged, the girl smiled broadly and the doll resumed her dance as the communal taxi inched forward.

The drive to Qalqiliya took her through one of the most fertile basins in the West Bank. Despite the dry season, the groves and orchards on either side of the road reflected a dark green in the morning light. Bernadette opened her window and filled her lungs with the crisp apparent wind.

As Projects Officer with UNRWA, Bernadette was responsible for both the payments to Palestinian households and for drafting reports to donors to describe how the money had been used in order to raise more funding. There was a whole series of variables strung together into an intricate formula to calculate net payments.

Bernadette loved to blend facts and figures with real situations and people. It was like cooking. You changed just a few ingredients and an altogether different dish was created.

A few kilometres outside Qalqiliya, Bernadette slowed down as she drove through a hamlet and came to a complete stop to let an old woman cross the road. The driver in the car behind her blared his horn and raised his arms angrily. She looked in her rear-view mirror and deliberately brought her hand out of the window, fingers and thumb touching, and waved in a gesture to signify, 'Be patient, asshole.'

It never ceased to amaze her how the very same drivers who could wait patiently for an hour at a checkpoint, had the staying power of a startled cockroach when it came to traffic lights and pedestrian crossings. This particular driver was being made to suffer an extra ten seconds, given that the old woman hobbled with a stick.

As soon as the coast was clear, he accelerated, causing his wheels to screech and overtook her, his open palm flopping down with resignation to signify, 'Woman driver — of course.'

She caught up with him at the last checkpoint outside Qalqiliya, waiting with a line of cars. She honked once to draw his attention and when the driver looked in his rearview mirror, she gave him a little clap to mean, 'Bravo, you've come far.'

This time, the driver shook his head and the open palm traced a sweeping arc to end at the chin. For the life of her, she didn't understand what that gesture meant.

Five-year-old Bernadette Shakour knew for a fact that it was the prettiest doll in the whole world. It had a lovely pink dress and white apron, brown eyes that came with retractile eyelids, and a little voice that said, '*Je t'adore,*' every time you pulled its string. She had received it fifteen days earlier, on Christmas Eve of 1975, from her very own Santa: '*Mon petit Papa Noël à moi,*' she had bubbled with delight.

It was the first day of term and she didn't want to start her second year of kindergarten just yet. Bernadette wanted to stay at home to play with her doll or, failing which, to take it to school and show it off to all her friends. Both options were unacceptable to her parents and her mother had to tell her off soundly before her father drove her to school on his way to work.

She cried all the way and, at the school gate, decided she hated three-year-old Michel for being too young to go to school.

When, halfway through the morning, her grandmother entered the classroom, Bernadette first thought that her parents had changed their minds and had decided to send the doll with Mémé. But then she wondered why this grandmother, who preferred to be called Mémé and who lived in Beirut not far from Papa's garage, had been sent instead of her other grandmother, Teta, Maman's mother who lived in Damour five houses down the road from them.

Mémé whispered briefly to the teacher and both turned to look at her oddly.

Outside the classroom, Bernadette asked in French, 'Where's my doll, Mémé?' Her other grandmother preferred to speak Arabic.

'Come,' she replied simply.

'You're squeezing my hand,' complained Bernadette. Mémé looked as if she was about to cry.

'Be a good girl, now,' she said. 'You'll be staying with me for a while.'

'How long, Mémé?'

'Maybe a week.' And then she muttered to herself in a language Bernadette didn't understand.

They hurried down the school corridor as though a monster were chasing them.

The weeks became months and several years, and it would take all that time for Bernadette living with her grandmother to understand the events of that day, and many more transformations to come to terms with them.

On 9 January 1976, at 11:00 am, Palestinian fighters surrounded the Christian town of Damour, approximately twenty kilometres south of Beirut. Within two weeks, the town of some 25,000 inhabitants was completely destroyed. In all, 582 men, women and children were massacred. Many of the bodies had been dismembered, so that the Red Cross volunteers who came to bury the dead had to count the heads to arrive at that number.

Among the dead were Bernadette's mother and little brother.

Bernadette never had another doll; and, soon after, she stopped believing in *Papa Noël*.

As a young girl, Bernadette came to believe that Palestinians were another species of creatures. They looked vaguely human except for their faces, which were always disfigured, and in the way they hobbled in dark places unlike the Christian champions who marched upright. They also caused Papa to be absent for entire months, even during the holidays. She'd heard one of Mémé's friends say that if every other Christian killed one Palestinian, then the disease would come to an end.

In that sense, it was like the fruit trees in Damour that needed a special spray every spring to stop the ravages of insects. While the town itself had become blurred as the memory of Maman and Michel, Bernadette remembered how she'd been forced to remain indoors for two days as a man in a mask aimed a metal pipe at the branches, spraying a white substance at all the trees in their garden. On the third day she'd emerged to see the powdery residue on the branches and leaves.

Bernadette was prepared to do her duty, and don the mask, carry a metal pipe and spray the Palesticide that would end the war.

But the problem was that, unlike cockroaches and mosquitoes, which could be Pif-Paffed to death, a special spray to ward off Palestinians had not been invented yet. She therefore spent most of her second Christmas at Mémé's trying to create such a repellent. She knew that the resulting substance had to be white as the snow on Mount Lebanon and free of fatty and sweet ingredients that only attracted rats. But beyond these obvious considerations, she didn't know how to proceed with her poison.

'Don't worry your little mind,' said Mémé with a sad, indulgent smile; she hadn't fully grasped her granddaughter's self-appointed mission: '*Le bon Dieu disposera.*'

So Bernadette started to pray twice a day and four times on Sunday until, five days before the Epiphany of 1978, the good God felt disposed to send her a gift.

The Maronite priest was administering the end of mass in the Church of Our Lady, which had unofficially been renamed the Church of the Refugees on account of the large influx of ex-residents of Damour and surrounding villages who used it as a meeting-place. Bernadette had only just begun the training for the First Communion so she remained seated as her grandmother joined the queue. After a while, a woman crossed herself and came to sit in Mémé's space.

'Bernadette,' she whispered. 'Look at you,' she marvelled softly. 'You look like a lady.'

'My grandmother is sitting here,' Bernadette whispered back.

'All grown up.' She seemed to inspect the girl for a moment. 'You don't recognize me, do you?'

She looked vaguely familiar; Bernadette shook her head.

'I'm Tante Hoda.'

The name was vaguely familiar.

'I lived next door to you in Damour.'

Bernadette nodded and wished Mémé would hurry back.

'How is your *Baba*?'

Papa, she corrected mentally and gave a curt nod.

'It's your duty now to look after him,' whispered Hoda

and, reaching inside a large bag, she placed a notebook on the girl's lap. 'This will help.'

Bernadette glanced down and then looked at the woman quizzically.

'This was your Mama's recipe book, Tante,' explained Hoda with sudden emotion. 'She made the best *riz-a'a-djeij* in Lebanon. She lent it to me before — ' her voice trailed off.

The handwriting on the cover was as vaguely familiar as the smell of her mother's chicken rice dish.

'I left with only my jewels and this book.' She cleared her throat. 'But I had to return it. Your Mama had asked me to before — '

'*Maman,*' corrected Bernadette.

She kissed the girl on her forehead. 'I knew I'd find you one day.' She rose to her feet and said, 'Take good care of it, Tante, and may it encourage you to prepare good food in these evil times.'

Bernadette opened the thick book at random and her index finger followed the recipe for *mahshi koussa b'laban,* stuffed courgettes cooked in yoghurt.

When Mémé returned and asked about the notebook in French, Bernadette replied in Arabic, beaming, 'Mama came down from heaven to give me this Christmas present.'

'Don't be such a foolish girl,' said Mémé crossly.

But Bernadette wasn't being foolish. She was convinced that, along with the usual recipes, Maman had written down a special poison that would affect only Palestinian creatures.

She immediately found what she was looking for as she

flicked through the entire notebook of 172 recipes. Between the recipe for *mhammarah* — walnut and chilli dip — and *sabeedaj jbeiliyeh* — tangy squid whose ink is replaced by equally black pomegranate molasses — she found an entry that was called simply, *La cure*.

That was it, she thought happily. The cure would make everything right again. All she needed to do now was to prepare enough of it to kill Palestinians. She couldn't wait to get into the kitchen.

Her father, Antoine Shakour, was not impressed with her poison.

Bernadette had mixed enough to fill a small pan. 'I can prepare more if you need it, Papa,' she said hopefully.

'She won't listen to me,' Mémé said to her son with resignation. 'You need to speak to her.'

'Fine. Let me deal with it.'

Mémé frowned at him. 'Since when do you speak to me in Arabic?' she demanded.

Antoine ignored her and, turning his attention to his daughter, indicated the pan and continued in Arabic, 'What *exactly* do you want to do with that?'

'I made it for you, Papa,' she said quickly, 'It's from Maman.'

'Eh?'

She showed him the entry in the large notebook.

Antoine's hand seemed almost to caress the page; he said nothing for a while. 'Yes,' he said at length, adding dispassionately and in French, 'This was for Michel's cough. You remember that, don't you Bernadette?'

She nodded. 'Yes, Papa.' She sounded very grown up when she added, 'But it's also the cure to the Palestinian disease.'

'The what?'

'The Palestinian disease,' she repeated evenly.

'I see,' he said, trying to appear serious though he did betray an amused smile. He asked, 'And how does it work?'

'Like Pif Paf,' she said simply. 'You spray it in their faces.'

'Right.'

He seemed to be giving that some thought; it encouraged Bernadette. 'It'll work. Honest.'

'We'd have to get really close to them though.'

'Stop playing with the poor child,' scolded Mémé.

It was Bernadette's turn to ignore her. 'Maybe we could use a really long hose like they do to spray the trees in Damour.' She added excitedly, 'This way we could go home.'

'This is your home,' interjected Mémé.

Antoine patted his knees for Bernadette to climb in his lap. He hugged her and kissed her.

This time Mémé spoke in Arabic, 'Tell her this is your home now.'

Antoine stroked his daughter's hair. 'I think we'll leave the poison for another time.' With his other hand, he opened the notebook at the recipe for *riz-a'a-djeij*. 'But we can have the taste of home,' he said gently. 'Why don't you get Mémé to help you make a real *riz-a'a-djeij*.'

Mémé immediately complained in French: 'I make a very good *riz-au-poulet*.'

Both Antoine and Bernadette looked at her with distaste; not even 100-per cent Francophiles ever called *riz-a'a-djeij* by its French equivalent. '*Oui, Maman,*' said Antoine, 'but why don't you help Bernadette with this recipe for a change?'

'A change from what?' she asked, suddenly perplexed.

'From your *riz-au-poulet*.'

She nodded slowly. 'What did you call it before?'

'*Riz-a'a-djeij.*'

'Of course it is,' she said, still frowning, which caused Bernadette to snicker.

Of the 172 recipes in the notebook, it seemed fitting to begin with *riz-a'a-djeij*.

There were as many versions of this dish as there were housewives in Lebanon. Maman's variety, duly reproduced by Bernadette, was a festive platter comprising minced lamb, raisins, roasted pine kernels and blanched almonds in addition to the rice (which was cooked in a broth of bone marrow) and chicken breasts. It served as a perfect accompaniment to turkey so that, in the course of ten Christmases until Mémé lost the ability to light the oven, she prepared the *riz-a'a-djeij* while her grandmother prepared the bird, and each tried to outperform the other.

5

ARON READ AVI's letter of convocation for military service and moved his hand to caress his son's curly hair. '*Çok güzel son,*' he said affectionately. You are very beautiful: it was the only sentence his Turkish-speaking S'faradi Sela had taught him. 'You are so much like your beautiful mother.'

Israeli men were required to carry out three years of compulsory military service from the age of eighteen and then at least a month a year of reserve duty until the age of forty. Those exempted from service included students of the Torah, Israeli Arabs and those with a criminal record or with mental or other, verifiable health problems. And while the law was less stringent on women, some choose to follow exactly the same military duties. This had been the case with Sela, who remained a reservist until the very end — until her coffin returned home, draped in the Star of David.

Aron pictured his son in an IDF uniform and remembered the first time he saw Sela. She stood at the far end of the massive Roman hippodrome on the outskirts of Tyre in South Lebanon, a slender figure made more vulnerable by the oval vastness of the old chariot track. She wore the tight uniform of an Israeli officer, which only accentuated full breasts and delightfully curved hips. Sela was the antiquities expert, a reservist attached to the army. The interview with her had developed into many meetings over the course of eight days and seven nights, with conversations that encompassed considerably more than Phoenician seafaring, Macedonian conquests and Crusader cathedrals.

'Dad, I refuse to join an organization that is dedicated to killing,' Avi said flatly.

The hand froze on Avi's head and slowly moved away.

Avi added darkly, 'I'd rather be locked away for life than kill a single child.'

'You're not being asked to kill children,' countered Aron. 'Your mother never had to kill a child.' Were it not for all the dust in the Middle East, Aron would also have served his country. As a naturalized Israeli, he should have become a reservist but was exempted from duty given his affliction.

'Mum lived in a different world and served a different IDF.'

'So that makes you shirk military duty?' asked Aron unsympathetically.

'Yes.'

'That doesn't make you a pacifist — it makes you no better than any deserter or common criminal.'

'According to Amnesty International, more than fifty children under the age of twelve were killed by the IDF in the first seven months of 2002 alone.'

'Where do you get that from?'

'From the Internet, where else?'

'And your point?' asked Aron impatiently.

'My point?' Avi glared suddenly at his father. 'My point is that you never get my point. My point is that young children are dying and that Israeli soldiers are killing them.'

Aron raised his tone. 'And Matea? Have you forgotten her? Have you forgotten all our little Mateas who are blown apart by fanatics every day?'

'No,' said Avi. 'We call those criminals fanatics, suicide bombers, Islamic extremists and much more besides. But do we have a name for our soldiers who kill their children? Don't you think it's strange — to say the least — that not a single one of these criminals has been brought before a tribunal? Not even on the lesser charge of accidental manslaughter.' Avi's green eyes were still grey. 'Children are not being caught in the crossfire — they're being actively targeted. And I refuse to be a part of that.'

'Then leave,' Aron shouted. 'Go live in London if you can't hack it here. Go be with your grandparents. They're too petrified of Israel even to visit.' Aron stopped abruptly. He hadn't meant to bring his parents into the argument: the rupture between the Lunzer and Lounger households was not at all relevant. That József and Dorika hadn't made the slightest effort to meet Sela let alone their own grandson was out of context here; that they had limited their contact to short phone calls and birthday cards with obscure Talmudic messages could hardly matter now.

As a child, Avi would have pouted at this point and withdrawn to his bedroom. But he now had the confidence and the cut and thrust of an eighteen-year-old. 'Nagypapa Józsi is also a conscientious objector,' he argued. 'On the contrary, he has the balls to follow his conscience and refuse to come to Israel.'

'*His* conscience?' Aron couldn't prevent his tone from turning derisive.

'Yes,' said Avi. 'Nagypapa doesn't believe in Israel, so he can't come to Israel.'

'Exactly right,' said Aron triumphantly. 'That makes him a lesser Jew.'

'A Jew who doesn't believe in Israel is not a lesser Jew.'

It was Aron who stormed out of the kitchen, with a final shot: 'Oh yes he is. *Your nagypapa* is a loser Jew.'

Avi waited a while in the kitchen, then moved resolutely to his bedroom, switched on his PC and immediately typed back his reply to the army, stating he was a pacifist and that his conscience did not permit him to serve in a military capacity.

Aron had headed to the bar for some whisky, and Avi could hear him swearing loudly to himself. He switched off his computer and picked up a pen to write in his pad:

They both talk in terms of purity. For Nagypapa Józsi, Judaism becomes impure in Israel because God intends Jews to wander eternally, growing in faith as they dream of the Promised Land

but never quite reaching it. And Dad talks about the purity of the
nation and how an influx of Arabs would sink the vision of Israel.

He tore out the sheet and swivelled in his chair to stick it on the wall on the Hungarian side. There was no actual space left, so the note had to cover partially a picture of broken crockery on a table (where thirty people had lost their lives in a suicide blast in Netanya on the first day of the Passover).

The wall reflected Avi's transformation over the years.

The portraits had remained and were now at the centre of a vertiginous spiral of pictures, articles, comments and graffiti that spun to the ceiling and floor. The pictures and articles were clippings from newspapers and magazines or were downloaded from the Internet. One of the most poignant images, on the side of the Janissary ancestor, was a snapshot of TV footage of a twelve-year-old Palestinian boy, Muhammad al-Durra, dying in his father's arms for a televised audience. The boy cowered behind his father, who tried to shield him with his arms from an Israeli sniper.

The banner beneath the central portraits had been replaced, leaving only the faintest of traces. Now Hungarian and Turk were circumscribed by a solid line and CARNIVAL was painted in such a way that the letters appeared as round watchtowers and the line as a barrier to separate Avi's great-great-grandfathers from the rest of the wall. The line was roughly circular except for a slight projection between the second and third towers, appearing like the silhouette of a nose to a man's head.

At the top of the wall and partially covering the crack running down from the ceiling was the destruction of the World Trade Center in New York and sixteen-year-old Avi's words:

The Twin Towers came down and the world watched. Today is the morning after the day before. I'm in a yarmulke — predictably enough, Dad doesn't see why I'm sitting shiva for complete strangers (3,000 complete strangers at the latest count!). I have heard on Arabic TV of the attack being called a 'work of art' because it was so perfectly coordinated and executed. So if this was a Degas, what would they call the Holocaust? A Matisse?

Aron poured himself another single malt, opened the heavy drapes and stared out at Jerusalem where the dust and exhaust fumes from all the traffic still ruled the skies of the Old City. The constant and very real threat from suicidal maniacs caused everyone to eye strangers with a mixture of dread and suspicion. This was a place where everyone drove like lunatics, sweating, cursing and blaring horns, and cut corners in business dealings as though somehow that would bring everyone home sooner.

After all these years in Israel, Aron still felt like a complete *goi*. Even his refusenik son was a thousand times more Israeli. He wondered suddenly how Sela would have dealt with Avi and how her death had shaped his own relationship with his son. He had trouble remembering the early years. That was the ultimate conspiracy by Mother Nature: you never knew what a drain your offspring could be until you had them. Even in the best of situations — that is, with two active parents and four grandparents — the young childhood years represented a weary blur of interrupted life.

That was why he felt an irrational sense of betrayal when Avi referred to distant Józsi as an affectionate Nagypapa instead of a neutral *Grandfather*, as though transformed into a principal caregiver.

He knocked back his drink and returned to the bar for another.

He remembered the celebratory phone call from Józsi and Dorika at the hospital when Avi was born, which was preceded, some two weeks earlier, by a card that read:

'Behold, a son shall be born to thee, who shall be a man of rest; and I will give him rest from all his enemies round about; for his name shall be Solomon, and I will give peace and quietness unto Israel in his days.' Chronicles 1 22,9.

And a week after they returned home from the hospital, Józsi had phoned again, this time to offer his very best congratulations.

'I saw Avi Lunzer,' he said to Aron with feeling. 'Last night I saw your son, my new grandson. I am very happy.'

'Thank you, Papa.'

'His name shines like a fire on the page. I can see he will be a son of light.'

'I'm pleased, Papa,' said Aron.

'Yes. He will be moved by the angel of tolerance and love.'

'I'm pleased you like the name Avi.'

'Of course, Solomon is a better name,' said Józsi. 'But what is more important is his God-given name, eh? And he is with Camuel just like my poor brother, your Uncle Aron. *Mazal jó-tov!*'

'So when will I see you, Papa?'

There was some hesitation. 'Yes. I ask myself this question every minute of every day,' Józsi said finally with feeling. 'When will your name light up my page?'

Despite the double-glazing, he could just make out the last call to prayer of the day from some minaret deep in the Arab quarter. The crier's voice heaved like some hounded beast. It was enough to make you seasick. At times it sounded like a strangulated cry; at others, it was strangely soothing and melodic. For a while, languages and voices became interchangeable.

Briefly, it sounded like the Hungarian lullaby that Dorika used to sing to Aron, which in turn Aron had sung to Avi:

'Csoda fia szarvas, ezer ága boga… Boy stag of wonder, with horns of a thousand branches. Thousand branches and of a thousand bright candles. Among its horns it carries the light of the blessed sun. On its forehead there is a star, on its chest the moon — '

Then the voice guttered back into a choked wail.

Aron closed the curtain on the eternal city that lived on borrowed time.

If Avi had been there, he'd have been surprised that Aron could have mistaken a Muslim prayer for an old Hungarian Christmas carol sung by his Jewish mother. He'd have been even more surprised to hear him mutter, '*De kar haval.*'

A week after the military service letter arrived, Avi was asked to appear before one of the conscience committees to explain his reasons. The committee studied his record of refusal to engage in military areas of his school curriculum and came to two conclusions to counter his request: first, his record of opposition to the army showed he had the character of a fighter that was clearly not that of a pacifist; and second, the best place for someone like him who refused to submit to authority and discipline was the army.

But what made Avi's case especially sensitive for the authorities was that his father was a reputable journalist — a success that Aron owed in part to Samiha.

Flying in on her brooms, as it were, every day for seventeen years, Aron had been able to work mostly from home, filing his reports from the pristine comfort of his study rather than from dust-swept locations or poorly ventilated newsrooms. It was similarly thanks to her, or at least thanks to her sudden absence, that he became something of a household name in Israel. His critical commentary on the nation's dependence on Palestinian menial labour was a result of his growing sense of despair as Samiha became unable to cross into Israel for work, and as the house progressively reverted to its unclean past.

Aron's piece had touched a raw nerve with the Israeli public. More to the point, though, it had been largely misinterpreted. He'd meant that Israeli society needed to buck up, swallow its pride and fill those empty posts internally, from a pool of Jewish labourers who would add favourably to the delicate demographic balance. Instead, even now, two years after that article had caused a sensation, he was credited for having swayed public opinion, which in turn facilitated the political decision that opened the door to blue-collar workers from the Indian subcontinent and the Far East.

That commentary had been especially well received by the ultranationalist Evshel party — the esrimist movement, which had grown so prominent that it now had a minister in the coalition cabinet and could muster enough activists to fill the Western Wall plaza several times over. It had certainly not been Aron's intention to cosy up to the ultras nor, for that matter, to end up with their current cleaner, a Chinese girl called Lin.

But Aron was able to use this leverage as a well-read if not well-known figure among the Israeli right to meet the brigadier general who chaired the conscience committee, and to discuss his son's draft with him. A week after that meeting, Aron was made an offer: if his son agreed to enlist he would be granted 'an easy service, without a gun, uniform or military training'. A job would be found for him in a hospital. And now Aron faced the harder job of convincing his son not to make any further protests.

Aron hurried into the Shalom Coffee opposite the central bus station, stepping inside with considerable relief and spluttering as his throat readjusted to a closed environment: an alien in the city out of its spacesuit.

He smiled blankly at the barista who made him an Americano, glanced at the only other customers — two businessmen in suits — and made for one of the comfy seats.

The businessmen were quarrelling; their hands alternated between slicing and punching the air as they argued their respective positions. One of them had a stack of notes that he'd point to every now and then, and which the other dismissed with a wave or a flick of his fingers.

The argument stopped abruptly as another customer entered the coffeehouse.

All eyes were now on the newcomer, who stood at the counter deliberating his order. He was dressed in the black of an ultra-orthodox *haredi*. The barista spoke to him in Hebrew and it was only when the *haredi* answered flawlessly that the tension eased. The hands of the businessmen shot up again; Aron went back to sipping his Americano.

Statistically, even those suicide bombers who wore the garb of ultra-orthodox Jews spoke at best a distinctly unorthodox and broken Hebrew.

The *haredi* nodded at Aron as he waited for his drink. Aron nodded back and turned to stare at the traffic outside the window and at a car that was weaving through pedestrians while overtaking a coach on the inside. The coach driver pushed down hard on the brakes and even harder on the horn for a full five seconds. The driver in the car blared his horn in response and raised his arms angrily, before driving off at breakneck speed.

The businessmen paused again, drawn by the commotion outside, and the *haredi* chose a seat furthest from the window.

Eventually, after another protracted siren-like blast, the coach turned into the bus station to discharge Avi and his fellow passengers from Haifa. Aron spotted his son, who was carrying a duffel bag and strode with military precision as he weaved through the traffic to cross the road.

Avi saw him in the window and gave a quick wave. He had spent the weekend in Haifa with a friend to attend a debate on the policy of targeted killings, and it had been Aron's idea to meet at the Shalom Coffee on his return. Braving dust and lunatic drivers, Aron wanted them to talk about the military service in a neutral setting, away from the flat. He also didn't want any interruptions from an annoying housecleaner.

'So how's the high life in Haifa?' Aron asked with a grin as his son joined him with a juice.

'Don't ask,' said Avi glumly.

'I should have asked you to bring back a broom from there.'

Avi looked at him quizzically.

'Lin and I had our own debate in your absence,' explained Aron. 'Apparently, our brooms are too short. And everything gets stuck on the bloomin' hairs.' Lin was a housedirtier — as he called her particular line of work — who neither understood his affliction nor showed the slightest sympathy. Consequently, the unwritten rules for cleaning the Lunzer residence were now spelled out in bold red letters of DO's and the DON'T-EVER's and posted in the hall next to the clothes brush. 'Ironic they should be too short, don't you think?' For Aron, it was a double irony given that Middle Eastern brooms were typically short and thatched together from bamboo shoots. 'Samiha never had a problem with our brooms.'

'*Her* brooms,' Avi corrected. 'She used to buy her brooms from a factory in Qalqiliya. She never asked us for any money for them.'

'Where?' Aron was genuinely surprised that his son should know that.

'Qalqiliya,' repeated Avi. 'In the West Bank. That's where they make the best brooms. She'd go there every six months to replace our brooms, always buying two: one with thick bristles for our carpets and one with thin bristles for the floors.'

There was a pause as they sipped their respective drinks.

To judge by their less violent hand gestures, the two businessmen in the Shalom Coffee franchise were on the verge of reaching some sort of compromise.

Aron had the written offer from the conscience committee in his pocket and he reached for it now and placed it on the table. 'I was wrong, son, and you were right. Your mum would have thought twice about joining the IDF now.' He smiled briefly.

'Somedays I feel I really do need to leave Israel and never look back,' Avi said distractedly.

'But you'd soon go mad if you lived with your grandparents in London.' He mimicked Józsi's pronounced Hungarian accent: 'You are pursuant of peace, my boy, but you are not a lover of people who brings them closer to the Torah.'

Avi grinned at that. 'Yeah.' He chuckled. 'You know, I actually thought of Nagypapa during the debate. I was so mad at the end that I stood up and shouted, "Carnival!". Of course, there wasn't a living soul there who knew what I meant by that, so I just got the weirdest looks. I wish you'd been there.'

'Why? What happened?'

'We lost,' replied Avi. 'Speaking for the motion was a lecturer of Western philosophy at the University of Haifa. He expounded his support for the ethnic cleansing of Palestinians, claiming this as the best means of solving the conflict in Palestine. The esteemed professor went on to stress the "purity of race as a precondition for national excellence".' Avi paused and his eyes turned dark grey. 'I don't know, Dad. I mean how could he, the child of a Holocaust victim, fail to realize the horror of that statement?'

Aron nodded; he was a nationalist, not a fascist. '*Michutz la-shurah*,' he said in gentle agreement. Causeless hatred drove people *michutz la-shurah*, beyond the bounds of common sense. It still bothered him that his critical commentary on the nation's dependence on Palestinian menial labour had been used as a rallying cry by the *evshelim*. He pushed the envelope to his son.

'What's that?' asked Avi.

Aron told him. 'This is an option, nothing more,' he said. He waited for his son to read the letter. 'If you still choose not to enlist, I will back you fully, even if that means you have to spend time in jail as a conscientious objector.'

Avi reread the offer by the brigadier general of the conscience committee and then, ever so deliberately, delivered a nod and said almost to himself, 'As long as I don't have to carry a gun or wear the uniform of the oppressor.'

Avi's duffel bag was packed again a week later as he left home to work in a hospital in the south of the country. His tongue-in-cheek parting gift to Aron was an interactive guide of al-Aqsa Mosque. 'I know it's just the dust and crowds that have stopped you from visiting it, Dad,' he teased. 'Now you'll be able to check it out from the comfort of your study.'

They hugged and kissed by the tidy rack of shoes.

Avi stepped outside with a final wave, and his son disappeared into the world.

If the sun disappeared out of the blue, it would take the world eight minutes to realize that it had gone. Nothing travels faster than light, not even emotions.

Several minutes went by until Aron became aware — really aware — of Avi's departure, the time it took to toss the interactive guide of al-Aqsa Mosque, still in its wrapper, in the cupboard in the TV room with all the other useless junk, and to pour himself a drink and move to his study.

It was at his desk that the sense of loss finally caught up with him.

Without Avi, Jerusalem became North London. In an instant, the light was sucked out of the flat and all the windows became smaller.

He just couldn't understand this sudden, gnawing reaction that felt sickeningly like bereavement. After all, Avi was only doing his military service — in one of the safest parts of Israel and without a gun. Besides, Aron had all but pushed him into it, cajoling, persuading but ultimately also shoehorning him into the army. He should have felt pleased by the outcome, proud even. So why was he down like a squashed cabbage?

He suddenly yearned for a friend to talk to; he wanted his Sela or his Avi — they were his only friends in the world.

At his desk, he opened the top drawer where he stored his most prized possessions and inspected them, like a Shylock or a Fagin, to make sure everything was still there under the yarmulke.

There was Sela's postcard from Rome — it was innocuous enough with a snapshot of the Colosseum that any tourist might buy. But they were Sela's last words to him and even more poignant than that was the sense of suspended time that it represented; thanks to some spectacularly gross postal inefficiency, the postcard had been mailed three days before her departure from Rome and arrived at its destination a full three weeks after the sender's corpse.

There, too, was a small piece of paving stone from Tyre, which Sela had given him on their first meeting and which had caused the patented dustometre to tip to the vomit scale when she'd said, 'This was once part of the Roman road that linked Constantinople all the way to Alexandria — just think of all the bare feet, sandals, shoes and boots that have trodden on this stone.' Even now he could barely touch it without feeling queasy and sensing two millennia of dust.

But he had opened his miniature treasure chest for the third item: an envelope with a lock of baby Avi's black hair from his first haircut. While he could never reach back in time to hold his baby, he could still feel his hair. He brought the lock to his nose and inhaled the fine, downy hair so deeply he could swear he caught a faint trace of baby shampoo.

He could tell because the smell got lodged in the back of his throat where the hard Semitic ĥ is formed.

Zadkiel
Angel of
prayer

Ibtihage
Zeitouni

6

In theory, at least, it was a straightforward request that any desperate father and soon-to-be grandfather could ask of his son-in-law.

Abu Nidal shook Fouad's hand warmly as soon as he was out of his car. 'Welcome home, son,' he said. 'How was your trip? Not too many delays at the checkpoints, I hope.'

'No, it was fine.' He was surprised by Abu Nidal's uncharacteristic effusiveness.

'Of course, of course,' grinned Abu Nidal as he pointed at the car's Israeli plates. 'Thank God for your number.'

As they were about to enter the house, Abu Nidal held him back. 'Let us talk for a minute, without the women and children to disturb us.'

'Yes?'

'I am very pleased that Nidal chose you.'

'Thank you.'

'I am honoured that you are my son-in-law.'

'The honour is mine, Abu Nidal,' he replied formally.

'And for this reason, we would like to extend our hospitality forever.'

Fouad brought his palm to his chest to accept the honour.

Abu Nidal reiterated: 'Please consider this your new home.'

Fouad gave a little bow. 'Again I thank you.'

Abu Nidal's smile broadened. 'Good, I'm glad that's sorted now,' he said, bringing his hand solidly on Fouad's shoulder. 'I know the family will be very happy to hear the news.'

He started to lead the way into the house, but it was Fouad's turn to hold him back. 'News? What news?' he said, perplexed.

Abu Nidal also looked momentarily confused. 'That you have just agreed to live here of course.' He added, 'But you should hurry before the Jews change the law.'

Given that Fouad was married to a girl from the West Bank, he was perfectly entitled under Israeli law to relocate to Qalqiliya — along with his car. Fouad was an Israeli Arab and, as an extension of that citizenship, his car had Israeli plates. And it was that very car or, more precisely, the two small plates at either end that could save the farm. With an Israeli-plated car and an Israeli Arab son-in-law at the wheel, Abu Nidal could commute to his land every day through the Hable gate.

'But I live in Haifa, Abu Nidal,' he protested. 'I have family and business commitments.'

'Your family and business are here now,' he countered. 'You will have a son as true as Palestine who will become the best olive farmer in the world.'

Fouad shook his head.

Abu Nidal took a step back. 'What do you mean no?' He frowned.

'I'm sorry, Abu Nidal, but I can't live here.'

'What do you mean can't? But I have already given you the farm,' he said with growing frustration. 'I signed the papers so you could have everything.'

Even the dowry, the notarized wedding gift that made his wife the sole inheritor of the farm, could not entice him to leave Israel.

'I don't want to live here.'

'But I've given you everything,' he shouted suddenly. He stooped down to pick up a rock. 'Even this coward of a stone is now yours.'

'I'm sorry,' said Fouad coldly. 'I really wish I could help you.'

Shahed emerged from his bedroom for lunch and they were all at the dinner table with the exception of Saddam. The eleven-year-old had visually marked a small crack on the Wall and could spend hours every day aiming stones at it. They could hear him outside whooping with joy every time he hit his target.

'I hope you will forgive our *balila*,' said Imm Nidal especially to her son-in-law both as an apology for the lack of kernels and good oil, and in order to ease the tension between her husband and Fouad.

Fouad and Nidal exchanged glances; he prompted her with his eyes.

Abu Nidal stared darkly at the dish of *balila*.

Imm Nidal held out her hand for Fouad's bowl and again apologized for the lack of proper ingredients.

'You should have asked,' Fouad said to her. 'I could have brought some pine nuts with me. We have the best pine nuts in Haifa.'

Abu Nidal's eyes shot up. 'This is how *we* eat balila. This is what *real* Arabs are being made to eat these days.'

The uneasy silence returned and Fouad's signals to his wife became more urgent.

Nidal's eyes were glazed.

It was Fouad who eventually broke the silence. 'We're moving to Haifa permanently,' he declared, placing an arm around his pregnant wife. 'Nidal and the baby will be better there.'

Abu Nidal's face became twisted as though he'd suddenly been stabbed. He spluttered and coughed and could only look at his daughter.

'Shahed,' said Imm Nidal quickly, 'go tell your brother that if he doesn't come in for lunch there won't be any left for him.'

As Shahed rose to his feet, his father ordered him to sit down again. 'Leave him alone.'

'But — ' she began.

'I said leave him alone,' he yelled suddenly. 'He's the only child left to me.'

'But Baba — ' implored Nidal and stopped.

Abu Nidal raised his hand and addressed his daughter and son-in-law, 'Eat your *balila* and go.'

Shahed spoke this time and said gently, 'I think it's the right decision and the only decision.'

'Who asked you?' he growled.

Shahed persisted. 'Nidal has a family now. She must look to its future. And its future right now is in Haifa.'

Abu Nidal's raised hand now turned to Shahed. 'Shut up. You're not too old to be slapped,' he threatened.

Shahed blushed and shrugged before dropping his eyes. 'That's what I think.'

'I don't care what you think. You could go live in Tel Abib and I don't care. But you,' he paused, and the hand returned to Nidal to wave hopelessly, 'I've given you more than everything and this is how you treat me.'

'She has to be with her husband,' said Imm Nidal.

'Everything, Baba?' said Nidal, ignoring her mother.

'How can I be a grandfather to your child?'

'But there's nothing left,' she said passionately.

He shouted, 'But we *can* have everything if that coward of a husband of yours will only live here with his car.'

Fouad jumped to his feet. 'I have better things to do with my life than drive you for three hours a day each and every day just to wait for you to pick stupid olives.' He stormed out of the room.

Nidal was also shouting now. 'You've given me exactly zero. What do you expect me to do all day? Throw stones at the Wall?'

'Yes,' he roared. 'Throw stones and eat *balila* without fucking nuts.'

The late stage of her pregnancy prevented her from leaving as dramatically as her husband. She rose slowly and spat, 'I hope you choke on your *balila*.'

'That's right,' he yelled. 'Go now and may you never return to this house, God-willing.'

Imm Nidal was unable to look at either her husband or her daughter.

It was precisely 2:20 pm — two minutes before the afternoon prayer of 10 November 2002 — when Shahed accompanied them to Fouad's car with its Israeli plates. He kissed them and whispered to his sister, 'Don't worry about Baba. He just needs time to accept your decision.' He paused and then added, 'Remember that this farm is yours. Come back whenever you want.'

But Nidal didn't seem to be listening. She was holding her belly and wincing as though in pain.

As their car sped away in the direction of Qalqiliya, Saddam came running in, excited. 'Baba, Baba,' he said. 'The crack's grown a bit. I swear it's grown.'

'Good boy,' said Abu Nidal with tears in his eyes. 'Come let me kiss you.'

The boy looked quizzically at his father and, moving towards him, he asked, 'Where's Nidal?'

Abu Nidal was too upset to reply. He could only shake his head and hug his boy.

It was precisely 2:40 pm when a car drove up to the Israeli checkpoint outside Qalqiliya. Corporal Sheena Baran was alone on checkpoint duty. She looked at the Israeli plates and then at the occupants. Sheena Baran was a first-generation Israeli. While she had emigrated from East London in the Cape Province and made aliyah at the tender age of fourteen, she still spoke Hebrew with a slight English accent, and her English vowels had never fully recovered from the South African influence.

It was almost three and a half hours before official curfew, but there had been a security alert so that the only gate into town had been closed since noon. She raised her palm and then crossed her hands together in a gesture to signify 'Stop. The road is closed.'

It never ceased to amaze her how some drivers were so thick that they misunderstood such basic gestures. The car inched forward forcing her to shout in both Hebrew and Arabic, 'Stop!'

She marched to the driver and ordered him to switch off the engine.

'I'm sorry,' he said in a strongly-accented Hebrew. 'But I have a medical emergency.' He indicated the woman in the passenger seat who appeared to be in pain. 'I have to take her to the hospital.'

The woman moaned loudly as if on cue.

'What's wrong with her?' asked Sheena suspiciously.

The man was flustered. 'I think she's having our baby,' he said desperately. 'It started as soon as we left her parents' house.'

He looked to be in his very late thirties or early forties, and she in her very early twenties; Sheena made no effort to cover her distaste as she demanded, 'Where do her parents live?'

He pointed vaguely at the road behind them.

Sheena addressed the woman, 'Where do your parents live?'

The woman seemed to be contorted with a bit too much pain and appeared to be cursing in Arabic. And while she certainly looked pregnant, she didn't seem to be on the verge of popping.

'She doesn't speak Hevrew,' explained the man.

'Hebrew, not Hevrew,' corrected Sheena. Arabs seemed incapable of distinguishing between *v*'s and *b*'s; she repeated: '*Ivreet, lo ibreet.*'

'Please,' he begged and repeated his request. 'I have to take her to the UNRWA hospital.'

'Papers,' she ordered unsympathetically. 'And open your boot.'

'I'm an Israeli citizen,' he said, handing over an Israeli passport. 'I live in Haifa.'

'I said papers.' She nodded to indicate the passenger.

He reached into his wife's bag to extract a Palestinian identity card.

Sheena did little more than glance at the Palestinian papers and then flicked the Israeli passport open, unimpressed.

'What's your name? Sugar?' Sheena had trouble reading the Hebrew transliteration. 'Foo-ad Ash-sugar?'

'Shuja',' he corrected. 'Fouad Ash-shuja'.'

'Well there's your problem, you see. You don't have an Israeli name.'

'I'm an Israeli Arab.'

'Now there's a perfect *oxymoron*.' She said it in English since she couldn't bring to mind the Hebrew equivalent. Then she resumed: 'You are either Arab or Israeli.'

'I'm Israeli.'

'But you're not. Look at you. Look at your wife. Look at the little Arab in her belly.'

She left them for a full five minutes as she searched the boot thoroughly. The woman's cries seemed to become more theatrical with every passing minute, and Sheena could hear the man talking to his wife in Arabic. She detected his tone that swung madly from frustration to desperation. At times, he even sounded vindictive.

She returned eventually to the driver and handed him the papers.

'Thank you,' he said, switching on the engine.

'Come back tomorrow morning,' said Sheena. 'The gate will be open at 6:00 am.'

The man looked at her with glazed eyes; he seemed unable to understand.

'Now closed. Tomorrow open.'

'But my wife's having a baby,' he whimpered.

His voice was completely drowned out by the woman.

Again, as though prompted, his wife raised both feet, placed them firmly on the dashboard and let out a strangulated wail.

'Only in Hollywood — ' began Sheena.

'What?'

She had to raise her voice above the woman's cries. 'Women give birth in cars only in the movies.' She pointed vaguely at the road behind them. 'Go back to her parents and come back tomorrow morning.'

'Her parents?' This seemed to touch a raw nerve. The snivelling tone became a shout: 'It's her parents who did this to her.'

Sheena shrugged. 'Then go to the Hable gate — '

'But there's no other hospital in this Godforsaken region.'

' — if you hurry you might still find it open.'

It was then that the amniotic sac broke, staining the woman's dress and filling the floor with a puddle. Later, Sheena would notice darker blots in the ochre liquid like congealed blood.

The man was too horrified to say anything.

Sheena hesitated for only an instant. 'Look,' she said, suddenly encouraging. 'I can't let this car through. But I will let you pass exceptionally. Do you have the number for the hospital?'

He shook his head, still stunned.

'Then run to the hospital and come back with an ambulance.' She indicated the other side of the checkpoint. 'It can wait there as you carry your wife across.'

The woman had fainted; he sat still, staring at her.

She opened his door and shook him. 'Now. Go. Run as fast as you can.'

He looked up at her with pathetic eyes.

'Go,' she shouted into his face.

He winced.

He got out of the car and took a couple of deep breaths like a sprinter before a race.

'Now. Run.'

He needed no further encouragement. He started to run as swiftly as his legs would carry him.

Sheena stared, nonplussed.

'Hey!' she hollered.

But he ran fast for a man of his age.

'Stop!' she tried again as he rapidly added more distance between them. 'You're going the wrong way!'

He just couldn't stop. Fouad kept running as far and as fast as he could away from all the madness.

Sheena's superiors were already planning to promote her for her apparent officer qualities, especially her ability to take sound, on-the-spot decisions. The man was still just visible and running away from Qalqiliya when she walkie-talkied the base and got them to phone the hospital.

Then she waited with the woman. 'Trust me, you're better off without him,' she told her in English. 'What a stupid fucking kafir.'

But the woman remained unconscious until the paramedics arrived. Nidal died, along with her unborn baby, roughly at the midpoint mark as she was being carried from the car to the waiting ambulance.

The car itself, with its Israeli plates, was repatriated two days later when a soldier at the base used it at the end of his tour of duty to return to Tel Aviv.

Sad, empty and unclean house.

Imm Nidal knew that in Islam, mourning was supposed to remain dignified. The Koran prohibited the expression of grief by loud wailing, hitting oneself or others, scratching, and breaking objects.

But Imm Nidal did all of those things.

She wept all the time and beat her brow repeatedly as if to correct some faulty wiring in her brain.

She was unable to pray during the three-day mourning period and the subsequent five days. She still heard the calls to prayer from the distant mosque, but a voice inside her made her scream, 'No.'

Five times a day, as the muezzin's call drifted to the farm, the crying only intensified, drowning in a consuming tide of anguish.

How could she pray when she was only half a person — Imm Nidal without Nidal?

She also couldn't lift a finger to clean the farm. How could she — the voice howled — when it was *his* farm?

The dam had broken the moment they learnt of Nidal's death. On the eighth day, the flood level had dropped sufficiently for the resulting carnage to become apparent.

'You killed her,' she shrieked at her husband. 'You murdered her. You murdered her unborn baby.' She thumped his chest until her muscles gave way. 'You're the father of all murderers,' she spat. He was *Abu al-Qotila*.

Abu Nidal just stood there, staring vacantly at some point above her head, while he took her blows. He never once opened his mouth.

For a second, she just glared at him, wiping the tears from her eyes, to look at him clearly. After all those years with him, only now could she see him for what he really was: an incomplete person, a partial man, nothing but an unfinished Abu.

She stepped back abruptly with that revelation. 'You're nothing,' she gasped. 'You're not a father. You're not even a man.' Then, just to prove her point, she stepped in again and slapped him hard on the cheek.

He barely flinched and his eyes never left the spot above her head.

'I wasted my life with you,' she yelled. 'Say something, you beast!' She spun around, picked up an ornamental bowl from a coffee table and flung it against a wall, causing it to shatter loudly. 'Speak, you coward,' she screamed, 'or God is my witness I'll break everything in this house.'

He remained like a cold statue.

'Damn your dead tongue!' With a blood-curdling screech, she attacked him again, scratching every part of his face she could get at.

His left cheek turned deep red and blood trickled down to his neck. And yet his arms never moved to block her, his head never ducked as her fingers moved on to ravage his right cheek.

But his eyes, still fixed elsewhere, welled up with tears.

It was Saddam who eventually made her stop.

The boy lay crumpled on the floor. 'Please don't do that to Baba,' he sobbed miserably. 'Please, Mama.'

She froze. For a while, there was a conflict in her mind. Part of her wanted to complete the job of stripping all the skin off, scratching until the nails scraped against bone.

'Please.'

Ever so slowly, her hands moved off his face, and she stared at her bloodied nails with a mixture of shock and horror.

So this was how demons took control of humans. This was how they spread their evil. They waited for the right moment — when the defences were down with intense grief — to turn a mother into one of them.

'*Bismillah!*' she moaned suddenly.

She couldn't bear to look at Abu Nidal; his mind had already been infected.

She took a series of deep, cleansing breaths and then turned to the only person in this house who still mattered.

Saddam needed her undivided attention, now that Nidal and her baby were gone and that Shahed was fast becoming like his father under the influence of the evil jinni in his room.

Reaching down to her crying child, she wiped away his tears. 'Come, Saddam,' she said gently. 'Come, my love.

We now have to pray more than we've ever prayed in our lives.'

But Saddam proved to be a poor *qareen*, a fickle companion in prayer. He only prayed with her that first time and even then he fidgeted with boredom. After that, he made sure he was outside and well out of earshot for every call to prayer.

For exactly twenty-one days, Abu Nidal didn't utter a single word.

He sat in his armchair in the living room, his head in his hands.

Shahed had a printout in his hand and was trying to find the right moment to hand it to him.

'He's become a vegetable,' said Saddam.

Imm Nidal looked at her youngest with shock. 'What did you say?'

'Well look at him,' waved the boy, scornfully. 'He's a vegetable. You said so yourself.'

'*Bismillah*! The jinni needs to be beaten out of you.'

'And who's gonna do it? You?' He laughed viciously and, pointing at Shahed, added, 'Or your last daughter?'

'Careful, Saddam,' warned Shahed, 'or your father will give you a good thrashing.'

'*My-father*? *Abi*?' He still laughed but his tone could not mask the boy's caution as he added, 'It'd be like being beaten by a cucumber — no, a lettuce.'

There was a moment's silence as all eyes turned to Abu Nidal. He remained motionless.

'See,' said Saddam, now more confidently. 'He's a fucking vegetable.'

'Apologize, Saddam,' ordered Shahed.

'You fucking faggot.' Saddam ran out of the house and shouted at the top of his voice, 'Shahed's a fucking faggot.' They heard him throwing rocks at the crack in the Wall and with every accurate shot, he yelled, 'Shahed's a fucking faggot.'

Imm Nidal collapsed in the armchair next to her husband's, but made sure that her back faced him. She had stopped even looking at her husband; he was *haram* to her eyes.

She looked at Shahed with visible pain. 'Have you no self-respect left?' she demanded. 'Why don't you defend your honour?'

'Honour, Mama?' asked Shahed, genuinely astonished.

'Yes. Honour. Will you never stand tall like a God-fearing man?'

'What would you have me do, Mama? Beat up a little boy who's only grieving for his sister?'

'*Allah.*'

He indicated the window with the hand that held the printout. 'That's how Saddam chooses to grieve.' The hand moved to the first armchair, 'And this is how Baba grieves,' before resting on the second armchair, 'And this is how you do it, Mama.'

'Me?'

'You blame Baba for her death and you pray more than you've ever prayed in your life.'

'We need more prayer.'

'You lock yourself away in your prayers,' said Shahed. 'Remember that you still have two sons.'

Imm Nidal stared at him and tried to recall the good son. 'And what about you?' she asked. 'How do you spend your days?'

'I write,' he answered simply.

'You write?' she said incredulously and looked at the paper in his hand with dread. 'What do you write?'

'I write about my grief.'

'Who to?' Imm Nidal already knew the answer and she pre-empted, warily, 'Dastmastur?'

'Yes.'

She closed her eyes for a second. Then she said the *shahada* and, turning away from Shahed, her eyes fixed a spot above Abu Nidal's head.

Eventually she said softly, 'Don't you see how you could become not even a man?'

Shahed frowned at that.

'Don't you see how he's brought all this evil to this house and still you communicate with him?' She turned to her son, her gaze moving away from just above the head of the nothing man.

'Evil?' This caused a sad smile to appear on his face.

'*Allah!*' She now looked at him long and hard. 'See how the kafir makes you laugh.'

'He may well be a kafir,' admitted Shahed, 'but he's not at all evil.' Shahed moved abruptly and purposefully towards his father as if to end the conversation. 'Baba,' he prompted gently.

'That's what false companions will have you believe,' she continued.

'Baba?' he repeated.

'Are you listening to me?'

'I know you didn't want me to but — ' Shahed hesitated, 'I put the tractor up for sale on the Internet with an asking price of $15,000.' He placed the printout in his father's lap. 'I got three replies, including one from — ' again he hesitated, ' — the neighbourhood.'

Abu Nidal didn't flinch so that, in this crouched position it now looked as though he were scrutinizing the printout.

'See how he makes you change the conversation,' accused Imm Nidal. 'See how he makes you ignore me? You call him your best friend but have you ever seen him?'

Shahed turned deliberately to his mother. 'No.'

'So you know he's as invisible as his name suggests.'

This caused him to frown again.

'Don't you think a true companion would be delighted to show his face to you?'

Shahed thought about that and nodded slowly. 'You're right, Mama,' he said at length.

'Of course I'm right, my darling.'

'Maybe I should see him,' said Shahed sadly. 'If we're such good friends we should see each other at least once.'

'But it's not meant to be.'

'I'll write to him and see what he says.'

'No,' she moaned.

She was about to add something when their attention was drawn suddenly to Abu Nidal, who sat up and stood up. Pausing only to nod curtly to his son, Abu Nidal walked out of the house with the printout of three contact numbers and addresses.

Abu Nidal broke his silence on 2 December 2002 and only to sell his tractor to a Jewish settler.

The Jew, a resident of the nearby settlement of Alfe Menashe, spoke in broken Arabic. 'When you buy?' he asked.

'In 1995,' replied Abu Nidal.

The settler whistled and waved his hand back to signify a long time ago.

'Solid,' said Abu Nidal. 'German.'

'*Allemanya*,' agreed the Jew as he climbed onto the tractor to investigate the levers. Presently, he indicated the casing covering the engine and said, 'I see?'

'Be my guest.'

'Ach,' he said, 'she see many todays.'

'And she will see many more, God-willing.'

'Yes,' he said with a look of doubt. He grinned suddenly at Abu Nidal. 'We buy your olive oil,' he said cheerfully.

'Buy?'

'Yes.' He waved his hand back. 'Buy it all years. Best olive oil in the life.'

Abu Nidal brought his palm to his chest in a formal acceptance of the compliment.

'No more?' asked the settler.

'No more.'

'*Haram.*'

'*Haval,*' agreed Abu Nidal.

Turning his attention once more to the tractor, he asked, 'How much?'

'As much as you like.'

The Jew looked at the wheels, examined under the tractor and, climbing back into the cockpit, said, '$2,000.'

'$3,000.'

He whistled again. '$2,500.'

'OK,' said Abu Nidal in English.

'OK,' said the Jew, reaching his hand down. 'I come tomorrow, yes? With friend and money.'

'Why bother your friend?' said Abu Nidal, shaking his hand. 'You drive your car,' he made a show of indicating the acceptable plates, 'and I'll follow you with the tractor.'

'Now?' The Jew looked uncertain.

'Why not? You can pay me later. Tomorrow, next week, whenever. We shook hands and that's good enough for me.'

The settler examined his watch: they had three and a half hours until curfew, time enough for a dozen round trips to Alfe Menashe. 'OK,' he said finally.

It was one of the shortest trips in Abu Nidal's life.

At the Hable gate, the settler spoke to the soldier and pointed behind him at the tractor. The soldier nodded and let both vehicles pass.

This brought them straight to his land on the other side of the Wall. For all too brief a while, Abu Nidal drove his tractor once more with his olive trees on either side. In the glare of the midday sun, the trees spread uniformly across the horizon like an army of thieves and murderers.

At the entrance to Alfe Menashe, the settler explained the situation to another soldier on checkpoint duty, who nodded and admitted them promptly.

Once inside, the settler switched off his engine and got out of his car.

But Abu Nidal kept driving.

The settler raised his palm to signify that he should stop.

But it was as if the Palestinian couldn't understand such a basic gesture.

The tractor moved dangerously on, forcing him to shout in both Hebrew and Arabic, 'Stop!'

Abu Nidal just couldn't stop. He kept driving as fast as his tractor would go.

The settler was too stunned to move out of the way.

By the time he realized something was seriously wrong, one of the front wheels had caught his foot and was fast climbing up his leg.

Once he finished with the settler, Abu Nidal drove over his car as well to crush its plates, and then he thundered off in search of another settler to turn to paste.

Abu Nidal had broken his vow of silence only to sell his tractor. So his mouth remained firmly shut even as

Israelis came charging out with their guns and riddled the tractor with bullets.

God is the greatest.

Imm Nidal closed her eyes to remain focused.

Of the five daily prayers, the *izhan al-asr*, or afternoon prayer, was always the hardest. Traditionally, *asr* was called when shadows were exactly as tall as the objects that cast them. It was the time of day when evil spirits became the most active like creatures stirred by the strong sun: when the invisible (*mastur*) rose from their seats of honour (*dast*) to whisper their spells in human ears.

The afternoon prayer always took the longest.

There was only God — He alone existed in the Singular. Everything else in the Universes of His Creation could be broken up into duals: humans and jinn, men and women, past and future. There were two deaths — the first occurred before birth and as a consequence of the original sin when humans and jinn failed to make a stand with God's absolute authority; and the second death, which terminated life in this world.

There were two Higher Heavens and two Lower Heavens — one each for humans and jinn — with profound differences between the Heavens. The Higher Heavens were reserved for those who had led a righteous life and had developed their souls sufficiently to the extent that they would be closest to God. In such fortunate cases, the angels of death simply invited them to the same Paradise where Adam and Eve once lived.

In the Lower Heavens, water did not flow so readily, fruits and meats were more limited, and pure spouses were not automatically provided. However, even these Lower Heavens were a coveted prize for those unfortunate souls destined for the last and most cramped of Universes: the Hell that would be created on the Day of Judgement.

It was written that all those who died before the age of forty, moving on before their souls had sufficiently developed, would go to the Lower Heaven. So Imm Nidal didn't feel she needed to pray for the soul of her daughter. Instead, she focused on Abu Nidal, who had allowed his mind to be possessed and who therefore now lived in the Purgatory for humans. His fate along with all the others in that Universe would be decided on the Day when the horn would be blown and half the residents of Purgatory would be redeemed and elevated to Lower Heaven, and the other half would be cast into the bottomless pit.

While her husband's fate was veiled — necessitating constant prayer — her son-in-law's was as clear as a full moon. Fouad Ash-shuja' was doomed to suffer an everlasting nightmare.

The events that led to the death of Nidal remained murky. But the fact was that Fouad had deliberately abandoned his pregnant wife at the Qalqiliya checkpoint. A well-wisher at her funeral had seen the Israeli-registered car cross into Israel, and Imm Nidal imagined the coward driving away from his obligations.

But God was just. He used subtleties to hint at His designs.

Fouad was thirty-nine when Nidal died. And the fact that he had not died alongside her and their unborn child clearly indicated that his soul did not deserve lower Heaven. Instead, it was predestined that the deserter should live a little longer, and return to Haifa en route to Hell.

'May you then become his constant companion,' Imm Nidal whispered, thinking of the jinni that lived in Shahed's bedroom.

Unlike the two Heavens and Purgatories, and so as to add to their mutual miseries, humans and jinn would be accommodated in the singular Hell.

She ended her prayer abruptly when she heard Saddam screaming and calling her urgently as though he were in pain: 'Mama, Mama. Come quickly.'

She ran to him. 'What is it?' she asked anxiously.

Saddam was standing at the entrance to Shahed's room and pointed. 'There he is, Mama,' he said with fear. 'Look. There's Dastmastur.'

For a second, she actually believed him and froze in her tracks.

It was only when she heard the boy chuckle that she summoned up the courage to peer inside.

Shahed was on his knees, unpacking a computer.

'See,' said Saddam impishly. He indicated the TV screen, the slit in the big box and the smaller box with a tail. 'That's its big head. Its arse. And its small prick.' Saddam added with a vicious laugh, 'Shahed's always playing with its dick.' His hand made a sweeping motion for effect.

Shahed ignored his brother and was busy connecting the cables.

'What is that?' Imm Nidal asked him.

'A computer,' he replied.

'I can see it's a *combyudar*,' she said dismissively. 'What's it doing here?'

'*Haram, haram*,' tutted Saddam as he took on a serious air.

'They gave it to me at work. It's an old computer.'

'So?'

'So I thought I might teach Saddam how to use it.'

Both Imm Nidal and her youngest were taken aback.

'I'm not playing with its prick,' countered Saddam quickly, his tone no longer amused.

'It's called a mouse,' said Shahed patiently. 'Computers can do some really cool things. And I'll show you.'

'It should not be here,' Imm Nidal said flatly.

'Cool?' scoffed Saddam. 'Can *combyudars* stand close enough to a tank to spit on it?'

'That's not cool. That's stupid.'

'You're stupid.'

'Take it back tomorrow,' Imm Nidal ordered Shahed.

'Why?'

'Because you're a coward like Fouad,' answered Saddam.

Shahed narrowed his eyes on his mother. 'Why don't you tell Saddam to go back to school instead?'

'School? What for?' snapped Saddam.

'Isn't that more important, Mama?'

'Stay out of my life, collaborator.'

'Do you actually know what Saddam does all day? Do you actually care?'

'Just shut the fuck up.'

'Do you know that he's always at those rallies organized by Hamas and al-Aqsa Squad? Don't you realize you're wasting his life?'

'We know what's important, don't we, Mama.'

'Stop!' she screamed. 'Both of you. Stop!'

Still addressing Imm Nidal, Shahed pleaded, 'At least let me teach him one thing that's not about violence and hatred.'

'You can't teach me anything that I need,' said Saddam darkly.

Shahed turned to his brother. 'But don't you want a better life?'

'I want a better afterlife.'

Shahed turned to look directly at his mother, his brown eyes moist and begging.

'I want to become a Martyr,' stated Saddam.

He wanted to become a *shahid*.

The Arabic word *shahid* and name Shahed were so similar that Imm Nidal didn't understand at first. 'You want to become Shahed?' she asked, bewildered.

Even for a child, he could already roar like his father: 'That stupid faggot? Are you deaf? I said I want to become a *shahid*.'

Shahed's eyes still begged her to say something.

'Take the *combyudar* back tomorrow,' she ordered Shahed.

Turning to Saddam, she warned him, 'And you can't be a martyr before you're forty.'

Flags and banners invaded the streets of Qalqiliya. Some of the protesters were adults, but the vast majority were children. All, including Saddam and his gang of friends, were armed with stones. Saddam hurled his and whooped with joy when it found its mark on the windscreen of an armoured personnel carrier. His friend was still congratulating him on his aim and was therefore completely confused when Saddam fell to the ground like a crumpled doll.

In the event, the computer stayed in the farmhouse for barely a week, until 10 April 2003, when the manager of the Internet café came to pick it up in his car.

The manager had ferried Shahed and his mother to the cemetery in Qalqiliya and now waited anxiously by the open boot of his car as his employee emerged with the monitor.

The shadow cast by the monstrous Wall, barely fifty metres away from the porch, was slowly engulfing the farmhouse, stretching and yawning as it rose to consume everything in its path. The grey pre-fabricated slabs, whose wide cement base was only visible in a brighter light, were fast becoming scales to a monstrous snake; and the four-metre-wide trench and barbed-wire fence that ran along it were turning into its winding tracks.

Five kilometres away due west in Qalqiliya, soldiers were already preparing to lock the only gate to the largest prison on earth, hanging up the one key for the night. The manager helped Shahed place the computer in the boot.

'You're a good lad,' he said sadly. 'Come back to work whenever you're ready.'

'I'll be in tomorrow morning,' said Shahed, standing awkwardly in his dark suit.

'Whenever,' insisted the man, taking in Shahed's blood-shot eyes. 'If you need anything — ' He let his voice trail.

Shahed nodded. 'Can I sleep in the shop?'

'Tonight?' He asked with surprise.

Shahed shook his head. 'Tomorrow and every working day after that.'

'What about your mother?'

The shadow cast by the Wall had overrun the entire house. 'I'll see her on the weekends.'

'If you wish,' said the manager — you couldn't turn away a grieving brother.

As he drove off, Shahed turned back and sat on the porch. He slumped back as he heard the radio in the living room, which Imm Nidal had just switched on.

The local radio station usually broadcast verses from the Koran non-stop with only brief interruptions for newsflash-es. Despite the cycles of the seasons, the last two prayers of the day were always approximately an hour and twen-ty minutes apart. In that time, Imm Nidal had the radio on and sat in her armchair for a full hour. This was an intrinsic part of her daily routine without which her mind would long have turned to the demons.

She could focus on the soothing voice of the recitals, recognizing every passage and admiring the unrivalled beauty of God's language, as the farmhouse became enveloped by the darkness.

But on 10 April 2003 and for a third consecutive day, the station dispensed with its usual programmes to broadcast live commentaries and analyses from Iraq in the wake of yet another Arab defeat.

Imm Nidal's mind ignored the actual commentary and heard instead: 'You alone we ask for help. Guide us in the right path, the path of those whom You blessed, not of those who have deserved Your wrath.'

Outside, Shahed wept openly, sobbing like a little child.

There were two Saddams.

An Israeli soldier shot the smaller Saddam with a rubber bullet at the last remaining section where the Wall was being built to seal in Qalqiliya. While four other stone-throwing youths were similarly hit in the upper body during that skirmish, they survived. In the case of smaller Saddam, the heavy metallic shard with a thin layer of rubber — which passes for a rubber bullet — penetrated his skull and proved impossible to dislodge. He had died the following day.

Barely an hour later, the statue of the bigger Saddam was pulled off its marble plinth in the centre of Baghdad, next to the Palestine Hotel.

7

A GIRL EMERGED from the Brahimi farmhouse and started to sweep the porch. Some distance away, Colonel Habib Ami peered at her through binoculars from his cover among olive trees.

'Who is she?' he asked his second in command.

'One of the daughters, I think,' replied Sheena Baran.

'Shit.'

'But we have tried to limit collateral damage.'

Every now and then the girl moved to the side of the house to clear her broom of the dirt and clumps of earth that had got stuck in the hairs of the broom. She knocked the broom five times against the wall: two short knocks on the smaller edge, swiftly followed by a stronger tap on the broad sides and two short knocks on the opposite edge. Pap-pap paaap pap-pap.

'How many civilians are there?' asked Colonel Ami.

'Can't be sure,' Sheena answered. 'But that's why we've chosen to do it on a Friday. The workers aren't there, and the mother and the youngest kid have gone to the mosque in town.' She paused and then asked, 'Do we have a green light, Colonel?'

He turned his field of vision to look at the main building that housed the broom factory, where, according to intelligence, as many as thirty Palestinian fighters were hiding — one of whom, Kalashnikov slung casually over his shoulder, was smoking outside and calling the girl. She ignored him; she looked with satisfaction at the porch and entered the farmhouse.

'Habib?' urged Sheena.

Colonel Ami's hands were tied. The terrorists were using the farm as a base from where they launched their attacks on his unit outside Qalqiliya and on the Jewish settlement of Alfe Menashe. It wasn't his fault that they were cowardly rats hiding among civilians.

By the time the girl re-emerged with a rug, he had given the signal to his captain.

The irony was not lost on him. While he was responsible for the operation to flush out the terrorists in the farm, it was his second in command who had come up with the code-name in English. Sheena Baran spoke briefly into a radio: 'Code one for *Clean Sweep*. I repeat, we have a code one for *Clean Sweep*.'

There, too, the Arab girl used a particular technique: she held the carpet aloft and, using the same broom, she struck the carpet twice in the middle, once at the base and once at the top, and repeated until no more dust puffed out.

The first strike was delivered within minutes. A jet swooped in low to drop its load on the main building and outhouses. Pap-pap paaap pap-pap. The girl and everything around her was suddenly consumed by a ball of fire.

Then, as an acrid cloud of dust rose high above the buildings, the armoured division moved in to fire its shells into what remained of the walls and survivors.

It was an uncomplicated and perfectly executed operation. The combination of surprise and massive firepower meant that there was almost no resistance, no Israeli casualties and no Palestinian survivors. In all, *Clean Sweep* took a little over half an hour, which included the time for the infantry to advance and secure positions in and around the farm.

The foot soldiers were given the task of finding the corpses, piling them in the demolished sitting room and arranging the dead meticulously according to sex and estimated age. The dead girls and women formed a separate and considerably smaller pile; the soldiers were still piling the men when the mother and her child returned from the mosque.

Sheena spotted them and called one of the infantrymen in her unit. 'Lavan, I need you.'

Corporal Hillel Lavan was a Palestinian Jew, that is, an Israeli whose family had lived in historic Palestine since time immemorial. As one of only two perfectly fluent Arabic speakers in the unit, Hillel Lavan was often chosen to act as interpreter.

'Tell her we need her to ID her husband and sons from the other corpses.' She waited for Lavan's translation and then asked, 'Were there any other civilians?' Her gaze moved down the woman's body to her hands and to an incongruous panda bear. The grip was so stiff that it seemed the Arab was trying to dismember the cuddly toy.

Sheena marched into the obliterated sitting room. As another soldier led the woman inside, propping her up, Hillel tried to stop the boy from entering. But the child was too small and quick and, moving deftly under the soldier's legs, he ran inside.

Rituals sustained holy men and good jinn alike. Habits could be made eternal and were therefore superior to people.

Imm Nidal still went to bed exactly one hour after the evening prayer, mostly to stare at the shadows flitting across the ceiling, and she still prepared her glass of sweet tea exactly fifteen minutes after the end of the dawn prayer, principally to entertain the spirals of steam clinging to the glass. Only the covetous and indolent needed more than a few sips of tea and a full night's sleep.

She swept the house and porch every morning of dust she no longer saw; cleaned all three bathrooms thoroughly every day even if only the smallest by the kitchen was ever used;

prepared meals for her family though she now lived alone. The world beyond the porch could drown in mess, but at least the Zeitouni farmhouse would always sparkle.

The set meals according to the days of the week also served to reaffirm her routine. She now cooked meat only on Fridays and always as *kibbé*, blended with cracked wheat to make the meat spread to a maximum (again without the luxury of kernels that elevated *kibbé*); lentils in the similar yet different dishes of *mjaddara* and *mdadara* on Saturdays and Tuesdays, respectively; runner beans in *loubya b'zeit* for Wednesdays; rice and plain yoghurt or *riz-oo-laban* on Mondays; and broad or black-eyed beans (depending on availability) to make *foul* or *fassoulya* on Thursdays. Given that it was a Sunday, she lined up the ingredients to prepare a *hummus balila*. The chores of life were truly a blessing. They sustained her and were her faithful companion.

'*Bismillah*,' she breathed as she served the food on two plates and sat down at the empty dinner table.

It was written that only the righteous donated their favourite food to the poor, the orphan and the captive. Imm Nidal washed her own plate and, as she did each day, she moved to the porch with the other plate to leave some lunch and a glass of water for that young Brahimi boy.

Feeding Mohsen Brahimi of the Brahimi farm, which used to make the best brooms in the world, had become a vital part of her routine. The jinnee in their farm had proved more powerful and malevolent even than Dastmastur. The demon had destroyed their buildings and killed every member of the poor child's family except for his mother, who had been transformed into a bird. Imm Nidal had seen the woman herself, flapping as she tried to fly away, overnight being unable to speak God's tongue and resorting to pathetic chirps instead.

The boy behaved more like a good jinnee than any human child. He needed her like no one before had needed her, not even her children. She rarely saw him but could feel his presence as he came, regular as the celestial bodies, to feed and leave the plates empty.

She remembered the first time she spotted him from the porch, fifteen minutes after the end of the dawn prayer. She was sipping her sweet tea when she saw a flicker of movement from one of the few remaining mature olive trees on this side of the Wall.

'Who's there?' she called, feeling a sudden chill through her thick dressing gown and abaya.

In the half-light of dawn, it seemed as if the tree was whispering something.

'Show yourself if you are God-fearing.'

The smallest of heads slipped in and out of view like a shy creature popping out of its burrow after a night of rest.

'Who are you?'

When there was no answer, Imm Nidal stepped off the porch and walked to the tree.

'Hello?' She moved to the other side and breathed, '*Allah.*'

There was no one there. She looked behind other trees, but there was no sign of the jinnee with the small head.

The following morning, she left a piece of bread and some water on the porch and then waited inside in the sitting room, peering out between a crack in the curtains.

She had to wait a full twenty minutes, but the shy thing came finally. He looked exactly like an elfin creature, cautious and crouching, his little head turning to the slightest sound. As his tiny hand reached out for the piece of bread, Imm Nidal hurried outside.

But again he was gone, vanishing once more as a *mastur* to its *dast*.

Imm Nidal was not frightened. She had seen and recognized the face.

'Mohsen,' she called. 'Mohsen Brahimi.'

But the boy did not return until lunchtime.

That day, and for the first time since the death of her daughter, Imm Nidal had prepared lunch with enthusiasm and a sense of purpose, and left a plate of *mjaddara* on the porch for her new friend. In all His wisdom, God had sent her an orphan to encourage her to be steadfast and to remind her of her duties.

Imm Nidal was still kneeling on her mat and nearing the end of the long afternoon prayer when she heard a knock at the door and a familiar voice calling out her name.

The woman entered and, seeing the praying figure, kept her distance out of respect.

Eventually, with a final '*Allah*' that sounded like a groan, Imm Nidal rose and turned to her visitor. 'Holiest of afternoons to you, Bernaytat,' she greeted formally.

'Hello, Imm Nidal,' replied the woman. 'How are you today? Third Sunday of the month,' she added cheerily, 'and already time for payday.'

Lebanese Christians were the brunt of Arab jokes for their poor command of Arabic, which rarely strayed too far from the dialectal, their vowels and most of their consonants, which had never fully recovered from the French influence, and, especially, their silly first names. In those senses, Bernaytat — or *hats* in Arabic — was a stereotypical Christian Beiruti. At least her surname, Shakour, was of good Arab stock.

'So it must be,' replied Imm Nidal, absent-mindedly. 'Then we'll have some sweet tea.'

Bernadette checked the time. There was two and a half hours until curfew. 'A quick tea.' As she followed Imm Nidal to the kitchen, she said, 'There's a plate of food on the porch outside — *hummus balila*, I think,' adding tactfully, 'Shall I bring it in for you?'

'Oh?' Imm Nidal stopped in her tracks and was visibly troubled. 'That boy never misses his lunch.'

'Shahed?'

Imm Nidal shook her head. 'No, my little orphan friend.' She panicked suddenly, 'Why hasn't he eaten?'

Seeing her agitation, Bernadette said gently, 'Perhaps he wasn't hungry today.'

'*Allah*, tell me nothing has happened to that Brahimi boy. He would die in a second without my food.' She frowned and added after a while, 'He's the reason I always cook lunch.'

'I never have lunch.'

Imm Nidal looked directly into Bernadette's eyes and her frown moved over the woman's spindly body. 'Never? But lunch is the most important meal of the day.'

'I haven't had lunch since I was fifteen.'

'*Haram.*'

'*Quel fromage*,' she agreed, causing Imm Nidal's expression to change to puzzlement.

She shrugged simply as an explanation.

Her mind returned to the orphan. 'But he must eat.' And she turned to her visitor. 'And you must eat, Bernaytat — never too much, and never too little.' Then, quoting from the Koran, she added, 'Jesus himself told his mother, "Eat and drink, and be happy."'

Bernadette was fifteen when her father gave her a newspaper clipping. 'I want you to read this and tell me what you think.' He added, 'And then I want you to write a 100-word précis in English.'

They could hear Mémé in the kitchen crashing pots and pans and tutting to herself as she prepared lunch. Mémé had taken to using Maman's book of recipes in part because she had come to accept that Maman's food was superior by several notches and also because the notebook provided a visual reminder of all the ingredients to a particular dish.

'I'll read it, Papa. But do I have to write?'

'Yes. A summary is a sign of real comprehension.'

From the kitchen, they heard Mémé moan aloud: 'Where's

the fresh coriander? How can I cook a *mahshi koussa b'laban* without fresh coriander?'

Bernadette rolled her eyes and called out: 'It's in the fridge next to the tomatoes where you put it.' And to Papa: 'Could I write it in French?'

'No. I want you to improve your English.'

'But you don't need English if you've got French — everyone knows that.'

'And everyone is wrong.' Antoine looked her in the eye. 'I want you to have all the opportunities I never had. French is a language of the past. English is the future. I want you to go to university and study in English to be the best. From now on, I'm going to give you an English text to work on every week.'

'But you don't speak English, Papa.'

'That's right. And that's why you must.' He indicated the article. 'I want you to be able to write like that one day.'

Mémé was still flapping in the kitchen. 'And just look at these courgettes.'

'To write so eloquently about even the most difficult subjects.'

'Have you ever seen smaller courgettes in your life?'

Bernadette was not unduly concerned; Papa would be unable to correct her English. Besides, he didn't spend enough time with them to enforce his weekly homework. She got up suddenly. 'I'd better help her,' she said. 'The last time she tried to core the *koussa* with a knife.'

'You do that,' said Antoine, 'and then read the article.'

In fact, Mémé had done very little in the kitchen. Bernadette cored the courgettes, stuffed them with minced meat and rice, cooked the yoghurt in a separate saucepan and then went to her bedroom to read the clipping, leaving Mémé to add the final touch of adding chopped coriander and crushed garlic to the *laban*.

She read the article three times, lying on her bed with an English-French dictionary beside her.

Were life to imitate art, Antoine Shakour would look grotesque on the outside. Portrayed in the larger-than-life characterization of a nineteenth century novel or of an early Hollywood movie, Antoine would have a crooked nose and dishevelled aspect and would be stooped with unthinking subservience in his role of sidekick to the Archvillain: Abaddon to the Devil. Reality is by far more fearsome and thought-defying than the best of fiction. Antoine does not materialize out of nowhere as a demon to wreak havoc on man. Rather he is a product of his society where massacres have become commonplace...

It was truly frightening how, in a blinding flash of perception, the ultimate champion could wither into a disfigured creature that was only vaguely human. The smell wafting from the kitchen that, only minutes before, had smelt so appetizing was now the most nauseating stench: stuffed cadavers cooked in blood.

Bernadette couldn't stomach lunch that day.

When they had settled in the living room with their glasses of tea, Bernadette opened her black briefcase, handed Imm Nidal an envelope containing $63 in financial assistance and asked her to sign her ledger. Imm Nidal complied without opening the envelope.

'Do you want to check the amount?' Bernadette asked politely.

And as usual, Imm Nidal asked, 'Is there a change?'

'No change from last month.' The aid to Palestinian families was calculated as a function of the type, size and head of the household. In the case of the Zeitouni family, Ibtihage Zeitouni — known as Imm Nidal — had joined the programme in January 2003 as a woman-headed household with two dependants, and the assistance had initially been set at $82.

'Then there is no need to check.'

'I saw Shahed in Qalqiliya the other day,' said Bernadette as she sipped her tea. 'I stopped by the Internet café.'

Imm Nidal nodded. '*Indranet*,' she repeated, with obvious distaste.

'He seems well.'

'Praise be to God,' she responded automatically.

'These are difficult times.'

'God redeems those who follow Him during the difficult times.'

'He was teaching algebra to his group of children,' said Bernadette. 'You must be very proud of him.'

'Those at your Lord are never too proud to worship Him and fall prostrate before Him.'

'He's a good teacher.'

'Upholding the teachings of profaners instead of God's Teachings.'

Bernadette frowned and felt she needed to repeat, 'He was teaching algebra, Imm Nidal.'

'*Al-jabr*.' She nodded sadly; the original meaning in Arabic meant a reunion of broken parts. 'And he sleeps in the same room as all those TV screens, on a cold floor instead of in his bed. So that he can avoid seeing me. I know.'

There was an uneasy silence, which was eventually broken by Bernadette. 'Imm Nidal, you know that Shahed is only avoiding the curfew. He doesn't want to get stuck at the checkpoint before 6:00.'

'Indeed.'

'Sometimes and for no apparent reason they'll just lock the only gate into Qalqiliya well before curfew.'

Imm Nidal stared at her with a glazed expression.

Bernadette stammered, 'Of course you know that. I'm sorry.'

'True believers are showered with forgiveness and a generous provision.'

'May our Lord soften the ground of our being,' said Bernadette formally, causing Imm Nidal to raise her eyebrows with clear approval.

She got up to leave. Then, almost as an afterthought, she asked hesitantly, 'Do I have your permission to mention your personal loss?'

Imm Nidal shook her head slowly. 'The boy will be back, God-willing. As you say, maybe he was not hungry today.'

'No, Imm Nidal,' said Bernadette quickly. 'I'm writing a report about the suffering of Arab women — about women who have — ' she paused, 'lost family members.'

Imm Nidal considered that briefly before asking, 'Who will read the report?'

'Anyone who's interested in Palestine.'

'And will you talk of the Israeli soldiers in your report?'

Bernadette appeared surprised.

'You have my permission if you mention the name of one Israeli.'

'One soldier?'

'Yes. One to represent all of them.'

'Why?'

'So that their hearts will be thrown into Hell.'

'*Yom huledet sameakh*,' said Avi on a crackling line.

'I was going to phone you when I got home,' said Aron, pleased. 'We must be telepathic.' This was the one day of the week that he spent in the newsroom and he had just opened an invitation card on his monitor that was addressed to all *Adlai* staff.

Aron looked up and smiled back at a reporter who had paused at his desk to give him a thumbs-up. Then he frowned as he took in what Avi had said. 'What do you mean "Happy birthday"?'

Avi reminded him that it was his Jewish birthday. The nature of the solar-lunar Jewish calendar created a lag with its Gregorian counterpart, so anniversaries always came later by Hebraic reckoning. Aron was born on both 25 October 1956 and 20 Cheshvan 5717, which Józsi often referred to as 'Bitter Cheshvan' because there were no religious holidays during that month. So his forty-seventh Jewish birthday in 5764 fell on 15 November 2003.

'Well thank you, son,' he said with a little chuckle. The last time Aron had celebrated his Jewish birthday had been with his parents in North London.

'Dad, I'm joining a unit in the West Bank.'

'Oh?' The publisher's secretary waved at Aron, and a subeditor saluted him from the other end of the room. Aron swivelled in his chair so that he was now facing the wall. 'Is there a field hospital there?' he asked.

'No, Dad. I've been given some training here and so I'll be shipped out tomorrow.'

'Training?'

'Military training.'

'You'll be going as a soldier?' exclaimed Aron.

'Yes, Dad. As a soldier in the IDF.'

'Are you sure?' Aron was momentarily lost for words. 'I mean are you sure that's what you want?'

'I thought you'd be happy. By the way, that was your birthday present.'

'Of course I'm happy, Avi. But only if you're happy too.'

There was a silence, which Avi eventually broke. 'You were right, Dad. I'm no pacifist. I'm Israeli — it's time I acted as one. It's time I slowed down that circle.' He paused, then repeated: 'Happy birthday, Dad. I've got to go. I'm running out of units.'

'Let me phone you back,' said Aron.

'No, Dad. We'll talk later. I'm in the canteen trying to eat God-awful falafels cooked, actually designed, by that megalomaniac chef who wants to shatter all our teeth. Bye.'

Aron held the receiver for a while and coughed to clear his throat.

When he swivelled back to his desk and put the phone down, he was confronted by several faces, all grinning at him and offering their mazal tovs.

He suddenly realized that he hadn't told Avi his own piece of news, which had arrived as a fancy evite a few minutes before the call, pinging all the network's computers simultaneously. It was a formal invitation by the publishers of *Adlai* to attend a dinner in his honour to pay tribute to his contributions to the paper. The soiree was to be hosted in four months on 21 March 2004, at the King David Hotel.

Aron did his best to smile at everyone.

'Give us a speech, Aron,' someone called out.

He declined with a raised palm. Aron was a writer, not an orator. He was self-conscious about his voice that could crack at the most importune moments. He came across as the prince of wit on a page and the pauper of social gatherings. He was simply not a born speaker, just as Avi was simply not meant to be a soldier. Aron was still shaking his head and was even able to chat with his colleagues while his mind tried to picture Avi in a military uniform. The image of his dead wife kept returning to him instead.

He was saved by Zach, the senior editor and the closest thing Aron had to a friend, who strode into the newsroom and shooed everyone away from his desk. 'You'll get his acceptance speech on the night.' Turning to one of the features writers, he said, 'Your piece on the IDF operation on that broom factory — mostly OK, but I need a stronger intro. Go,' he said and added more loudly, once the writer had stepped away, 'And make a clean sweep of it.' The writer understood the reference and grinned back.

He sat on the corner of the desk and said to Aron, 'You'd think the IDF would come up with less corny codenames.' He paused as he took in Aron's expression. 'So what's with the black face?'

'What?'

'My senile grandfather has a happier disposition. What's the matter?'

'Nothing.'

'Well, then, give me a face that says: "I'm about to get the *Jew-litzer*".'

Aron gave the thinnest of smiles. 'Just thinking about my son,' he admitted.

'Good, good,' said Zach, pushing himself off the desk.

'He's joining a military unit in the West Bank.'

'Excellent. You must be very proud,' he said, but he wasn't really listening. He stepped away to check on another news feature and with a backward glance, said loudly, 'Remind him to keep 21 March free.' He added to the newsroom, 'And that applies to everyone here.'

Aron wasn't sure that Avi would be entitled to a leave so soon after his transfer to the West Bank. He suspected that he'd be attending the event in his honour on his own, and the general buzz of the newsroom only accentuated this feeling of loneliness.

8

THERE WERE MORE Israeli soldiers at the gate than usual.

Corporal Hillel Lavan spotted first the UN plates of the car and then the driver. His face lit up. He grinned and with a short bow said formally, 'Holiest of late mornings to you, sweet Miss Shakour.'

Bernadette smiled back. 'Hello, Hillel,' she said in her colloquial Arabic, 'and how are you today?'

'Praise be to God,' he said, nodding, 'and yourself?' They exchanged a few more pleasantries and then the soldier asked, almost apologetically, 'Do I have your permission to check your boot?'

'Of course,' she said, surprised. Her boot was always checked on the way in, but never before on the way out; the IDF searched more thoroughly those who entered Qalqiliya than those who left it. 'Why the extra security today, Hillel?' she asked him when he returned to her window.

'We lost one of our men last night,' he answered, adding almost in a conspiratorial tone, 'It was a suicide attack. It happened just there.' He indicated the location with a quick flick of his head over his left shoulder.

Bernadette took in the other soldiers who were milling around the site, her gaze resting on one of them in particular: a blonde with a deeply freckled face who was busy writing notes in a pad.

'May the Lord have mercy on his soul,' she said finally.

Hillel's hand went to his chest in a formal acceptance of the condolence and then swung out in a sweeping arc to authorize her to leave the town.

The entire Middle East simmered with misnomers and paradoxes.

For instance, you could be a Palestinian Jew, loathing the radical transformation of your land as wave upon wave of Ashkenazim and European S'faradim gradually westernized Israel, or you could be an Israeli Arab, an alien in your own land forced into accepting a foreign passport. Similarly, you could be an Arab and still feel most at ease in a Western tongue and culture; or a Maronite, priding yourself on your Aramaic roots, and still actually understand little more than the Lord's Prayer:

'Cosmic creator of all radiance and vibration, soften the ground of our being and carve out a space within us where your presence can abide. Fill us with your creativity so that we may be empowered to bear the fruit of your mission. Let each of our actions bear fruit in accordance with our desire. Endow us with the wisdom to produce and share what each being needs to grow and flourish. Untie the tangled threads of destiny that bind us, as we release others from the entanglement of past mistakes. Do not let us be seduced by that which would divert us from our true purpose, but illuminate the opportunities of the present moment. Amen.'

God is the greatest.

Imm Nidal was kneeling on her mat and had just begun the last prayer of the day when she heard a woman's voice calling out an unfamiliar name.

'Ibtihage Zeitouni? Ibtihage Zeitouni!'

Facing towards the Kaaba and at three forearms length away from her sutra, Imm Nidal raised her hands to her shoulders, fingers stretching to the earlobes. Then, with this last *Allahu Akbar* of the day completed, she folded her hands over her stomach with the right hand covering the left hand to restrict every movement.

'Ibtihage Zeitouni!' There was a loud thump at the door.

Imm Nidal forced her eyes back to the exact spot on the mat and tried to empty her mind of common thoughts.

The door handle turned and two Israeli officers stepped into the farmhouse.

They always came in twos: the first to deliver the blow, and the second to protect the rear and ensure a hasty retreat from potential danger.

However, in this case it was the second soldier, a blond woman, who took the lead. 'Ibtihage Zeitouni?' prompted Captain Sheena Baran when she saw the kneeling figure.

'She's praying, ma'am,' stated the first Jew in Hebrew.

'And well she should,' retorted Sheena. 'Tell her to get up.'

Corporal Hillel Lavan nodded. He hated that there was only one other fluent Arabic speaker in the unit and, therefore, that he was often chosen for such assignments. He cleared his throat and said in formal Arabic with a flawless Palestinian accent, 'Imm Shahed, we disturb your prayers because we come with news for you.'

Imm Nidal flinched but remained otherwise motionless.

'Up, up,' ordered Sheena impatiently as she moved towards her.

'Will you please rise, Imm Shahed?'

Unable to focus on the mat, Imm Nidal closed her eyes briefly. When she opened them again, the blond soldier was standing next to her, blocking her path to her sutra. '*Bismillah!*' she cried out suddenly.

Sheena was momentarily surprised by her outburst and took an instinctive step back. 'We got your attention now, woman.' She motioned to Hillel to speak.

But it was Imm Nidal who spoke, quoting from the Hadith, the sayings of the Prophet Muhammad: '"If only the one passing in front of another performing prayer knew the magnitude of the sin that he committed, he would prefer to wait for forty days, months or years rather than to pass in front of him."'

'What did she say?'

'That you have committed a major sin, ma'am,' replied Hillel, 'by walking in front of her during prayer.'

'Sin?' Sheena gave a humourless laugh. 'That's rich coming from the mother of a terrorist.'

'Imm Shahed,' began Hillel. He paused, cleared his throat again and delivered a statement in perfect Arabic that had become lodged in his brain: 'Pursuant to Regulation 119 of the Defence Regulations, your house is to be demolished and the land on which it is built is to be confiscated, thereby prohibiting you and any of your family or friends from rebuilding or constructing a new house.'

Imm Nidal turned finally. She looked at the soldier with horror.

'Do you understand what I've just said, Imm Shahed?' he asked unnecessarily.

She shook her head slowly. When she spoke, her voice was like that of a little girl's, 'But I'm busy. I have work to do.'

'The bulldozer will arrive tomorrow morning,' continued Hillel. 'Please ensure that you have vacated the premises by then.'

'But I have work to do,' she repeated helplessly.

'You must leave before it arrives.'

'But who'll clean the house and who'll cook for my boy?' she moaned.

Hillel looked away.

'What's she saying?' asked Sheena.

'She wants to know when the bulldozer will be here, ma'am.'

'Tell her first thing in the morning.'

'Pack all your belongings tonight, Imm Shahed.'

'But who'll feed that young Brahimi boy?' She was distraught. 'He will die without me.'

'Tell her she's lucky to get some warning,' said Sheena. 'That's more than our boy got when her son blew him up.'

Hillel hesitated and then said gently, 'Our Lord will provide for him.'

Imm Nidal looked straight into his eyes; for an instant, his uniform was blurred in the periphery of her vision.

'Come on, Corporal,' ordered his superior as she moved to the door. 'Our work here is done.'

'What's your name?' asked Imm Nidal.

He told her.

'It's a good Arabic name,' she said sadly. Reluctantly, her eyes moved away from his to settle on his belt with its holster. 'But why are you doing this, Hillal Laban?'

'You should have stopped your boy, Imm Shahed. You know this is what the army does to the houses of terrorists.'

Imm Nidal was beside herself with grief. '*Allah*,' she cried. 'Is that why he missed his lunch? That orphan is too young to be a martyr!'

'Orphan?'

'Just like Saddam was too young. How can little boys with stones be terrorists?'

'He was armed with explosives,' corrected Hillel.

'But Mohsen Brahimi was my *qareen*. How can I live without him?'

Their eyes met.

Hillel frowned. And for an instant, he considered that they had made a mistake and that this house might emerge unscathed. 'Are you not the mother of Shahed Zeitouni?'

'Shahed? Yes, Shahed works in Qalqiliya.'

Captain Sheena Baran repeated her order, 'Come on, Lavan.'

'Yes, ma'am,' said Hillel about to turn to the door. Again he hesitated. It was difficult enough informing people of the imminent destruction of their homes. He almost whispered, 'Then may our Lord have mercy on your son's soul.'

More enduring than a thousand words of sympathy was the gesture: a single nod, a curt downward swing of the head as though preparing to bow. That gesture was full of respect, honouring the living with their dead.

The elegant Ambassadors' Hall at the King David Hotel was fitted out for a gala dinner — a true white-glove service suitable, if not for kings, then for leaders of warring nations. The podium was closest to the head table at the far end of the hall. On it was the crystal trophy, moulded into the shape of a broadsheet, refracting the overhead lights from the chandeliers to cast a miniature rainbow on the ground.

Aron's neighbour on his left, an attractive woman in her thirties, prompted, 'Is it true? Did Begin and Sadat hold their peace talks here?'

Aron was about to reply when his other neighbour leaned forward and said, 'Quite true, my dear, quite true. First, the peace talks, followed by the peace dinner.' He pointed vaguely at one of the far corners. 'I was sitting all the way over there,' he chortled, 'far enough not to make a nuisance of myself.'

Aron nodded and smiled politely. The man was in his sixties, spoke monotonously and was so seriously over-weight that Aron had trouble picturing him as anything peskier than a sloth. Gamaliel — or Gam as he usually in-troduced himself — was the publisher of *Adlai*, a position he'd held for much of Aron's career with the paper. And over the years they'd exchanged barely a handful of per-functory conversations. Aron never found anything to say to him — a situation that was not facilitated by the man's severe body odour which seemed to go straight to Aron's throat. You could smell he was a working man.

To make matters worse, Gam always made a conscious effort to wear nothing over his shirt with its rolled-up sleeves and visible armpit patches. Even at this gathering, he'd removed his blazer as soon as he found his seat at the top table.

Still addressing the woman, Gam draped an arm around Aron as he added proudly, 'The same menu has been recreated for our very special boy.'

Aron coughed to clear his throat.

'Wasn't the main course game?' asked Zach in English with a twinkle in his eye. 'I don't see that on tonight's menu.'

People smiled; someone even laughed. *Gamy* was the long-standing nickname that Zach had given his boss.

'No,' answered Gam with a smile, not realizing he was the brunt of the joke. 'We had lamb, like tonight's meal. Kosher and halal.' His smile broadened, ending with another chortle. While this had clearly been a joke to Gam, his audience listened politely as he went on, 'The Egyptian delegation tried to come up with some Hebrew words. And we did the same with the Arabic equivalents. It was a game.'

'Aha,' exclaimed Zach causing more people to laugh.

'Yes, indeed,' said Gam enthusiastically, pleased by the response. 'We thrashed them soundly. All they could say was *shalom, kosher* and *haval*.' He laughed, causing a ripple effect on his shirt-enveloped belly.

The banter moved on, splitting up into so many conversations that Aron didn't know which way to look.

Aron was disappointed that Avi hadn't called him. It was Sunday, 21 March 2004, the first of spring, and also the day after *Shabbat ha-Chodesh*, 28 Adar 5764, and therefore his twenty-first wedding anniversary by Hebraic reckoning. His son was a very sensitive young man; Avi had certainly never missed wishing him a happy anniversary before.

'That's what I always say,' Zach was saying to his neighbour. 'Give the pundits something to mull over and then something to chew on. Do it the other way round and you end up with a severe dose of indigestion.'

'That's right,' cut in Gam. 'First, the talks.' His hands flapped like butterfly wings to mimic prattling conversations. 'Then, the eats.' The palms turned inwards to wave back and forth at his mouth to denote gluttonized eating.

His jollity faded suddenly, his attention drawn to the main entrance.

'Excuse me,' he said to everyone as he rose to his feet with a parting nod to Zach. 'Get this show on the road. I'll be right back.'

Everyone turned to look at the main entrance where two IDF officers had appeared.

Aron recognized the expression on their faces. He'd seen it twice before for Sela: once for the news itself as he opened the door to them and coughed violently, and once for the coffin draped in the Star of David. They always came in twos: the first to deliver the blow, and the second to fill in should the first falter. Standing upright like archers, fingers already pulling at the longbows.

The leading soldier spoke to Gam.

Zach was already at the podium, speaking into the microphone. 'Cutting to the paper chase, we all know why we're here,' his voice boomed. He fingered the crystal prize, adding, 'We've come to celebrate one man's extraordinary career.'

Gam turned to look with dismay at Aron.

'By the same token, we're celebrating one extraordinary paper. They go hand in hand. Without *Adlai*, there can be no Aron Lunzer to touch people's hearts and souls. And without our Aron Lunzer, there is only a feeble pulse and blurred vision.'

Aron stared at the leading officer.

Their eyes met.

And for an instant, it seemed he might emerge unscathed.

Zach was waving grandly at the head table. 'Ladies and gentlemen of the press, I give you tonight's star.'

For a second, it seemed the soldier might look to another.

Aron had seen it all before.

The soldier hesitated —

No.

— and stiffened —

Please God, no.

— and delivered his nod.

The hall erupted with applause as, ever so deliberately, Aron's world collapsed.

9

Aron had his own wailing wall to mourn the death of his son — Avi's wailing wall, with its haunting images of death and destruction. The pictures, articles and notes yearned to be peeled back in the reverse order with which they had been put up, starting with Avi's last note on the purity of the nation, which partially covered a picture of broken crockery on a table, and ending with the framed portraits of his great-great-grandfathers.

In this vacuum of grief, he could turn the clock back to whenever he wanted; even entropy had fallen off a cliff. He opened his eyes and saw his son for the first time.

He stood awkwardly in Sela's hospital room, clutching three sunflowers, as he took in the shock of black hair in the crib by her bed.

He wept and coughed helplessly.

A nurse looked at him with astonishment and asked Sela whether she should bring him something.

Sela shook her head. 'It will soon pass.' Turning to Aron, she said, 'Thank you, sweetheart. You know they're my favourite flowers.'

The baby, on its back, opened its eyes and stared intently at the bright flowers.

'Look who's awake,' cooed Sela and lifted him gently first to show Aron. 'Avi, say hello to your dad.' Then she moved him to her breast.

'He's so — ' Aron's voice trailed off.

'Beautiful,' she completed, offering the baby a nipple.

He nodded and wept.

When one death has already set you on a collision course with a lifeless neutron star, another death ends up sucking out every atom that's left, leaving you in a spinning place where even light is cornered by the sheer weight of grief.

All notions of time and space lie curled up in a ball on the floor, next to pools of congealed vomit and bottles of whisky. These can also reverse time — appearing empty one moment, then progressively filling up to the top, only to repeat countless cycles.

It gets to a micro-moment, a chronon of time, when unscrambling scrambled eggs becomes physically easier than breathing.

And yet even if your lungs have collapsed, your heart still beats because the dead are too ashamed to have you now.

It's only later — much later — when you're already with-drawn to a dot, that a crack in the wall can grow, progres-sively becoming as wide as an open gate. There is no white light on the other side, no relief from the pain. But at least it is elsewhere. At least, it's not this place of timelessness where even the walls howl and wail — literally, tangibly, really.

'*Mamash.*'

It was the first word he'd spoken in eons and it sound-ed so dispirited and detached that it sounded like someone else's voice coming from somewhere other than the bedroom floor. It seemed to come from the crack itself, running down from the ceiling.

'Chabad.'

It was definitely coming from the crack, reminding him of the Chabad in Galilee where twelve-year-old Avi had found meaning and purpose.

'Fuck you.'

This time it was his voice and the crack remained silent.

He swigged his whisky in three gulps.

He wasn't yet ready to leave his black hole. He wasn't quite small enough to fit through and emerge on the other side.

Lake Merom was too small to be considered a sea, unlike the popular Lake Tiberias, due south, which had devel-oped into the Sea of Galilee. It was the most desolate and, consequently, the most stunning of the inland waters of

Israel. Comparatively few tourists ever came to Lake Merom, partly because of the narrow and winding route that linked it to the rest of Galilee. But a more compelling reason was its close proximity to death. Given that the northern border was a mere five kilometres away, Israeli jets routinely flew on reconnaissance missions, breaking the sound barrier, and bombs and Katyusha rockets from Lebanon often landed in the vicinity even during interludes of peace.

Aron had been sitting still on a rock for so long that a rabbit, popping its head out of its warren, hopped out and twitched its nose at him curiously.

He ignored it, his attention riveted to the surface of the lake.

The morning mist had just lifted, leaving the surface perfectly flat like a hospital sheet stretched from the scree at Aron's feet to the opposite bank. It now reflected a faithful image of a craggy hilltop and the blue sky beyond.

He coughed suddenly and reached for the inhaler in his pocket.

The rabbit started and hopped straight back into its warren.

A sudden breeze shimmied across the lake, fragmenting the reflection into a thousand spirals as a young man came walking along the path, dressed in the black suit of an ultra-orthodox *haredi*. He came to stand at the water's edge and turned to nod at Aron.

Aron frowned back and returned his gaze to the lake.

A single cloud appeared and the ripples ferried it across carefully to the opposite bank. After some time, another, larger cloud tried to follow. But the wind had died down and the lake remained perfectly still — so the larger cloud was confined to its patch of the sky.

'I've seen you at camp.'

It had been quiet for so long that Aron jumped when the *haredi* spoke. 'Hm,' he replied brusquely.

Aron had finally found the energy to move off the floor in Avi's bedroom in the first week of June. Now in his third week in the Chabad camp in Galilee, a hundred kilometres north of Jerusalem, he still had trouble recognizing the officiating rabbi and his assistants, let alone his fellow 'campers'.

The young *haredi* sat on a rock and joined Aron in contemplating the inland water.

Chabad houses and camps provided children and adults with a spiritual retreat — in the case of the latter, they were especially meant to bring those who had fallen by the wayside back into the Jewish fold through study, prayer and group sessions. But Aron hadn't come here for any lessons on the Torah or the extra counselling in spiritual life offered by the rabbi; he'd had quite enough *davening* as a child to last a lifetime.

He had come to this particular Chabad in Galilee to keep the memory of Avi alive in his mind. Beautiful Avi, who, as a four-year-old, had answered every question with an irritating bray. Or baby Avi, barely into his second month of his second year, who had pulled himself up to a standing position and stared at Sela's postcard in Aron's hand. With a pudgy finger on a tear flowing down Aron's cheek, he had uttered his first recognizable words: 'Daddy bou-hou-hou.'

At first, he had planned to spend just one night in the place that twelve-year-old Avi had called the most perfect spot in the world. But the solitude of Lake Merom had exerted a pull on him.

The *haredi* tried to make eye contact with Aron again, but he got up to leave.

It took only one person to break the isolation. He walked one mile in the direction of Lebanon, back to camp, and coughed as he donned the yarmulke to enter the gates.

Often, over the past three months, he wished he'd remained Arnold Lounger and had never made aliyah to Israel.

The *haredi* was back the following day and again exchanged nods with Aron. He sat at the same rock and looked at the lake.

This time it was Aron who broke the silence. 'Will you be returning soon?' he called out. In a broader sense, it was a euphemism for rejoining the Jewish community. In theory, all the adults who went to a Chabad — fervent believers as well as the merely lackadaisical and profaners in matters of faith — had one goal: to graduate to the level of 'Master of return', *Baal teshuva*, and to emerge, subsequently, as fully-rounded, fully-practising members of orthodox society.

'I have already returned,' he answered. 'I'm a student of the Torah.'

'Right,' said Aron, disappointed. He had meant it in the narrower sense of returning to camp.

Often, even *haredis* attended Chabad to go through their scriptures. He left his rock and came closer to Aron.

'Do you mind if I sit with you?' He indicated the space next to Aron.

'Yes.'

The *haredi* hesitated.

With a resigned shrug, Aron waved him to a rock next to his.

'And you? Are you prepared to return?'

'Hmm,' replied Aron. 'I'll have to soon.' He didn't relish the thought of returning to his empty flat in Jerusalem.

The man looked at him quizzically.

'Just waiting for my golden chariot,' added Aron, who was already getting tired of the man's company. 'Any minute now.' He was referring to the holy *merkava* — chariot of God — that came to take the prophets on divinatory adventures.

'Really?'

'Yes, *mamash*.'

The man was suddenly fascinated. 'Is that why you come here a lot? I've seen you — you stare a lot. Especially here.'

Aron looked at him properly for the first time. The face was younger than the dark clothes would suggest. He was young, so young — perhaps Avi's age — but with broad shoulders and a muscle tone that seemed at odds with the garb as though he'd lost his way to an athletic event and ended up in a religious camp by mistake.

'It's true,' continued the young man, 'that if you stare at an object long enough, the mystery of Ezekiel's vision will become known.' His eyes grew wider.

'What's your name?'

'Yitzhak Krickstein.'

'How old are you?'

'Twenty, almost twenty-one.'

'Well, Yitzhak Krickstein. If you want my advice, go now and get yourself a life.'

The *haredi* looked at Aron, who waved at the desolate lake. 'This is a place for sorry old men like me, not for someone with a future. Go away from the Chabad and travel, feel things, fall in love. Don't just sit with old scriptures.'

'If you're not here for the Torah,' said Krickstein, his eyes narrowing, 'why are you here?'

He was about to answer with some lie when he had a sudden and brief coughing fit.

The *haredi* looked at him with alarm.

'It'll soon pass,' he spluttered mechanically.

Eventually, with a final cough, Aron said flatly, 'I lost my son.'

It surprised him that he had said it; it was the first time he'd actually uttered it. He'd thought it every waking moment since that wretched day in March, but this was the first time he'd expressed it to another living soul. It surprised him even more that he had chosen to say it to an ultra-orthodox Jew. But then the man was only just older than Avi. 'An Arab fanatic took him away from me.'

There had been a spate of suicide attacks in Israel lately. 'A suicide bomb?' asked the young *haredi*.

Aron nodded. While the rest of the world was gripped by the very real images of abuse in Iraqi jails, Aron kept imagining and reliving Avi's final moments in the West Bank. In his recurring nightmares, the face of the terrorist always appeared smudged like the genitals of the tortured detainees on the news; only the fatal belt of explosives was in perfect focus, flashing as the victory smiles of prison guards.

'So you've come here,' said Krickstein gently, 'to find the reason why he died written in the Torah?'

Aron's expression was full of contempt. 'I'm more likely to understand why from newspapers.' The macabre irony was that he was considered something of an expert in suicide bombers and had appeared several times on CNN to argue the link between the home-grown terrorists and the global conflict against al-Qaeda.

'So what do the newspapers say about the death of your son?' insisted Krickstein.

He shook his head. Such discursive reasoning now echoed nauseatingly hollow; Avi grew to be just another statistic for March 2004. It was not enough that some faceless horror had blown himself up along with his Avi, or that the fanatic's house had been destroyed and his family made homeless. Nor did he gain anything more than the coldest comfort from the fact that the Israeli military had officially classified Avi as a war hero. 'You see,' he said at length and almost conversationally, 'my family is full of heroes of Israel.' Israel was so full of dead heroes that she was bursting at the seams.

Above them, two Israeli jets broke the sound barrier as they flew north into Lebanon, the sonic booms causing the lake's water to crawl. They watched the ripple effect in silence.

After a while, Krickstein said slowly, 'I find deeper justice in the Talmud.'

Aron put his hands on his knees, preparing himself to leave.

'I was in the army,' the *haredi* added and shook his head sadly. 'I left just a few months ago.' He gave a humourless chuckle. 'Actually I had to leave because I almost became a hero of Israel myself — ' His voice trailed off.

Aron moved his hands away. 'What do you mean?' he prompted.

Krickstein spoke with feeling. 'The Talmud helps you to see things more clearly. I was lost back then.' He continued in a softer tone, 'But the more I read, the more I understand my role. This is the endless war between the sons of light and the sons of darkness.'

Aron groaned, and his hands returned to his knees. 'You sound just like my father.'

'Really? Is he a rabbi?'

'No,' said Aron. 'He's just — '

'A master in Kabbalah?' Krickstein asked hopefully.

' — very religious.' Aron stood up.

Krickstein jumped to his feet. 'I would love to meet your father.' He held out his hand. 'I'm sorry, I don't know your name.'

Aron told him as they shook hands.

'*Aron Lunzer*?' repeated Krickstein. His face turned suddenly pale. 'Aron Lunzer of *Adlai*?'

'Yes.'

Abruptly, the young man mumbled something about forgetting a group study at camp and walked briskly away.

How curious, thought Aron. Even diehard readers of *Haaretz* who absolutely despised *Adlai* would not have been so rude. Then again, people who read *Haaretz* would probably rather be dead than be seen wearing the black of a *haredi*.

As the breeze picked up, Lake Merom joined him to shrug at the *haredi*'s sudden departure.

'I'll also be going soon,' Aron informed the lake softly. 'I won't be coming back, but I will miss you.'

Lake Merom had sat an extended shiva with him, proving the most accommodating and understanding of grieving companions. But he had to leave because June was coming to an end and, for much of July, the fierce *khamsin* winds would sweep in from North Africa and turn the whole area into a giant dust fest.

The postcard was waiting for him in the post box when he returned to Jerusalem, buried among bills and promotional leaflets. It was innocuous enough with a snapshot of the Western Wall that any tourist might buy. The note simply read:

Qalqiliya in the West Bank

Aron stared at it blankly.

For a second, he relived another moment, when he'd picked out a different card from deep within the post box, with its picture of the Colosseum. He wondered briefly whether this, too, was a case of major postal cockups, with the card arriving well after the sender's death.

But it wasn't Avi's handwriting. He looked at the front and back of the card, and at different angles as if to catch the reflection of a concealed signature or some other distinguishing mark. He frowned when he couldn't find one.

Of course, he immediately recognized the name of that town — it had played its part in most of his nightmares over the past three months. It was at the checkpoint in Qalqiliya that a Palestinian madman had blown himself up, taking Avi with him. Qalqiliya was also where they made the best brooms — it annoyed Aron that he should remember that trivial detail now.

Who had sent him the card, he wondered, and why? He was also amazed by his reaction. For a second, he almost felt like going to Qalqiliya to experience the pang of standing exactly at the scene of the crime.

He switched all the lights on in the flat and checked all the rooms, even poking his head in Avi's bedroom, like a released prisoner not quite daring to step into his former cell.

He poured himself a whisky and, with his drink and the postcard in one hand, he went to his study where he switched on the TV and his computer. Sitting at his desk, he briefly watched CNN's extended coverage on Iraq and then turned to the monitor. He hesitated and then went through the motions of checking the temporary files, history and recent documents folder. This was part of the routine whenever Aron switched on his computer. It was a habit that first began when he suspected his young Avi had found a way to crack the parental control on the browser in order to surf the Internet for porn. He realized how ridiculous it was for him to be doing that still, especially now, but it was a habit he found impossible to kick.

He stared at the postcard for a while and then eventually launched his browser, downloaded a map of the West Bank centred on Qalqiliya, which he printed, and Googled Avi's name in another window.

The result yielded two solitary links; by stark contrast, 'Aron Lunzer' was mentioned in more than 1,000 web pages. The sheer difference served as a painful reminder of his boy's premature death: Avi hadn't been given the chance to grow even in cyberspace.

The first link was an old page from Avi's school where his name simply appeared in a list of 'boys 12 & under' who had been involved in a swimming competition in the summer term of 1996. Being confronted by the electronic wraith of his eleven-year-old son was poignant if otherwise unimpressive — it was ultimately normal that his son's old school should have some record of his participation, no matter how banal.

It was the second of the two results that awakened the dormant beast in him.

The Google result took him to the UNRWA website and to a report in PDF format, entitled *Situation Analysis of Palestinian Women, 2000–2004*. Avi's name was mentioned in the 157th footnote in the context of the Palestinian who had murdered him. He printed out the entire document, but only read and reread the two footnotes on that page:

[156] The second intifada is equally known as the al-Aqsa Intifadah in reference to the incendiary visit by the current Prime Minister of Israel, Ariel Sharon, to al-Aqsa Mosque on 29 September 2000.

[157] The Israeli soldier was named Avi Lunzer.

That Avi had been mentioned at all in such a context and report astonished and infuriated him by equal measure. Irrationally, Aron was also incensed that his son should be down as a footnote, instead of in the main text.

He was still glaring at the pages when he reached the very last sheet. It took him a while to realize that it wasn't actually part of the report; it was the map of Qalqiliya, which he'd cleanly forgotten about and which had been printed first and so appeared last in the batch of sheets.

He was about to scrunch it up when something about the layout of the Palestinian town caught his eye. The security barrier was marked by a bold red line that descended from the northeast and went off the page southeast of the town; the central section, bulging with a full catch of fish, neatly circumscribed Qalqiliya to end in a bottleneck at the eastern approach. In fact, it appeared like a line-drawing silhouette of a man's head, with nose and neck, looking up towards Jordan.

Aron blinked.

He realized with a jolt where he'd seen that silhouette before.

He practically ran to his son's bedroom and switched the lights on.

He held up the printout and looked at the wall with amazement.

Since March, he had spent so many of his darkest hours on the floor, too stricken to even try to draw any sense of the disfigured wall, with its leitmotif of death and destruction.

He remembered how it was initially meant to represent a dialogue between Józsi's and Lilah's grandfathers, Hungarian and Turk. With time, as the wall changed progressively over the years, so too had the tenor of the conversation. Now the ancestors appeared to hurl recriminations at one another in a vertiginous spiral of pictures, articles, comments and graffiti.

Aron shuddered as he remembered his many attempts to join the argument, their haughty expressions remaining impassive to his shouts. On several occasions over the past months, he'd even come very close to pulling everything off the wall in his anguish, of tearing and shredding all those images and articles of death.

But the image of his twelve-year-old dragging a pencil on the wall had kept appearing, forcing him back.

He knew every part of the wall intimately in the way that the most detestable face sears the mind until death.

He could close his eyes and still see exactly how the letters of CARNIVAL formed watchtowers to the fortress around the great-great-grandfathers. He could recreate from scratch the unexpected gap between R and N, as though Avi had simply run out of ink or patience to fill in the line. And there, too, was the slight projection between the second and third towers — A and R — which appeared like the silhouette of a nose to a man's head.

But until that moment, Aron's attention had focused especially on the most intriguing element of the mutilated wall: the graffiti splashed messily onto the surface in bold colours, written in both English and Hebrew, that wound clockwise towards the window and curved anticlockwise to end at the light switch.

He looked at the wall with amazement as though, even after all those weeks and months of growing thinner from staring at it, he was only now seeing it for the first time.

He took a step back with the printout still in his hand.

There was no mistaking it: Avi's lines matched almost perfectly those on the sheet. There, in the middle, was the Palestinian town where the Hungarian with his curled moustache and Turk with his beard cohabited.

A shiver ran down his spine as he looked at this giant, disfigured map of Qalqiliya and at the gap between R and N, which, transposing onto the real map, marked the Qalqiliya checkpoint where Avi had been blown up. His son had drawn the exact spot where he would die.

But Aron's solution opened up a whole set of other conundrums.

Why had Avi drawn a map of Qalqiliya on his wall? More to the point, that part of the wall had been drawn when Avi was seventeen — a full year before his call-up papers — so why would he even have been interested in a Palestinian town?

Aron left the bedroom in a greater state of confusion than he had entered it. He spent an agitated evening, which even his whisky was unable relieve, and a restless night, which was only exacerbated by all the dust particles that had invaded the flat in his absence.

The following morning, he woke up with a start and a violent cough. Mechanically, he reached for the inhaler on his bedside table and found the postcard instead.

He almost vomited as it brought to mind the jumble of thoughts from the previous evening.

His more impulsive half had saved him in the past, driving him away from gloomy North London and the resigned, predestined attitudes of his parents. The same quiet impulse had urged him to follow the IDF into Lebanon, where he'd found both a wife and a career.

But it wasn't this investigative half that niggled him now — it was plain guilt. There was no denying that he had forced Avi into the IDF; over the past months, every little scrap on the wall had served to remind him painfully of that fact. And now the wall seemed to be screaming at him again, ordering him to Qalqiliya if for no other reason than to see for himself where Avi had spent his final months.

He switched on the TV and opened the second drawer of his desk to check that his British passport was still valid. It was, and Aron tapped it absentmindedly against the desk with some disappointment.

Under Regulation 126 of the Defence Regulations, Israeli civilians were strictly banned from travelling to the West

Bank. So that the part of him that dreaded even the notion of travel had hoped to use the excuse of an expired foreign passport not to visit Qalqiliya.

In the background, CNN reported on the preparations by the coalition forces in Iraq to hand over limited sovereignty to a new, post-Saddam government, and he began to prepare himself mentally for a flying visit to Qalqiliya.

One death necessitated one resurrection.

He would adopt his alter nomen and trace his son's last steps as the British citizen and freelance reporter, Arnold Lounger.

If he had time and patience, he might even try to meet the author of the UNRWA report — a certain Bernadette Shaker — who'd relegated Avi to such a lowly footnote.

This was his *Baal teshuva*, not quite a Master of return. If March went out like a slaughtered lamb, then July returned like a slightly more emboldened goat. He was prepared to brave all the dust and terrorists in the world very briefly just to see where Avi had died.

10

Qalqiliya was once a prosperous market town. Endowed with nearly half the water of the West Bank, the municipality boasted one of the most fertile agricultural basins in the entire region. Before the arrival of the Israeli settlements and the construction of the Wall, the local community had been comparatively wealthy, benefiting from exports of fruit and vegetables to Israel and the Gulf.

The shops were now shuttered and the streets empty of traffic.

The Hotel Baghdad on the northern side of the town square had also seen better days. It was late afternoon and the sun shone on the main, western facade of the building, highlighting the years of neglect, shadows of grime that crept up the walls and moved through cracks in the windows. The rot had spread to the hotel sign as well, separate bold letters running vertically down the building on iron supports. Only the top and bottom three letters had survived and Aron read:

HOT   DAD

The air conditioning in his rental car had been on the internal circulation setting for the entire trip from East Jerusalem, recycling the air so many times that it actually started to affect his throat. It was as though his own smell had been copied countless times to turn into the super-stench of a crowd. But even a bubble of stale air was preferable to the dusty roads of the West Bank.

Aron stared at the sign and kept his engine running.

A young man dashed from the hotel entrance and was about to open the car. Aron quickly raised his palm and wiggled an index at him. The man was still moving to open his door so Aron shouted, 'Stop!'

The young man paused and started to wait by the driver's door. He was dressed in jeans and a nondescript shirt, and the only item of clothing that linked him in any way to the hotel was a worn out cap with the monogram HB.

Aron needed time to think.

He'd been so preoccupied with driving in the West Bank — finding his way on the byzantine road network and out-manoeuvring insane Palestinian drivers — that this was the first opportunity he had to question his decision to come here.

He'd booked his room for two nights over the phone, but since the hotel hadn't asked for his credit card details he was perfectly free to cancel even at this stage. Part of him offered congratulations on a mission already accomplished; he had made it to Qalqiliya and had even stopped and seen the gate at the entrance to town where Avi had lost his life — albeit fleetingly and from the confines of his car. For a second, he was tempted to believe that he could now return home.

But he had also phoned ahead for a meeting with Avi's superiors at the army base, scheduled for the next day — the same IDF that sustained Israel and for which many martyrs had given their lives. He could never cancel on the IDF.

He finally switched off the engine with a deep sigh and allowed the bellhop to open his door.

The alien world's atmosphere had an immediate effect on his throat as soon as he stepped out of the car. He coughed, spluttered and coughed even more violently until he was doubled over, desperately scrabbling for the inhaler in his pocket.

He was still coughing when he checked in as Arnold Lounger and hopelessly tried to clear his throat as his bellhop had a brief run-in with another youth for the privilege of carrying his bag to the room.

As the only guest staying at the Hotel Baghdad, Aron was put in the executive suite. It consisted of a queen-sized bed but with sheets for a single bed — judging from the bare mattress at the sides — and an en suite bathroom, which he now made for, to retch over a stained toilet.

After a while, he flushed the toilet and turned the tap on in the sink. The plumbing groaned at the simultaneous request and knocked like a trapped beast. It yielded a trickle of water to refill the toilet tank and for a full ten minutes, until it had finished with that task, hissed air out of the tap.

Aron returned to the room and switched on and off a faulty TV that relayed the sounds of the various local stations to accompany a flickering pinprick of light at the centre of the tube. And when he discovered that even the phone didn't work, he went down to the lobby and demanded to see the manager.

The man shrugged helplessly. He did, however, fish out a cell phone from a pocket to tackle the last of Aron's long list of complaints. 'Please,' he said, holding out his phone, 'be my guest.'

Aron did use the manager's phone later that evening, after a plain dinner of strained yoghurt that soothed his throat a bit and made his voice marginally less croaky.

But he still didn't sound quite like himself when he contacted Bernadette Shaker to arrange a meeting. He made a mental note that she spoke with a pronounced American drawl and with that degree of informality and earnestness that only Americans seemed to take pleasure in.

Sheena's antipathy towards journalists had its roots back in South Africa when she, along with her parents and many other whites, blamed the international press and accused them of bias and of presenting their country in a poor light that perpetuated the harsh economic sanctions, which eventually led to her family's emigration. It was therefore ironic that she should have been assigned the responsibilities of an army spokesperson given this thinly veiled dislike of the media.

She felt that the international media suffered from a similar myopic vision when it came to the conflict in the Middle East. Foreign reporters wore their impartiality as flak jackets — once in the safe confines of their pressrooms, they pitched pieces that were tipped towards the Arabs. You could always tell from the subtle language: fewer adjectives were used when suicide bombers struck their innocent victims; comparatively more were used to describe defensive operations by the IDF; and such words as 'wall' and 'militant' were used instead of 'security fence' and 'terrorist'. European journalists were worse than Americans; topping that mound of prejudiced reporting were the British, particularly those employed by the *Guardian*.

But she was especially scathing of the bias that crept into several Israeli publications. Among these was the *Jerusalem Post*, which needed to start writing for Israelis rather than catering to a foreign readership and which had to be cleansed of its senior editors, most of whom were corrupt and couldn't even speak Hebrew. And the lowest of the low, *Haaretz*, which couldn't stop dreaming about peace with al-Qaeda, al-Aqsa Martyrs' Brigade and Hamas, rather than supporting a country and a world at war with terrorists.

Indeed, the only foreign or local newspaper she bothered to read regularly was the daily *Adlai*. At least that publication ran even-handed reports and commentaries that were relevant and specific to Israelis.

Paradoxically, it actually made perfect sense for Sheena to have been promoted to press spokesperson for the base. She was naturally more guarded whenever she was in the presence of a journalist.

The soldiers who accompanied the visitor to the camp gave her a half-hearted salute. 'Mr Lounger,' she greeted as she held out her hand, 'my name is Sheena Baran.'

His left hand moved to cover his mouth as his right hand met hers. He coughed, tried to clear his throat and coughed more violently.

She instinctively took a step back. 'Can I get you something?'

He shook his head and reached for the inhaler in his pocket. 'It'll soon pass,' he spluttered.

In addition to the natural defence provided by its geological vantage ground at the top of a hill, the military camp was watched over by two towers and protected by the northern section of the wall that encircled Qalqiliya.

Sheena turned to catch the reflection of the early morning sunlight from one of those two triangular tops, the freckles on her face like so many ellipses on a page waiting impatiently for the man's fit to subside.

On the rise, midway up the hill, squatted a tank, its gun pointed in the direction of the town; below, a bulldozer shifted the ground, turning a ramshackle orchard into mounds of deep red earth. There was a heap of shorn olive trunks and branches, and a group of Palestinians were busy loading this firewood onto the back of their truck.

'Sorry,' said the man at length, clearing his throat one more time. 'I'm a patented dustometre.'

'Right. It's a long walk up the hill without a car,' she said, but her tone was not sympathetic. She led the way to her office.

When the visitor remarked on the tidy arrangement of the barracks and the wide and straight roads in the camp, which were in stark contrast to the urban chaos of Qalqiliya, she inferred an unvoiced criticism and replied coolly, 'The sense of law and order is more deeply ingrained in Israeli society.'

Once in her office, she frowned at his press card and, tapping on a sheet of paper with her pen, said, 'There's no expiry date.'

'I'm an old timer — ' he began.

'I can see that.'

'We didn't need them then.'

'Issued in 1982,' she said, unconvinced. Sheena had been a young girl then, living on the Esplanade in East London and trying to shimmy stones off the snowy surf of the Indian Ocean.

'Yes. I was covering the Peace for Galilee.'

Sheena looked up; a reporter from the *Guardian* or the BBC would have said, 'the invasion of Lebanon'.

'I think there's been too much focus on the greater conflict, on the clash of civilizations. Even in terms of terrorist attacks on purely civilian targets, the attention tends to be drawn to the scale of the carnage and the political implications. I feel that the Islamic fanatics get way too much favourable coverage in the West.'

Sheena found herself nodding at his acceptable choice of terms and adjectives.

'There's an urgent need to correct that,' he continued, 'a need to write about the personal tragedy that comes from such horror tactics. In a very real sense, there's a need to personalize the human drama beyond mere statistics.' He added passionately, 'I wish to write about one such case, the case of Private Avi Lunzer whose one misfortune was to be in the direct path of a fanatic.'

'One soldier?'

'Yes. One to honour all of them.'

'Why that particular soldier?'

'This full-length feature will be pegged as the 20,200th Israeli soldier who has fallen since the State of Israel was established.'

Sheena considered that for a full minute, clasping her hands together with the pen sticking out between her thumbs.

Eventually, she asked, 'And your readership will be interested in such a story?'

He gave her a knowing look. 'I believe this will benefit anyone who's interested in Israel.'

'Very well, Mr Lounger,' she said, finally. 'How can I help you with your research?' She relaxed her grip on the pen.

She looked very vaguely familiar, like some face from his neighbourhood encountered on the way to work.

Aron had to remind himself that there was no story; he was only pretending to be a British journalist in order to bypass the travel ban on all Israeli citizens, even grieving fathers.

It was particularly ironic that the feature was only a ploy since Aron was genuinely interested in writing about the IDF and had done so from many different angles over the course of his career. In a sense, even this gung-ho treatment of the IDF — looking at what it took to be an Israeli soldier — was an act of revisiting a piece that he'd written twenty years ago.

He recalled the high spirits of the IDF in 1982, at the start of the invasion of Lebanon, when the army took pride in promoting a humanistic goal among its members and in seeking to avoid unnecessary bloodshed and civilian casualties whenever possible. He'd written about this concept, known as 'purity of arms', in one of his early freelance pieces for *The Daily Telegraph*, which he'd subsequently recycled and repackaged for *Adlai*.

Sela had proved the inspiration for that piece, detailing this unwritten code of conduct as Aron steered her into a café and schemed of ways to remove her delightfully tight uniform.

The truth was that, sometime after her death and well before Avi's, he'd lost his journalistic urges. He'd been sitting in his flat in Jerusalem for such a long time that he thought he'd forgotten what made a good story and how to chase it. He'd also forgotten the thrill.

His faithful dictaphone — a veteran analogue recorder that had accompanied him on the skirmishes in the Bekaa between the Israeli and Syrian armies — was in the same pocket as his inhaler. And he had two small pads in the other pocket, ready to be filled with thoughts, ideas to pursue and transcribed notes to cover the story — a sequel to purity of arms.

But the dust everywhere made sure he never forgot the real reason why he was there.

His throat remained inflamed throughout that day as he toured the camp, ever ready to force a violent cough lest he stop thinking about his son. And while he was largely successful at striking a balance in his body language between sympathy and detachment, he couldn't resist wincing imperceptibly when Sheena handed him the official report of Avi's death.

Aron copied it in his first pad:

Private Avi Lunzer died at exactly 4:35 am on 21 March 2004 as a result of a bomb detonated at close range. He was on check-point duty when he became suspicious of a man attempting to leave Qalqiliya 1 hour and 25 minutes before the end of curfew. The man, a Palestinian youth named Shahed Zeitouni, refused repeated calls to stop. Having succeeded in crossing the barrier, Private Lunzer fired three warning shots in the air, forcing the Palestinian to stop 22 metres away from the checkpoint. As Avi Lunzer drew closer to investigate, the Palestinian shouted 'Alla-hu Akbar' and detonated his charge.

Another officer joined them outside the mess hall. 'This is Corporal Caleb Sharett,' said Sheena, introducing him to Aron. 'I've assigned him to be your guide for the rest of the day.'

The young officer looked vaguely like a fairer version of Avi except for the eyes. He flashed a smile of perfect white teeth. 'How's it hanging?' he asked Aron, shaking his hand. He spoke English with a strong Israeli accent.

They were standing next to a large notice board on which were tacked two sheets, written in English and Hebrew, respectively, and entitled *Arafat's rules of engagement*. Sheena made a mental note that the journalist glanced at the Hebrew before turning to the English version.

The five golden rules that pro-Arab media follow in order to produce dramatic results are as follows:

1. See the Middle East only through Arab eyes. NEVER EVER consider the Israeli perspective.
2. Treat Arab governmental statements as hard news and be sure to SUPPRESS or MINIMIZE all the news unfavourable to Arabs.
3. Muddy the waters WHENEVER necessary.
4. NEVER EVER discuss the fundamental moral issues posed by suicide bombs; use ONLY the language of incitement.
5. Credit ONLY Arab claims, even if wholly unfounded; NEVER EVER pay attention to Israeli assertions, no matter how self-evident.

Sheena allowed the thinnest of smiles to creep across her face. It had been more natural for her to draft Arafat's rules in English. So she'd written them first in her mother tongue, then translated them into Hebrew for the benefit of her fellow comrades, and posted both versions to try to win over biased journalists visiting the base. 'Most reporters don't understand Israel's predicament and show little sympathy to our cause.' She scrutinized the man and waited for his nod before adding, 'Besides, these golden rules are good for the morale of our boys and women. Isn't that right, Caleb?'

'Yeah.'

Sheena exchanged amused looks with the corporal. She was visibly pleased that the journalist was taking notes, tickled even by the thought that her list of Arafat's rules might make it to print, even if it was an English daily. 'Private Avi Lunzer was the 20,200[th] Israeli soldier to die for Israel,' she explained to Sharett and told him about the feature that the reporter wished to write and about where to take the visitor.

'Cool,' said Sharett finally.

In fact, Aron was also jotting down notes about the casual air at the IDF base. Relations between reservists and their officers had always been informal. Saluting was almost an option and it was common for reservists and officers to address each other by their first names and to argue as equals. This informality extended to such exterior symbols as smartness on the parade ground and military appearance and bearing. The general feeling was that, as long as the level of performance in combat remained high, stringent spit-and-polish prevalent in other armies was unnecessary and ran counter to the egalitarian traditions of Zionism. This aspect of purity of arms had not changed since the 1980s.

A sudden coughing fit forced him to abandon his notes and reach for the inhaler.

Corporal Sharett went off to bring him a glass of water.

'I'm your man,' he said when Aron was in a state to listen. 'I'll tell you everything you need to know about the IDF.'

Aron cleared his throat. 'Did you know Private Lunzer?'

'Sure. Avi was my pal. If you're in the army, everyone is your pal.' He paused and then added, 'Well, not Yasser Arafat.'

'I'm sorry?'

Sharett found his joke more amusing the second time round and laughed as he said, 'If you're in the army, Yasser Arafat isn't your pal.'

He led the way out down the main road in the camp.

'Seriously, man,' Sharett was saying, 'you know he created this intifada with his own two hands, don't you.'

Aron caught a flash of light and looked up to see some soldiers in one of the round watchtowers. One of them was looking down at him through binoculars. Aron waved mechanically.

'That criminal says peace of the brave and you and your English friends — no offence, man — kiss his ass, and in Arabic he tells Palestinian children to become suicide bombers.'

The IDF base outside Qalqiliya consisted of various offices in separate portacabins, a mess hall and five large buildings that were numbered above each door using the first five letters of the Hebrew alphabet. Next to each number in a smaller font were pithy military attributes, appearing like operation codenames. As they walked past the successive buildings, Aron read *Aleph: Proven Force, Bet: Able Sentry, Gimmel: Retribution* and *Dalet: Uphold Order*.

'Arafat takes all the money that you Europeans give him and puts it in his wife's bank account in Paris.' Sharett turned left to enter the fifth building and held the door open for the visitor.

Aron read the Hebrew sign: *Hey: Restore Peace.* 'I see,' he said. 'And how long have you been at this base?'

'Long enough to know Arafat's true colours.'

They stepped into a corridor and then down a long, empty dormitory with a line of beds on either side.

'I guess you'll want to write about Arafat in your story, right?'

'Not really.' Aron could already see the salient points of the IDF feature. 'I plan to describe things as they are. In the West, we're bombarded with the everyday hardships of Palestinians. It's high time we showed it's not all fun and games for the soldiers who serve their country. I want readers to hear the dawn wake-up call, to feel the constant irritation of sweat and dust, and to see, smell and taste the good work that you do here.' He paused to clear his throat, which sought to remind him that he wasn't really there as a journalist. He added, 'Through the experiences of one dead soldier.'

Sharett stopped halfway down the dormitory. 'Sure, man,' he said. 'But if you're writing about us, you need to know that we all agree that Arafat should be killed or at least expelled from Israel.' He indicated a bed. 'Well that's where your dead soldier used to sleep. That was Avi Lunzer's bunk.' He continued, 'We'll only stop mourning once Arafat has choked on pita and *hummus.*'

Aron succeeded in stifling the itch in his throat. He approached the bed and tried to picture his son sleeping there, his purely S'faradi features in the dark.

Sharett turned his attention to another soldier who had entered the dormitory.

Corporal Hillel Lavan peered at the two suspiciously. 'What are you doing here, Caleb?' he asked in Hebrew. 'And who's that?'

'Showing this *goi* around,' replied Sharett sharply. 'Captain's orders.' He told him briefly about the journalist's feature on the IDF.

Aron looked at the neat arrangement of pictures and postcards stuck to the wall by the bed, and he could only imagine how messy it would have been if it had still been Avi's private space. Another young soldier had since moved into Avi's bunk. Aron couldn't stop the creeping envy as he stared at one picture in particular that showed the young man posing with his girlfriend at some resort. He coughed.

He was only vaguely listening to Sharett who said in Hebrew, 'I don't imagine he'll want to write about you,' and then in English, 'That's Corporal Lavan, the officer in charge of this building. He doesn't talk English.' He flashed a smile of perfect white teeth. 'But he does cough like an Arab.'

'What are you saying about me?' asked Hillel.

'Just that you're the head of *bayit-pagom*.' Each building had its own corporal to act as lead officer and, with the exception of the fifth building, was usually referred to only by its Hebrew letter. Sharett was the head of *aleph*, Proven Force. But Restore Peace had acquired a nickname and was commonly known as *bayit-pagom*, reject-house.

'Ashkenazim bring us nothing but shame,' the other said darkly.

Sharett momentarily lost his grin. 'You talking to me, sheikh?'

Aron heard the exchange in Hebrew and flicked open his notebook to and scribbled: *less camaraderie than in the 1980s?* His eyes shot up. 'Tell me about Avi Lunzer,' he interrupted. 'What sort of young man was he? How did he spend his days?' He directed his questions at Sharett, but glanced at the other soldier who gave him an evil stare.

Sharett noticed, his grin returning. 'Ach, don't worry about him, man,' he said. 'He only barks and only if your skin isn't as dark as his.'

'What about Avi?' persisted Aron.

'Avi was the best sort,' replied Sharett without hesitation. 'Great guy, made you laugh just by looking at him. He loved to have fun.' He shook his head sadly, 'He's a real hero.' He nodded first at the bed and then at the exit. 'Avi slept there, but he spent most of his time with his real brothers in *aleph*.' He laughed good-naturedly. 'That's alpha-house to you. That's how you should call it in your article.'

On the way out, Aron spotted a copy of *Arafat's rules of engagement* on a board. Next to it was a checkpoint rota for July and some of the names on the list were highlighted in yellow.

'That's for the Qalqiliya gate,' explained Sharett.

'What does the yellow mean?'

'*Rejects*,' he let slip in Hebrew, but said in English, 'All the soldiers in this building. Come, I'll show you our checkpoint rota in *aleph*. We use a red pen and you'll see the difference on the page. You'll see how much more duty me and my boys do.'

'How does the checkpoint duty work?' asked Aron, opening his pad. He coughed when they emerged to walk back up the road towards *aleph*. 'How many soldiers man the checkpoint?'

'Always a minimum of two,' he replied. 'If they're from back there,' he said nodding back at *bayit-pagom*, 'we always put one of theirs with one from my house or from *bet*. It's safer that way.'

'So there was at least one other soldier on guard duty in the early morning of 21 March.'

'Sure, man. Why March?'

'That's when Avi Lunzer died.'

His eyebrows twitched imperceptibly. 'Right.'

'So who was with him?'

'I don't know,' he said. 'Can't see why you need that in your article.'

Aron stopped in his tracks, forcing the soldier to turn around. 'Well how about because he survived — just for starters.' He added adamantly, 'He would have the inside story of what it's like to come to within an inch of death and live through a terrorist attack.'

Sharett shrugged.

'I thought you said you were my man.' Aron tried to smile. 'Surely there must be a copy of the checkpoint rota for March kicking about. It would be very useful if I could get a quick peek.'

'I'll see what I can do,' Sharett said.

'Thanks, man.'

By the time they emerged from alpha-house, word had spread about Aron's feature. They returned to the mess hall for lunch and he was promptly surrounded by soldiers, gathered around him like excited schoolchildren, each wanting to talk about Avi so that their names would be in print.

They were all so young. Aron switched on his dictaphone and just let them talk; his throat was so inflamed anyway that even the mass of bodies around him didn't bother him so much.

He did not reveal his Israeli persona to them for more than just practical reasons relating to the travel ban. As a British journalist with, theoretically, no emotional interest in the demise of one soldier, it encouraged them to talk more openly, to describe the true nature of the young man he had held as a baby. When they spoke of Avi's valour, they did so persuasively, conscious that his worth would be measured, analysed and written about by a complete stranger.

A young reservist declared that Avi had been too good for the fifth house, Restore Peace.

He was quickly silenced by another.

'What do you mean?' Aron asked the first soldier.

There was an abrupt and uneasy silence.

'Off the record,' he told them.

There was a deafening sound of lunch being consumed, cutlery scraping against plates and glasses banging on tables.

Aron used Sharett's word in Hebrew: '*Bayit-pagom.*' He made a show of switching off his dictaphone. 'I don't need it for my piece, but what does *pagom* mean?'

The tension lifted as promptly as it had descended; several soldiers laughed, someone called out provocatively, '*Pagom, pagom, pagom.*'

Now they all vied to be the first to explain to the *goi* the finer points of the five houses at the base.

When reservists joined the base they were assigned a house according to their backgrounds, age and, especially, military school records. The houses were colour-coded and ranked such as the most combative recruits ended up in *aleph*, red, followed by *bet*, orange, while the least warlike were housed in yellow *hey* — *bayit-pagom*.

'Avi was orange,' someone at the back called out.

'No way, he was blue.'

While there was some debate as to which colour best described Avi, they all agreed that he should never have been yellow.

Aron put in a new tape in his dictaphone when, after lunch, Captain Baran took him to see the commander of the base, Colonel Habib Ami.

'That is why Avi Lunzer is a hero,' stated Ami. 'He lost his life so that mothers and their little children would be spared. Lord knows which of our cities that terrorist would have hit, and how many more innocent civilians that Muslim would have butchered.'

The man was speaking in Hebrew, so Aron waited for her translation before nodding. He noted that she had changed 'Muslim' to 'Islamic fanatic'.

'Even the bomber's father was a terrorist who infiltrated

Alfe Menashe and murdered a civilian, leaving his four children without their father. Terrorism spits on the young and old. This war knows no generation gaps.'

'What would you say now to the family of Avi Lunzer?' asked Aron.

'I would tell them of the worthy sacrifice of their son,' he replied. 'I would remind them of the many such noble sacrifices that have gone into building the only democracy in the Middle East. I wish from my heart of hearts that our many terror victims heal quickly and regain fresh and vibrant spirits.'

'But would you tell the family that their son had been placed in *hey*?'

Colonel Ami frowned.

'Isn't it true that it's called the reject-house?' He made a show of consulting his notes. '*Bayit-pagom*?'

'No one is a reject in the IDF,' he replied evenly. 'We are all brothers and sisters under God and in the army.' He paused to make sure that Sheena had finished translating. 'But we do group our soldiers so that they will work better together.'

Aron was about to argue that point and ask if the colonel didn't think that the elitist housing system ran counter to the egalitarian traditions of Zionism. He was going to ask whether the IDF had lost sight of purity of arms.

But Aron's constitution chose that moment to react to the dust in the office. Even as he coughed violently, he made a mental note that you could hear the bulldozer working on the orchard outside the town, filling the air with noxious particles and transposing the dust to new breeding grounds.

'He suffers from allergies,' Sheena explained to her superior.

Colonel Ami rolled his eyes. 'How do you expect *gois* to understand what we're going through,' he said deprecatingly, 'when they can't even breathe our air.'

Aron wrote in his notebook:

impurity of arms — because of Lebanon and the intifada?

In recent commentaries for *Adlai*, Aron had warned American GIs in Iraq not to repeat the mistakes of the IDF in Lebanon, namely, not to ignite the Shiite mesh that would turn the army of liberation into one of occupation. While the policy to withdraw from Lebanon had been sound, the timing couldn't have been more ill-conceived: the IDF should have moved to the Israeli side of the border and locked the gate when the last PLO fighter left Beirut. Instead, Israel had had to suffer the ignominious images of Hizbullah 'liberating' South Lebanon. He now wondered if those images, along with the stress caused by the intifada, had mortally wounded the reputation and morale of the IDF.

While previously it had been unheard of that reservists — especially among elite units — should even attempt to evade duty, commanders now struggled against increasing swathes of reservists who tried to avoid service for medical or other reasons. In fact, the conscience committees, including the one that had ruled on Avi's case, had been established as a consequence of this growing trend.

A reservist escorted Aron down the hill from the base with fifteen minutes to spare before curfew.

As they drew nearer to the checkpoint, he recognized one of the two soldiers on duty. Sharett waved at him and then brought his arms down, propping up the barrier casually like a customer at a bar.

In the past, such relaxed discipline had added an egalitarian dimension to purity of arms. But now, this sense of informality worked against the IDF.

Aron was shown the very spot where Avi had been blown up. For a moment, he just stood there with his eyes shut.

'Will you be seeing us tomorrow?' Sharett asked.

He opened his eyes to see the corporal's broad smile of perfect white teeth. 'Yes.'

'Good. Because remember, I'm your man.' He turned to the other soldier manning the checkpoint and said in Hebrew, 'My name's going to be in an English newspaper.'

'Hey, Caleb, how come you get all the attention?'

'Because I told this *goi* I was Lunzer's bum chum,' replied Sharett, causing the other to snigger. Turning to Aron, he added pleasantly in English, 'I have something for you.'

Behind them, a Palestinian family was waiting patiently to cross the checkpoint.

Sharett took out a folded sheet of paper and handed it to Aron. It was the checkpoint rota for March. He immediately looked at the entry for the night and early morning of 20/21 March. Next to Avi's name was another that had been highlighted in red. In the reject-house, Avi's name on the board would have been highlighted in yellow.

Aron read the name: *Krickstein*. The name sounded familiar. 'Krickstein?'

Sharett nodded. 'But you don't want to put him in your story.'

'Who, Krickstein?' Aron was still frowning. 'Why not?'

'No way, man. Some people just don't get the military life. You know how Avi Lunzer was more than yellow, well Krickstein was a lot less than red.'

'So what happened to him?'

During this conversation, the Palestinian family had still been waiting. The father began to gesture for permission to enter.

Sharett ignored him and shrugged at Aron. 'Who cares? He's a civilian now.' He laughed, 'I hear he's hoping to become a rabbi.'

It suddenly dawned on him. '*Yitzhak* Krickstein?'

'That's right, man.'

Fortunately for Aron, the Palestinian in the car had just said something in Arabic, his hands still gesturing permission to enter. Sharett spun around to glare at him and missed Aron's look of complete astonishment.

'Wait,' he growled at the driver in Hebrew. 'Stop,' he snarled in Arabic and turned back to Aron to add in English, 'These people are just retards.'

'I'll see you tomorrow, then,' Aron said hastily, moving away.

It was one thing to entertain such private thoughts. But it was altogether a different matter to express it so openly in front of the subject who was as likely to understand English as Aron was of understanding Hebrew. Besides, Aron was still shaken and needed to rush back to do some serious thinking.

He did glance back, though, curious to see if the Palestinian had reacted; he hadn't. But then that didn't prove anything. Aron, too, had been smarter than to blow his cover when Sharett had made fun of his dead Avi.

Aron reached his rental car, which was parked on the Qalqiliya side of the barrier and, once inside, he stared in the rear-view mirror. Even from that distance, Sharett's snarl was easily visible. The corporal pushed the Palestinian back and brushed his hands together to signify the end. He pushed the man again and, with the other soldier, locked the gate and closed Qalqiliya for the night.

It was a snarl that appeared often enough on the bearded faces of terrorists.

But it was substantially more shocking to see it on the face of a young, educated man who could be your neighbour's son.

It reminded him of that francophone Lebanese in Beirut, the Christian militiaman he had interviewed decades ago for his last feature for *The Daily Telegraph*. He'd sported exactly the same snarl as he described, in fluent French, his reasons for massacring Palestinian women and children in Sabra.

11

THERE WERE NO sushi bars in the West Bank. Little girls were more likely to wear veils than miniskirts and fishnet stockings. And the sense of community was still strong enough to welcome foreigners.

Communities in the West felt so disenfranchized from the ruling majority that they closed in on themselves and regarded strangers with suspicion and even hatred. But in traditional Arab societies, communities were so well rounded that they could afford to extend the hand of friendship to outsiders. Orientalists marvelled at that and called it Arab hospitality; Arabs themselves called it a duty. According to the unwritten codes of this hospitality, if it was in your power to help someone in need, then you were morally obliged to do so.

But Bernadette was not guided by Arab hospitality when she agreed to meet Arnold Lounger in Qalqiliya.

Papa often said that the only person who'd ever really understood him was the young English journalist who had interviewed him and with whom he'd spent little more than two hours. 'You could see it in his eyes,' he recalled. 'They were deep green with sympathy. They were just like your brother's green eyes.'

It was the fortnight after he'd given her Arnold Lounger's article to summarize, and Bernadette waited anxiously for him to read what she'd written.

'He had Michel's cough too.' He smiled briefly. 'Almost threw up in my garage when I removed the air filter of the car I was working on — I should have given him your mother's cure.'

He turned to her handwritten assignment and read:

Antoine Shakour lost his wife and son to Palestinian gun-men so that when he talks of his remaining daughter, there is more than the ordinary hopes and aspirations of a caring father, more than the usual concerns about the cost of living and school fees. Antoine is a mass murderer for his daughter and justifies his acts as a personal crusade to safeguard her future as a Christian living in the Middle East. He speaks in a refined French and describes rationally why he along with fellow militiamen stormed the Sabra Refugee Camp on the fateful day of 16 September 1982.

From the first reading, Bernadette had understood the deep sense of disgust the journalist had intended. That Papa had failed to pick up on his sinister caricature and had forced her to read Arnold Lounger's article proved his poor grasp of English. Even her 100-word précis impressed him for all the wrong reasons.

'I like your style,' he said appreciatively, adding after he'd perused her text a second time, 'and it shows that you really understood the piece. The humanity of the subject really comes through. Bravo, *ma petite*. Good job, my darling. *Ça c'est du bon travail.*'

Bernadette said nothing.

'Tell her to eat,' said Mémé to her son.

'Eat,' he said automatically to Bernadette.

'No.' Mémé shook her head impatiently and then waved her index finger to suggest the girl's spindly body. 'Look at her. She hasn't had lunch in two weeks. A real father would be around more often to know these things.'

'Two weeks?' Antoine frowned at his daughter. 'Is that true?'

She gave a half-hearted shrug.

'Do your friends at school tell you you're fat?'

'No, Papa.'

'Good. Because you're not.' He was silent for a while and then asked, 'Do you have a boyfriend?'

'No.'

'Good. Because you're too young. And you remember what we said about sex?'

She nodded; he'd come up with the slogan himself and repeated it often enough with the pride of a copywriter's first jingle.

'Well?' he prompted.

'*Une verge est un piège pour une vièrge.*'

'That's right,' he said. 'So listen to your Mémé and have lunch. OK?'

'OK.'

'Promise?'

She nodded again. A promise that was left unuttered could not be broken just as a penis could hardly be considered a trap for a virgin.

The article on Papa had caused her to abandon lunch, an initial act of disgust that had slowly developed into a regular habit and that served to maintain the barrier between them. She felt that she could dissociate herself from her father as long as she remained true to her midday fast. It was for that same reason that she didn't rush to correct the mistake when, several years later and upon gaining admission to the American University of Beirut, the registrar mistakenly Anglicized her surname to Shaker.

She had Googled Arnold Lounger's name some years ago and had been disappointed when the search had come back with only a handful of archived articles, with the 'The Human Face of Evil' at the top of that list. She assumed that Arnold Lounger had either stopped writing before the rise of the Internet or had died. She was therefore doubly amazed when he phoned her — out of the deepest blue — to ask for her help in sorting out some details for a piece he was writing on suicide bombers.

She was not guided by Arab hospitality when she agreed to meet him. Nor was she acting out of a sense of duty towards Imm Nidal when she inferred that Shahed would figure prominently in his article. Of all the journalists in the world, he would be able to see past the tit-for-tat reporting on the violence.

Bernadette had agreed to meet him for altogether more profound reasons. It was his article on Papa that had set in motion her slow transformation, leading her inexorably to the West Bank. It was the same article that had taught her to learn and ever so gradually fall in love with the English language.

More than that, it was Arnold Lounger who had driven her to replace lunch with the Lord's Prayer the second she realized she was the daughter of the Butcher of Sabra.

She would have met the British journalist anywhere and under any pretext.

The entrance and lobby were visible from the hotel's coffee lounge, the grandly if misleadingly named Café de Paris. The only features that were even vaguely French were a faded poster of the Champ de Mars, with lawn, crowd of people and Eiffel Tower in the same ubiquitous grey, and a *trottoir* feel in that the café encroached onto the pavement.

Aron spent most of his time there, his notes strewn across the table, for the principal reason that it seemed just about the only place in the West Bank where his throat did not react violently to the surroundings. The area was closed off by glass, the floor tiles were not covered by carpets, the metallic chairs had only the thinnest of cushions, and the tall plants, which were positioned such that they offered a maximum privacy from the rest of the pavement beyond the glass wall, were all artificial and hosed down every day.

Aron had extended his stay and was still the only guest. He had made full use of the Café de Paris and its six seating areas over the past three days. By late morning and for the entire afternoon, the sun would rise above the town to delineate a western trajectory along the glass roof, forcing Aron to follow suit, moving all his notes progressively along the tables in search of shade.

It was noon and he was preparing to move to another table by a fake yucca when he spotted her.

The young woman strode purposefully to the entrance carrying a black briefcase and in a matching suit. In any major city, the woman could have passed almost unnoticed as a corporate executive rushing to a meeting. In Qalqiliya, though, there were no businesses, no scheduled appointments and certainly no need for formal attire. Her trousers flared slightly at the hem and flickered perfectly at the waist.

The woman's face appeared to belong to the region. Her long black hair, dark eyes, off-white complexion and long nose were 100 per cent S'faradi. He found himself wondering if she spoke Turkish.

Aron saw her talking to the receptionist and it was only when she was indicated the Café de Paris that he realized with a start that the pretty woman was coming to see him. He quickly gathered his notes on the table.

Bernadette Shaker did not remotely look like her phone voice; he'd conjured up Midwest not Mideast, complete with cheerleader smile and bouncy blond hair. He was having trouble recapturing the infuriation he'd experienced at finding Avi's name in her report. Irrationally, he thought he might have felt more resentment had she been less attractive.

'Arnold?' she prompted as she held out her hand. 'I'm Bernadette.'

He stood up to shake her hand and a pile of notes slipped out of his grip onto the floor.

'I'm sorry,' she said, bending down to help him gather the sheets.

'No, I'm, er.' He stopped and forced his peripheral vision to focus on picking up the paper. 'Thank you,' he said when she gave him the sheets she'd collected.

'Are those notes for your article?' she asked sweetly as they sat down, adding a bit too quickly, 'I've read some of your fine work.'

Aron accepted the compliment politely though he knew it to be disingenuous. He'd written fewer than a dozen articles with the byline of Arnold Lounger, and the woman could barely have been in her teens the last time he'd written under that name. Her flushed cheeks seemed to confirm the white lie.

'Çok güzel son,' he tried.

'Sorry?'

He made a show of clearing his throat. 'So we're even,' he said to change the subject and succeeded in bringing to mind the offending footnote number 157. 'And I've read some of your work — the *Situation Analysis of Palestinian Women*.'

'How did you find it?'

By Googling Avi's name. But he replied by waving his hand in a noncommittal way.

She nodded in agreement. 'Please feel free to send all your complaints to my editor.'

'Oh?'

'He gave it his own spin.'

'I see.'

'Yep. Toned it right down to easy reading for political reasons.'

'Oh.'

'But I'm sure you know what I mean,' she continued as he nodded absently. 'You write about things as they happen on the ground only to have your copy changed by some smart-aleck who's never been here and can't begin to understand the suffering.' She shrugged helplessly. 'The golden rule on UN house style: always treat the two sides to any conflict with total impartiality even if one side is ethnically cleansing the other.'

'I see,' repeated Aron.

'It's like the Balkans or Rwanda.'

Over the course of his career, he'd come to think that making facile comparisons was almost a human condition; the brain needed everything to be exactly like something else, no matter how tenuous the actual link. The West Bank was about as removed from the Balkans as Iraq was from Vietnam. 'As I said on the phone, I was particularly, er, taken by the last annex of your report.'

She nodded and said soberly, 'In the unedited version, the tragedy of the Zeitouni family appears in the main body of the text — not hustled to the back.'

'What can you tell me of the suicide bombing?'

'The death of Shahed Zeitouni?'

'Yes.'

'Shahed had everything to live for.'

'I expect the family of the Israeli soldier he killed would say the same about their son.'

'Yes,' she conceded. 'But I didn't know the soldier. I knew Shahed. Shall I show you where he worked?' she asked suddenly. 'It's sure to help you with your story.' Her gaze took in the bundle of sheets on the table.

There most certainly was a story, but it had nothing to do with fanatics who blew up innocent people — that was just a plain, open and shut case of murder. The story wasn't even about Avi.

He gave her the thinnest of smiles. 'Of course, please.' He indicated the exit of the Café de Paris. 'Just let me drop off my notes.'

In an ironic twist, the more he'd pretended to be reporting on the IDF, the more he actually wanted to do it. After all those years, it had taken only two days in the most infected neck of this desecrated territory for his journalistic instincts to come alive again. And like a real reporter, he had sniffed out a gem of a story and was keeping his cards close to his chest. The IDF still believed he was writing something of a PR piece for them, unaware that he had already started his report tracing the demise of purity of arms in the Israeli army.

A real journalist also knew when to follow a lead that might feed different articles down the line. That was called pork — material gathered for later use if needed. 'I'm curious, Ms Shaker,' said Aron presently as she led the way out of the hotel.

'Bernadette, please,' she corrected.

'What do you think my angle should be? Where do you see the story going?'

Her reaction took him totally by surprise.

She stopped in mid-stride and laughed. Her face lit up and she was a beautiful S'faradi. 'You're a genius, Arnold. And you're such a tease. You certainly don't need a poor Arab to help you with your story.'

Aron's left hand moved to cover his mouth as he coughed violently.

She instinctively took a step towards him. 'Are you OK?' she asked with concern.

Aron nodded and reached for the inhaler in his pocket.

'You don't actually wheeze,' she stated. 'Must be all that dust that sets you off.'

He nodded helplessly and made a mental note that this was the first time anyone had immediately understood his affliction.

'I had a little brother who suffered the same way,' she said gently. 'My mother had a cure for it. I could send it to you if you wish.'

He shook his head, cleared his throat and gave a final cough. 'I'm fine now.'

'It's not a long walk,' she encouraged.

The woman's Arabism became more apparent in the midday sun. As they turned northwards from the town centre, she pointed at the separation barrier in the distance and said in flawless French, '*Ceci n'est pas une pipe.*'

'What do you mean?' asked Aron.

'Magritte's tobacco pipe.'

'I know the picture.'

'Well look at it.' Her finger now arced from left to right. 'Can it honestly be called anything other than what it is — the Apartheid Wall.'

And, once they turned into a small shop, she switched to Arabic with the manager. The shop had a rickety sign that was openly nonchalant about the cringing use of an ampersand. It read simply: INT@RNET.

Aron heard her introduce him as an 'English journalist', and she turned to him to say, 'I'm hoping we can turn this place into a technology community centre some day.'

The manager, a scrawny man in his thirties, eyed him with suspicion.

Aron was tempted to share his conviction that it would be easier to raze the building to the ground and start afresh; instead he said, 'Be sure to change the sign first.'

Technologically speaking, it was like entering a time warp. There were eight bulky PCs that seemed to have just scraped into the Pentium age. These were connected by cables underfoot to form a rudimentary network and, adding to the fire hazard, by two wires along a wall that ended in a dot matrix printer and an electric generator.

But while the Internet café was as shaky as its sign, the group of a dozen or so young users were equally indifferent about its shortcomings. The teenagers were mostly playing computer games and whooped, moaned and generally created a din of excitement at their terminals.

Aron's attention was drawn to a solitary boy who was staring at a monitor as another child controlled the keyboard. He had dark circles under his eyes, shiners that seemed to result more from malnutrition and sleep-deprivation than through violence.

'Kids in the West shoot hoops or kick balls with other kids,' said Bernadette. 'The games are more lethal in Palestine — the kids throw stones, and the men shoot bullets.'

The scrawny manager's English was as rudimentary as his Int@rnet. 'Israelis bad men,' he confirmed.

'I see,' said Aron, adding, 'So Shahed Zeitouni came here to play computer games.'

Bernadette ignored that and indicated a teenage girl in a wheelchair, a few paces away from the boy with the shiners, who was also a spectator and egging on a friend. 'All these kids have suffered very real injuries or deep psychological traumas from the violence.' She turned to Aron. 'Now let me tell you about Shahed Zeitouni,' she began. 'Shahed was only nineteen when he died.'

The same age as Avi.

'He tried to change the game. He taught all the kids you see here and many more besides.'

'To play computer games?'

'Yes. And to surf the Internet, write documents, do maths. He single-handedly established courses to teach these kids all kinds of subjects you and I take for granted.'

'Shahed good boy,' affirmed the manager and, pointing at a patch on the floor, added, 'He teach here. Many children.' Leading the way to an adjoining boxroom, he said, 'He sleep here.'

'The family farm was outside Qalqiliya,' explained Bernadette, 'so Shahed would sleep in the shop to avoid curfew. He tried to give the children something other than the occupation to think about.'

'He no like Uncle,' agreed the man.

'Uncle?' prompted Aron.

'*Amo* is the nom-de-guerre of the local commander of al-Aqsa Squad.'

'You mean al-Aqsa Martyrs' Brigade.'

'No, Squad.' She raised her eyebrows as though he should have known that as a journalist. 'It's a splinter group of the Brigade that's particularly strong in these parts.' She continued, 'Shahed believed in non-violence and tried to draw the kids away from such organizations.'

'How ironic then that he should become a terrorist himself.'

The woman gave him a cold look for the first time since their meeting.

There was a strained silence that was eventually broken by the scrawny manager. He had clearly not moved on with the conversation. He still pointed at the patch on the floor and repeated, 'Shahed sleep here.' He looked at them quizzically. 'Every day he sleep here,' he insisted. *'Ma a'ada as-Sabbat wal-Ahad.'* He translated for Aron's benefit, 'No Saturdays. No Sundays.'

Bernadette frowned at this but Aron appeared unimpressed so the man turned to him and, pointing again, said, 'Here. Shahed good boy.'

So where did he sleep on those nights, she wondered and asked: *'Wayn kan yenam bil-weekend?'*

The man smiled, partly because of her use of a foreign word instead of the Arabic equivalent, and, especially, because only a Christian Lebanese would consider Saturday and Sunday to be the weekend.

His answer caused the lines on her brow to deepen. She spoke almost to herself, 'He says that Shahed spent every weekend with his mother on the farm. And yet she hadn't seen him in over a month.'

'The best assassins are the ones you least expect,' said Aron dispassionately. 'Perhaps he taught computing during the week and attended Amo's lessons on terrorism every Friday and Saturday.' He added to the man, 'He sleep with Uncle on *Shabbat*?'

'No, no,' disagreed the man vehemently. He moved his two hands wide apart to signify different poles. 'Shahed and Amo like this.'

The boy with the shiners glanced at Aron with interest, his bruises drawn out like stretched question marks.

Bernadette seemed withdrawn as they left.

'Don't be so hard on yourself,' he said kindly.

'Sorry?'

'You are what you are,' Aron said lamely as he tried to sound comforting. 'In the final analysis he just proved to be a bad seed with bad intentions.'

'Despite what you may think, Shahed was a good young man,' she retorted without missing a step, her briefcase swinging at her side. 'I just wish I could find some way to make you see that.'

It was perfectly normal for her to be in denial.

They were taking a different road back to the town centre, past the municipality building with a frayed Palestinian flag drooping in the still air. 'Are you Palestinian?' he asked.

'Would that make it easier for you, Mr Lounger?'

That was taking denial to an irrational extreme. 'Hold on,' he said crossly and quickened his pace to keep up with her. 'Why the personal attack?'

'Personal? Hah!' she snapped. 'And to answer your question, I'm Arab, French, Syrian, Lebanese and Phoenician. Depends on who's asking. To you I think I'll say I'm an al-Qaeda operative.'

'You thought I'd write about the terrorist, is that what's bothering you?'

She proceeded to swear at him in Arabic; he knew she was swearing because of the way her hands moved and the way her lips curled all the way back. This was how pure S'faradim cursed.

'Have lunch with me.'

He caught her off guard; her briefcase came to a full stop.

'Have lunch with me,' he repeated.

'I don't eat lunch.'

'That's OK,' said Aron with a little smile. 'We can be Zen and say, "the food is not the lunch."'

'I was mistaken about you.'

And about the terrorist, thought Aron, but he said, 'That's right. I'm not the bad guy.'

'I thought you'd write about Shahed's humanity. I was pleased when you phoned me — you can never know how pleased,' she continued, 'I took it as a sign. I hoped — no, I believed — that you of all the journalists in the world would be able to see past the tit-for-tat reporting on the violence.' She added sadly, 'You must have changed.'

'But you don't know me,' exclaimed Aron.

'No, I don't,' she agreed. 'And frankly, it's just as well.'

She marched off.

The Israeli soldier at the gate grinned at her and gave a small bow.

'Happiest of afternoons to you, sweet Miss Shakour,' he said formally.

'Oh lay off, Hillel,' she said in her colloquial Arabic. 'Just let me out.'

'What happened to "Hello, Hillel"?' Corporal Lavan peered at her, taking in her red eyes. 'Are you all right, Bernadat?' he asked with concern.

She wiped her eyes. 'It's all this damn dust.'

Hillel looked over her shoulder at the foreigner. 'Has he done this to you?'

'I tell you it's the dust. Now let me out.'

He glared at the journalist. 'Shall I shoot him for you?'

A thin smile appeared on her face.

'Anyone who offends the prettiest lady in Palestine deserves a thousand and one deaths.'

Her smile broadened. 'But you wouldn't want to kill him,' she said sweetly. 'He's one of yours.'

'Not one of ours. One of theirs,' said Hillel. 'What does the West know about us?'

'Well spoken, brother.'

He nodded formally to let her pass before turning his gaze on the foreign reporter who was now doubled over as though searching for something on the ground. That's right, *goi*, thought Hillel, keep looking. He almost wanted the stranger to unearth the filth about Lunzer, to dig deeper to reveal the truth about that hypocrite.

They'd been forced to lie at the base. That soldier was no hero. If Hillel had been assigned the story, he'd have written about that poor woman, Imm Shahed. It took more courage to live as she did.

The *goi* seemed to be sick; Hillel paid no attention and turned instead to admit a Palestinian family into Qalqiliya without bothering to check the boot of their car.

12

Arnold Lounger was in fact like the worst dish in Maman's recipe book.

The first time Bernadette made *kishek* as a young girl, she almost vomited. The very preparation of this most Lebanese of delicacies was repulsive enough — *kishek* was dried yoghurt that was encouraged to rot and then combined with cracked wheat and salt until it became a coarse, sallow powder. The resulting smell was of unwashed socks left to fester over summer, and the taste was about as appetizing.

If, by some chance encounter, their paths were to cross again, she would tell him that he was like *kishek*.

Aron woke up with a violent cough. Mechanically, he reached for the inhaler on the bedside table. It was the early hours of his seventh day in Qalqiliya and 120 days almost to the hour after Avi's death. It was 19 July 2004 and also 1 Av 5764 by Hebraic reckoning: *Rosh Chodesh Av*, marking the beginning of the annual period of mourning observed by Jews worldwide over the destruction of the Temple.

He couldn't go back to sleep so he switched on the TV and sat staring at a pinprick of light as he listened to a religious programme on the significance of the new month of Av. 'Being Jewish often means being able to see the bright side of bad times, and not forget the sad note at happy times.'

The pinprick of light flickered to the beat of the speaker's voice. 'The Torah emphasizes unequivocally the need to clear Israel of the Palestinians, who will grow to become "thorns in your eyes", "pricks in your sides" and harass decent Jews "in the land wherein ye dwell". Every means towards that end is justified, even ordained. And let us never forget that Jerusalem is in the centre of the land of Israel, and that the sanctuary is in the centre of Jerusalem.'

The light in the centre of the TV flickered in agreement. 'In Evshel, we believe that with our hearts, minds and deeds. We believe that we will soon merit the coming of the Messiah and the rebuilding of the Temple — and everything that goes with it — and that our joy will become untarnished and complete. *Evshelim* are the true underwriters of the Zionist ideal.'

Bloody esrimists, thought Aron with disdain. They wanted to build the Temple at all cost, oblivious to the orthodox view that such a construction would in effect force God's hand to usher in the messianic era. A considerably thornier issue was that the historical location of the Temple was currently occupied by al-Aqsa Mosque.

'We have prayed for the rebuilding of the Temple for the past 2,000 years. This prayer is a formal part of our thrice daily prayer services. To us, it means everything; to Muslims, it is only their third holiest site — '

'*Michutz la-shurah*,' groaned Aron, switching off the TV. Way, way beyond the bounds of common sense.

As a child, *Rosh Chodesh Av* marked the beginning of the lowest point in Aron's calendar, when the gloomy flat in North London became all but a mortuary. But he suddenly had a brief yearning to travel back in time, to sit on the floor with his parents and listen to József wax lyrical about Moses' brother, Aaron the High Priest.

He had spent six days and nights on the wrong side of the security barrier, most of which — both by choice and by order of the curfew — had been in the solitary confinement of the dingiest hotel ever built by men. On this side of the string of Crusader castles, he had dreaded the seething hotbed of lunatics taking to the streets every day to shout abuses and burn flags and makeshift effigies of leaders of the civilized world. Instead, the fanatics had turned out to be worried fathers pleading with soldiers, children whiling away the time at antiquated consoles, and educated women who were prettier and smarter than your neighbours. The most shocking image had been the inert eyes of a little boy with shiners.

Officially, Avi had died to protect the free state from the hordes of barbarians.

But in Qalqiliya and from a Western perspective, the new cultural war of the twenty-first century had been waged and won eons ago. When you walked in the town, you walked in a decaying orchard of buildings. People clung to their houses like oranges and pears ready to drop at any instant from their rotting balconies. Every day, it was like stepping in a graveyard from a world war, fully aware of the justifications for that war, but realizing that the world had changed sufficiently to avoid similar horrors.

It had taken 20,200 Israeli soldiers to subdue this and similar towns and villages.

On the eve of the war of independence in 1948, Arabs had bragged that all they needed were 'a few brooms' to drive the Jews into the sea. That boast now lay crumbling among the dead houses and buried shops.

What the abject residents needed most of all were many brooms to clean up their town and many more computers to brighten their outlook and open up to the modern world.

Aron moved to the rickety table next to the TV, picked up his pen and wrote in a notebook marked *Ideas for future stories*:

Jews on the far right have become the new radical muftis. Their calls to the impressionable youth are pure and simple: kill modernism wherever you find it, this is pleasing to God. Has Israel finally caught the Arab disease?

As if on cue, he heard the first prayer of the day. The main mosque in Qalqiliya was on the other side of the square so that the muezzin's call boomed out of loudspeakers, causing the window pane to vibrate rhythmically.

'It tolls for thee,' he said under his breath.

He wondered whether even the High Priest could have resisted the causeless hatred that had become endemic in both Israeli and Palestinian societies. He rather suspected that Aaron himself would not have been *meurav b'daat im ha-b'riyot*, bound with his fellow creatures in love.

It reminded him of the Chabad in Galilee, the spiritual retreat that was so out of synch with the modern world that it didn't even have a landline, let alone a TV or a computer.

Aron had borrowed the hotel manager's phone to call the Chabad head office in Jerusalem only to be told that their camp in Galilee could not be contacted even in an emergency.

That was so ridiculous, especially given the camp's close proximity to the northern border, that he'd exclaimed, 'But what do you do if there's a war, send an angel down to warn them?'

He was trying to get hold of Yitzhak Krickstein, the young man who had traded his military fatigues for the black uniform of an ultra-orthodox *haredi* and had moved from *aleph* to the Chabad.

While he wondered at the twist of fate that had caused the encounter at Lake Merom, at least one mystery had been solved. It was the Lunzer name that had triggered the *haredi*'s sudden departure. Krickstein had recognized the surname since he'd been on checkpoint duty with Avi, who must also have told him of Aron of *Adlai* fame.

According to the military records, which Captain Sheena Baran had readily supplied, Krickstein dropped out of the army two days after the terrorist attack. She had also given him a copy of Krickstein's affidavit on the events of 20/21 March, which had been used for the official report on Avi's death.

Aron began to suspect that Krickstein had sent him the postcard of the Western Wall and he realized, with a pang, that the *haredi* was officially the last person to see Avi alive. He resolved to seek him out upon his return to Israel to ask him about those final hours.

The first rays of sunlight arrived from Jordan to cast a tentative beam on the wall opposite.

His work in the West Bank was done.

He had seen the exact spot where Avi had died, had met his superiors and most of his peers, and had even gained an insight — albeit unbidden — into the young Palestinian terrorist who had killed him.

He packed his bag and sat on the bed to reread his piece on the IDF.

It was perhaps the best piece of investigative reporting he'd written in years and yet he still felt desperately hollow.

Ever since Sela's death, he'd learnt to recognize the degree of emptiness, from absolute nothingness to bitter isolation. He knew that the emptiness he now felt was of a different order to the grief over Avi or Sela. This was more of a niggling sensation like a mild toothache, as though part of him refused to accept that he'd accomplished his mission, and balked at the prospect of returning to Jerusalem so soon.

The fake plants in the Café de Paris were hosed down shortly after the end of curfew; Aron waited until 6:30 am before heading downstairs for breakfast. His waiter brought him bowls of strained yoghurt and olives and two notes that had been left for him at the lobby.

The first note was handwritten and read:

My mother's cure for your allergy:

1. *Chop a raw onion and extract the juice from it.*
2. *Crush six cloves of garlic into a fine puree and progressively add drops of olive oil and lemon juice until the substance turns milky white.*
3. *Add one teaspoon of the onion juice to every two teaspoons of garlic paste and blend thoroughly with half a teaspoon of fresh turmeric powder.*

A teaspoon of honey can be added for taste. This remedy should be taken two or three times a day. Avoid foods that form catarrh, including white bread, meat, sugar, puddings and pies.

Bernadette Shaker

He folded it carefully and turned to the second note, a typed sentence that read:

If you want to know what motivates martyrs, then meet me at 10:00 am today in the clinic of Dr. Hamid Abdullatif, on the second floor of the building behind the central mosque.

Aron reread it.

The name and, especially, the choice of 'martyr' for terrorist were immediate markers of the writer's political affiliations. His first impulse was to rip up the note and resume his breakfast.

He read it one more time, which provided time for the inner journalistic beast to cock its head with curiosity.

He had planned to check out in the morning; he now decided to postpone his return trip till the afternoon. After all, he reasoned, it wasn't as if anyone was waiting for him back in Jerusalem.

Aron reached the second floor of the derelict building. Under the doctor's name on the door were the words *Certifiable Padiatrist*. The door was open and the phone began to ring as soon as Aron stepped inside. A bald man with round spectacles answered it, looked across at Aron and spoke briefly into the phone.

The man got up to leave.

'Wait,' said Aron. 'Are you the doctor?'

The man nodded and left.

Aron paced up and down the clinic, pausing only

momentarily in front of a faded poster from the 1970s of a child suffering from polio. On another wall was an equally faded poster by the World Health Organization warning new mothers of various infantile infections and diseases caused by poor hygiene. Those, along with rudimentary weighing scales and a tape measure tacked to the wall, provided a more accurate indication of the doctor's branch of medicine than his sign on the door.

Aron had waited no more than five minutes and was about to leave when he heard footsteps coming up the stairs.

A burly man in a balaclava helmet walked in and stopped for a second as his dark brown eyes looked around the room. He reached Aron in two long strides and proceeded to give him a rapid body search.

'No,' said Aron quickly as he saw a blindfold in the man's hand.

The man insisted wordlessly.

'No,' repeated Aron. 'If you want to talk, then we'll talk here.'

It was unclear whether the man understood English. His response was to grip the blindfold and to narrow his eyes.

'I've changed my mind,' Aron said lamely.

It all happened suddenly.

The man swung his body to throw Aron deftly off his feet. Then, pinning him on his front, he reached around to tie the blindfold so tightly that it pressed into his eyeballs causing constellations of stars to swim by.

Aron tried to shout but discovered that his mouth had

already been expertly gagged. He spluttered and let out a series of muffled coughs as a combination of gag and dust from the floor inflamed his throat.

He tried to kick his assailant but ended up being kicked in the stomach and having his limbs tied with razor-sharp wire. As he was carried to the boot of a car, he realized with rising dread that, officially, he was no longer a reporter, just another Western hostage to terrorists.

When they came to change him from the car to what sounded like a van, Aron was cursing himself for his poor judgement and for making the biggest mistake in his life. They drove around for what seemed like hours and long enough for self-pity to set in. And for the first time in his adult life, he used the Hungarian-Hebrew stress of his parents on himself.

A cockroach paused to wave its antennae cautiously at Aron before deciding it was safe enough to move to the dining area. The burly man still in his balaclava helmet spotted it and squashed it in one quick step as though extinguishing a cigarette. He left the room in three long strides.

Goliath's den was a squalid room suitable, if not for humans, then for a host of insects. The room was separated into a living area where a TV blared out cartoons in Arabic and a dining area where flies hovered over dirty dishes on a table.

Only the blindfold had been removed so that Aron found he was tied to a chair at the centre of the living area. Directly ahead of him, next to the grimy remains of the cockroach was a camera clipped to a tripod; behind that, a spotlight shone into a white umbrella to fill the room with a diffused light. There appeared to be a small hole in the umbrella, which caused the light to refract and cast a miniature rainbow on the ceiling above the flies.

Aron's neighbour on his left, the only other person in the room, was a boy sprawled out on a torn sofa watching TV. He recognized the child with a start only because of the shiners. The inert eyes returned to the screen as soon as the burly man came back with a smaller and older man whose face was also concealed by a balaclava helmet.

The newcomer seemed as out of place in this setting as the photographic equipment. He wore clean jeans and an ironed white shirt — and even his helmet, with 'Timberland' stitched under the chin, was a fashionable ski mask in light blue.

He spoke in Arabic to the other two.

The man removed Aron's gag; the boy turned down the TV only marginally.

'If I were a reporter, I'd want to be a photojournalist.' The man spoke English fluently, with a generic Mediterranean accent. He nodded to himself as he moved to the tripod. 'Don't you think photography is the greatest human invention, far greater than computers and the jet engine?'

'Who are you?' asked Aron. 'Untie me.'

The man ignored him. 'It's the language of angels, capturing the very essence of joy, anguish and horror. A photograph transcends culture and the spoken language.'

The man turned to the boy sprawled on the sofa and formed a rectangle with his fingers. 'Such innocence,' he said, peering through the fingers. 'Such purity.' He made a clicking noise with his tongue — click-click — as of a camera taking a picture.

Hearing the man clicking his tongue, the boy turned. '*Bass, Amo*,' he piped.

Amo? Uncle? Aron shuddered. The leader of al-Aqsa Squad was known as Amo.

'Hmm. Memory itself consists not of written texts or moving images but of such snapshots in time. That's why photographs tug at the very soul of man.' He moved back. 'Think of such images as the female American soldier loosely holding the dog lead and the naked and destroyed Iraqi prisoner on the other end. Shocking, disgusting.' He shook his head in wonder. 'Photographically, a masterpiece. A million words of moving text cannot begin to compare with this potency.'

He turned suddenly to stare at Aron, a penetrating gaze that caused Aron's flesh to crawl. 'Who is Arnold Lounger?'

'You contacted me,' he stammered.

He seemed to give that some thought. 'Don't you just love the Internet?' He asked abruptly. 'You can download the most incredible pictures.'

'What do you want?'

'You can search for just about anything you can think of: sex sites, if that's what you're after,' he gave the boy an avuncular grin, 'or names of people.'

Without a face to frame the eyes, the stare was that much more piercing.

'Have you ever tried Googling your name, Arnold?'

'What do you want from me?' repeated Aron. The sense of dread was rising from his gut to lodge itself in his inflamed throat.

'Of course, not everyone is on the net.' He gave him a thin smile. 'I'm not. But then I'm not a journalist. I don't have a byline that can be picked up by search engines.' He opened his palm. 'Five results for Arnold Lounger.' He tutted. 'You make sure all words are spelled correctly, you try different keywords and try more general keywords — and still you come up with five, old results for Arnold Lounger. Curious, wouldn't you say?'

'I haven't written much,' said Aron deliberately.

'Hmm.' He started to fiddle with the camera. 'Have you ever heard of the triangular relationship in photography? Any fool can take a good picture these days — simply auto-focus and press the shutter, especially with these new cameras that tell you when the lighting is too low and you need a tripod.'

'Please let me go.'

'But a master photographer must first graduate as a psychologist, must understand the triangular relationship between subject, viewer and author. If your intention is to shock the very souls of your viewers, then it's not enough to click an image of suffering. When you look at the picture of a monster, say the iconographic image of a South Vietnamese about to blow the brains out of a Viet Cong, you react sympathetically to the victim but the image stops there. Your mind stores the image and then lulls you into complacency: such appalling horrors — you tell yourself — exist in the wider world, out of your personal experiences. Do you see what I mean?' He asked Aron but nodded to the burly man who left the room.

'Now take exactly the same scene but have a little girl skipping rope behind the Viet Cong. Now that's immortality.'

The burly man returned with a stained cleaver.

'Please.' Aron began to sob.

'You see, as the photographer, you must construct your image such that the gruesome blends in perfectly with the banal and the photographs become a deliberate part of the torture.' He was still fiddling with the camera settings. 'The language of photography will again prove its power.' He paused. 'Now let's take that picture.'

The hooded man grabbed Aron's hair, pulled him back and held the blade as a butcher preparing for a kosher and halal banquet. The man in the white shirt looked through the viewfinder one last time.

The boy watching TV turned to meet his eyes; his shiners were so stretched they seemed to have consumed his face.

'Good,' he said. 'Hold that pose.' Click-click. He pressed down on the shutter.

That moment has a head, a body and a tail.

First there is the sense of detachment as you look upon your own terror and as the cleaver prepares to cut your throat. At the outer fringe of the snapshot, the young child looks on helplessly.

Next comes the *corpus momenti* in pockets of extended time as all the neurons fire simultaneously like a 1,001-gun-salute. The mind, knowing it has one last heartbeat, plays a random compilation of memories in unison.

Aron loves only the dead. At the warped tail of that moment, as the mind prepares to burn the closing image, he realizes he does love himself. He has much to offer. If only he had just a bit more time. Given all the time in the universe, he could come to love all its precious creatures.

The conservation of love — that is the ultimate law of physics that applies everywhere equally. When a creature dies, its love is redirected and redistributed among the living.

For only the shortest chronon at the precise end of that moment, Aron looks at the boy and gives him all his love.

13

At first, in the Café de Paris, Bernadette had been drawn to his penetrating green eyes that only added to her nervousness. Ever since Papa had told her that the journalist had her dead brother's green eyes, she'd been able to picture them often in the centre of an otherwise featureless face. And yet she was taken aback more by the eyes: they were at odds with the lined face and the thinning blond hair. The eyes sparkled with youth and seemed capable of soaking everything up with the curiosity of a child, even her innermost thoughts.

At that stage in the meeting, he was still living up to her idolized image of him to the extent that when he uttered something that sounded like '*çok güzel son*', she panicked that he could genuinely read her mind.

He also had Michel's cough, which only endeared him more to her.

But then his angle became crystal clear. He was as biased as any European or American journalist who never raised the fundamental moral issues posed by the Israeli occupation.

Bernadette waited for Lounger's call and progressively became more impatient. He hadn't contacted her, not even to thank her for Maman's cure for the cough. The Englishman was rude as well as bigoted, and she hoped she would never see him again.

Amo cast a critical eye on the picture he had just taken through the camera's display. 'Practice makes perfect,' he said. 'Now let's see if we can get it absolutely right for the real thing.'

'No, please,' moaned Aron.

He was finding it hard to breathe, and for once it had nothing to do with dust.

'My name is Aron Lunzer,' he sobbed.

'Aron Lunzer? Hmm.' Amo was busy zooming in on the image and shaking his head. 'And so who is Arnold Lounger?'

The burly man still held the cleaver like a butcher.

Aron told him everything: the Lunzers of Budapest who became the Loungers of London to revert to Lunzers of Jerusalem.

'Who do you work for, Aron Lunzer?'

'I work for *Adlai*. I write columns.'

'*Adlai*.' Amo looked up from the camera. 'Very conservative pictures in *Adlai*, wouldn't you say?'

'Yes.'

'Even *The Daily Telegraph* is more risqué.' He nodded to the man who released Aron's hair and took a step back. 'Of course the *Telegraph* used to be a lot more risqué in the past.'

Aron still found it hard to breathe.

'So tell me, Aron Lunzer, what are you doing here? Hmm?'

'Avi.' The sudden image of his boy gave him strength. 'I came to see where my son died.'

'Your son?'

He had no secrets left. 'Yes. My son. Avi Lunzer who was killed by Shahed Zeitouni in March.'

'Shahed Zeitouni,' repeated Amo pensively. 'Don't you just love mysteries?' he asked as a smile crept over his face. 'I have two things to show you,' he declared suddenly, adding cryptically and with a vicious chuckle, 'but will only show you one of them.'

He stepped briskly out of the room and returned presently with a couple of printed sheets. Aron immediately recognized the masthead of *The Daily Telegraph* on the top sheet.

'I'm glad you came sniffing around here,' he said. 'Otherwise I would never have had any reason to Google you and I would never have found this little gem.' The man gave a conspiratorial grin as he gazed at the page. 'I will never travel without this article.' Amo revealed the full-page feature, entitled *The Human Face of Evil*. His hand trailed reverently down the text, and then stopped at the lead picture. 'Sublime,' he said softly. 'Bloody brilliant.' Click-click.

Aron could only gawp at his article.

'I have seen the light.' He chuckled again and waved the sheets. 'And I now have my very own scriptures to turn to.'

He peered at Aron as though evaluating him. 'And here you are. The world has indeed become a village.' Amo moved closer and indicated passages in the text that had been underlined with a red pen. 'You're responsible for this.'

Aron's confusion only deepened.

'Of course there's no way you could recognize me.' Amo pointed at the picture.

In the foreground was the subject of the piece, the militiaman Antoine Shakour; at his feet were six corpses lying haphazardly. The man's finger moved beyond the smiling militiaman to three others in the background and to rest finally on the one with disfiguring bruises on his face.

'And besides, I didn't look quite myself then,' he said. 'But notice the bottles of beer in each hand. A drink after a hard day's work — humans the world over can relate to that. Such a simple detail that turns this ordinary picture into the divine.'

'But,' stammered Aron, 'but you're in the uniform of a Christian militiaman.'

'And you,' said Amo wryly, 'you turn out to be Israeli. How twisted is that?'

He put the pages down on the table and nodded to the burly man. 'And now, despite my deepest respect for you, I'm going to have to bid you adieu. But it was a pleasure meeting you.'

As the burly man took a step forward with his cleaver, Amo returned to his spot behind the camera. 'As I said before, let's see if we can get it absolutely right this time.'

'Why?' Aron cried. 'Why do you want to kill me? Tell me why I have to die. I don't understand.'

The burly man had already caught hold of his hair and pushed his head back again.

'I have a plan,' he said. 'And that plan doesn't sit well with foreign journalists talking to the IDF.'

'I don't understand,' he repeated miserably. 'At least tell me why my son had to die.'

Amo actually shrugged. 'Israelis are born and so they must die.'

'Shahed Zeitouni — ' Aron was still struggling for breath, ' — was no martyr.'

'I quite agree,' said Amo without a trace of hesitation. 'He was a dog, not a martyr.'

He was saying that, Aron thought quickly, because his terrorist had failed his mission.

The skinny boy across the room was now madly flicking channels. Amo's gaze turned to him, betraying a hint of affection.

Aron noticed that look, framed in the blue ski mask.

'But his little brother, Saddam Zeitouni, used to sit there. Now there was a good boy with all the makings of a martyr. Unfortunately, Saddam died before his time.'

'So what does it take to become a martyr?'

'Time and patience,' replied Amo, returning to the camera. 'Especially time, which I'm afraid you've run out of.'

'Let me write a story,' Aron said desperately. 'Let me write about the human face of martyrdom.'

'Why?'

'Because stories are immortal. You can kill me today and forget me in minutes. But in twenty years, you'll still want to take my article on Sabra wherever you go.'

Amo stopped fiddling with his camera and peered intently at Aron.

'And how do you propose to write about martyrdom?' he asked slowly.

'I'll write about one martyr,' Aron replied urgently. 'This feature would be radically different from any that has ever been written — a close-up account from behind the eyes of a martyr.'

'One martyr?' Amo glanced at the boy.

'Yes. One or more — you can choose.' He added passionately, 'I would make the reader *really* know what it means to be a martyr.' But it was what Aron said next that finally convinced him: 'Together we can deliver the story that will never die. I'll write the words and you supply the pictures.'

Amo found himself nodding slowly. 'But what guarantees do I have that it will be published? A story is only as good as the paper it's in. I need a leading newspaper that will be picked up by any search engine.'

'Then Google my real name,' he said, 'and just see what you get with Aron Lunzer. I'm the star columnist of *Adlai*. I can get anything published.'

'Very well,' said Amo, finally. 'I will check your name.' He clicked the lens cap back on the camera and nodded to the burly man who let go of Aron's hair.

Aron was still tied to the chair and the pain in his wrists had spread to every inch of his body. But he was alive for now. That was all that mattered.

He was in limbo for what seemed like an eternity.

The child still watched cartoons and the burly man with the cleaver watched Aron.

Eventually, Amo stepped back into the room. 'You haven't written anything in three months,' he stated.

'I've been in mourning.'

'Hmm.' He smiled suddenly. 'But I liked your piece on the *evshelim*. You and I are kindred spirits, Aron. We see life through the same prism — even if our angles are somewhat different.' He told the burly man to untie Aron. 'Allow me to introduce you to the subject of your piece,' he said almost affably. 'Here is our future martyr.'

Even though he was indicating the boy, Aron failed to understand at first and glanced instead at the burly man.

The cleaver returned to the kitchen along with the burly man who had prepared falafels for lunch.

'I have named him Shahid, which means "martyr" in Arabic. When you write about him, please use that name.'

Amo was still talking, but Aron had turned to stare helplessly at the boy's darkly underlined eyes.

'But I must insist that you write Shah*id*, not Shah*ed*. That's crucial. The names may sound similar in English, but they have two quite opposite connotations in Arabic.'

Again, Aron thought about Amo's terrorist who was a dog instead of a martyr because he had failed his suicide mission. Indirectly, Aron was now the prisoner of the same man who had caused Avi's death.

Countless flies buzzed desperately when the burly man entered with a copper tray full of greasy brown balls; not even the stale cigarette smoke could mask the stench of deep-fried instant falafel.

Amo indicated a seat at the table in the dingy dining room. 'But now you are my guest. Let's eat.' He told the boy to join them.

'Will you let me go once I finish the story?'

'Of course. You have my most sincere word. Please.' He gestured for Aron to begin eating. 'Everything about us is different, even our falafel mixes.' He added, 'Jews seem incapable of adding fava beans to the chick peas. But you need those beans to get that extra dimension.' Amo used one hand to wave the fumes to his nostrils as though to appreciate a subtle perfume, which made the gesture all the more exaggerated since his nose was still covered by the light blue mask. 'Try it, Aron, you'll see. You'll never taste better falafels in all of Zion.'

Aron declined wordlessly.

'You offend Arab hospitality,' he tutted and then turned to scold the child who had reached for three balls and was busy stuffing all three in his mouth. '*Shway shway*, slow down, *Shahid*.'

Foaming falafel at the mouth, Shahid ignored him and reached for two more.

The burly man swung his massive arms every so often to shoo flies away from the heavy platter.

'I look forward to doing some good work this afternoon, Aron.' He pinched one ball delicately between thumb and index, causing it to puff steam. 'And later this evening, I'll lend you my laptop so you can write the story. Then we'll be able to put our baby to bed, yes?' Click-click.

It was unclear to Aron whether his abductor meant the piece or the skinny child who was now fighting a losing battle against all the flies.

Amo bit into his falafel daintily so as not to stain his ski mask. 'Man is such a carnivore.' He nodded to himself. 'In Europe they make vile burgers out of soya. At least we've got our falafels. Vegetables can only give you that deep sense of satisfaction when they're made to look like meat.' He indicated the food. 'These balls are the food equivalent of trick photography. Please have one.' He reached across the table for the platter, causing Shahid to snatch two more balls, and brought it under Aron's nose. 'Will you change your mind?'

Aron shook his head and rose to his feet.

Amo indicated he should sit down again. 'We haven't finished our meal.'

'I need the bathroom,' Aron replied urgently and was accompanied by the burly man in three long strides.

The boy watched Aron's exit with interest, his shiners stretching into exclamation marks as he chewed his food.

The empty platter remained on the table of the dingy dining room throughout the interview.

Aron, taking notes on a pad, asked the questions. Amo interpreted only those questions that he approved, and then translated Shahid's replies into English.

Aron was writing a sympathetic account about a fanatic who wanted to blow up innocent people. The fact that the terrorist was himself a victim — a scrawny child who had been deprived of real food and love by equal measure — made the prospect that much more unpalatable.

The boy had been abused by everyone. Of course, while the terrorist's own use of the child was by far the crowning turd on the dung heap, the Israeli military had done its bit to cultivate the budding martyr.

You couldn't radicalize a child when he was that young, but you could rob him of his childhood and show him that nothing except violence really mattered. By his own account, he had witnessed enough loss and death to warp Moses himself.

The boy was almost eleven when a band of armed Palestinian militants had arrived at the Brahimi farm and threatened to kill everyone if they refused to allow them to stay. They proceeded to use the farm and its broom factory as a base from where they launched their attacks. The IDF retaliated massively on Shahid's birthday, obliterating the farmhouse and making no distinction between the armed guerrillas and the boy's father and five siblings. The boy and his mother were only spared a similar fate because they happened to be in town at the time of the attack. They returned to find the corpses piled high in the sitting room, with its one wall still intact and still miraculously covered by a tidy line of brooms.

The mother and child were left to separate stranger from kin.

And later, the boy was forced to fend for himself for almost four months until the commander of al-Aqsa Squad took him in.

'What happened to your mother?' Aron asked Shahid.

Amo didn't translate the question. 'You don't need to talk about her in your story,' he said simply.

'Background info,' countered Aron. 'So that I can understand Shahid better.' He'd already used that argument to understand why the IDF had singled out the Brahimi farm, and the fact that it had been swamped by Palestinian fighters had been offered strictly off the record.

'Not for publication,' said Amo, warning him with a finger. He waited for Aron's acknowledgement before interpreting the question in Arabic, and then shrugged as he offered the boy's reply, 'She was abducted by *ibreet*.'

'*Ivreet*?' said Aron, frowning. 'Taken by *Hebrews*?'

'Something like that.' The index was up again. 'But I don't expect to read about that.'

Shahid nodded, flapped his arms and made an odd tweeting sound.

A more accurate name for the town would have been *Laramallah* — God-*did-not*-will-it-so.

Ramallah — God-willed-it-so — was the result of either a gross misnomer or of a particularly messy and indifferent deity. The urban design seemed to have been set on a desert dune in the middle of a dust storm. This could explain how major intersections crept up on you without the slightest warning and why derelict tenements vied for space with gangly apartment blocks all bundled together hazardously like kindle of varying lengths. The few gardens, adequate pavements and modern buildings were isolated pockets of planning in a morass of disorder. These were largely confined to the centre of the temporary capital of the Palestinian Authority, roughly delineated by the compound where its president had remained in virtual house arrest ever since Bernadette had come to the West Bank.

As Projects Officer with UNRWA, Bernadette was responsible for calculating the payments to Palestinian households according to an intricate formula of many variables. In the case of Imm Nidal, for instance, the death of Shahed had cut her monthly allowance given the loss of a dependant. However, the demolition of her home had increased that allowance as had her subsequent move to Ramallah, where the price of living was indexed higher than in Qalqiliya. In all then, Imm Nidal's current situation had changed and had — in the crudest statistical sense — improved by seventy-three per cent.

Imm Nidal's sister, Samiha, lived in a squat house, squashed among skyrises like a dirty street child being ignored by a mass of busy pedestrians.

Imm Nidal's nephew opened the door, admitted Bernadette wordlessly and retired as Imm Nidal entered the drab living room.

'Holiest of late mornings to you, Bernaytat,' she greeted formally.

Bernadette caught herself thinking of tomato: we say *banadoura*, and you say *bandowra* — the linguistic disagreement in Arabic was as palpable as the transatlantic rift in English.

'You come in time for some sweet tea,' added Imm Nidal pleasantly.

Bernadette was offered the only seat in the living room: a rickety armchair whose arms were hugged so close together that she had trouble holding her glass of tea. Imm Nidal sat opposite on a bed that, despite many cushions and a rug to cover the mattress, failed utterly to pass for a sofa.

Imm Nidal signed the ledger to receive the envelope containing $63 in financial assistance and asked, as usual, 'Is there a change?'

'No change from last month.'

'Then you are giving me too much now,' she said. 'I don't cook as much as I used to. And Samiha says I don't clean as well as she does. But she uses less detergent so how clean can that be?' Her arm swept across the room as she added conspiratorially, 'Tell me honestly, Bernaytat, was my house ever this dusty?'

The room appeared spotless if completely cheerless, but Bernadette said, 'Never.'

'Even as children she always envied me. Even now, when I have nothing left, she envies my faith. But the transgressors never succeed.'

Imm Nidal finished her tea in one gulp, topped up Bernadette's glass and refilled her own.

'I have spent 126 days here,' she said despondently. '126 days away from home.' She quoted from the Koran: '"God's guidance is found in houses exalted by God, for His name is commemorated therein. Glorifying Him therein, day and night." And that's why I need to go home, Bernaytat.' She looked at Bernadette desperately. 'I have a boy,' she said suddenly. 'Back in Qalqiliya, I have a boy who needs me. You must help me find him.'

'A boy?' asked Bernadette, frowning. 'Another son?' For an instant, she considered that they had made a mistake, and that the financial assistance would have to be recalculated to reflect the extra dependant. 'You have another son?' she repeated incredulously.

'A boy like Shahed before the kafir seduced him.'

'Who?' Bernadette was confused.

Imm Nidal spoke softly, 'The evil jinnee who brought all the evil to my house.' She paused. 'Shahed communicated with him. But I rejoice that he's now dead and awaiting final judgement.'

Bernadette felt it prudent to remain quiet, but her frown deepened.

'See?' Imm Nidal indicated her empty glass. 'I can now drink my tea again. Now that the false companion is no more.'

'Who killed him?'

It was Imm Nidal's turn to frown. 'The Israelis of course.'

'Of course.'

'He roamed the earth corruptingly, destroying properties and lives. God does not love corruption.' She added suddenly and almost chattily, 'I have proof of the communication. Would you like to see?'

Bernadette nodded, still utterly mystified.

As Imm Nidal stepped out of the room, she paused to say, almost as an aside, 'I haven't even shown it to Samiha. But I'm showing it to you because you and I are more like sisters, Bernaytat.'

Bernadette accepted the confidence by bringing her palms together.

Imm Nidal returned presently with some loose sheets. 'I took these from Shahed's bedroom on that last night before — ' her voice trailed off.

She placed the sheets in Bernadette's lap. 'I left with only my clothes and this.' She cleared her throat. 'I had to keep this to remind me of the evil.' Imm Nidal closed her eyes and muttered the *shahada* to herself as Bernadette read the words.

It was a printout of several emails between Shahed, who went by the online name of Squaring-the-Circle and a character known as Dustmaster. The conversations were very informative in the way eavesdropping can bring with it certain rewards, but they seemed hardly malevolent.

There was a long pause even after Bernadette had finished.

'Dustmaster?' she said at length, her tone hesitant.

The name still caused Imm Nidal to shiver. 'Long may he suffer the torment of the bottomless pit.'

Bernadette scrutinized the sheets again to see if she'd missed anything and then decided that Imm Nidal's grasp of English did not extend much beyond the alphabet.

Bernadette looked up and prompted gently, 'Is Dustmaster your lost son?'

'*Bismillah!*' moaned Imm Nidal. 'That fiend who was as invisible as his name?!'

This caused Bernadette to frown again.

'That Dastmastur?' Imm Nidal was upset. 'Did you not hear me? I told you he's dead and awaiting final judgement. That snake who took my beautiful Shahed from me.'

'I apologize for my mistake. Forgive me, Imm Nidal,' Bernadette said formally. 'I'm confused because you talk of another son.'

'Another boy,' corrected Imm Nidal, 'not another son. The Brahimi boy.'

'Brahimi?'

'Yes,' she said sullenly. 'Mohsen Brahimi. That poor orphan I used to feed when I still had my home. I fed him almost from the day they took his mother away.' She paused. 'They came for her that day, poor woman, the very same day they picked up her dead family.'

'Brahimi of the Brahimi farm?' asked Bernadette. 'Your neighbours down the road?'

She nodded sadly. 'They used to make the best brooms in the world. *Haram.* Their farm was surely possessed by a more powerful jinnee.' She added in a hushed voice as though fearing invisible spies, 'But that poor woman was weak. She opened her mind to the jinnee who turned her into a bird.'

'I'm sorry?'

'When they took her away, they had to tie her arms in a white jacket because she was flapping them so much. She thought she could fly away, you see. She'd stopped speaking the Arabic of our Lord and could only make little bird sounds.' She reached across to squeeze Bernadette's arm. 'But that poor boy.' Imm Nidal became suddenly emotional. 'I had already lost everything but my faith.' Tears started to well up in her eyes. 'Shahed was spending all his time with *combyudars* and those other evils — '

Imm Nidal wept.

Bernadette moved to sit on the bed and placed her arm around her.

'God is the greatest,' she sobbed. 'Why are we so weak, Bernaytat? Why?' She took a couple of deep breaths. 'I was not as you see me now. I was — ' she almost whispered, 'filled with doubt.' She nodded emphatically as the image of her nails digging deep in Abu Nidal's cheeks came to mind. 'One more day and Dastmastur would have defiled my mind. Two more days and they would have sent a van with a cage to lock me up like a mad dog.'

She patted Bernadette's knee and gave her a reassuring smile.

'God is the greatest,' she repeated. 'In all His wisdom, he sent me the orphan to encourage me to be steadfast and to remind me of my duties. It was a cold day in November when I first saw Mohsen Brahimi. For four months, he came to me like a good jinnee and for four months I fed him. And so it was every day.' Her smile now turned sad. 'He is more than a human child — he's my *qareen*, my faithful companion. Mohsen made me cook when there was no one else to cook for. That sweet Brahimi child stopped me from turning like his mother.'

Imm Nidal's hand now held Bernadette's firmly. 'Please help me find that boy,' she entreated. 'He needs me but I need him more.'

Bernadette hesitated for only a second. 'I'll try,' she promised.

Imm Nidal brought the hand to her lips.

'I will do my best,' she said.

They held hands for a full ten minutes until Bernadette got up to leave.

It was almost as an afterthought, as she spotted the printouts on the armchair, that she asked, 'May I photocopy these sheets?'

Imm Nidal looked shocked. 'And reproduce the evil? Heaven forbid! Why would you do such a thing?'

'This could interest a journalist who might write a story about Shahed.' Not Arnold Lounger, thought Bernadette, but some other, less biased writer.

She shook her head firmly. 'I would rather a story about Mohsen.' She indicated the sheets. 'They are a witness to the communication. I need them.'

Bernadette read the printout again, committing the salient points to memory, before handing it back to Imm Nidal.

'Please don't wait till next month to bring news of the boy.' Imm Nidal led the way to the door just as her nephew emerged from a bedroom. 'It's fortunate you don't eat lunch for I have none to offer you.' She added snidely, 'His mother won't let me in the kitchen.'

Bernadette smiled awkwardly and left.

She had relocated to the West Bank partly to rediscover the Arab roots of her ancestors. So it was with an overriding sense of duty — the unwritten codes of Arab hospitality — that she drove away from Imm Nidal and aimed straight for the psychiatric ward of the UNRWA hospital in Qalqiliya. She had to see if any of their patients flapped their arms like a bird and generally fit the description of Mohsen Brahimi's mother.

It all reminded her of Mémé.

The entire Middle East simmered with misnomers and paradoxes. For instance, a church could still be widely known as the Church of the Refugees even if the massacre of Damour had become a dim memory and most refugees had either moved on to other parts of Beirut or had filtered back to rediscover their properties. And you could be the daughter of the Butcher of Sabra and yet still love your father.

Papa accompanied them to the midnight mass of Christmas 1992 several months before Mémé's vanishing act, and what would transpire to be her last Nativity. Mémé and Papa stooped their heads as though in deep prayer and mumbled the Aramaic and Arabic passages. While in Mémé's case, the burble was down to a clinical mental block, Papa was a

Christian only in times of war when he could wear the uniform for all to see. You could tinker with German cars during the day and still harbour dreams of fighting the good fight; and you certainly didn't need to know the prayers by heart.

At the kiss of peace, Mémé refused to acknowledge her son. He refused to shake the hands of strangers, accepting only a quick peck from his daughter and responding to her Aramaic 'Shlomo' with the meaningless 'Shlomo mashlomo.'

Alzheimer's has that particularity that, once accurately diagnosed, it's usually already at an advanced stage. All the early warnings, brushed away as little more than signs of old age, become obvious symptoms of the disease: forgetting what was served for breakfast two hours earlier, but remembering with crystal clarity a best friend at kindergarten from 70 years ago; mistaking a son for a brother or a grandson for a nephew; and losing track of time, believing yesterday to be last year and the other way round.

It is one of the most inhuman of diseases not so much for the agony that it causes — the pain is restricted to the inner mind — but because of its debilitating characteristics. It is far better to suffer sudden and complete amnesia than to live through the degenerative loss of faculties, to experience the gradual unstitching of the neural networks and to lose ever so deliberately all the information and skills learnt over the period of a lifetime. In the final stages, a sufferer even forgets how to smile.

Every patient's return to infancy traces its own route. In Mémé's case, she began to believe that she lived in the affluent suburbs of Alexandretta of her childhood, oblivious to the fact that the coastal town had been renamed Iskenderun by invading Turks in 1938, and that the invasion had caused her family to emigrate to the poorer end of East Beirut.

Equally, in her last year, she started to switch languages. While in the past, Mémé had prided herself on being trilingual, she had in actual fact been bilingual, with some rudimentary Turkish to complement her Franco-Arabic. However, in a chronological sense at least, she had acquired Turkish first by virtue of the Armenian nanny who had looked after her in the first six years; and Arabic last since her father had been a diehard Francophile.

Consequently, as the dementia progressed, Arabic was the first to go. Unfortunately, this coincided with Papa's own gradual switch from French to Arabic as the years spent hunkered with Arabic-speaking, Arabic-thinking militiamen took their toll on his linguistic abilities.

Of course he could still speak French, but whenever he used an Arabic term for a forgotten French equivalent, she howled and screamed blue murder, causing the neighbours from the flats opposite to look across with concern.

'Who's this monster?' she moaned at Bernadette. 'Tell him to leave our house.'

'That's your son, Mémé,' said Bernadette gently.

'He's a murderer.' She looked at him with terror as she whispered to her granddaughter, 'He's come to rape us.'

'That's Antoine, Mémé.'

Mémé sobbed like a child. 'Please make him go, Raphaelle. I beg you. *Je t'en supplie.*'

Bernadette had stopped being a granddaughter for some time. For a while, when Mémé could still string together some basic Arabic, she had become her own dead mother, that is, Mémé's daughter-in-law. It had been a particularly poignant phase when, chattily, Mémé would ask after the health of the children, and whether the homemade recipe for young Michel's cough was working. But at this later stage, Bernadette had become her own great-aunt, Raphaelle, Mémé's older sister who had died of tuberculosis at the age of eighteen back in 1940.

Papa left and his visits to see them became even fewer and further between.

Eventually, as Bernadette began her second year at university, she became Anike, the Armenian nanny. She studied political science during the day and basic Turkish at night so that Mémé would understand such basic commands and questions as 'Eat your dinner', 'Have you done pipi?' and 'Go to sleep now'.

She found a neighbour who, for a fee, looked after Mémé every morning when Bernadette went to her lectures.

Mémé wailed every morning as soon as she saw the neighbour entering the flat. 'Anike *stay*,' she cried. 'Anike don't go.'

'I go to work,' said Bernadette firmly. 'You be good girl.'

'Pretty girl?'

'Very pretty.'

'More pretty than Raphaelle?'

'Yes, more pretty. You're very pretty.'

'Again?'

'*Çok güzel son,*' repeated Bernadette.

Mémé went missing just before Bernadette's midterm exams. By all accounts, she slipped out when the sitter was asleep and somehow managed to end up halfway across the city to a slum that was as far removed from affluent Alexandretta of the 1930s as could ever exist.

It took the police three weeks to track her down — a hunt that owed its success largely to the trail left by the conspicuous pink nightie and matching slippers that she was wearing and to the fact that she stopped passers-by to ask for directions in prattling Turkish.

Mémé had ended up in Sabra. Of all the places in the world, her grandmother had chosen to lose herself for exactly twenty-two days in the very same camp where, a decade earlier, her father had run amok.

The Palestinian camp was designed as a labyrinth with tortuous paths skirting around and under windowless dwellings, which in turn were stacked high and adjoined like mad Lego blocks. The aim was twofold: to maximize the habitable surface area available to refugees, and to provide a medieval defence mechanism from invaders. However, with hindsight, it was a structure that not only proved ineffectual in warding off Papa and his blood-crazed comrades, but actually encouraged greater bloodletting given the high population density.

Bernadette and the Lebanese policeman who accompanied her would never have found the correct dwelling without the help of the two young guides, a boy and a girl, who waited for them at the main entrance to the camp.

The two outsiders followed their giggling guides, matching their every step, as they hopped, skipped and jumped over unsavoury rivulets and ducked their heads where sharp masonry jutted out for no other apparent reason than to injure careless pedestrians.

Bernadette could not have come to this shantytown on her own. Every so often she held on to the policeman's arm not so much for help through the obstacle course but for the reassuring grip to counterbalance all the macabre images that haunted her. She could never quite dispel the leading photograph that ran with Arnold Lounger's article: a picture of Papa drinking Almaza beer while six cadavers lay rotting at his feet.

They came eventually to an open door and were ushered into a dark room.

The air was musty and not even the stale cigarette smoke could mask the strong traces of urine. Indistinct bodies surrounded her, faceless and ageless, as her eyes slowly adjusted to the dim lighting.

A woman's deep voice boomed, 'Have you come for her?'

Bernadette reached for the policeman's arm again and squeezed; he answered for her: 'Yes. Where is she?'

'How are you related to her?'

By contrast, Bernadette's voice sounded frail and vulnerable. 'I'm her granddaughter.'

The darkness lifted gradually. Bernadette could now discern an old woman among the crowd who was perhaps Mémé's age and was busy scrutinizing her.

The old woman bowed formally. 'Then you are most welcome here,' she said at length. 'A relative of the Lady is a friend of this house.'

The bodies drifted apart as she moved in to embrace Bernadette and kiss her three times on the cheeks.

The crowd, which Bernadette mistakenly assumed had gathered to meet them, turned out to be four generations of the same family sharing the same cramped space. The head of the household ordered a daughter or granddaughter to prepare some coffee as she led Bernadette by the hand. She described how Mémé had been found wandering aimlessly in the camp and how, with nowhere else to go and no one else to take care of her, she had been adopted by the family and named *as-Sitt*, the Lady. Later, as they sat for coffee with a wholesale number of children, grandchildren and great-grandchildren milling around, she would provide details of Mémé's stay in Sabra: how the family would take turns bathing her, changing her and feeding her.

'We'll all be sad to see her go,' said the old woman, leading the way to the far end of the room. 'But none more so than young Ali here.'

The youngest member of the household was probably two years old. He'd been unconcerned by the arrival of the two strangers. He was showing off Bah-bah, a worn teddy bear with disproportionately long arms, to his best friend.

'Bah-bah,' he said to her, grinning. 'Bah-bah,' he insisted as he reached for her hand and then closed her fingers around the bear.

Someone marvelled, 'No one else is allowed to touch Bah-bah.'

Mémé's smile made her face glow.

Bernadette was dumbstruck; she couldn't remember if she'd ever seen her look so delighted.

Mémé sat in the best armchair in the room, the only chair that still had both its arms, all its legs and its original upholstery.

'Bah-bah,' said the little boy.

'Bah-bah,' agreed Mémé.

They laughed at their private joke as the grownups looked on.

Mémé's cheeks turned the deep red of fleshy tomatoes that are native to the Maronite hinterland. She glanced at Bernadette and completely failed to register her granddaughter.

14

ARON HAD EARNED himself little more than some extra time.

He didn't believe for a second that his captors would simply let him walk out of Goliath's den. They would kill him eventually, perhaps holding off the execution until his piece on Shahid was published.

It was partly because of that cold assessment and partly thanks to his renewed journalistic instinct that he came up with a second, even more exciting article to buy himself some more time like Scheherazade.

The idea came to him as he gathered the background information on the world's youngest suicide bomber. 'How will the death of a little boy achieve anything?' he asked, matter-of-fact. He had asked the Butcher of Sabra a similar question about murdered Palestinian children and in the same nonjudgmental way to encourage him to talk.

They were still at the table, while the burly man sat on the chair in the middle of the living area, smoking cigarettes.

'If an adult suicide bomber is a poor man's weapon of mass destruction, capable of a ton of destruction, then a child bomber creates a megaton,' answered Amo. 'Imagine the aftershock, the emotional bombshell that travels the globe at the speed of broadcast. Imagine innocence and purity being driven to the final sacrifice by sheer despair — that's true poetry.'

'Yes,' said Aron, 'but how will it achieve anything? In other words, what do you actually hope will change with his death?'

'Everything.' He paused to choose his words carefully. 'It will be the definitive suicide mission.'

Aron waited patiently.

'The specific details will become apparent after the mission.' He brushed the point aside as though it were less significant. 'These will be in the paragraph before the article — what do you call it — the lead?'

'Strap.'

He nodded. 'All you need to know for your story is that Shahid will spark the third intifada — an event even more catastrophic than that which caused the second. This third uprising will dwarf the second in the way the second put the first in the shade.'

Aron frowned.

'All the best wars come in three instalments.' He handed Aron a large black-and-white picture. 'That's the image I would like to use for the piece,' he said. 'I'll leave it with you so that it might inspire you.' Click-click.

Aron did little more than glance at it and then placed it on the table, next to a laptop.

'I've shot worse.' He showed his teeth suddenly and because of the mask, Aron thought at first that he was snarling. 'The Israeli army could certainly tell you that. And sometimes you get the most rewarding pictures even in poor lighting and even when you're crouched uncomfortably behind an old olive tree.' He was still laughing at his private joke as he got up. He indicated his laptop and picture. 'I think you have everything you need now.'

'But how did you choose Shahid?' Aron asked quickly.

'You don't need that for your story.'

'You're right,' agreed Aron immediately. 'But I would need it for the second, follow-up story.'

He stopped smiling and even the light blue mask couldn't hide his baffled look. 'What second story?'

By contrast, the burly man's eyes remained as impassive as ever.

'A second profile — with your permission, of course,' said Aron. 'A feature as strong as the first that could be released a week later, when the media world had just finished digesting the first. A double whammy.'

'What's the subject?' Amo asked suspiciously.

'You are,' he said simply.

For a full two seconds, Amo simply stared at him. Then he laughed abruptly. 'You don't come across as a joker, but you're a true comedian.' He got up and started to move to the door as he mimicked Aron's earnest tone, '"You are."' He chuckled to himself.

'Let me take you back to 18 September 2001. How do you suppose the world would have reacted if on that day some newspaper had published a profile of Khaled Sheikh Mohammad?'

Amo stopped.

'The mastermind of 9/11.'

'You have me confused with a different group,' Amo said slowly.

'Imagine — the world's leaders are slowly coming around from the biggest blow in a century and are desperately scratching their heads to find the culprit and,' he slapped the back of one hand against the other, ' — bang — out pops the profile. As a blind interview, the story reveals nothing of his whereabouts or identity, simply his philosophy and ideas for the world. Can't you just see the stacks of newspapers hot off the press, websites across the world scrambling to carry the feature, blogs everywhere adding their personal views on it? It's bloody sensational and you know it. Damn, your intelligence alone would persuade millions around the world.' Aron even tapped into his captor's perverted sense of art, with a final shot, 'You know it's a winner, artistically speaking.'

Amo turned to face him only once he'd reached the door. 'We'll talk about this tomorrow,' he said, 'once I've read your piece on Shahid. I hope my picture inspires you.'

Aron turned to stare sullenly at the boy who had crashed out on the sofa.

Even asleep, he seemed to be watching TV as though he were wired into it so that his eyes would only open in the morning once the broadcast resumed.

The burly man still sat on the chair in the middle of the living area; the balaclava helmet never left his face, and his eyes never left Aron.

Aron nodded nervously. When the man failed to react, he indicated the copper platter on the table and then the laptop and the notes. 'I need more room on the table,' he said.

The man got up, placed the heavy tray on the floor and returned to his seat.

'Hm. Could you take it to the kitchen?'

By way of a reply, the man drew his legs out and lit a cigarette.

'OK.' Aron stretched, yawned and switched on the laptop. 'This is going to be a long night.'

He was immediately greeted by his own look of horror as the burly man prepared to cut his throat with a cleaver. That particular picture had been set as the desktop background clearly as a twisted joke.

'OK,' he said again, removed the background and added humourlessly, 'Oh my, what big hands you have, Grandma.' He began by opening the recent documents folders as he added in a deep, Arab accent: 'All the better to cut your throat with.'

He could churn out the piece with his eyes tightly shut. He had written about terrorists in so many past commentaries that all it took was an adaptation of the angle and changing 'Islamic fanatic' and 'terrorist' into 'hero' and 'freedom fighter'.

It was an open and shut case of abuse and murder: the death of Shahid — as well as of those indistinct bodies, faceless and ageless, that would scatter around him — that was as senseless as Avi's. That was the real nut graf of the piece. He reached for the black-and-white photograph that Amo had left on the table. Aron had to admit it was front-page material.

But he began by checking the temporary files, history and recent documents folder on the laptop. He realized how ridiculous that habit was, especially now. But just as he'd had no scruples about spying on his young son, seeing it as his duty to protect Avi from Internet porn, he had even fewer qualms about tracking the Internet history of his captors. With the brute stretched out before him, Aron discovered a mix of offline pages, ranging from a government portal of the Foreign Ministry of Egypt to unsavoury Islamic sites that, in Arabic and pseudo-English, called for the '*Detrication of the Terorist Israel and her satinic lover america*'.

He launched the word processor and started to type madly like someone possessed. He finished the article in record time under the unblinking stare of Mr Wolf.

It was one of his best pieces; he just hoped the terrorist called Uncle would agree and commission the next feature. He looked once more at the black-and-white photograph that Amo had left him.

The picture was taken with a wide-angle lens. At the far end of the room in sharp focus was an unbroken line of brooms — perhaps as many as a hundred — arranged meticulously according to brush size and thickness of the bristles and bundled together into tidy packs of six.

By contrast, the rest of the image was the epitome of mess and chaos. The wall with the brooms was the only one left intact as if the brooms themselves offered some protection from the encroaching disorder. There was a gaping hole in the western wall, further distorted by the lens, which prepared to consume the entire room with its jaws of blown-up masonry. Closer still were the remnants of a humble sitting room: armchairs whose arms had been pulled out of their sockets, a ramshackle collection of seats with missing backs or legs, a coffee table charred to the bone, and a TV set with gouged vision.

The dust was everywhere. In this monochrome setting, it gathered in thick whorls of grey, stitching the most immutable of blankets. In a sense, the dust was more unsettling than the scene of devastation: it was incongruous to have so much dust when there was a neat stack of brooms nearby, waiting patiently to be used. After a while of staring and to satisfy a growing itch, Aron felt he could reach inside the picture, to pick out a broom, preferably a bigger brush and with thinner bristles, to do the spring-cleaning himself.

Indeed, it was only with time, once his vision strayed from the centre of the photograph to the fringes, that another absurdity became apparent. Where the eastern wall had been all but obliterated and what at first he had mistakenly thought a small boulder was, upon closer inspection, the figure of a child — the young boy. The dust had settled on Shahid as well, perfectly camouflaging his thin body and leaving grimy streaks on his face. He sat hugging his knees and watching TV with all the intensity of a child the world over watching a favourite cartoon. The absurdity clearly lay in the hollowed TV and in the fact that the viewer was compelled to share the photographer's twisted joke at the expense of his miserable subject.

It was a deliberate act of manipulation by Amo: first, you saw the brooms, then the destruction and dust, and finally the child.

The nights came and went in the terrorist den that was about as far removed from his flat in Jerusalem as could ever exist. And while Shahid was not remotely like Avi, there were moments when he felt transported back to his study, with young Avi watching TV as Aron alternated between pacing the room and sitting at the desk and the PC. His captors brought them food on plates, ignoring the heavy copper tray. It had remained on the floor ever since the first meal of falafel as though on a daring mission to attract a maximum number of ants and cockroaches.

By the end of the second day, he found himself scolding the budding terrorist. 'You watch too much TV.'

Shahid responded by burying an index in a nostril.

'And stop that — it's disgusting.'

'Stop that itz-dizgusting,' mimicked Shahid.

'What?'

'What.' The boy looked up at Aron timidly.

'Are you a parrot now?'

'Ahryu aparot naoh.'

'Go make yourself some homemade maracas and march to Mozart music.'

Shahid hesitated.

Aron grinned. 'Got you there.'

Then, given his face was so gaunt, the boy's sudden grin stretched from ear to ear.

They heard footsteps approaching from the adjoining room; Shahid's grin vanished as abruptly as it had appeared. He brought an index to his lips. 'Shh.'

'Shh?'

He nodded and added in an urgent whisper, 'Click-click.'

'Click-click?'

'Click-click come.'

In the event it was the brute, not Click-click, who stepped in to check on them; it was Aron who chose his new nickname. He bent down to whisper in the boy's ear: 'Grrr-grrr.' To Aron, he would always remain a wolf in burly man's clothing.

'Grrr-grrr,' agreed Shahid, his grin returning slowly.

They laughed at their private joke as the brute looked on visibly irritated.

On the third day, Grrr-grrr and Click-click stepped into the room together.

'Have you read the piece?' He kicked himself for sounding too anxious like a rookie journalist waiting for his editor's feedback.

'Yes.'

He tried to sound nonchalant. 'Well?'

'It's OK.'

'OK?' Aron could not hide his irritation. 'It's a masterpiece.'

'It reads a bit too much like the Butcher of Sabra.'

'Which has become your holy text,' Aron reminded him. 'You never leave home without it.'

'Yes, I lied' he said absentmindedly. 'I never take texts with me, only pictures.' But he added after a while, 'Come.' He indicated the dining room. 'Interview me and let the story begin with the Butcher of Sabra and his friends.'

It was supposed to be a blind interview: a story that would reveal little of his past. But by the end of the session, the terrorist had disclosed so much about himself that Aron knew he would never make it out alive.

Amo was born in 1948, somewhere on the road between Haifa and South Lebanon, and born a second time in the Sabra Refugee Camp on 16 September 1982.

He is the champion exit strategist and knows instinctively how to emerge from intractable situations. Six years earlier, in 1976, when the Phalangists besieged the refugee camp of Tell az-Za'atar outside Beirut, he was able to escape, disguised as a Red Cross worker a day before the camp was razed to the

*ground. At the checkpoints, he rounded his vowels and aban-
doned some consonants in his speech so that he sounded less
Palestinian Muslim and more Lebanese Christian.*

It is a linguistic skill that served him well again in Sabra.

*Given his affiliation to the rival Abu Nidal organization, the
PLO high command had refused to include him on the list of
fighters being evacuated from West Beirut. And with the Israeli
siege still in place, he forged some papers, assumed the distinctly unArabic name of André, and paid a fellow fighter to beat
him to a pulp and lock him up in a detention cell in Sabra with
other bona fide 'Christian' prisoners.*

*Amo's timing was perfect. His face was still swollen and lacer-
ated when he was liberated by Christian militiamen, the same
who went on the rampage in Sabra, slaughtering old men,
women and children.*

*His moment of rebirth occurred when he emerged outside and,
with a rising sense of detachment, took in all the heads without
bodies, and bodies without limbs. This was the moment the real
Amo was born.*

*His liberators gave him a bottle of beer, and he clinked with
them and drank to their health, dribbling in the process because
of his inflamed lower lip. A photographer appeared and they all
turned and grinned with their trophies of dead civilians at their*

feet and toasted the camera. Amo's smile would have been the broadest were it not for his disfiguring bruises.

For Amo, nothing can ever match that heartbeat when he first realized how much he loves the look of death and destruction. Even with all the time in the universe to take pictures of every person at their moment of death, nothing will ever compare to that first rush.

That, he says, is true immortality...

The TV was switched off for much of the fourth morning as Shahid and Aron played chess on the laptop.

It surprised him that the boy knew all the basic chess moves. There was something strangely captivating about watching him play chess, the way his brow would furrow and the way his finger remained poised on the mouse as if on a chessman as he contemplated his next move. They didn't play real chess, that is the variety that Voltaire qualified as reflecting 'most honour on human wit'. Instead, they played to lose. And Shahid was particularly good at suicide chess.

When the boy won the second game he blurted out something which Aron at first mistook to be in Arabic.

'What's that?'

The boy repeated his phrase; the accent was atrocious, but it was intelligible Hebrew.

Aron frowned and repeated in Hebrew: 'Die, you Arabs, for the greater good of Israel.'

The boy nodded, pleased, and repeated it slightly more fluently.

'Why would you say that?' said Aron.

When the boy didn't answer, he asked him instead why he wanted to die. He had to use a lot of hand gestures, pointing at Shahid, making an explosion with his hands and then playing dead. 'Why?' he asked gently, pointing at the boy again.

Shahid answered, '*Mish rah mout la'aneh rayeh dirghe a'al-janna.*'

'What does that mean?'

The boy shrugged.

'*Mish* — ' began Aron and stopped as he forgot the rest.

Shahid repeated his answer several times. Every time he said it, Aron was able to commit slightly more to memory.

Eventually, Aron tried, '*Mish ra-mout laan rayekh dirghe al-janna.*'

Shahid grinned and waved his hand to mean so-so.

Later, Aron sat on the sofa next to the boy as they watched Tom and Jerry. After a while, he asked, 'What's your name?'

'Shahid.'

'Your real name?' He tried again: 'Your other name?'

'Jerry,' said Shahid impatiently. He was clearly annoyed at being interrupted from his cartoons.

It reminded Aron of Avi's collection of Tom and Jerry comic books. 'You look like my son when you do that,' he spoke mostly to himself. 'Would you like to see a picture of him?' Aron reached for his wallet in his back pocket and extracted a wrinkled picture. 'He's younger here — maybe only a couple of years older than you are now.'

He presented the picture of his Avi, but the boy couldn't take his eyes off the mouse on TV who was using a shrill whistle to call his canine ally.

'Look,' insisted Aron.

Shahid ignored him.

Aron's hand wavered. 'And just why would you be interested in my son.' He turned the picture back towards himself to take in every detail of his grinning teenage boy. 'He's just an Israeli soldier to you,' he said without a trace of recrimination. 'And why should you care when you have your own death to look forward to.' He closed his eyes. For a full twenty-four hours on twenty-four-hour news channels, Shahid was destined to become news, views and opinions — the toast of the global village. People from Jakarta to Johannesburg would become experts in dissecting his cause and specialists in analysing his motives. He nodded slowly. 'That's me, see?' he said vaguely.

Shahid turned away from the hapless cat being pummelled by the dog to glance at the man with interest. 'Tom?'

'That's right. I'm Tom.'

Shahid nodded and, needing no further explanation, he returned to his cartoon.

Aron continued, 'Tom writes so that others will become experts, so that others will care. That's what Tom does for a living. Tom is paid to write about people like you when you're dead.'

His sudden tears were triggered as much by Avi who was no more as by the stabbing realization that, because he was too weak to change a single event, this boy wouldn't even make it to adolescence. 'Oh fuck I'm sorry,' he cried. 'I'm so fucking sorry.'

Shahid turned again, this time with astonishment. 'Why Tom cry?'

'Avi was lucky, don't you see?'

He repeated, 'Why Aron cry?'

'His death wasn't important enough to be probed by reporters like me. But you — you'll be a shooting star, my son.' Aron wept helplessly. 'You're already dead.'

'Jerry not dead.' Shahid pointed at the immortal mouse. Since that didn't console him, he placed a hand on the man's left shoulder and patted him tentatively. Then he teased the picture out of the man's grasp.

Aron was sobbing so loudly that he didn't hear the boy at first.

Shahid repeated softly: 'Abi. That is Abi. Nice Abi.'

Aron fought back the tears as he tried to focus on what the boy had just said.

In a frustrating mixture of body language and very basic and extremely broken English, Shahid told him that Avi had taught him suicide chess. If it was astonishing to the extreme that the boy should have known his Avi, it was downright mystifying to think that an Israeli soldier would be playing chess with a Palestinian boy.

In the event, Aron was deprived of the extra time he needed to investigate Shahid's connection with Avi. Mr Wolf came in the middle of the night to swoop up the sleeping child in his massive hands. Standing at the door, his master said, 'His name will soon be on everyone's lips.'

'What if he fails his suicide mission?' Aron said desperately. 'Will you call him a dog instead?'

Amo narrowed his eyes on him.

'That's what you called Shahed Zeitouni. You called him a dog because he failed you.'

Amo spoke very slowly. 'Shahed Zeitouni was a dog because he worked against me.'

Aron was confused. 'No. You sent him. My son stopped him and that's why he died. You killed Avi.'

He shook his head; his ski mask was a pale grey in this light. 'I'm afraid not,' he said, 'much as I'd like to take the credit for the death of one more Israeli soldier.'

The two appeared at the Qalqiliya gate at 2:30 am, as father and son, and squinted when the torches were shone in their faces. By contrast, the two soldiers on the other side remained dark silhouettes.

The father placed a protective arm over the son.

The lights danced briefly to take in the father's suitcase, the boy's backpack and the clothes they were wearing before returning to their faces.

'Do you speak English?' It was a woman's voice.

'No. I doesn't speak English,' he replied.

'*Ivreet?*' she tried.

'*Lo.*'

Both torches lit up the boy's face; he looked particularly frightened.

Her light returned to the father's face, his lingered a while longer on the boy. 'All Arab kids look the same.'

'Keep your voice down,' ordered the other soldier, adding, 'I guess you'd better open the gate to Hell for these two.'

Bernadette was a latter-day crusader. It pained her that Papa could not see that. That she could not tell a Kalashnikov from a Molotov did not make her any less militant; that their fights should be diametrically opposed did not make her an inferior warrior. Her battles were neither for a deity nor for a national identity. Her defence of the Maronite Mount Lebanon was not limited to that particular community and nor was it contained in that precise geographical area. It applied equally strongly to the Shiite south, Sunni north, Greek Orthodox centre and, beyond the borders, to the myriad of other communities scattered around the Middle East. Others branded her a Marxist for her outspoken views on Western nationalism, but in truth she was a communitist, not a communist. Socialist structures and institutions were just as much a product of Western nationalism and were, if anything, even more repressive of minorities.

In the two historical and opposed models of governance — Roman versus Ottoman and Austro-Hungarian — she fought with the underdog: the latter two empires that had left economic and social issues firmly under the authority of individual communities. In the Roman model, a community that was at odds with the ruling political majority was labelled *communitas non grata* and was suppressed often violently through pogroms for the greater good of the majority and for the benefits that came from nation-building endeavours. Arabs had never wanted to build nations and, fundamentally, the West's war on terrorism was simply about failing to understand that.

In a sense, Bernadette's transformation was the antithesis of Mémé's Alzheimer's: it was a gradual stitching of the neural networks that progressed from the unquestioning hero-worship of a little girl, to the denial of late childhood, to the deep revulsion of the teen years. Papa was no less disfigured than the Palestinians who had massacred her mother and younger brother; the PLO killers, by reverse extension, were no more monstrous than the man who had given her life.

She had a barely cognizant Mémé to thank for the final transformation. It was as Bernadette braved the uncharted shantytown of Sabra to retrieve her grandmother that, unwittingly, she found a way to reconcile the mass murderer with the parent who had held her for three straight days and nights during a severe dose of German measles, a way to focus on the man who still wept in secret over the loss of his wife and child rather than on the madman who could so deliberately aim at Muslim women and children.

Beirutis had become all but Westernized. During her confused walkabout through the capital in her pink nightie and slippers, Mémé had been as likely to find a helpful stranger as on the streets and boulevards of Paris, London or New York. It was left to the poorest of the poor to dress her in old but warm clothes and to share their cramped space and limited food with her. Mémé had found care in Sabra: an isolated island of the Ottoman model in a Roman ocean.

When Bernadette asked the matriarch what had motivated her to adopt Mémé, her question was greeted with real surprise: 'Wouldn't you have done the same thing, Barnitat, had you found me wandering all alone in my nightie speaking Frankish?' To purely Arab ears, all foreign languages sounded like Frankish. 'We have to look after others like we do our own no matter their age and their sickness.'

It was a revelation for Bernadette. She had grown up accepting that the modern world equated automatically with progress. But this great-grandmother of refugees described a life that was as far removed from the West as you could possibly find: they dressed as their forebears, prepared their food according to timeless recipes handed down from mother to daughter, and respected other communities as they did their own and as their ancestors had instructed.

On three separate occasions, Papa gave three separate reasons why he couldn't attend her graduation ceremony.

Bernadette couldn't face being surrounded by the proud parents of fellow graduands so she gained her degree in absentia. It especially pained her that Papa had never realized how good her English had become.

But Papa gave only one reason to explain why he couldn't attend his mother's funeral, and all his friends and most of Mémé's were equally absent. In the case of Mémé's friends, this was down to the fact that they were mainly ill, senile or similarly dead. But for Papa and his former brothers-in-arms, the unwritten rules of engagement prevented them absolutely from mingling with the enemy, even for the purpose of honouring the dead.

However, the Church of the Refugees was full nonetheless with bona fide refugees. An entire Muslim Arab tribe retraced Mémé's final journey, walking halfway across town to pay their final respects to the Lady who had been one of theirs for only twenty-two days.

At the kiss of peace, Bernadette shook the hands of her new friends and, since they would not understand the Aramaic equivalent, she said, '*As-salaam a'aleykom.*'

Aron's captors would never let him leave his cell, and he had run out of articles to write for them. Where before he had suspected that the leader of al-Aqsa Squad would not live up to his word and set him free, he now knew it to be a fact. Aron was already dead and decapitated in Amo's eyes.

The first story on Shahid was a masterpiece and yet Amo had actually preferred the second story, the profile that revealed a bit too much about him. To Aron, the second piece almost read like an obituary, summing up a lifetime's achievements with little analysis.

It occurred to him just then that perhaps that had been Amo's intention all along. The second article was pork; the terrorist leader was keeping it in reserve for the days following his own death rather than Shahid's.

It wasn't therefore a big deal if he revealed too much about his life since the piece would be made public posthumously and since, more to the point, Aron would have been the ghost writer in more ways than one.

Aron sat at the table and reread his story with rising anger and recrimination.

He stared with resentment at the passage that described how Amo went about recruiting child suicide bombers: always on the lookout for candidates wherever the predator could find them, vetting them as they played on the streets, threw stones at tanks or emerged onto balconies to smoke cigarettes surreptitiously. He would recognize potential martyrs from their behaviour and expression. He was drawn to a particular type: he looked for sadness in the eyes, a sense of craving to belong and to be loved. But just as importantly, the child's body language had to appear aggressive or uncaring; it was 'pointless getting melancholic wretches who could only cry like babies'.

Later, Amo would befriend the child, would explore the boy's background to see if he had experienced any tragedies such as the loss of a parent or the demolition of a home, and whether he had a grasp of the Koran. The ideal candidate — one who could be fashioned into a *shahid* — would know real grief and little Islam beyond the virgin brides in heaven.

And finally the training itself for the 'budding squaddy' — how he now loathed that he'd come up with that, changing into almost quaint what was horribly grotesque: practise walking and running with several kilogrammes of Semtex around their middles.

Officially, the little boy Shahid would soon die, killing innocent bystanders in the process, to ignite a third intifada. And Aron too would die, in this hellhole, as just another Western hostage.

He stared furiously at the copper tray on the floor. A cockroach paused to wave its antennae cautiously before scuttling across the room and slipping under the door. This was soon followed by the sound of a boot stamping on the ground. Grrr-grrr was there, thought Aron bitterly, on the other side of the locked door.

'Hey!' he shouted. 'Can you take this fucking tray away?' He kicked the tray, causing it to crash against the wall. It made such a satisfying clanging sound that he kicked it several times.

He reached down to hold it firmly in both hands. 'Stupid fucking tray.' It was heavy, but he was angrier. He started to bash the table with it and all the chairs to a gratifying din.

He moved to the living room area and struck the shelves and the TV, denting everything he could.

He was so absorbed in his mad vandalism that he didn't notice that the burly man had entered the den.

He turned and saw him now.

It all happened suddenly.

'Grrr-grrr!' Aron roared like a lion, his heart pounding.

The burly man took two giant strides towards him, preparing to strike him down with his massive arms.

Aron yelled the only Arabic he knew, '*Mish ra-mout laan rayekh dirghe al-janna.*'

For barely a second, the man looked at him with a mixture of amazement and confusion.

And in that split second, Aron lunged to do the only thing possible — he swung the copper tray straight into the man's balaclava helmet. The head spun round like a toy, but the man was still on his feet, so Aron struck him again and again, looking to cause a dent in the head. Even when the man finally collapsed with a loud thud, Aron kept hitting him until a constellation of stars swam by.

In the end, it was a sudden coughing fit that caused him to stop.

He dropped the tray in shock and saw the man's blood seeping through the mask to end in a pool by Aron's feet.

The door to his cell was now open and he sprinted towards it. He paused to peer very cautiously outside at a landing. There was another door opposite that was shut and a stairwell, with steps leading only up. There was the dimmest light from a small bulb on the landing and he had to fumble to climb the stairs. He didn't mind, though, as the obscurity would conceal him from any other roving wolves.

It grew progressively lighter until he reached the ground floor where he saw the daylight, blinked several times dazed, and realized with a start where he was. It was his point of departure — the same derelict building where, on the second floor, a *padiatrist* practised his brand of medicine.

He must have been driven around in the boot just to disorient him. But he didn't pause to consider that any further. With only a quick backward glance at the stairwell from where he'd emerged, he hurried outside and ran all the way back to Hotel Baghdad.

He sprinted as, behind him, the muezzin's call boomed out of the central mosque's loudspeakers to call the faithful to the afternoon prayer, when shadows were exactly as tall as the objects that cast them.

15

SHEENA BARAN MARCHED down the hill from the base to stand at the Qalqiliya gate with Corporals Sharett and Lavan, the two soldiers on checkpoint duty.

Hillel Lavan stiffened when he saw her and gave her a half-hearted salute.

Caleb Sharett flashed a smile of perfect white teeth. 'How's it hanging, Sheena?' he asked in his strongly-accented English. 'You get much sleep?'

'How's it,' she responded automatically, which was how friends greeted one another in South Africa. Then she added in Hebrew, 'You haven't seen that English journalist around have you?'

Sharett shook his head.

Their exchange in English and especially their conspiratorial looks caused Lavan to regard them with distaste. She caught his air and he turned his attention to an old Peugeot that was serving as a communal taxi.

'Lavan,' she called out. 'You missed one.' Lavan had collected the identity cards of all six adults in the car and was about to check them. He glanced at her questioningly as she indicated a little girl in the back seat.

He spoke to the driver in Arabic who turned to the girl's mother who ferreted in her bag for the missing document, found it and handed it over to the driver who passed it on to Lavan. Everyone in the car looked at Sheena with a glazed expression, even the doll in the little girl's hands.

But she ignored them as she took in the line of cars. The fifth car waiting patiently to enter Qalqiliya had UN plates. Unlike her dislike of the media, her deep resentment of the United Nations was not remotely veiled. It was a world body that was Arab or sympathetic to Arabs from its twisted horns to its scaly tail.

There was an IDF directive to check all UNRWA vehicles thoroughly. This was issued some two years ago when an UNRWA ambulance travelling in Gaza was found to be transporting explosives rather than a woman in the throes of labour as the driver had claimed. In fact, a week after that directive was issued, Sheena had had her own experience with a pregnant Arab who had died at the checkpoint. At least that woman with the kafir husband had been genuinely in the throes of labour.

The car with the UN plates was now third in line; Sheena stared at the female driver.

She was clearly local staff and her face looked vaguely like the pregnant woman's.

Bernadette had given up waiting for Lounger's call and decided to confront him instead at his hotel and tell him of the emails she'd read that pointed to Shahed's innocence. She was doing it out of duty for Imm Nidal and because of her feelings for Shahed himself; she was certainly not doing it for Aron's green eyes.

There were three Israeli soldiers at the Qalqiliya gate — two men and a woman — and Bernadette recognized one of the men.

She grinned and said, 'Hello, Hillel, and how are you today?'

He looked at her oddly as he asked for her papers.

'My papers?' she said with surprise. 'You know them by heart, don't you?' She handed them over.

Sheena asked in Hebrew, 'What's she saying?'

'She wants to know when the gate will be shut today, ma'am,' replied Lavan.

'Just check her boot,' she ordered Lavan.

'Hey, maybe she needs a full body search,' Sharett sniggered. 'When does she open her gate? Go on ask her, Lavan.'

Hillel hesitated and then said gently, 'Would you mind opening the boot for us, Bernadat?'

As he moved to the back of the car he knocked into Sharett's shoulder.

'Cool it, *bayit-pagom*,' he said, adding to Sheena in English, 'She must be his girlfriend. Maybe he plans to see her later.'

Bernadette stared at him blankly.

Sharett chuckled. 'Shame they don't talk English.'

But by the time Lavan returned with her papers after a perfunctory search of the boot, her hands had formed tight fists and her lips had curled all the way back.

Hillel handed back her papers and nodded formally to admit her. Then, speaking under his breath, he said spitefully, 'Ashkenazim bring us nothing but shame.'

Bernadette looked at him crossly. 'I believe he's one of yours, Mr Lavan' she said finally as she sped off into Qalqiliya.

'Caleb, come with me into town,' Sheena said. 'We need to check if the Limey has checked out of his hotel.'

'Oh man, I hate going to that shithole.'

Sharett stared at the car with the UN plates that accelerated away from the checkpoint and casually waved the next car into Qalqiliya without bothering to search the boot or even to look at the occupants. Then he climbed into a jeep and waited for his captain.

On the rise above them, the bulldozer had now gone — only the tank remained, its gun aimed immutably at the town.

There were several hours left before sunset. Therefore, by Hebraic reckoning, 8 Av 5764 would soon come to an end with the sun's dying embers, marking the beginning of *Tisha B'Av* and the lowest point in the Jewish calendar. For traditionalists like Józsi, the mourning that had grown in intensity since 1 Av peaked on 9 Av.

It wasn't quite *Tisha B'Av*, but it was already the third worst day in Aron's life.

He had just killed a man.

A brute, a terrorist, a mute monster who would otherwise have killed him, but also a man. He had caused the death of a human being, who had been left on the floor for all the insects in the world.

He stared blankly out of the window in his hotel room, his mind replaying the nightmare of the past eight days, with its haunting end projected in slow motion. His peripheral vision spotted a military jeep pull up at the hotel. He turned slightly to focus on the captain and the corporal, and then he picked up his packed bag, which had been waiting for him all this time in his room, and rushed downstairs to meet them.

He needed to tell the IDF about Shahid.

They met in the lobby. 'Mr Lounger,' said Sheena with surprise and a trace of irritation, 'you've been absent for over a week. We thought you'd finished your story and left without saying goodbye.'

'I need your protection and your help.' His heart was still pounding and the vision of the pool of blood caught in freeze-frame came back to stab him.

He looked unwashed and had let his beard grow into a fine fuzz. Were it not for his green eyes, he could have passed for an Arab just then. 'I think we've already gone out of our way to help you, Mr Lounger,' she said coldly.

Aron switched to Hebrew, 'I need the army to protect me and to find a boy, a young child.'

'You speak Hebrew,' gasped Sharett, repeating unnecessarily to Sheena, '*Hoo m'daber ivreet.*'

Her eyes narrowed. 'Who are you?' asked Sheena.

'I'm an Israeli citizen.' The image of the young Shahid came to him as did, inevitably, that of the dead Mr Wolf. 'I need the IDF to find the boy — it's a matter of life and death.'

Sharett had trouble seeing him as anything other than a British journalist. 'But what about your feature on the IDF, man?' he asked incredulously in English. 'What about the story on Avi Lunzer?'

'I've written three stories since I've been here,' he told them in Hebrew. 'And not one of them is about my son, Avi.'

'Your son?' Sheena was too stunned to think clearly.

'Fuck me sideways,' breathed Sharett.

It was at that moment that Bernadette stepped into the lobby. Aron spotted her behind the soldiers and switched back to English. 'My name is Aron Lunzer. Avi was my son.'

Bernadette was about to turn away, but what he said next caused her to freeze in her tracks.

'I was held hostage by al-Aqsa Squad — they almost killed me. They've groomed a boy to become the world's youngest suicide bomber. We've got to find him before it's too late,' he pleaded. 'I can describe him.'

Sheena needed to take control of the situation. 'Since you claim to be an Israeli citizen,' she said frostily, 'I'm going to need to see your passport. And your British passport as well.'

He took them out of his bag and handed them to her.

'And you're going to have to come with us.'

'Of course,' he said immediately. Mr Wolf would soon have friends baying for his blood. 'If you have an artist in the camp we could work on a sketch of the child.'

'This isn't Hollywood, Mr Loun — Lunzer,' she corrected herself.

'But the IDF must find him,' exclaimed Aron. 'They're going to use him for a massive suicide mission to ignite a third intifada.'

'How do you know?' she asked suspiciously.

'They made me write his story,' he admitted.

'How did you escape?'

Aron blinked nervously. 'They let me go when I finished writing for them.'

'The Arab Islamists just let you walk out the front door?' said Sheena with disbelief, tossing his passports back at him.

'Pants on fire,' agreed Sharett with a chortle.

'So where are they? Where were you held?'

'I don't know. They gagged and blindfolded me and tied me up in the boot of a car,' he replied — that part at least was true. 'They dumped me outside the hotel.' He wasn't at all prepared to tell them about the man he'd killed. 'But it's the child you need to be looking for,' he added passionately. 'He's a small kid, looks half starved and has huge shiners.'

'That's every other Arab kid in the West Bank,' she stated coldly. 'So assuming, just for a second, that your gut feeling about a suicide attack is right — '

'It's not a bleeding gut feeling,' he retorted.

' — do you know their target?'

'No.'

'Can you describe their leader?'

He shook his head.

'Or any other member of the group?'

He hadn't dared to look under the burly man's blood-soaked mask. He said quickly, 'But that's why the boy's description is so important.'

Bernadette chose that moment to step in. 'I can help.'

The soldiers spun around to look at her with complete surprise.

'UNRWA has an e-fit program. We often need to release facial composites of missing people,' she said. 'I can help you with the sketch of the boy, Mr Lunzer.'

'She talks English,' gasped Sharett.

'Yes,' said Aron with a thin smile. 'She *speaks* English considerably better than you do.'

Sheena crossed her arms. 'I don't think much of your game of deceit,' she told him. 'You should have told us you were Private Lunzer's father.' Her tone softened marginally and a hand moved to wave him to the exit. 'But you are Israeli and we'll make sure you get back home safely. Come with us, Mr Lunzer.'

Aron hesitated and looked at both women.

Eventually, he shook his head and said to Bernadette, 'Let's go see that artist of yours.'

Sheena stiffened, her open hand closing into a fist. 'I am disappointed in you, Mr Lunzer — you of all the journalists.

And to think I used to love your columns in *Adlai*.' She went on to warn him, 'You're in violation of the IDF ban on Israeli citizens. You have twenty-four hours to get out of the West Bank or you'll be under arrest.' Sheena turned smartly on her heels. 'Come on, Caleb, our work here is done.'

Sharett brushed past Aron and almost whispered to Bernadette, 'I'll be seeing you.'

'*Zil bashlama waqree shlamé lawahayk,*' she replied.

'I don't talk Arab.'

'It's not Arabic,' she said evenly. 'It's Aramaic for "Go in peace and give my best to your parents."'

At first the e-fit computer program generated a face that looked more like a flabby middle-aged man than a shrunken boy. But as the shapes, sizes and positions of each facial feature were altered, the picture gradually evolved into an approximate representation of Shahid.

'The eyes are wrong,' said Aron. He brought to mind the image of Shahid while Mr Wolf prepared to sever his throat with a cleaver. 'They were darker and more slanted, and big shiners the size of plums.'

The UNRWA operator opened various windows for Aron to select the eyes from screens of alternatives. He added the shiners, olive complexion, gaunt expression and even the oddly shaped mouth that — in a grin — would stretch from ear to ear.

'That's better,' he said. 'But the hair needs to be longer. Way longer and scruffier — you can't really see his ears.'

Eventually, when they had a sketch that Aron was reasonably sure matched the boy's features, he asked Bernadette, 'Do you recognize him? I first saw him with you in that Internet café. You must have seen him.'

She shook her head.

'But you do believe me, don't you?' he appealed.

Bernadette was captivated by his expressive green eyes: they were now so hopelessly miserable that she longed to comfort them. She nodded. 'Yes.' She allowed a sad smile to appear. 'I should have seen that you have more angles than Pythagoras.'

He looked into her eyes; they were 100 per cent tender.

'I'm truly sorry about your son.' She made a mental note that there was no longer any point of talking about Shahed's emails.

The operator printed out the image and handed it to her. 'Could you also email it to me,' she asked him, adding to Aron, 'I'll forward it straight away to IDF central command.'

Aron nodded distractedly. 'He's just a little boy. A little boy I was unable to help.' His voice cracked suddenly with pent-up emotion. 'You can't see that in the eyes,' he said, indicating the printout in her hands. 'You can't begin to see the level of abuse he's had to suffer from both Arabs and Israelis.' He recalled his background notes on Shahid.

She resisted the urge to reach over to squeeze his hand.

He was suddenly feeling extraordinarily tired. He sat back in his seat and stretched out his legs. He closed his eyes as the picture that Amo wanted to run with the piece now floated into his mind, with its line of brooms in sharp focus. 'Bloody brooms,' he sighed.

'Sorry?'

The image was replaced by another — drawn purely from his imagination — of Avi in the uniform of an IDF soldier teaching the boy suicide chess. Shahid was not *his* boy in the way Avi was *his* Avi. 'I don't know his real name — they call him Shahid. But we should tell the army to check out the Brahimi farm — that's where he used to live. Maybe he's gone back there.'

'Did you say Brahimi?' exclaimed Bernadette.

'Yes.' He needed to come clean and tell the IDF about the basement flat in the padiatrist's building and about the man they would find on the floor with a head full of copper. They would understand, he felt, and besides *aleph* males like Sharett would probably only congratulate him for the manslaughter of a terrorist. 'Could you tell them for me?' Aron rubbed his eyes. He'd never felt so dizzy in his life. He needed to sleep to stop his mind from spinning like a gyroscope. 'Can I stay with you tonight?' he asked. 'I don't know where else to go. I'll leave tomorrow — I have to.'

She didn't seem to be quite listening. 'Mohsen,' she said almost to herself as she peered at the composite image. 'Is this what you look like?' She added incredulously to Aron, 'I'm also looking for the Brahimi orphan.'

As she drove him the short distance from the UNRWA headquarters to her flat in town, she told him about her mission to find the boy, but he was too tired to listen. And once they were inside, Aron collapsed on a sofa and muttered,

'*Mish ra-mout laan rayekh dirghe al-janna.*'

The accent was appalling, but it was intelligible Arabic. Of the three versions of Arabic, this was the one Bernadette was most at ease with and so she responded, 'Well, I'd rather you didn't tonight.'

'Hmm?'

'Heaven,' she said to him. 'Well you can't die on my sofa.'

He sat up abruptly and looked at her bewildered. 'What?'

A small smile appeared on her face. She repeated what he'd said in her colloquial Arabic. 'You really don't have a clue, do you?'

'What does it mean?'

'I'm not going to die because I'll go straight to heaven.' She paused and then asked him, 'Why would you say that?'

Aron winced 'Shahid said it.' He paused to think about that. 'Heaven?' he repeated, adding sombrely, 'But that kid isn't going to heaven. He isn't even going to end up in a coffin. He's just going to be despised by the thousands who will have lost their loved ones.' He paused again. 'By people like me, you see. My wife and son are martyrs of the state.'

He shook his head weakly.

Bernadette couldn't resist it any longer; her hand reached over to hold his.

'No, don't,' he warned but made no effort to remove his hands from hers. 'I'm the common denominator. I make things cancel and disappear.'

He'd yelled it at the burly man before striking him down with the copper tray.

It was as if his eyes were connected directly to his hand because the more pressure she applied, squeezing warmly, the more his eyes filled up with tears. 'I killed a man today,' he confessed and told her about Mr Wolf who had almost cut his throat twice with a cleaver.

'I'm Aron Lunzer, don't you see?' he moaned finally. 'I'm the cockroach in the room. Don't get too close to me or you might die as well — just like my wife and my son. Just like Shahid.'

She spoke very softly, 'Aron Lunzer is not cockroach.'

'And how would you know?'

'Because were life to imitate art, Aron Lunzer would not look grotesque on the outside.'

Aron was too tired to recognize the words at first.

She continued: 'Aron does not have a crooked nose and dishevelled aspect. And he is not stooped with unthinking subservience in his role of sidekick to the Archvillain: Abaddon to the Devil.'

The words sounded familiar from a deeper past.

'Because Aron Lunzer is in fact a beautiful man.'

He stared at her helplessly.

She nodded. 'My full name is Bernadette Antoine Shakour. I am the daughter of the Butcher of Sabra.'

'You can't be,' he stammered. 'You're,' he struggled to find the suitable word, 'good.'

She used both hands to pull his to her lips and said, '*Shlomo.*' Then she leaned over to place her arms around his neck and gave him a deep kiss.

Sheena Baran

Shabriri
Angel of blindness

16

Colonel Habib Ami entered Sheena's office with a fax, which he dropped on her desk. 'We need to talk,' he said to her.

She glanced at the sheet of paper. The fax was a composite facial of a child, and at the bottom of the sheet were the words:

Courtesy of the United Nations Relief and Works Agency for Palestine Refugees in the Near East (UNRWA).

'Sure, Habib. What's on your mind?' She looked up from her desk as he paused at the window to stare out at the base, his hands behind his back.

'We've received a directive from central command about a suicide attack,' he said at length.

'Well, what's new?' Intelligence reports on potential terrorist missions came in so frequently they sometimes felt like corporate newsletters.

'This one's big apparently.' Ami turned away from the window and began to pace the room. 'It involves our district.' He indicated the fax. 'And that young boy is the suicide bomber.' He shook his head. 'What a mad, sad world.' He stopped at the wall behind her desk where a panoramic photograph had caught his attention.

Sheena peered at the composite image and moved it to the sunlight so she could have a better look.

'Is that what constitutes IDF intelligence these days?' she said sceptically. 'Tipoffs from UNRWA?'

'The brass wants us to look into this anyway.' Indicating the grinning girl in the picture, he stated, 'You haven't changed much.' It was a picture of a very young and very blond girl with freckles standing with her hand on a signpost while behind her in the background stretched what appeared to be a pristine sandy beach.

Sheena glanced only briefly at the picture of her younger self. 'He looks like every other Arab kid,' she argued. 'Are we supposed to detain every Arab boy in Qalqiliya simply to satisfy some biased female recruit of UNRWA?'

'What female?'

'I already know about this,' she said. 'It's a cockamamie story that was drummed up by that English journalist who's in cahoots with her. Do you remember him?'

'The *goi* who couldn't breathe our air?'

She nodded. 'Turns out the *goi* isn't actually a *goi*. He's Israeli — Aron Lunzer's his name.'

'Lunzer?' he said with a frown.

'That's right. Private Avi Lunzer's father.'

The colonel's frown deepened. 'Why would he pretend to be — '

She finished off his sentence. ' — an English journalist called Arnold Lounger?' She nodded. 'Because he's convinced that his son's tragic death was part of a greater plot. So rather than grieve for his son like an honourable man, he lied his way into the West Bank and into our base to shit-stir.' She paused. 'That story of a child bomber — honestly, pure bull. I'll write a report about that if you need it.'

He nodded, turned to look at the picture again and said, 'Good piece of investigative work, Sheena. Where's the journalist now?'

'I sent him packing.'

'Shame. We should have locked him up and thrown away the key,' he said, joking.

'Yes.' She wasn't smiling.

The colonel pointed at the picture on the wall. 'Where was it taken?' he asked.

'Just down the road from my hometown in South Africa.'

When Sheena lived in the Cape Province, there was only one golden rule for using the beach outside East London. It was posted on a large, rusted signpost where the rocks gave way abruptly to the white sand and snowy surf

of the Indian Ocean. The one rule, written in bold black
capitals and in three languages, read:

THIS BEACH	OLULWANDLE	HIERDIE STRAND
AND AMENITIES	KUNYE NEZINTO	EN GERIEWE
THEREOF	EZISETYENZISWAYO	DAARVAN IS VIR
RESERVED FOR	ZIGGINELWE	DIE UISLUITENDE
EXCLUSIVE	ABAMHLOPHE	GEBRUIK VAN
USE OF	BODWA. NGOKO	BLANKES
WHITE PERSONS	MTHETHO. ISIBA	AANGEWYS
BY ORDER	WE DOLOPHU	OP LAS
J.J. HUMAN	J.J. HUMAN	J.J. HUMAN
TOWN CLERK		STADSKLERK

'What are the other two languages?' he asked.

'Xhosa and Afrikaans.'

'Kosa?' said Ami, intrigued.

Sheena repeated the hardest of the three Bantu clicks,
'Xhosa.'

He made no attempt to click his tongue as he remarked,
'There's no Kosa for town clerk.'

'Bantu languages are less sophisticated,' she said, matter-
of-fact. 'There are huge gaps in their dictionaries.'

'But isn't there a Kosa for human?'

'That's a South African surname, Habib,' she said. 'It
doesn't need to be translated.'

'It's an interesting picture,' he said finally, adding, 'Write
that report, but don't make it too intelligent. I wouldn't want
to lose you to central command.'

She smiled as he stepped out of her office and gazed distractedly at the wall.

Next to the picture were *Arafat's rules of engagement* and another sheet of paper with the heading: 'The Palestinian Theorem'. Sheena had come up with the formula, which, she found, had an algebraic beauty all of its own:

The more belligerent the Arabs are (y) = The more land they lose (x).

From the dark days of the partition, when the colonial powers ruled that Israel should consist of little more than a fraction of historic Palestine, the state had progressively acquired more land only thanks to the wars sparked by Arabs, albeit with some behind-the-scenes blessings and encouragement by Zionist groups.

The trick to retaining the land was to make Israel always appear as the victim in the conflict, so that any reaction to Arab violence would be perceived as being wholly justified. The war that followed the declaration of independence, the Six-Day War and the Yom Kippur War all followed the same template and served the Israeli cause.

The one hiccup was the Israeli involvement in South Lebanon, a territory that was not on any Zionist map and therefore a mistake as far as Sheena and others in her party were concerned.

The intifadas, too, were good news for those who could read the situation and appreciate the general trends beyond the immediate loss of life and property.

The more suicide bombers detonated their charges in Israeli towns and cities, the more land could be Israelized under the mantle of security necessities.

The separation barrier across the West Bank was only a first step on the agenda. It permitted the authorities to confiscate land, which would eventually be redistributed among Israeli families. But the barrier had proved more effective in keeping out terrorists than many had hoped. Certainly in terms of large-scale attacks in Israel proper, the second intifada was fizzling out.

According to Aron Lunzer, the next attack would kindle a third uprising. Sheena doubted that. Just as she hoped for a wider regional war but doubted that Arabs would ever get off their collective arses. They were just full of hot air. Nothing short of a direct Israeli strike on Mecca could ever provoke Muslims into a regional war. And unfortunately, in this day and age, such a direct approach would only have negative consequences for the nation.

Her gaze returned to the picture.

That photograph was perfect. It had nothing to do with technique or lighting. You didn't need to see an image of destruction to be moved. In fact a real photograph, worthy of its frame and its pride of place as one of the most cherished possessions, had to be a private affair: a shared secret, a buried moment in a secluded alcove that only the photographer and subject could revive.

A good picture was immortal for its snapshot of oneness. There was the past and the future during which photographer and subject lived different lives across generations in separate continents and with diverse impulses, tastes and motivations. But in that one, infinitesimal moment, the photographer — her English teacher and friend of the family — and subject were truly one, feeling the warmth of the same African morning sun on their bodies, hearing the identical waves that crashed on the shore.

That image of a very young Sheena was worth a thousand memories and as many emotions. She still remembered how she'd tried to appear as glamorous and seductive as the women in her mother's magazines.

Immortality meant taking your secrets to the grave with you.

They left her flat together in the morning just after the end of curfew and drove the short distance to the UNRWA headquarters where he had left his rental car. They popped into her office just long enough to print out a batch of the boy's facial composite, which was now framed by the question 'Have you seen him?' in Arabic and Hebrew, and UNRWA's contact number. They divided the stack of sheets between them and each carried their pile to their respective cars.

There was an uneasy moment when they couldn't decide whether to kiss or shake hands.

Bernadette made the first move and opted for a peck on the cheek. 'You're not coughing,' she remarked. 'Have you made my mother's cure?'

Aron cleared his throat and found it surprisingly free of phlegm. 'Partly, I suppose,' he said. 'No meat, puddings and pies for me — in fact no real food for over a week. Thank you for that as well.'

Bernadette accepted his thanks with a quick grin.

'I don't suppose they'll ever let me back into the West Bank,' he said with a humourless chuckle. 'I've probably been blacklisted to high heaven.' He stepped into his car.

In fact, Aron wasn't going very far at all. He was going to try to stay in Matan, the first town on the Israeli side of the wall — a mere two kilometres away from Qalqiliya. At little over a stone throw's distance, he was staying as geographically close as he was legally entitled. Moreover, they had decided in the night that while Bernadette would continue to search for the boy in the West Bank, it made sense for him to cover Israel, particularly the closest border crossing.

'So you'll have to come over if you get any news of Shahid,' he said.

'I need special passes and permits for the West Bank and I can get those. But even with my UN laissez passer, I'll need a formal invitation from an Israeli citizen. Someone who'll be responsible for me.'

Aron didn't hesitate. 'Then consider yourself formally invited.'

They drove in the same direction for a while, down empty steets, until they reached the main intersection leading out of town. She watched him turn east to the Qalqiliya gate while she headed in the opposite direction to drive an even shorter distance to the Int@rnet café.

The manager was just opening his shop when she arrived and he greeted her warmly and offered her a coffee which she declined politely.

He shook his head at the e-fit picture of Mohsen.

'Are you absolutely sure?' she asked. 'He was seen here last week. Are you sure you've never seen him before? He's in terrible danger.'

'No, I'm sorry.'

Indicating the entrance to the Int@rnet café, she asked, 'Could I stick one up on your door?' she added, 'And maybe you could ask all the children who come here today if they've seen him.'

He nodded. He wanted to talk to her about UNRWA's plans to turn his shop into a technology community centre, but she was already walking back to her car.

'I have to go to Ramallah now,' she said. 'I'll be back this afternoon. But please phone me immediately if you hear anything about this boy.' She was back in her car and lowered her window to call out, 'By the way, maybe this afternoon you wouldn't mind if I looked at the computer Shahed used?'

'Shahed?' said the man with a frown. 'Why?'

'There's something I need to check.' She smiled at him and gave him a little wave.

Travelling through the Palestinian bantustans between Qalqiliya and Ramallah, a trip of approximately forty kilometres, involved crossing sixteen checkpoints and a three-hour journey.

It was the same road, along the groves and orchards of the West Bank, that Bernadette took every month to deliver the financial assistance to Imm Nidal. Given that it had only been a week since the last payment, Imm Nidal opened the door and immediately asked, 'Do you have news of my boy?'

'No, Imm Nidal,' she replied and showing her the facial composite, she said, 'But is that him?' She had driven all this way to identify the boy, to make sure that the child called Shahid and Mohsen Brahimi were one and the same.

'*Bismillah!*' moaned Imm Nidal. 'What have you done to his face?'

Bernadette explained gently that it wasn't a real picture.

'But you have turned him into a fiend, Bernaytat!' She was inconsolable. 'I want my *qareen*, not this fake idol.'

'Since we don't have a picture of him,' said Bernadette, 'an artist drew this to help us find him.'

'We know that Satan is incompetent.'

She still hadn't actually identified the boy, so Bernadette said, 'Is this *very* rougly what Mohsen looks like?'

'No, no, no, Bernaytat,' replied Imm Nidal miserably. 'That is *exactly* what Mohsen looks like if Dastmastur has twisted him.'

Bernadette stayed briefly, just long enough for some sweet tea.

Sitting on the bed in the cheerless living room, Imm Nidal asked why the picture had some Hebrew text.

'The Israeli army is helping us. And we will find him, Imm Nidal.' She couldn't tell her that her *qareen* had been recruited by al-Aqsa Squad to become the world's youngest suicide bomber. She remembered Mohsen's words to Aron and said, 'What would you say if someone claimed he wouldn't die because he'd go straight to heaven?'

'I would call that man a profaner,' said Imm Nidal without hesitation.

'Why?'

'Because everyone dies.'

Bernadette nodded; she hadn't inferred any hidden meaning either. She was getting ready to leave.

'Every child of Adam has to die before they see paradise. Except, of course, for the Prophet, peace and blessings be upon him.'

Bernadette frowned. 'The Prophet Muhammad didn't die before going to heaven?'

Imm Nidal forgave her ignorance; she was after all just a Christian.

'The Prophet, peace and blessings be upon him, is the only Muslim who visited heaven *before* his death. He rose up from the blessed al-Aqsa Mosque. That's why it is our third holiest site.'

Aron drove to Matan, a small border town where peak traffic consisted of a single school bus and the grocer's antiquated van.

He followed the van to the shop and showed the grocer the picture of Shahid.

The grocer shook his head warily.

'Could I stick this up on you window?' asked Aron.

The man shook his head again.

'It's a matter of life and death,' insisted Aron. 'The man who's with that boy is a suicide bomber.' He didn't want Shahid to be shot accidentally and besides, technically, he wasn't lying since it was the man rather than the child who actually wanted to kill innocent people. 'They might still be in or around Matan.'

He had a sudden coughing fit and reached for the inhaler.

The grocer didn't wait for his fit to pass. He opened a crate of tomatoes and carried it to the vegetable section of his shop.

Aron joined him presently. 'Your customers might have seen them.'

He looked up and, indicating the contact number on the sheet, he said coldly, 'Then you should have put the IDF ho-tline number.'

As the only retail outlet in town, the shop sold a bit of everything. Aron walked down the aisle that had stationery products to pick up a black marker pen and pointed at an old, second-hand cell phone under the glass counter. 'How much for these?'

He crossed out the UNRWA number on the sheet and added the IDF hotline as well as his new number.

When Aron asked if he could now stick the picture on the window, the grocer shook his head again. 'That's just for my promotions,' he said. He placed a hand on the counter. 'But you can leave it here.'

And he shook his head a fourth time when Aron asked where the nearest hotel was.

'The closest is in Kfar Saba,' he said, waving in a vague westerly direction. 'Not many tourists ever come to Matan.'

'What about hostels?'

'No. Only houses and farms.'

'Campsites? Chabads? Anything?'

The shopkeeper perked up suddenly. 'There are some houses available for short-term leases. I could get the real estate agent for you.'

'Yes, that would be fine.'

He went to the back of the shop and called to his wife. 'You've got a customer,' he shouted up the stairs.

He returned, picked up the sheet off the counter and said almost conspiratorially, 'Why don't we make an exception this time.'

Aron coughed a thank you.

While the grocer stuck Shahid's picture on his window, Aron gathered the ingredients to make Bernadette's cure for his cough: onions, garlic, olive oil, lemon juice and turmeric powder — he dispensed with the honey since he didn't need the mixture to taste good. He also bought a squeezy bottle, a flask with a rotating spout so that it was leak-proof when closed and squirtable when open. It was small — compact enough to fit snugly in his pocket — and clearly aimed at young schoolchildren to judge by the side sticker of a grinning teddy bear.

The grocer's wife cum estate agent noticed the flask. 'Will your family be joining you?' she asked. 'There's a beautiful house with lovely views of olive trees on the east side. It's a family home. It would be too big for just one person.'

'Let's go there.'

That morning, he stayed in his new accommodation just long enough to prepare Bernadette's recipe. He pounded and mixed all the ingredients, sniffed the resulting white substance, made a face and then forced himself to swallow a tablespoon full. It was too soon to know whether it was having its desired effect on his throat. But it seemed to clear up his head, so he poured the remaining liquid into the teddy bear flask. With the spout between his lips, he squeezed the plastic bottle and swallowed another dose, noting that this time there was a burning sensation as the milky liquid trickled its way down the gullet.

He got back into his car and drove northwards along the Green Line of the Six-Day War, stopping in every town and village to ask whether anyone had seen the child and to drop off his e-fit composite.

By the middle of the afternoon, he had driven so far north that he'd reached the banks of Lake Tiberias in Galilee. Since Lake Merom was now only a few kilometres north of there, along the narrow and winding route, he kept to his northerly bearing.

He decided to go to the Chabad to track down Krickstein, the *haredi* who had been on that last checkpoint duty with Avi and who had dropped out of *aleph*, moving down from red to reject.

He looked for him first at the lake itself, pausing briefly to stand at his spot and nod at his erstwhile grieving companion.

But Krickstein wasn't at the Chabad either. The rabbi was pleased to see Aron and thought, at first, that he had come to begin another session with them.

'No, my dear Aron,' he said once Aron had explained the purpose of his visit. 'Our brother made *baal teshuva* many months ago.' He went on to explain that Krickstein's 'master of return' had translated into a new mission: to teach the love for the Torah to young children in Netanya.

Aron wrote down the address and drove the 120 kilometres straight back to his rented accommodation in Matan — a trip that took him just under two hours.

It was early evening and his flask of Dustblaster was empty.

That was the name he'd given to Bernadette's recipe. Even if it was merely a placebo, the stuff was already doing wonders for his throat. He returned to the kitchen to make a second and bigger batch of Dustblaster. He briefly considered adding honey to the next batch and then, just as quickly, decided not to in case honey lessened the curative effect.

This time he poured the substance into a glass, in the absence of whisky, and sipped it as he moved to the living room.

For a while, he just sat and stared at his phone.

No one had phoned him about Shahid.

He dialled his number in Jerusalem almost to see if the second-hand mobile actually worked. He accessed the answering machine remotely and listened to several messages.

The first two were from Zach, his editor at *Adlai*, wanting to be called back as soon as Aron was ready to show the slightest sign of life. This was followed by a similar if sadder and less witty request from Józsi that sounded like an eleventh commandment.

In the fourth message, recorded perhaps a week after the first two, Zach sounded considerably less sympathetic: 'Hi Aron,' he heard. 'We're in the process of revamping the op-ed page and I need to know when we can expect to receive your contributions again. I've gone with a couple of best-of-Aron fillers but frankly the powers that be are on my case about re-runs. Would appreciate if you could find the time to call me back. Cheers.'

He was about to phone him, but then stopped and dialled Bernadette's number instead.

They were only a few kilometres apart and yet the reception was so poor that they could have been talking from different planets.

'Do you have any news?' Aron had to raise his voice because of the poor line.

Her response was mostly garbled, but he heard her mention al-Aqsa.

'What about al-Aqsa Squad?'

'No, Mosque.'

'No mask?' He now tried to picture Amo without the light blue ski mask or free of the disfiguring bruises as he posed with her father.

'Al-Aqsa Mosque. I've spoken to a Muslim friend — ' and the rest of her sentence was consumed by static. Then she was back again for a moment, 'And I need to tell you something about Shahed.'

'Shahid? Have they found him?'

'No, *Shahed*,' she had to shout. 'Shahed Zeitouni, the young — '

This time she was gone for good.

He tried calling her several times and cursed every time he got a busy signal.

He downed his Dustblaster and poured himself another.

Why had Bernadette mentioned Shahed Zeitouni? He was just the mad youth who had blown up his Avi. Yet, Amo — the god of fanatic lunatics — had called Shahed a dog. Why would he lie?

He tried Bernadette's phone one more time.

'Damn you!' he shouted and strangled the phone.

He dropped it on the floor and stared gloomily at it for a while.

Then he spread his notes out on the coffee table. Even though it had barely been a week ago, so much had happened since his capture by al-Aqsa Squad that they read as if they had been written by a different person altogether.

He turned his attention to one sheet in particular where he'd summed up the inconsistencies surrounding Avi's death.

1. You can hear the bulldozer from the base and yet few soldiers seem to have heard the explosion; most soldiers learn of Avi's death hours later during breakfast.

2. There is no high alert status that such an attack would ordinarily call for.

3. There is a rota of checkpoint duty whereby every soldier performs such a duty an average of twice a week and for three hours per shift. But on the night of 20/21 March, Avi and Krickstein are recorded as having manned the gate for a total of five and a half hours, from 11:00 pm on Saturday until 4:35 am on Sunday when Avi died (the checkpoint duty should have ended at 5:00 am). No reason is given for the double shift.

4. The Palestinian was stopped leaving Qalqiliya. But where was he going? If it was to bomb Alfe Menashe to avenge his father (the official line), then he should have started from the family farm outside the town to avoid the checkpoint.

5. And why not wait till 6:00 am and the end of curfew?

6. Where did he spend that Saturday night? Clearly not in the farm otherwise he'd have been stopped entering

Qalqiliya. Did he spend it in some secret hideout in town, a safe house for Hamas or al-Aqsa Martyrs' Brigade (or is it Squad)?

7. These terrorist organizations are usually quick to claim a victory when Israeli soldiers die. Why have none of them claimed responsibility for Avi's murder?

He picked up his pen and now wrote two more points:

8. Why did Amo call Shahed Zeitouni a dog?
9. When and where did Avi teach Shahid to play chess? And was Krickstein there?

He tried Bernadette's number again, but it was switched off. So he phoned his editor and immediately regretted it.

'Well if it isn't the prodigal son in person,' said Zach. 'Where the devil have you been? The production people here are squeezing my nuts and bolts about you and I'll be screwed if I have to wait again for you to call me. So, where are you?'

Aron wasn't given a chance to answer.

'I mean you're making me sweat, Aron. I'm already seven on the *Reek*ter scale. Pretty soon, I'll be the new Gamy. What's happening with you? Are you still with us? You've been through shit, Aron, and you know I've always backed you through thick and chunky. But I need something from you, anything to keep you on our payroll.'

'So I'm a supernova in *Adlai* one day, and a black dwarf the next?'

'It's been four months, Aron. You know how it hustles —
that's four years on a daily. Listen, if you're not feeling particularly inspired right now, I can help you with some ideas.'

There was an uneasy pause.

'Are you giving me a yellow card?' Aron asked at length.
It felt like a demotion from red *aleph*.

'We're way past yellow, my friend. You're out there on
the bench and I'm breaking my balls with the knobs to field
you again.'

'Well I've got a piece for you,' said Aron. 'An introspec-
tive on the IDF.'

'What?'

'A report on the slipping standards of the army,' explained
Aron. 'How the concept of purity of arms has been smeared.'

'We didn't commission that,' he said a bit coldly. 'I'll need
to take a look, but I hope it's not like something I'd read in
Haaretz.' He paused and then added more encouragingly, 'But
what I need right now are a thousand of your finest words by
tomorrow. The Shabbat edition will be an Egypt special for
Abdul-kader's visit. So write like an Egyptian. I'm easing you
back in. You could almost recycle that piece you did on Camp
David — but you didn't hear that from me — Egyptians failing to patrol their side of Gaza and so forth. Just pinch that
angle a bit. OK? Egyptians are our friends today.'

'Abdul-kader?' He frowned; he'd seen that name somewhere very recently.

'God,' groaned Zach. 'Egypt's foreign minister, remember? Where *have* you been these past few weeks?'

Aron was tempted to offer a chronological account: in the dingiest hotel in the West Bank and in a terrorist cell of al-Aqsa Squad. This was when he remembered where he'd read that name — in the temporary folder of the terrorist's laptop.

'Catch up, tomato-head. Abdul-kader's addressing the Knesset tomorrow, meeting the other side the day after and praying in al-Aqsa on Friday.'

'OK,' Aron said, simply. He was preoccupied, trying to recall the actual content of the offline pages.

'Good man. Let's touch base again tomorrow.' There was a brief pause. 'And Aron,' he added, 'I do really mean tomorrow.'

'Right.' But Aron was still trying to conjure up possible links between Uncle of al-Aqsa Squad and Egypt's foreign minister.

When faced with the choice between saving his career and tracking down Krickstein, Aron settled on the latter. More than just clearing up the inconsistencies surrounding Avi's death, Aron wondered whether Krickstein had some leads concerning Shahid, whether he too had participated in teaching the boy chess. He even rationalized his decision along patriotic lines: that it was by far more urgent to try and thwart a suicide attack on Israel than it was to write a commentary on an Egyptian dignitary.

He left Matan at dawn and drove to the Temple Israel School in Netanya. It was still early morning when he arrived and a small crowd of parents and children had gathered to wait for the school gate to open.

The sound of the bell caused a sudden commotion as though a starting pistol had just been fired: parents tried to kiss their children, who ran wildly to the gate. Aron stepped out of his parked car and crossed the road in a sprint.

He had spotted Krickstein.

The young *haredi* froze when he saw Aron approaching him.

'Mr Lunzer,' he said with astonishment. 'What are you doing here?'

'I've come to see you, Yitzhak Krickstein. Can we talk?' He held out his hand.

'I, um — ' He was taken aback by Aron's directness and shook the hand automatically. 'Yes, of course. But I have lessons all day. If you — '

'This is a matter of life and death,' interrupted Aron. 'I'm sure your students will understand.'

'Oh.' He looked worried. 'What's it about?' Krickstein was still dressed in the black of an ultra-orthodox *haredi*, and his facial hair had grown to droop in wispy strands that he started to tug at now.

'Let me buy you coffee,' said Aron and indicated a Shalom Coffee outlet at the far end of the street.

'I don't drink coffee.'

But Krickstein knew it wasn't about coffee. He exchanged a few words with a fellow teacher and followed Aron to the Shalom Coffee.

Aron showed him the sketch of Shahid as soon as they found their seats. 'Do you recognize him?' he asked.

Krickstein shook his head.

'Are you sure?' asked Aron, disappointed. 'You never saw him with my son, Avi?'

'Avi?' Krickstein's eyes grew wider. 'I'm sorry I left you in Lake Merom — ' he said faulteringly, ' — without telling you that I knew your son, Mr Lunzer.'

'That's why you bolted, isn't it?'

'I felt bad about that.'

'Is that why you sent me the card?'

'Yes,' he admitted. 'It came to me in a vision. It's like I was awake and Ezekiel told me what to write.'

'Then Ezekiel should have told you to sign it.' Aron was *hiloni*, not *haredi*, with little time for Talmudic nonsense. 'So Avi told you about me.'

'Only that you work for *Adlai*.'

'And you never saw him with this boy.'

'No, sir. Who is he?'

Aron ignored his question. 'Were you Avi's friend?'

'Not really, sir. You don't go in the IDF to make friends.'

Aron peered at him for a while. Eventually, he asked, 'So what happened, Yitzhak? Describe the last checkpoint duty. Lead me up to the point when Avi died.'

'I'm really sorry about your son,' said Krickstein quickly. 'It was a bomb. There was an Arab terrorist who — '

Aron interrupted him. 'I've read your affidavit on the events of 20/21 March,' he said. 'In fact, I have a copy with me.' He tried a different tack. 'So how come everyone at the base thinks you're a coward?'

His eyes shot up. 'I'm not a coward, sir.'

'You quit,' stated Aron. 'You couldn't hack it.'

'I'm now a student of the Torah.'

'You're not real IDF material, are you Yitzhak? That's it, isn't it?'

'No, sir.' He was upset.

'You were *aleph* and then you became yellow.'

Krickstein looked at him with dread in his eyes. 'You went there?'

'*Pagom, pagom, pagom.*'

'No!'

'That's right — no, you're worse than *bayit-pagom*. You're the biggest reject on the face of this planet.'

'They made me do it!' he cried suddenly.

'What?'

'I didn't want to, I swear,' he sobbed.

'What did you do?'

'They made me sign a report that it was a suicide bomb and that I'd seen it. But I wasn't there.'

'They? Who?'

'I didn't want to — '

'Yes?'

'They told me it was my duty as, as — '

He was stuttering so much that Aron completed his sentence for him. 'As a soldier?'

'No, an *evsheli*.'

'Evshel?'

Krickstein nodded. 'And when I refused, they threatened me with all sorts — disciplinary actions, court martial. But it was when she came back with two reports that — '

'She?'

'Baran. Captain Sheena Baran.' His hand shook as he brought his bottle of water to his lips. 'She gave me the choice: either I sign the first report, or she signs the second.' He paused. 'And she made me read the second. It said that I'd been shot in the line of duty. That I deserved full honours as a fallen hero of Israel — ' His voice trailed off.

'So you signed the first.'

'She made me read my own death certificate,' he said, haunted. 'They kicked me off the base a couple of days after that.'

'So tell me about your checkpoint duty that night.'

He was quiet for a moment, his hands still shaking, so Aron repeated, 'What *really* happened?'

'Avi and I always did checkpoint duty together. Whenever it fell at night, he sneaked off. It wasn't a big deal until that last time.'

'Sneaked off?' pressed Aron. 'Where to?'

'I don't know,' he said guiltily.

'Avi went off, leaving you alone at the checkpoint?'

'Yes, sir.'

'Why did you let him?'

Krickstein's cheeks turned red as he confessed, 'He paid me.'

'So that night,' recapitulated Aron, 'Avi went off, leaving you alone at the checkpoint. And then what happened?'

'At 2:00 in the morning, Baran came to ask me where he was. I didn't know so they locked me up.'

'It was 2:00 am?' Aron flicked through his notes. 'Why wasn't Avi back before then?'

'We were supposed to be relieved at 2:30, not at 2:00.'

'But didn't you have a double shift?' insisted Aron. 'Weren't you supposed to be on checkpoint duty from 11:00 pm on Saturday until 5:00 am on Sunday?'

'We were supposed to be relieved at 2:30,' repeated Krickstein. 'But they were half an hour early.' He paused. 'So they took me away and went looking for your son.'

'How did they find him?'

'I don't know, sir.' Krickstein looked suddenly petrified. 'Maybe he was walking back. Maybe they just waited for him.'

Aron narrowed his eyes on him. 'You knew where he was, didn't you?'

His eyes turned red.

'And you told them where to find him.'

Krickstein couldn't look him in the eyes.

Aron hissed, 'You may be fitter than me, but I'm still going to beat the shit out of you if you don't tell me, you fucking esrimist.'

Krickstein almost whispered, 'The destroyed farm down the road.'

'Where?'

'The Brahimi farm,' said Krickstein.

Aron turned to glare with fury at the picture of Shahid, the Brahimi orphan whom Bernadette had called Mohsen.

Krickstein groaned with dismay. 'She made me tell them. I swear Baran is the most evil human being.' Then, tugging nervously at a long lock of hair, the black-clad *haredi* said, 'I'm not in Evshel any more.'

Aron shouted when he was very angry. But when he was this furious, his tone turned icy cold. 'I can see that, you fucking esrimist.'

Bernadette phoned him when he was back in Matan.

The line was clear and he heard her frustration perfectly. 'The IDF aren't doing anything. I spent the whole morning in central command until some junior officer finally agreed to see me. He told me that they had looked into Mohsen's case and decided it wasn't worth pursuing, that it was probably a hoax anyway. They said they received a hundred threats a day and couldn't go chasing every one of them. No offence, Aron, but the Israeli army really sucks.'

He was beginning to agree with her. He told her about Krickstein's forced confession.

She exclaimed, 'But that's the only hard evidence they had against Shahed Zeitouni. I knew Shahed was innocent, didn't I tell you?'

'It doesn't prove he's innocent,' countered Aron darkly. 'He was there in the middle of the night during curfew — that's a fact and that's still very suspicious.'

'Maybe,' she said. 'Or maybe he just went to see his Israeli friend.'

'What friend?'

'I was trying to tell you last night,' explained Bernadette. 'I found some emails in Shahed's computer. His best friend and lover was an Israeli soldier.'

'Lover?' Aron said, intrigued. His throat started to tickle and so he reached for his flask.

'Yes. In fact most of the emails that he saved were about sex.'

'A woman in an IDF uniform,' he let slip, thinking suddenly of Tyre.

'A *man* in an IDF uniform,' corrected Bernadette.

'Gay sex? Shahed Zeitouni was gay? Are you sure?'

'Oh, absolutely,' she said. 'I don't know his name, just his online name.'

Aron sipped the white liquid while Bernadette read out passages from a couple of the more revealing emails.

'In the last email, Shahed tells his friend that he's looking forward to meeting him and losing his virginity to him.'

Aron frowned. 'I don't get it,' he said, bringing the flask to his lips. 'How could he be having sex then?'

'It was online sex up to that point,' she said.

She read out parts of the last email that she had found and duly printed in the Int@rnet café.

'The Israeli arrived in Qalqiliya on 16 November.'

That had been the day after Aron's forty-seventh Jewish birthday, the day Avi had joined his unit in the West Bank.

'He'd been doing his military service in a hospital in Israel.'

Aron choked on the Dustblaster.

'Hello? Aron, are you OK?'

He erupted into a raging fit, coughing and spluttering. 'Avi —' was all he could manage to utter for a while.

'Your son?' she exclaimed.

Any lingering doubts he might have had that it was his son vanished as soon as Bernadette added, 'Was he Dustmaster?'

He was transported to Avi's bedroom and to the most intriguing element of the wall: the graffiti written in both English and Hebrew. Winding clockwise towards the window, the English text read:

HE'S SQUARING THE CIRCLE AND I'M THE DUSTMASTER.

Its Hebrew translation dragged across the corner with the floor, curving anticlockwise to end at the light switch.

Bernardette waited patiently on the line, but when the coughing worsened, she said with concern, 'Try to take deep breaths.'

When he finally spoke, it was barely louder than a murmur. 'Squaring the circle.'

'That's right.' He heard her say. 'That was Shahed's username.'

'Phone you back,' he said abruptly, dropped the phone and ran to the bathroom.

The dustometre had tipped to the black alert level — the most extreme defence condition. Even the paving stone from Tyre hadn't caused such a cataclysmic outbreak of vomit.

He heard the phone ringing intermittently from the bathroom.

Eventually, when he felt there was nothing left in him to push out, he lifted himself up off the floor. He turned the water on in the shower, stripped and waited a full ten minutes before stepping into the cubicle. He started to cough again.

The phone hadn't stopped ringing.

He answered it. His throat was so inflamed that he rasped, 'You're wrong. You think I wouldn't know my son? You think he could keep such a thing from me? I know my Avi and that's not him.' He added bitterly as though that would prove everything, 'He even tried to force himself on a girl once.'

Aron fell abruptly silent.

'You really do have a lot to learn about people, Aron,' she said gently.

He suddenly realized that, with the exception of Matea, Avi had never brought a girl home. But then, he'd never brought a boy home either. Aron had just assumed that his son had been less interested in sex.

'You're wrong,' he repeated, but with less conviction. The coincidences were stacked up against him. 'Avi was 100 per cent man.'

'You really understand only what you want to understand.'

He winced at that; Sela had told him exactly the same thing when her belly protruded with — as the facts could not deny — a homosexual infant. 'It's just so unnatural.'

'Why?'

'Because,' he stammered. 'Because — ' And he left it at that, his hand throttling the phone.

'It's like *kishek*,' she said simply.

'What?'

'It means that Shahed would not have murdered his best friend and lover.'

She carried on, but Aron had stopped listening. For several minutes, he started to picture Avi at various stages of life, playing the slides at random: twelve-year-old Avi placing sunflowers on Sela's grave, eighteen-year-old Avi leaving home with his duffel bag, four-year-old Avi answering every question with an irritating bray. He wished he were back in Jerusalem to feel his baby's hair from the first haircut. He could even imagine smelling it now: the fine, downy black hair with the faintest trace of baby shampoo. It was still substantially better to have a gay son than no son at all.

Bernadette was saying, 'What Mohsen Brahimi said to you is really strange.' When he failed to react, she prompted, 'Your Shahid.'

That brought him back into the conversation — Shahid was *nothing* like his son. 'I'm glad you find it strange that a little boy should want to kill himself,' he said grumpily.

She persisted, 'But that's the point, remember, he doesn't actually think he's going to die. He told you he'd go straight to heaven and avoid death.'

'Right,' he said crossly. With virgins waiting at the pearly gates. 'I'd like to know what exactly a prepubescent child is supposed to do with a virgin bride.'

'Yes,' agreed Bernadette. 'But either he's too young or else — and that would really explain why he sees himself as a living martyr — he knows where the attack will be and he's hoping to emulate the one Muslim who visited heaven *before* his death.'

Aron frowned. He concentrated fully on what she was saying. 'The one Muslim?'

'Muhammad rose up to heaven from al-Aqsa.'

Muhammad was such a common Arab name that at first he didn't make the link with the prophet.

'Al-Aqsa Mosque,' she stressed.

Muhammad was the prophet who had made his *baal teshuva*, master of return, from al-Aqsa. It all snapped into place.

'Only trouble is,' she said, 'I just don't see how that helps.'

But Aron did. He suddenly understood why the terrorist had been checking the Egyptian Foreign Ministry website and even why Shahid had to say a line in Hebrew. No Muslim would ever dare to conceive, let alone carry out, such a crime against Islam; the boy had to *appear* Jewish and he had to sound like an ultra, *evsheli* or *haredi*. The terrorist called Uncle was a chess player, but so too was Aron. His voice became little more than a whisper. 'I do. And I think I even know *when* it's going to happen.'

'When?'

'Friday.'

'Tomorrow's Friday.'

He spoke urgently. 'So can you meet me in Jerusalem tomorrow morning?'

'Why?'

'Because I can't go to a mosque on my own.'

Amo was the champion exit strategist.

He was not, on the other hand, one for making a grand entry. Compared to his spectacular escapes from the Palestinian camps of Tell az-Zaatar and Sabra, his return to the fatherland — by way of the splinter represented by the West Bank — was mundane to the extreme.

According to their forged papers, they were Israeli Arabs. And as far as the neighbours were concerned, they were an uncle and nephew from Haifa visiting their relatives in East Jerusalem.

He switched the bedroom light on and Shahid bounced on the bed.

It was late and the boy needed his rest. 'Settle down now,' he ordered.

With one last bounce, Shahid landed neatly on the pillow and in one fluid movement slipped his legs under the blanket. 'That's how a superhero goes to bed.'

'Yes, Shahid,' said Amo. 'Now go to sleep.'

'So am I a superhero now?' the boy asked.

'Of course,' replied the man. 'You're more than a superhero.'

'A wizard?' he asked.

'That's right. You are art for the sake of art.'

The boy frowned. 'What does that mean, Amo?'

'It means you're a wizard capable of wonderful magic.'

Shahid nodded drowsily. 'I want wings. Will my chest be red as a robin's?' He yawned. 'As red as *Abi*'s?'

'Yes,' Amo answered, not quite understanding. 'As red as a robin's and your father's.'

'Not *my father*,' he said sleepily. 'Abi who was Shahed's friend.'

'Sure. Why not.' Amo switched the light off and left the boy to his dreams.

This would be their safe house in the city for just one more night, and the boy would sleep in that bed or in any other for just this night.

He took out four photographs from his breast pocket and gazed at them lovingly. He never travelled without them.

Technically, only one of them was a masterpiece: the black-and-white picture of the devastated Brahimi farm where he had first met Shahid and which would serve as the lead picture to Aron Lunzer's story. Of course, the story itself would only be published later, considerably later once the regional war was well underway and unstoppable. Only then would readers learn the story of a destitute Palestinian child so totally abandoned by everyone that he had chosen to strike out against his own people and religion. It was a sublime triangular relationship between subject, reader and author.

But he had succeeded in getting this far thanks to the other pictures: damning photographs of Israeli soldiers, which he had used to blackmail his way into Israel.

These, too, had been taken in the Brahimi farm, but at a different time, when Amo had returned to see if Shahid was starving enough to join the Squad.

Finally, after a decade of scheming and conniving, everything was fitting together like matching jigsaw pieces. And yet Amo couldn't sit still. Now that they were only hours away from the mission and the greatest work of art in the history of the region, he just couldn't stop his leg from shaking with impatience.

Only the most outrageous act could provide the catalyst for Muslims everywhere to declare war against Israel. A third intifada could only escalate into a truly regional war if the most populous Arab state was brought on board. Egypt had to break its peace with Israel.

From the very start, Amo had planned to bomb al-Aqsa Mosque, the third holiest site in Islam, synchronizing that attack with a visit by a leading Egyptian dignitary.

Ammar
Ash-Shuja'

Abbadon
Angel of
destruction

17

THE COMPLEX OF religious buildings in the heart of old Jerusalem is known as both the Noble Sanctuary to Muslims and the Temple Mount to Jews. Enclosing more than thirty-five acres of fountains, gardens, buildings and domes, Muslims regard the entire area as a mosque though, in actual fact, al-Aqsa Mosque is at the southernmost end; dotted around are several domes of which, at the centre, is the celebrated Dome of the Rock facing Mecca and the direction of prayer. This is the exact spot where, according to the faithful, the Prophet had visited heaven while still alive.

Leading progressively away from the dome, through an imposing arched doorway, is a central courtyard, a narrow corridor and an atrium, which serves as the entrance to the mosque.

There is a water fountain in the atrium, squirting fine jets a little distance in the air before landing in an octagonal marble basin. It is situated closer to the right side of the main entrance such that it copies the asymmetry of baptismal fonts outside Crusader churches.

Two gigantic columns support the arched doorway, and of all the principal, load-bearing columns, only these have an unimpeded vantage of the entire compound. From there, a tutor could stand at a safe distance all the while keeping a watchful eye on his pupil.

The main crossing point to Jerusalem from the West Bank was set up as an international border between two equal countries, complete with its phalanx of border guards and customs and immigration officers, and large notices everywhere, written in Hebrew, Arabic and English — three languages and scripts to accentuate the customs and security regulations before entering Israel. It all looked so official and perfectly organized that it was easy to forget that only one of the two states actually existed, that no other country aside from Israel recognized that border and that, especially, the line severed the other budding nation from its capital in East Jerusalem.

Aron spotted her immediately. Bernadette stood out in the crowd waiting to cross the checkpoint, partly because she was among the first in the mass of heads, but especially thanks to a bright red shirt that she'd chosen to wear.

The customs and immigration officer looked at her and at her Israeli sponsor with suspicion. He flicked through her Lebanese passport and the UN laissez passer, and checked the details against both the invitation form, duly completed and signed, and Aron's Israeli passport.

'Lebanese are not permitted to enter Israel,' he said eventually.

'Rubbish,' retorted Aron. He had written a piece on the thousands of Lebanese, mostly members of Israel's proxy militia, the South Lebanon Army, who had fled south with the retreating IDF. Many had chosen to remain in Israel rather than face charges of treason or acts of retribution by Hizbullah. 'She's a Lebanese Christian.'

The officer peered at Aron and hesitated.

'Besides,' insisted Aron, 'she's entering on a UN document.'

'Are you Aron Lunzer from *Adlai*?'

'Not any more.' Zach hadn't bothered to phone; he'd just sent him a curt email when Aron had failed to deliver his piece.

Aron's reply appeared to satisfy the officer. 'I found it suspicious that a reporter for *Adlai* would invite an Arab.' He stamped her UN document as he added softly, 'I've always hated *Adlai*.'

The ornate ceiling in the atrium caught the reflection of the early morning sunlight so that the Koranic verse, *Ya Sin*, commissioned in the sixteenth century by Suleiman the Magnificent, glimmered, and the etched and deeply intricate script chased its shadow into the limestone. Two tidy racks, with their little cubbyholes for the worshippers' shoes, stretched across the lateral walls of the entrance hall and rose from the ground to the height of a tall man. These were empty, with the exception of two pairs of shoes and one pair of slippers, which belonged to the groundsmen who entered the empty mosque carrying a carpet.

Unlike the many rugs scattered around the pulpit, this carpet was both finer and considerably more expensive. It was one of very few surviving examples of a *Farsh* from the eighteenth century, fit for an emir, and was brought out only on rare occasions. The groundsmen reached the spot directly under the dome and spread out the carpet in preparation for the visiting Egyptian dignitary and his entourage.

The main roads in the old quarter had been closed off as a security measure for the Egyptian foreign minister and all the traffic had been diverted onto the narrow and tortuous side streets, causing one of the worst congestions East Jerusalem had ever experienced.

It was already almost noon and they had been stuck in the bedevilling traffic jam for two hours.

'Fuck,' swore Aron. He twisted in his seat to reach for the flask of Dustblaster in his pocket and proceeded to drop it under the seat. 'Fuck,' he repeated. He now had to unbuckle his seat belt in order to stretch all the way down.

Bernadette looked up at a little girl on a balcony who was staring at all the cars. 'Traffic jams, bombs, maniacs — you take me back to my childhood days in Beirut.'

'We're not going to make it,' he panicked. He squeezed the bottle and almost seemed to be inhaling the white substance rather than ingesting it. As he returned the flask to his left pocket, he shuddered and asked, 'When do Friday prayers start anyway?' He shuddered again.

'I don't know.'

'Great,' he said bitterly. 'The only Arab I know well would have to be Christian.'

'Is the mosque far?'

He indicated a westerly direction and the other drivers on the road. 'Five minutes if these bastards would just disappear. Ten hours at this rate. Sorry, I shouldn't have asked you to come. As it is I don't know why I did. I mean, what can you do? Fuck, what can I do to stop it? Shit, I really shouldn't have asked you.'

She smiled at him. You had to be amused by life and death when you lived in a war zone — more than anything else it was sarcasm that had helped Beirutis endure decades of bloodshed. 'That's right,' she said. 'You take me to a suicide bombing on our first official date. A fine gentleman you are.'

'Don't you realize the situation? You could die, I could die. Thousands could end up in a billion pieces.' He stared sullenly ahead.

They inched forward in silence and then he turned left at first opportunity, down a street that was even more log-jammed. 'Is everyone off for prayers today?' he grumbled.

Bernadette said suddenly, 'Why don't we run to the mosque?' She pointed. 'Isn't that it over there?'

They could just make out the top of the golden Dome of the Rock above the buidings.

'Yes,' he said, switching off his engine. 'Let's go.' He opened his door.

'Aren't you going to park your car?'

'At this hour? In the old quarter?' He shook his head. 'No space and no time.'

She joined him and the driver behind them blared his horn. 'You can't just stop here. Are you mad?' the driver shouted, his whole torso sticking out of the window.

'Yes, I am,' replied Aron, expertly tossing him his car keys. 'Happy Hanukkah.' And to Bernadette: 'Let's go.'

The driver turned in amazement to his neighbour in the opposite lane. 'He thinks it's Hanukkah. He's mad. He's really fucking mad.'

They sprinted away as a cacophony of horns and curses erupted around them.

The sunlight no longer reflected off the atrium floor. In the midday light, the intricate script in the ceiling was all but obscured and lost on the flow of worshippers. The tidy racks with their little cubbyholes were already so full that latecomers had to leave their shoes and slippers in less precise rows on the ground.

Inside the mosque, men and boys sat on the rugs, first filling the area closest to the pulpit from where the imam would preach. The magnificent *Farsh* directly under the dome was still empty and became ever more a gaping hole in a human fabric as more worshippers gravitated towards the centre.

While most waited like spectators before the show, sitting casually and exchanging pleasantries with neighbours in hushed tones, some used the time to meditate, sitting upright on their haunches, their hands neatly folded over their stomachs with the right hand covering the left hand to restrict every movement. Soon enough, with the first *Allahu Akbar*, the congregation would act in unison to face the imam, using him as the compulsory sutra, and raise hands to shoulders as one body and stretch fingers to earlobes.

For now, those inside al-Aqsa waited patiently as a steady stream of faithful were channelled through the compound, taking turns at the taps for their ablutions and leaving the central courtyard to aim for the massive arched doorway and its two imposing columns.

The Egyptian foreign minister's motorcade drew up to the compound as a little boy in a keffiyeh came to stand by the column marginally further from the water fountain. In the past, before Yasser Arafat injected it with political overtones, the keffiyeh had been an uncomplicated headdress to cover the heads of peasants and farmers in the way baggy *sharwal* trousers covered their legs.

Even now, were it not for the distinctly urban setting that surrounded the Noble Sanctuary, the boy could easily have been mistaken for a farmer's son.

He, too, waited and fiddled nervously with the keffiyeh as he stretched his neck all the way back to look up the giant column. Every now and then, a Muslim on his way into the atrium would pause to ask if he was all right or whether he needed a companion to enter the mosque. Indicating the courtyard with the Dome of the Rock beyond the corridor, the boy answered automatically that he was waiting for his father.

Shahid was lying.

He pointed to where he knew Uncle was also waiting. More to the point, it was his mother and not his father who, any minute now, would glide down from heaven and envelop him as her wings took them to their new celestial farm.

His press pass clipped to his shirt, Amo seemed to be taking pictures of the Egyptian's entry into the central courtyard; in fact, his lens moved from the minister's bodyguards to the Israeli guards at the periphery of the compound and back, scanning the crowd. Click-click.

There didn't appear to be any extra security. Over the years, Amo had trained himself to take in every detail of a scene in a blink set at its highest shutter speed.

From a distance, he could make out his boy standing by the designated pillar. You didn't need a megaton of explosives to bring down a load-bearing column just as you didn't need to saw right through a thick trunk to bring down the tallest tree in a forest. The trick was to localize the explosion, creating just the right shock in the right place, and let gravity and moments of inertia do the rest. He didn't expect the entire mosque to crumble — just the atrium facing all the cameras. That would do the trick.

The child was fidgeting with his keffiyeh, as though preparing to remove it.

Not yet, my boy, don't show them your skullcap just yet. Wait for the Egyptian to come a bit closer. There's a good boy.

'There he is,' panted Aron. They were by the Dome and, beyond the corridor, they could just discern a small figure standing by the main entrance. He'd been right — Shahid was there, standing by one of the pillars.

Muslims could be fair, but not as fair as a European Jew; Arabs could have green eyes, but never quite so green. But considerably more telling than his features was his female companion: no true believer would ever bring a woman to the male section of a mosque, especially not for Friday prayers, and especially not with her long black hair visible for all to see and a bright red shirt that had harlot written all over it.

Therefore, neither he nor she was Muslim, and the crowd immediately closed in on them to block their path.

The bodyguards kept a wary eye on the newcomers as they hurried the Egyptian minister to his ritual wash.

'Let us through,' Aron demanded in Hebrew. An old man, barring his way, pushed him back as two younger men came to join him and folded their arms. More and more stopped their procession to the mosque to face the intruders as a solid wall.

Bernadette tried pleading in Arabic and waved her arms desperately.

They heard the foreign, Christian accent before the actual words, and it was a while before the stony expressions softened.

Amo caught the woman's wave and zoomed in on her. Click-click.

Then he saw her male companion and panicked.

He was still blending in perfectly so that he seemed to be busy fiddling with focal stops as his mind brooded over Aron Lunzer. He was furious that the journalist had escaped, let alone discovered the mission.

He raised his lens again to scan the crowd, quickly checking to see if the Israeli soldier he'd blackmailed was there. J.J. was not in the mass of heads and he turned to focus on the guards one more time: they appeared cautious but otherwise unperturbed. Either the journalist hadn't informed the authorities, or else undercover agents were concealing themselves particularly well.

And either way, it didn't matter any more. The Egyptian had finished his final ablutions and was a few steps away from the atrium.

'I beg you, faithful followers of the Prophet — peace and blessings be upon him — to help us find our young son.' Her voice was desperate: 'He entered this holy place by mistake. He suffers from a terrible disease and will die if he doesn't get his medication.' She got Aron to show them all his flask of Dustblaster. But it was her next words that finally caused a breach in the human barrier: 'I beg you to help me as I would help you if your sons were lost and about to die in our churches and synagogues.'

According to the unwritten codes of Arab hospitality, if it was in your power to help someone in need, then you were morally obliged to do so. And among all the Arab communities in the world, none are as well rounded as the faithful who attend Friday prayers regularly.

The boy had removed his keffiyeh. Click-click.

Good, my lovely boy, good. And don't forget your Hebrew now.

Amo was already moving back, away from the courtyard as part of his exit strategy.

The Egyptian foreign minister paused to look at the boy's skullcap with curiosity.

Shahid's hand moved under his shirt and felt for the wire.

He looked up at the blue sky and grinned suddenly as he heard his mother calling.

'Mohsen! Mohsen!'

He would have pulled the wire there and then except that he had to utter the magic phrase in *ibreet*. That was the condition; otherwise she wouldn't fly down to carry him away.

'Mohsen!'

'*Die, you Arabs* — ' But what was the rest of the magic spell? '*Die, you Arabs* — ' he tried again. How could he have forgotten?

'Here, Mohsen!'

'Mama,' he whimpered suddenly. 'Mama!' What was it again?

'Look over here!'

He saw her through the tears in his eyes and immediately recognized her: she led a host of angels, her black hair caught the wind, her arms flapped playfully, and her chest was bright red as a robin's.

She flew up to be with him while the angels kept a respectful distance.

Bernadette hugged the little boy who had collapsed in her arms. Carefully, she reached in to remove the hand from under his shirt.

She hadn't lied — her son looked ill around the eyes and had a delirious look about him. Since she had already explained the situation to them, the Muslims didn't bat an eyelid at the boy's skullcap.

Amo could have gone.

He was the champion exit strategist and instinctively knew how to emerge from intractable situations. He could have lived to plan a future attack. But after a decade of scheming and conniving, he couldn't face losing when he had already pinched victory so delicately between thumb and index.

In a blink, he knew exactly what he had to do.

'Mama,' Mohsen sobbed. 'I'm sorry.' He'd forgotten the spell and he hadn't pulled the wire. 'I'm sorry,' he wept.

'Everything will be all right,' said Bernadette warmly, caressing and kissing the boy as though she had known him all her life.

Aron bent down to them and urged, 'Let's go.' Still holding his flask of Dustblaster, supposedly to treat his son's life-threatening condition, he asked Shahid, 'Is Amo here?'

The boy saw him and then turned to Bernadette. 'You're not my Mama,' he piped sadly.

'No, but I'll take you to see her.'

As a teacher, you had to be willing to go through what you preached, and as an artist, you had to be prepared to die for your art for the sake of immortality.

Only Shahid recognized him as he approached them, one hand hugging his zoom lens, and the other in his pocket.

Both Aron and Bernadette read his press card, clipped to his shirt and ostensibly from a Christian Lebanese newspaper.

'This is not a good time,' said Bernadette in her colloquial Arabic and, thinking she was talking to a fellow national, she added the first name on his card: 'André'.

Amo could easily round his vowels and abandon some consonants like her speech, but this was no longer the time for deception. Today, he was Ammar Ash-shuja', born in March 1948, somewhere on the road between Haifa and South Lebanon as his branch of the family opted to flee their ancestral home.

'I couldn't remember the words,' Shahid explained pathetically.

He ignored both the woman and the child to address the man in English: 'This was not part of our deal,' he stated coldly.

Aron jumped as he recognized that voice.

'Good Aron, hold that pose now.' His other hand brought out a pistol and turned to the boy, aiming for his middle. Click-click.

In that split second, Aron lunged to do the only thing possible — he squeezed his bottle of Dustblaster with its caustic mix of garlic, onion and lemon juice.

That second has a head, a body and a tail.

First, a fine stream of white substance streaks across the air, forming a perfect arc that lingers to join all the dots between the end of the spout and his left eye.

Next, in pockets of extended time, all the neurons fire simultaneously in a blinding flash of pain and the gun shoots its bullet, hoping it's still on target.

But it was not the white substance that brought him down like some lethal spray — the true Palesticide was an Israeli bullet fired from God knows where. He looked briefly at his shirt that was fast turning red at the chest and was surprised that the ground had chosen that precise moment to rise to his face.

The last thing he saw, before the stinging pain caused his right eye to close as well, was the teddy bear on the squeezy bottle. In this continuum, the grinning bear turned to wink at him.

It was the ultimate trip. The mind, knowing it had a handful of heartbeats left, played a random compilation of memories in unison.

The conservation of art — that was the goal of immortality. When a person died, the art must be redistributed among the living.

For only the shortest chronon at the end of that second, Ammar raised a hand to Aron and knew what his last words must be.

An Israeli agent assigned to protect the Egyptian minister stood far off, halfway down the corridor, and was still aiming his rifle at the fallen man as, all about him, worshippers ran for shelter.

Even though his eyes were shut, Aron knew that the terrorist was beckoning him. He hesitated.

Bernadette's arms were still wrapped around the boy; they were both unharmed. Aron knelt down to look at the face without a mask as his blood formed a pool. It was already conjealing in places to form little chunks of liver on his shirt.

'What?' Aron moved his ear down to the dying man.

Climbing Everest was easier than speaking. 'I liked what you wrote about me.' He paused to catch one of three final breaths.

Everything about men was art for art's sake.

He used a leaden finger to indicate the blood-encrusted camera: 'Take my picture now.' He was suddenly too tired even to click his tongue.

18

*ABOON DABASHMAYA NETHKADASH shamak...*The cosmic creator of all radiance set over the eternal city and the last *Allahu Akbar* of the day drifted in through the open window.

Aron stood awkwardly by the bed.

She took his hands and guided them to her soft breasts, encouraging them to carve out a space between them. His head moved down her neck to rest for an instant, lips attaching themselves to the top of her shoulder. She responded in kind, brushing her cheek against the side of his head and stroking the nape and top of his back to send shivers down his spine.

His mouth moved on downwards to savour what the fingers had already thoroughly assessed.

Her nipples became so sensitive she gave an involuntary twitch.

He stopped. 'Sorry,' he said breathlessly. 'I'm a bit rusty.'

'I know rust — my father's a car mechanic, remember?' She reached down to feel his erection. 'Trust me, that's not rust.' She confirmed that with the sense of taste — the same sensors that learn to love the aftertaste of *kishek*.

They made love five times over the course of the evening, night and early morning when they stirred to lock together like fitting jigsaw pieces. On two of those occasions, their lovemaking was timed inadvertently to the call to prayer from the main mosque. Rather than diverting them from their true purpose, the first prayer of the next day woke them to illuminate the opportunities of the present moment so that the bedsprings creaked to the rhythm of the muezzin's chant.

Kishek is among the oldest recipes in the Levant — Canaanite urns containing traces of the stuff attest to this long culinary tradition. Before the advent of the modern age, turning yoghurt into the coarse, sallow powder that is *kishek* provided a healthy if unsavoury way of storing dairy products during the lean winter months.

Lebanese are deeply proud and traditional folk when it comes to their food; they deliberately foist the substance on their children, force-feeding them so as to overcome the assault on the olfactory from an early age.

While it would be easier to consign *kishek* to a quaint and pre-refrigerator past, there is in truth something delectable about the taste of rot. After that first impression of desiccated vomit — an initiatory stage that usually takes at least five years — there is little in the Lebanese culinary repertoire that can match *kishek* in terms of satisfying contrasts: chewy yet melting in the mouth, pungent foretaste yet warmly nuanced aftertaste.

Aron Lunzer — as indeed his article on Papa — was equally something of an acquired taste.

Arnold Lounger's feature had caused her to abandon lunch. But the more Bernadette had read it, the more she had seen past the initial sense of revulsion. By the time she came to write her thesis, she agreed with Papa that the English journalist was a genius. He had succeeded in portraying Papa's humanity beyond the nauseating deeds of the mass-murderer. The man who was her father was not grotesque on the inside; Papa's narrative came through vividly only once his monstrous shadow was blotted out.

And it was the man, Aron Lunzer, who twenty years later, had unwittingly encouraged her to make her peace with Papa.

They had avoided all contact ever since Mémé's death. Papa had found it impossible to forgive her for the mass of Palestinians who had turned up to his mother's funeral.

It was his birthday and Bernadette entered Papa's garage with a peace offering on a tray, covered in aluminium foil.

He looked up from the open hood of a Renault, recognized her with a start and then returned his attention to the air filter.

He had become an old man and was having trouble lifting the heavier tools.

Bernadette stood awkwardly for a while, staring blankly at the empty wall opposite and at the workbench.

She broke the silence. 'I've made some *kishek* pizzas.'

'I can smell them from here,' he said simply.

It might have ended there. Bernadette waited a full ten seconds and was about to leave when he grunted, straightened his back and let the hood drop shut with a loud bang.

'They smell good.' He moved several tools to make some room for the tray on the workbench.

'Happy birthday, Papa,' she said as the tray found a new home among screwdrivers and spanners.

'*Merci.*'

'How are you, Papa?'

'As you see me.'

'Papa, I forgive you.'

That took him by surprise. He frowned and said dismissively, 'I don't need your forgiveness.'

'But I need you to know that.'

'And have you come for my forgiveness?'

She looked at him questioningly to which he shook his head disapprovingly.

'I didn't raise you to go begging in Sabra.'

'That was a long time ago, Papa.'

'It's like yesterday for me.'

'I don't beg in Sabra or anywhere else.' Bernadette had

gone to the Palestinian refugee camp to retrieve her grand-mother, and she said so: 'I went to Sabra for Mémé.'

'The real Mémé would never have gone there. My real mother died well before she went to that cesspit.' His tone turned vindictive. 'She died when she stopped recognizing her own son.'

There was an uneasy pause; then he asked, 'And what *exactly* are you forgiving me for?'

Bernadette started with the lesser sins: 'For not being there when I needed you, for not being more understand-ing with Mémé.' She almost whispered, 'For what you did in Sabra.'

'I see,' he said darkly. 'The angel of mercy comes to save the sinner on his birthday.'

'No, Papa. It's not like that.'

'And what about those who massacred all the Christian women and children? Do you forgive them?'

'Yes, I do.'

He was genuinely surprised. 'You forgive those who killed your own mother? And your own brother?' he de-manded incredulously; his tone was a mixture of grief and rage. He roared suddenly with anguish: 'You can for-give the fucking monster who can cut off the head of a pregnant woman? And then turns to hack at the neck of a three-year-old?'

There was a stunned silence.

'Maman was pregnant?' Bernadette was shocked. 'You never told me.'

'Was there any point?' he shouted.

After a while, he continued in a more subdued tone: 'We wanted three children. It was all going according to plan. A girl, then a boy, to finish with another girl.' He was hurt and bitter. 'A girl who would have respected her father. A girl who would truly have understood her Papa.'

'But I do respect you, Papa.'

'I still see them. All three of them. Suzanne has your mother's looks and my fiery spirit. She's studying to become a journalist. And Michel — well he's an established engineer with a family of his own now. We are doting grandparents to his first boy.' He closed his eyes as a single tear moved down his stubbly cheek. 'Your mother and I have given the best that life has to offer to our young. We are so proud of them.'

'And what about me, Papa?'

'You are not in my dreams,' he admitted sadly. 'You are the one we lost.'

'Oh, Papa.'

'I would turn the clock back in a second. But I would not stop at Sabra — they all deserve to die. I would take us back to Damour. Do you remember the snow on that last Christmas?'

Bernadette was too upset to speak.

'No. You were busy with that doll of yours. And Papa Noël had given Michel a toy plane that was too big for him to carry. Your mother and I went out to the garden. We drank some wine as the first snowflakes started to fall, and we laughed because we lived in the most beautiful country in the world.'

Papa turned to the tap in his garage and, reaching for a bottle of detergent, he scrubbed his hands clean of the grime.

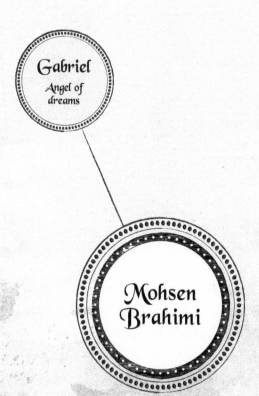

Gabriel
Angel of
dreams

Mohsen
Brahimi

19

ARON AND BERNADETTE led Mohsen into the courtroom. The boy kept putting his hands in his pockets nervously.

'Don't do that,' scolded Aron. 'And keep your middle button done up.'

He fussed over Mohsen, buttoning up the blazer and then brushing the back.

'He's worse than my grandmother,' teased Bernadette in Arabic to Mohsen, which caused the boy to grin.

Aron had bought the blazer, trousers and black shoes for Mohsen's day in court.

They'd waited almost a year for this day and Aron wanted everything to be perfect, including the boy's posture. 'Remember, always walk with your head held high and your back straight,' he told him.

As a former *shahid*, Mohsen should really have been

called Shahed — Aron remembered the pointed distinction offered by the terrorist called Uncle.

Mohsen was a witness to the murders.

The defence lawyers raised objections concerning the reliability of a Palestinian boy's eyewitness account, but were promptly overruled.

When Mohsen was called to the stand, walking tall and with his hands out of his pockets, he provided such a detailed account that even the presiding judge was visibly shaken and swayed in his chair.

Aron could not have been prouder of Mohsen if he'd been his own son.

It had been the worst birthday ever. There was no cake, no special meal — in fact no actual meals other than tinned food for the subsequent six days — and he had set his heart on a Spiderman doll but his mother bought him a cheap panda bear instead. At the store in Qalqiliya, she told him Spiderman was too expensive and that, anyway, what was the point of playing with a doll that pretended to be a man that pretended to be a spider. She turned to the panda on a lower shelf. 'He's so cute. Don't you think, Mohsen?'

Mohsen had just turned eleven. He wasn't into cute. He wanted joints that moved — even the wrists could be forced back to spin an imaginary web.

They argued all the way home, and he refused to hold the bear so that she was forced to carry it like a baby in her arms.

The Israelis were everywhere when they reached the farm. They waved their guns and scrutinized them. One of them tried to stop Mohsen from going to the demolished sitting room, but he moved deftly between his legs to join his mother. She had been taken to distinguish his father and brothers from the other corpses — his sisters had already formed a smaller pile.

The Israeli attack to dislodge the Palestinian fighters hiding in the Brahimi farm had fallen on a Friday. So his mother was spared because she always attended prayers in the mosque, in the screened annex reserved for women, and so too were the three employees who helped stitch the reeds into brooms, load the delivery van and sell the end product to wholesalers. Mohsen was spared because his mother had promised him a birthday present after the service, and he had waited patiently for her outside the mosque, convinced that such good behaviour would entitle him to a Spiderman.

But now, the stupid panda bear was being wrenched this way and that by his mother as they waited for the empty coffins to arrive. It deserved to die. Mohsen was pleased to see that, by the time the undertakers arrived, it had lost two of its limbs and one of its button eyes.

His mother's expression had already turned lifeless as the panda's as they arranged the bundles meticulously according to sex and kin, and the Israelis loaded the largest stack into their own delivery van. The undertakers and half the town came for the smaller pile. There were only a few hours left before sunset so everyone worked as a team, rushing to clean and load their cargo.

This was when Mohsen first suspected he had the power to become invisible.

One minute they were all dashing around him like ants about a pebble, and the next they were gone, taking the full coffins and his mother with them.

She never returned.

And because she couldn't see him either, she didn't actually say anything other than odd tweeting sounds.

The following sunset, when no one came looking for him, he returned to the same spot by the eastern wall to watch what had once been the TV, in the midst of the armchairs without arms, seats without backs or legs and the coffee table that was charred to the bone.

Suddenly, a man entered with a camera. Mohsen froze as the man casually changed the lens and started to take pictures. Eventually the man stopped and seemed about to leave. Clearly, Mohsen was invisible; perhaps he was also invincible.

But instead of leaving, the man settled by the rubble of the western wall.

They sat in complete silence as the day turned slowly into night.

The crescent moon, glowing with the setting sun, was now joined by the brightest stars in the constellations. The other stars slowly popped out and soon the sky was swarming with them.

'What's your name?'

They'd been sitting in their respective positions for so long that Mohsen had almost drifted off.

'What's your name?' repeated the stranger.

Mohsen didn't breathe, hoping the man would think he was still a rock.

'You look like a Shahid.'

The man was obviously a superhero with x-ray vision.

Mohsen stirred.

'Are you?' insisted the man.

'I'm Mohsen,' he said finally.

'So tell me, Mohsen, would you like to be a Shahid?'

Mohsen shrugged.

'I can make you a Shahid. Do you know what that is?'

The boy shrugged again.

'I can make you the greatest Shahid ever.' The man rose to his feet. 'Do you know the mosque in Qalqiliya?'

He nodded.

'Behind the mosque, there's a building with a doctor's clinic on the second floor. The doctor's name is Hamid Abdullatif. If you want to become a hero, go there and tell the doctor you've come to see me. Tell him you've come to see Amo.' He paused. 'Do you understand?'

Mohsen nodded at the silhouette.

By the fourth day, he had consumed all the crumbs and scraps that he could find in the bombed-out kitchen. He had also given up hope that the undertakers would ever return with his mother. So he resolved to go to Qalqiliya looking for food and the doctor's clinic when, instead, Shahed Zeitouni and another man came to him.

Had it not been for them, he would have been a Shahid a lot sooner.

Mohsen was eight when he had first met Shahed and he hadn't been able to see him clearly for the tears in his eyes, his bloodied nose and his face that was being shoved in a muddy puddle. For no apparent reason, Shahed's brother Saddam, who was almost eleven, had turned up at the farm and picked a fight that the older boy proceeded to win easily.

He was still pinned down by Saddam when they heard a shout.

In his blurred vision, Shahed appeared to have two heads and four arms. One pair of arms moved to pick Saddam off him, pulling the bully up by the ear, and the other pair lifted Mohsen gently off the ground and brought a tissue to his nose. While one of the heads scolded the truant brother severely, reminding him of the duty to their sister on her wedding day, the other head spoke soothingly to Mohsen, making sure he was all right.

On that occasion, Shahed took him home and forced Saddam to apologize formally to his mother, then they turned to walk the two kilometres to the Zetouni farm, the conquering hero in his black suit dragging a yelping boy.

When they next met, on 27 November 2003, on the private lane linking the Brahimi farm to the main artery into town, Mohsen was again caked in mud and dried tears. This time, Shahed had a man with him — in the uniform of an Israeli — and was holding his hand, not his ear.

The two men had come together barely an hour before at the Qalqiliya gate, neither shaking hands nor daring to show any form of recognition beyond slight nods. Shahed had led the way straight to the presumed seclusion of the Brahimi farm. It was only as they left the main artery and started to walk up the tree-lined private road that Avi had nervously reached for his friend's hand.

Shahed recognized the boy and immediately let go of the other's hand. 'Mohsen Brahimi? Is that you?' he exclaimed. 'What are you doing here?'

'I live here,' replied Mohsen automatically.

Again, Shahed's gut reaction was to take him back to his mother — but to his own mother this time.

'My Mama is tired,' said Mohsen, nodding vaguely up the lane towards the demolished farmhouse. 'She needs to sleep.' He looked down at his feet. 'And I need to find some food for her.'

The Israeli stared at him but with kind, green eyes.

'Then let me speak to her,' insisted Shahed.

'No,' he panicked. 'She's very tired and hungry.'

'Mohsen,' said Shahed gently. 'Your mother is not there.'

'Yes she is,' he moaned suddenly. 'And I have to be here when she gets back.'

In its rush to bury the family, the community had lost count of the exact number of dead. The mother had gone mad with grief and the de facto orphan had been overlooked.

'I know someone who can find you a good home,' said Shahed, thinking of Bernadette Shakour of the UNRWA.

'I live here,' repeated the boy desperately. 'Mama has just gone to get me a Spiderman. She's coming back, you'll see.'

Shahed put his hand on the boy's shoulder. 'Your Mama is in hospital,' he said tenderly.

'You're lying,' he spat. 'You just want me to leave so you can have our house.' He addressed Shahed but glared defiantly at the Israeli.

Shahed looked at the boy guiltily. He explained the situation to his friend and then admitted in Arabic, 'You're right.' He added formally, 'Do we have your permission to come to your house?'

The boy looked quizzically at them. 'What for?'

'Because this is my friend,' he confessed, adding as he indicated the uniform. 'And because Israeli and Palestinian friends must meet in secret.'

Mohsen nodded wisely. He knew what a secret was and, more to the point, he understood that one secret could set the scales for another. 'Only if you swear not to take me to another home.'

They sealed the agreement with a handshake after a brief hesitation.

Under normal circumstances, Shahed was too responsible and true to his word to accept such a deal. In his usual frame of mind, he would have turned down the boy and cancelled on Avi in order to take Mohsen straight to Imm Nidal for a hot bath and a square meal or else to UNRWA for a foster home.

But these weren't normal times. Even as he shook the boy's hand, he could neither resist the rising excitement of spending the next two hours with Avi nor dispel the thought that he would finally lose his virginity.

He offered his own deal within a deal: 'But you have to promise to stay away for the next two hours.' He added, 'Go to my mother. Tell her I sent you there for some food.' Again, ordinarily, he would have taken him to Imm Nidal in person.

For a few short months after that first night, the Brahimi farm was partially resuscitated. The main rooms almost sparkled as the two men set about restoring and cleaning their space like exuberant newlyweds enjoying their first home together.

Except that the couple of nineteen-year-olds already had an eleven-year-old charge, a little boy who refused to sleep anywhere but in the sitting room, huddled and camouflaged like a small boulder by the poorly restored eastern wall.

Avi and Shahed were more like brothers to him than parents — better, in some respects, than the two older brothers he had lost.

They could be irritating, particularly Shahed with whom he spent the most time and who insisted on teaching him English at home and computing in the Int@rnet café in town. It was as if Shahed were making amends for their pact, adding more clauses to the original deal by forcing the boy to study hard. Being the last to leave and the first to arrive at the café, he claimed to sleep among the computer cables when in fact he sneaked off to the Brahimi farm every night so Mohsen wouldn't be alone. Avi would join them for parts of a couple nights a week, tiptoeing past Mohsen in the living room to enter the bedroom, and a full morning here or a full afternoon there.

Avi was more fun. Sometimes he turned up at the farm when Shahed was at work in the café and they would play games like chess or hide and seek. Mohsen learnt more English trying to communicate with Avi than he did formally with Shahed's red pen correcting his mistakes.

Even when they prepared for the short but cold winter, Shahed went about the task of installing a small wood-fired heater solemnly, with the sense that it was a duty to ensure that they — and especially the boy — stayed warm. Avi, on the other hand, turned everything into a game. With a tub of filler and a scraper each, Avi and Mohsen would see who could fling the most accurately and from the greatest distance to cover all the holes in the walls.

Mohsen was confused by Avi: friend yet Israeli. And whenever he didn't understand something he just turned to his daydreams.

It was the last night in the Brahimi farm. Mohsen froze when he felt a sudden chill on his face. The front door opened with barely a creak and two men entered waving torches like lasers. Since they weren't expecting to see anyone on the floor of the living room, they didn't. They crept past Mohsen, one of them almost stepping on him, as they moved directly to the bedroom.

They charged in without knocking.

He heard shouts in *ibreet*, accompanied by vicious laughter and dull thumps. This time, when Shahed and Avi moaned, it was from actual pain.

Petrified, Mohsen heard Avi's voice, shouting back in their alien tongue and then to Shahed in English: 'Are you OK?'

One of the intruders ordered in broken Arabic: '*Yalla*, get dressed, whore.'

In the densest and most archaic Arabic, Shahed shouted from the bedroom: 'Hark! Conceal thyself in true fashion, ye who may hear my voice!'

The headlights of the jeep returning to the checkpoint caught Sheena's frown.

At first, when she saw the absconder leading the way with his hands on his head, she planned a straightforward chastisement by the book for clear dereliction of duty. Krickstein had already been locked up, having obligingly informed them of Lunzer's whereabouts.

But she swiftly changed her mind when she saw the Arab behind him stepping off the jeep and when a grinning Sharett described how they had been caught with their pants down and their cocks up.

It was sinful enough to befriend an Arab; it was an outright *haval* when that Arab was also a lover. But when the Arab lover was of the same sex, the needle went way off the moral indicator on the scale of abject depravity. By comparison, even perfidious Arab Israelis who worked for the biased UN were saints.

Sheena Baran decided there and then to scare them to death.

Avi stiffened when he saw her and gave her a half-hearted salute. 'Captain,' he pleaded. 'It's really all my fault.'

'Is it,' she said automatically as she looked at the Arab with disdain.

'I forced him,' he said. 'Please let him go.'

'Did you have fun then?' she said almost chattily. Turning to Sharett, she asked, 'Which one's the woman? I can't tell.'

Avi decided to change tack. 'There's nothing wrong with what we were doing.'

Sharett tutted disapprovingly; his grin hadn't left his face.

'Nothing wrong?' She jerked her head as though to correct her hearing. 'You abandoned your post, soldier — '

'You came early,' admitted Avi, adding, 'Where's Private Krickstein?'

' — in order to fuck some Arab. I'd say you were deeply fucking wrong.'

'Carnival,' he said under his breath and in English.

'What did you say, Lunzer?' she shouted with disbelief.

'Nothing, Captain.'

She moved her hand deliberately to the pistol in its holster. 'Repeat what you just said,' she ordered.

It was Shahed who answered for him, talking rapidly: 'He just said carnival. That's all he said. Carnival.'

'He talks English,' gasped Sharett.

'Yes,' said Avi, his eyes never leaving Baran. 'He *speaks* English considerably better than you do.'

'Carnival?' she mused. She had actually heard Avi, but was just taken aback by it. After all those years since the Wailing Wall, it was still the most unexpected word anyone had ever said to her. Was he the same brat who had crashed into her in the plaza?

'It's just something I say, Captain,' he said truthfully. 'It's a long story. I think I should see Colonel Ami.'

'And disturb Habib's sleep with your sordid story?' She shook her head emphatically. 'I think not.' In the course of her distinguished military career, the commander of the base as well as her previous superiors had spotted her ability to take sound, on-the-spot decisions. 'Well why don't you tell me about carnival as we return to your love nest.'

'Oh man,' groaned Sharett. 'Don't tell me we have to drive back to that shithole.'

'It means the greatest shame,' said Avi. 'It means that what you're doing is so literally wrong, it will rub out that part of your soul that once recognized it as shame. Then it moves on to another part of your soul, like a degenerative disease, feeding on other tangibly wrong deeds. In the end, when there is nothing really left of your soul, you even forget what you were like and that you were once born a perfect and happy baby.'

For a second, she simply stared at him as if he were craziest person she'd ever met. Then, in one fluid motion, she removed her pistol from its holster and aimed it straight at Avi's head. 'Oh, I'm sorry,' she said sarcastically, 'is this really bad for my soul?' She nodded towards the jeep. 'Now move it, kafir-bugger.'

When they returned to the farm and led them away from the jeep, Sharett thought he detected some movement next to an old olive tree. He heard a clicking sound and told himself it was cricket.

They were the same two voices — a man's and a woman's — that Shahid would hear again, four months later, on 25 July 2004, as he crossed into the land of the *ibreet* with Amo. And again he would see them only as dark silhouettes with their torches and tremble with fear.

Sheena addressed Sharett: 'Where were they, then?'

He led the way to the bedroom, treading carefully and shining his torch only briefly at the dark obstacles.

The men were now in the bedroom; she stood in the doorway. 'Well isn't this the perfect secluded alcove,' said Sheena. 'I don't suppose you boys have brought your swimming trunks.' She waved her pistol. 'Off with your kit. Now.'

Avi stood his ground. 'No.'

She betrayed a thin smile as she ordered, 'Show us your privates, Private.'

'You're sick.'

'Come on — chop, chop — assume the position.' And then to Sharett: 'Why don't you help them get it right?'

'You're fucking mad.' Avi's voice cracked. He coughed several times to clear his throat.

'Why are you doing this?' Shahed asked evenly. 'We've done nothing to you.'

'You're here, aren't you?' she retorted spitefully. 'Isn't it bad enough that we have to live with you cancerous lot?'

Avi struggled to speak. 'You'll never get away with this.'

'Au contraire. If you don't strip right now, I will shoot both of you and say that you, fallen hero of Israel, lost your life as you fought this Islamist terrorist.'

'And if we do as you ask?' said Shahed.

'Then I'll let you live like the cowards that you are.'

Shahed started to remove Avi's clothes, one by one, tenderly.

'There's a good Arab,' said Sharett gruffly. 'Knows how to put on a show.'

Avi, naked, turned to his friend to repeat the compliment.

'Call it scientific curiousity,' she said. 'I'd now like a demonstration of a few of your favourite positions.'

When they didn't comply immediately, she brought her pistol arm to eye level and aimed. 'So you're on top, Lunzer. Do you always grip the sheet — ' She stopped and spun around. 'What the — '

Mohsen couldn't help it. When he saw the woman aiming her gun, he let out a muffled cry. And now he couldn't stop sobbing quietly. He thought she was going to shoot his brothers.

Sheena's pistol turned to aim at a dark bundle by the eastern wall.

Avi thought she was going to shoot Mohsen. He didn't blink. In that split second, Avi lunged off the bed with the white sheet trailing behind him like a matching cape to his white body. He slammed his body against hers, knocking her off her feet.

Her first shot ricocheted off the heater. She was a trained soldier; he was a pacifist drafted into the IDF, a *pagom*. It was no match. She had to punch him only once to break free and then, deftly on her feet again, her second bullet found its mark on his chest.

Sharett's torch lit up the growing circle that had appeared and that was as strikingly red as a male robin's.

Shahed didn't bother with classical Arabic. 'Run!' he roared. 'Run, damn you! And don't ever stop!' He stood tall. He shouted with such ferocity that, had Abu Nidal lived to witness this moment, he would have had tears of pride for his son.

Mohsen did as he was told. While the two were temporarily preoccupied with Shahed, he started to run.

It was a child. He seemed to have appeared out of nowhere and promptly vanished again by the time Sharett sprinted to the front door and shone his torch into the night. Sheena was not unduly concerned though and called Sharett back. No one would listen to a little Arab and, besides, they still had much work to do. Given the turn of events, she decided to use the situation to her advantage and prove that, unlike other bases, theirs could stop would-be suicide bombers from crossing into Israel.

They dressed the bodies in their respective clothes and lugged them to the jeep. It was dawn by the time they finished recreating the suicide bombing at the checkpoint. She ensured that they were on their sides and hugging a grenade between their chests so that the impact would be equally strong on both and in order to muffle the sound. This was pure Hollywood.

Mohsen didn't stop running until he reached the doctor's clinic behind the mosque in Qalqiliya. He waited until the end of curfew and walked between two Palestinians, timing his paces to theirs so that the guards wouldn't see him.

It was 10 November 2004 and Sheena Baran had just started her lunch in the mess hall when Colonel Habib Ami entered with two soldiers who were not from the base. Others looked up but no one stood to attention or saluted their commanding officer.

Sheena scooped up some hummus with some pitta bread as the three moved straight to her table.

'Hello, Habib,' she said jovially. 'You look serious today. What's up?' She put the food in her mouth.

His nod was directed at one of the accompanying guards; it was then that she noticed their military police armbands. They always came in twos.

'Captain Sheena Baran?' prompted the first MP.

'Yes?'

'We have a warrant for your arrest. Will you please follow us?'

She choked on the hummus.

She coughed violently and spluttered, 'Wh-what?'

'You are charged with the murder of Private Avi Lunzer.' The MP looked at the card in his hand as he added, 'And of the Palestinian, Shahed Zeitouni. You are not obliged to say anything at this point. Just stand up and come with us if you please.'

'This is a joke.' Her eyes turned to appeal to Ami.

'You heard him, Captain,' said Ami, dispassionately. 'Just go now.'

'Colonel,' said the MP, 'if you could just point out Corporal Caleb Sharett as well, we'll take it from there.'

Mohsen's testimony, damning though it was, would not have been enough to convict Baran and Sharett. However, in combination with some equally damning pictures, there was evidence beyond any reasonable doubt to prosecute them for premeditated murder.

Four photographs had been found on the dead leader of al-Aqsa Squad: the picture of the devastated Brahimi farm; a shot of Baran and Sharett leading Avi and Shahed, their hands on their heads, away from a military jeep at gunpoint; and two further pictures as they returned to the jeep, carrying one of their dead victims in each shot.

The prosecutor entered the three photographs of Baran and Sharett as exhibits, and motioned to move them into evidence.

The defence lawyers immediately objected and tried to disallow the pictures. They questioned their credibility just as they had raised objections concerning the reliability of a Palestinian boy's eyewitness account.

They were overruled again.

At the end of his deliberations, two weeks later, the presiding judge said those responsible for the 'unacceptable and un-Israeli' conduct had to be dealt with severely such that they would serve an example to other would-be offenders in the IDF.

Sheena Baran and Caleb Sharett were court-martialled and sentenced to fifteen years and five years, respectively. She was found to be guilty on one count of manslaughter and one of premeditated murder; his role was ruled to be complicit, thereby justifying the shorter prison term.

The sentences covered the lesser indictment of acting in ways unbefitting officers: a general charge to describe how they'd forced their victims to strip, before dressing them up again and blowing them up in order to conceal their crime. Their time spent in jail since their arrest — almost a year until the trial — would also be taken into account.

This was not the landmark ruling that Aron had expected. The military judges deemed that Avi's death had been accidental. It was Shahed who had been killed in cold blood.

Aron was so enraged by the decision that he threatened to pursue the case through the civilian District Court and, if necessary, all the way to the Supreme Court.

Two days later and when Aron had returned to Jerusalem, an army spokesman came to his flat to placate him. He explained the IDF's position and hinted that a handsome gesture would be forthcoming if Aron dropped the case. The officer reached in for a folded sheet of paper and slipped it over to Aron. There was a six-figure number written on it.

Before his transformation, even the army's offer to settle out of court would not have appeased him. But now he had the well-being and future of other people to think of. 'Shekels or dollars?' he queried.

This caused the major to chuckle. 'Are we the Bank of America?'

'Is this to pay off two murders?'

'There was only one murder, Mr Lunzer,' he replied evenly. 'Your son's death was a tragic accident.'

'So the entire sum is for the family of Shahed Zeitouni,' checked Aron.

'Yes.' The officer avoided his eyes as he added, 'But of course there's no way for the IDF to know how much of it you choose to remit to the Arab family.'

'I see.'

Aron folded the piece of paper and brought it to his forehead as he considered his options.

'You know that's a generous offer, Mr Lunzer.'

'You just don't want the bad publicity that would result from a public trial.'

'This is a win-win situation,' said the officer persuasively. 'You will lose if you take this further. We will fight like Gideon himself and we will prevail even if it's through countless appeals.'

'I'm interested in a deal,' admitted Aron.

'Good. That's the right decision.'

'But with some amendments to the current offer.'

The officer frowned and asked warily, 'Such as?'

'Shahed Zeitouni was murdered by an officer in the IDF.' He waited a full minute for the major to nod impatiently before continuing. 'Therefore he was not a suicide bomber.' Another nod. 'Therefore Regulation 119 of the Defence Regulations should never have applied to his family's home.'

'What are you saying?' he asked though he knew already where all this was leading.

'The family suffered two crimes committed by the IDF.' Aron pocketed the paper. 'In addition to this sum, all of which will go to the Zeitounis as blood money, I want their farmhouse to be rebuilt by the army.'

The officer's chuckle sounded less genuine this time. 'Who do you think you are anyway, one of the patriarchs?'

Aron shrugged and said affably, 'That's the price for your redemption.'

That day, the officer picked himself up and marched to the door with a hasty, 'We'll see you in court then.'

But he was back a week later, the day after Aron officially filed a public lawsuit against the IDF.

Aron got his landmark ruling, albeit out of court and out of the public eye. That was their deal within a deal. In addition to the usual release papers that he signed on behalf of Mrs Zeitouni, they had to agree never to disclose the army's mistake nor its move to correct it. The IDF operated through private contractors so that, to all intents and purposes, the family was solely responsible for reconstruction.

Aron volleyed back with his own deal within a deal. The army accepted both his architectural plans and his insistence that the new farmhouse be rebuilt on the other side of the wall so that the Zeitouni residence could be reunited with ninety per cent of the estate.

20

THE SHORT-TERM LEASE in Matan had rolled over so many times that even the grocer's wife cum estate agent had tired of the paperwork and encouraged him to sign an annual contract.

Aron's kitchen had an uninterrupted view of an olive grove, which in the early morning light, stood rank and file in sea-green uniforms. Behind the grove and two kilometres over the hill was the Green Line of the Six-Day War: the future border between two states that had so much in common that they were the worst bickering twins in the family of nations. A further three kilometres due northeast and all the olives up to the separation barrier belonged to the Zeitounis.

He began to wonder if Aaron the High Priest himself had become bound with his fellow creatures in love on account of his years spent as a stranger among Egyptians. As a child, he remembered Józsi telling him that the ancient Egyptians called the landless Israelites *Habiru*, which was derived from *apiru* or foreigner and which over millennia changed modestly to become *Hebrew* in English. Another English word, Palestinian, was derived from the Hebrew *philashtim* or foreigner and originally referred to Aegean Greeks. Etymologically at least, everyone in Biblical Israel was alien to the land.

Aron had forgotten the specific reason that had caused him to leave his warm bed. He yawned and moved to his study, which was a perfect copy of his old study down to the alignment of the armchairs with respect to the desk. The top drawer of his desk still contained his miniature treasure chest: Sela's postcard, the small piece of paving stone from the ancient Roman road in Tyre and the lock of Avi's black hair from his first haircut.

But there were some new additions in the study, such as Mohsen's first essay written in English (with Aron's corrections in red) duly stored in his treasure chest, and the Lord's Prayer, written in cursive Aramaic script, which was framed and nailed to the wall between the Ottoman and Austro-Hungarian ancestors.

It was Bernadette who helped him to see that, from a certain angle, any geometric shape could be made to look like any other. In politics, religion and sexual orientation, you had squares and circles, and a myriad of polygons between them. There was certainly a clash of civilizations if by clash one meant mismatch rather than conflict. The deep fault lines created by religion, history and language were like so many jigsaw pieces waiting for the perfect bridging sections to link them all up.

He was surprised that he didn't miss Jerusalem. At first, he'd kept the house ostensibly to supervise the construction of the new Zeitouni farm.

In truth, he actually liked living in a house with a garden. Now that he was doubly protected, he could even enjoy it. In addition to his Dustblaster, he had been reunited with Samiha, who diligently searched and destroyed all the dust particles in their hideouts. Blessed Samiha, who was more upset by Avi's death than by Shahed's, her own nephew. He often wondered at the twist of fate that had brought the two families together.

Although he could find a thousand perfectly rational excuses for moving from Jerusalem, he knew that the most honest reason was that he was now closer to Bernadette. From Matan, she could easily commute to her work in the West Bank.

'But I can't live in Israel,' she'd said, when he had first proposed the idea to her. 'I'm a foreigner.'

'Not to worry,' he'd replied, waving away her concern. 'Everyone in Israel is Hungarian.'

It was now 4:40 am according to the traveller's clock on the desk and he was still trying to remember why he'd got up. He checked the living room and adjoining dining room.

His suitcase was in the hall, waiting to be packed. This jolted his sleepy memory. He hummed a bar of 'Happy Birthday' and returned to the kitchen.

Anniversaries always came later by Hebraic reckoning. Aron was born on 20 Cheshvan 5717; so his jubilee in 5767 fell on 11 November 2006.

But Józsi had phoned him on his Gregorian birthday for a change and had offered him some Leviticus as a special treat: '"And ye shall hallow the fiftieth year, and proclaim liberty throughout the land unto all the inhabitants thereof; it shall be a jubilee unto you; and ye shall return every man unto his possession, and ye shall return every man unto his family."'

Aron was amazed how he could still quote entire passages of the Tanach.

'I bought you a horn for your birthday,' said Józsi at length.

'Thank you,' answered Aron automatically.

'Then if you blow your own horn on your birthday, I will put a prick up my ears to hear.'

Jubilee was derived from the Hebrew *yovel* for 'ram's horn' or 'trumpet', and was the year following seven times seven years, during which a trumpet blast on the Day of Atonement would signal a year of rest for the land. During a Jubilee year, all debts were to be cancelled and private property returned to its rightful owners.

'It is like yesterday that I lost you,' said Józsi with regret. 'You are already half a lifetime older and all ready to make proclamations with a horn.'

It was also a special time when you were encouraged to follow the example set by Aaron the High Priest and restore *shalom bayit*, peace and harmony between parents and children.

'If you give me your new address, eh, I can send it to you?'

'Why don't I pick it up in person?'

'Eh?'

The new Aron could be just as impulsive as the old Arnold who had left North London decades ago in order to make aliyah.

Dorika, who had been listening in on another phone, interjected excitedly, 'You can come? Arnold dear? Will you?'

'Yes, Mama, but not alone.' So impulsive, in fact, that he could invite Bernadette to visit London without consulting her first. 'I'll bring a friend with me.'

'An old friend?'

'A good friend.'

'Does he *bentch* and *daven*?' asked Józsi.

'No, but *she* speaks Aramaic.'

'Aramaic?' He hesitated only briefly. 'Then I shall be happy to speak to her in Aramaic like the Chaldeans to their king.'

Dorika offered her own endorsement more prosaically: 'If you're a happy man and woman then I am happy.'

In the main, he was a happy man, happier, at any rate, than he had been for decades. Today, he just had to get through the day and, more precisely, lunch with Mrs Zeitouni. Frankly, they had little in common, even with Bernadette or Mohsen acting as interpreters. It was his idea that they should buy Mohsen a computer, and Bernadette's harder task to persuade Mrs Zeitouni that computers were not, in actual fact, filled with malevolent trolls and hobgoblins. He found he had more to say to Samiha and her children.

Still, they — especially that cheeky Mohsen — had insisted on this shindig for his birthday. But Aron knew he'd be a lot happier once they were back from the Zeitouni farm and started to pack for their first overseas trip together. They were taking the scenic route to North London, via Paris, which oddly enough, his francophone girlfriend had never visited.

It was banal thirst that had woken him. It was nothing more than juice that he'd come looking for and promptly forgotten. He opened the fridge and reached for the carton.

He had his glass of juice and was about to close the fridge when, instead, he opened a cupboard and a drawer for a spoon and a bowl. The main course that Bernadette had prepared for his birthday lunch was in a large, oval dish covered in aluminium foil.

He reached in, peeled back a corner of the foil and stopped, guiltily.

He heard Bernadette moan from the bedroom. He waited for a full minute to be sure she was still asleep, then, as quietly as possible, he lifted more of the foil to scoop some chicken rice in a bowl. There was so much anyway, that no one would notice. Besides, it looked so appetizing.

In addition to the rice and large chicken breasts, there were pieces of minced lamb, raisins, roasted pine kernels and blanched almonds — a panoply of contrasting ingredients coming together to form the most festive of meals.

Aron felt he was entitled to a little taste. After all, you only lived to turn fifty twice if you were fortunate enough to be Jewish.

God is the greatest.

Imm Nidal almost slept through the first prayer of the day. She was still in bed when she heard the faintly audible call to prayer from distant Qalqiliya and, jumping out of bed, she made a mental note that her internal clock was running several minutes slow.

She rushed to the prayer mat and hurried with her *shahada* to catch up. At three forearms length away, in the direction of Mecca, was the eastern wall of her new bedroom acting as her sutra. Her bedroom in the new Zeitouni farmhouse was considerably bigger and better designed than the one she used to share with Abu Nidal. Where the previous bedroom had a blank wall, this one had a large window with double-glazing that would twice refract the light of the rising sun.

She made another mental note that her new bedroom and more comfortable bed were the true culprits for her delay, and quickly followed that with a third note to admonish herself for failing to empty her mind of such common thoughts.

She forced her eyes back to the exact spot on the mat and folded her hands over her stomach with the right hand covering the left hand to restrict every movement.

Come to your good. Come to your good.

And, since it was the dawn prayer, there was an extra couplet: *Prayer is better than sleep. Prayer is better than sleep.*

Prayer was always better than sleep if you woke up in time.

She could tell instinctively that no one else was awake. While Mohsen could be excused because he was young, she considered it *haram* that her own sister and her two adult children remained snug in bed like the slothful creatures that they were. Samiha only prayed to God when she needed a favour from Him. In that, as in other ways, she behaved more like a Christian than a true believer. Ever since Mohsen's guardians employed her to clean their house, Samiha strutted around like a peacock, hinting often that it proved she was the better cleaner. But did she ever lift a broom on the farm? No, not Samiha. She was now too precious a cleaner to do a stroke where she lived — where she and her equally indolent children had been invited to live.

Now that the Zeitouni farmhouse had acquired a fourth bedroom, an extra guest bathroom and extra space in the living room and kitchen, it took considerably longer to do the daily chores; an offer to help on occasion would have been proper.

And today, of all days, the farmhouse really had to be spotless. Mohsen had invited his guardian, Haroun Lanzara, to celebrate the man's birthday on the farm. As Samiha's employer, he would judge for himself who cleaned best and whose house truly sparkled.

There were of course other reasons why her guests of the day had to be received like a king and queen.

She had met him on several occasions and still couldn't decide what to make of him. He was Israeli, but seemed good to Arabs, and his name was Arabic, yet of question-

413

able stock. While on the one hand, Lan-zara, or *he-never-visited*, had swooped down from Heaven like a redeeming angel to give her back her home — and for that she would always be indebted to him — he had a dubious influence on Mohsen. This was exemplified by the *combyudar* that was in the boy's bedroom.

But fortunately, Mohsen was not Shahed. The boy was more attached to the Koran than the screen. The house was too new and Mohsen was too pure to accommodate an evil jinnee.

She looked forward to their afternoons, sitting and reciting the Holy Verses together every day after *izhan al-asr*. It was added to her routine and was already the high point of her days. They developed their souls together, sitting gladly side by side, reading, interpreting and, later with the radio switched on, listening to the soothing words of God and admiring the unrivalled beauty of His language. He sustained her and was her faithful companion. They shared beliefs on a level that was alien to his guardians.

Habits were easy to break once there was a strong enough reason to break them.

In the old farm, she used to sip her tea at dawn come spring and over the course of the long summer months. Now, weather permitting, she moved to the porch with her glass of tea even in autumn — her first of many seasons in this house, God-willing — to watch the sun rise over the fields of olive trees. Behind the farmhouse was the Wall that stretched uniformly across the horizon. Since it was out of sight, out of mind, the first rays of sunlight could once again shine from Jordan straight onto the porch and handrail, to settle on the fine layer of dust that gathered overnight and that reflected those rays like glimmering dew.

The youngest tree from her vantage stretched its branches delicately, unfurling them to witness the dawn of a new day — she had named that one Mohsen. Respecting what was already a ritual, she raised her glass and toasted the young olive. Then she closed her eyes for a moment and thought of the day ahead.

She had to clean the house but at least she didn't have to cook for the guests, though she wondered about her friend's culinary skills. While she respected and liked Bernaytat more than a sister, how good could the Christian's food be, particularly since, until recently, she would never eat lunch? They were bringing a dish of *riz a'a djeij* — but frankly, if it was anything like her Arabic, it would be rice peppered with chicken nuggets and served with ketchup and mayonnaise.

The olive trees in the field looked like so many upturned brooms, their clumps of wrinkled green olives messing up the otherwise bare branches. Instinctively, Mohsen was tempted to pick up each tree by its trunk and give five rhythmic raps against some imaginary wall to liberate the fruit: two short knocks on the first smaller edge, swiftly followed by a stronger tap on one of the broad sides and ending with another two short knocks on the opposite edge. Pap-pap paaap pap-pap. Just as you would to clear a broom of dust and dirt stuck in the hairs. There was no other way to do it.

This was his land as were all the trees as far as the eye could see. He would never weave a single broom, which suited him since brooms and the Brahimi farm left him dead cold. Instead, he was happy to learn about olives so that he could become the greatest Zeitouni farmer ever.

He saw Imm Nidal standing on the porch in her black abbaya and he felt a sudden rush of affection for her. With the exception of her hair, she was more like his mother than Bernadette could ever be, more familiar in her speech, mannerisms and faith and, over the course of a year in Ramallah, in the way she scolded him and caressed his hair according to her mood. His debt to her was greater because, while Aron and Bernadette had saved his life, she had given that life a true purpose by formally adopting him. According to Muslim custom, the farm would eventually belong to him and he dreamed that he would one day make the best olive oil in the world.

He had hoped to slip in without being noticed, but she seemed to be staring straight at him. He grinned sheepishly, called out her name and waved.

Her eyes closed, she dreamt for a second that the young olive tree was actually calling her.

Imm Mohsen finished her tea in one gulp, sighed with content and turned to get the house ready for Haroun's birthday party.

London, 2006

Józsi believed he was still awake when he heard his son's jubilee horn from downstairs.

It was the month of suffering, but also the month of eternal joy. It was the day of death for Aaron the High Priest, and the day of birth for the Messiah, who would be born to mankind for the construction of the final Temple. This was *Tisha B'Av*, trumpeting the ultimate triumph.

It was also the exact moment in time when two sheets that had been joined at one point for fifty years finally became unstuck.

Józsi opened his eyes and drifted down to the living room, heading straight for the cabinet that contained his folder of names. Of the two sheets, at the top of the pile, only one mattered now.

He dropped the first one, with the central name of Arnold Lounger, and held the second with awe.

Among the angels and demons orbiting Áron Lunzer, one now shone off the page, casting its glow in the dark flat.

Józsi was unable to speak at first.

'My boy,' he gasped at length. 'My beautiful, beautiful son.'

His hand didn't dare to cover the angel's name, his fingers skirting around the shimmering edges of the letters. They lingered reverently for a while then reached for a red pen to draw a bold circle around MIHÁLY.

'Of all the angels,' he whispered, 'you would choose to be their king.'

He paused and then wrote his son's ascendant angel in English, below the Hungarian, out of respect for the language of his adopted land.

He gazed at the name one last time and finally returned it to the folder, proclaiming, 'Now I see you.' He grinned. 'I am happy now.'

Michael

Angel of
miracles

Áron
Lunzer